BEFORE
AND
AGAIN

BEFORE
AND
AGAIN

BARBARA DELINSKY

ST. MARTIN'S PRESS ❧ NEW YORK

BEFORE AND AGAIN. Copyright © 2018 by Barbara Delinsky. All rights reserved.
Printed in the United States of America. For information, address St. Martin's Press,
175 Fifth Avenue, New York, N.Y. 10010.

www.stmartins.com

Designed by Anna Gorovoy

The Library of Congress Cataloging-in-Publication Data is available upon request.

ISBN 978-1-250-11949-0 (hardcover)
ISBN 978-1-250-11948-3 (ebook)

Our books may be purchased in bulk for promotional, educational, or business use. Please
contact your local bookseller or the Macmillan Corporate and Premium Sales Department at
1-800-221-7945, extension 5442, or by email at MacmillanSpecialMarkets@macmillan.com.

First Edition: June 2018

10 9 8 7 6 5 4 3 2 1

To my two Ws—Wrenna and Will—with love before, again, and always

PROLOGUE

Mackenzie Cooper had no idea where she was or, more critically, why she hadn't already arrived. Her navigation screen said she was still on the right road, in the right town, but all she could see were woods left and right and a curve of macadam ahead. The turnoff was to have been five minutes past the café in the town center, and they had easily gone ten. During that time, she hadn't seen anything remotely resembling a turnoff, much less the red mailbox that allegedly marked it, although a red anything would have been easy to miss. The fall foliage was a tangle of fiery shades, its leaves crowding the roadside like families at a parade.

A glint in the rearview caught her eye. Braking, she steered to the side until branches brushed the car. She toggled her window down, but before she could get an arm out in a plea for help, the pickup steered around her, sped past, and disappeared over the hill ahead. Assuming the driver knew where he was going, she accelerated and followed, but by the time she hit the crest, the pickup had taken another curve, and by the time she made that one, her car was alone.

She glanced at her phone. It was cradled in a vent holder at the perfect spot for viewing, which had served her well until her map app had frozen. The upper-left corner of the phone showed an ominous No Service where bars should have been, meaning that she couldn't even call or text for help.

"Are we there yet, Mommy?" came a plaintive cry from the five-year-old safely strapped in the back. It wasn't the first such cry, just the first that Mackenzie couldn't honestly answer.

"Almost, sweetie," she said, white-knuckling the wheel through another sharp turn. When the road straightened, she touched the SUV's map screen to zoom in. The larger view showed tendrils where driveways might be—and, *oh*, she just passed one, she realized, but it was a barely there thing, thin and rutted, with no mailbox of any sort.

Turn around, her sane self ordered. But the red mailbox was likely around the next curve, she reasoned, and, if not that, her phone would wake up. Besides, she didn't see a place to turn around. Her SUV was big, the road narrow, and it was snaking wildly through a forest that had no business being this close to the city.

Actually, this place wasn't close to the city. Lily's school was. But being a private school, many students traveled distances each day, which translated into playdates in the boonies. Lily's new best friend had already been to their place twice, easily arranged since the Coopers lived close to school, but this was their first playdate at Mia's. And why would Mackenzie hesitate? Lily wanted to go. She had asked repeatedly, had *begged*. Besides, Mackenzie liked this family. She liked that they didn't live in an oversized shingle-and-stone rebuild, that the dad was a carpenter and the mom a struggling writer, that Mia was on scholarship. Edward, too, felt an instant connection—as if the Boyds were people they had both known in earlier, more modest lives.

Mackenzie had made the arrangements with Mia's mom, including drop-off and pick-up times, clothes to bring for playing outside, Lily's love

2

of peanut butter and aversion to chocolate. She hadn't thought to ask about cell reception. Her carrier was the best in their own neighborhood, clearly not so here.

The map screen switched to night mode for several beats, seeming as confused as Mackenzie. She knew it was a glorious fall day. Glimpses of blue could be seen through the high canopy, along with shards of fire where sun lit the leaves, but in every other regard, the day-darkness was unsettling.

"Are we lost?" came Lily's worried voice.

"We are not," Mackenzie said with determination. "Mia's driveway is off this road."

She just didn't know where it was, and, no matter how often she glanced at the phone, it remained dead. Eyes shifting between the road and the SUV's map screen, she zoomed the view out once, then again until she saw an intersection, which was good. At this setting, though, she couldn't judge how far off it was. She was an artist, not a mathematician.

"All I see is trees," Lily said, more curious than complaining. "Maybe Mia lives in a *tree* house."

Mackenzie smiled into the rearview mirror. As dark as the woods were, her daughter's blond hair sparked with light. "Maybe a *fairy* house. What do you think?"

"With fairy dust around it? And popsicle-stick windows and clay walls? *That's* silly, Mommy."

"Why?"

"Only *our* fairy houses have those. Besides, fairy houses aren't real. Mia's house is made of wood. Her daddy built it, and he's a . . . what did you say he is?"

"A carpenter."

"Uh-huh. Are we *almost* there?"

"I think so. But will you look at these trees, Lily? They're yellow, like your hair. Know why?" she asked as a diversion.

"The green stuff."

"Chlorophyll. It dies off when the nights turn cool. Remember, we talked about that? The colors we see now were always there. We just couldn't see them until the green was gone."

Lily was silent through another twist of the road, then asked, "Are you sure we're not lost?"

"Do I ever get lost?"

"You did when we were driving to the ocean."

"Excuse me, little love. I got us to the ocean, just not the part Daddy wanted us at, but he was sleeping." In the passenger's seat. After a late night of work. "No, we are not lost." But Mackenzie was thinking of turning around and retracing the road to town. If she had a working phone, she could call Mia's mom for directions. Of course, there was still the turning-around problem. The road was undulating with a frequency that made narrowness all the more of a challenge.

"Why's it taking so long?" Lily asked.

"Because I don't want to drive fast on a road I don't know."

"Will you know how to find me to take me home later?"

"Absolutely," Mackenzie said with feeling, though she was thinking it might not be a problem if she didn't get them there in the first place.

"I love you, Mommy."

"I love you, too, baby."

"Mommy?"

"What, hon?"

"I have to go to the bathroom."

"We're almost there, almost there."

According to the map screen, they were nearing the crossroad. Hoping to get her bearings there, perhaps see a sign or regain her cell signal, at the very least have room for a turnaround, she zoomed in to identify it, to bring the name into view, leaning closer to catch it.

Too late, she remembered that the GPS display of her current position trailed reality by a number of seconds. Too late, she realized that the momentum built climbing another hill would have her barreling down the far side without knowing how close the intersection was.

She never saw the STOP sign hidden by leaves of the same color, never saw the van speeding at her from the right. She felt the terrifying jolt of impact, heard a high-pitched scream from the back seat and would have blindly reached for Lily if the SUV hadn't hurtled into a spin that defied gravity.

She felt another impact, then nothing.

1

The trouble with waking up in the morning is that you look like who you are. That's great if you like who you are, but not so great if you don't.

I don't. My face is pale and my eyes haunted. Five years have passed since the accident, but after a night with my head on the same plane as my heart, the scar on my forehead is a bright red. At least, it looks that way to me. When I touch it, I find a smooth ridge, but my fingertips remember the earlier roughness. And then there's the picture taped inside the medicine chest, where I'm sure to see it when I reach for toothpaste.

Mug shots are never pretty. Heartache is written all over mine. Size-wise, the print is small enough, but that doesn't dilute its impact. It's a reminder of what I did, a little dose of daily punishment.

Duly tweaked this Thursday morning, I closed the medicine chest and leaned into the mirror. I dabbed a long-wearing concealer over the scar and under my eyes once, twice, then a third time because last night was a bad one. After setting it with a breath of powder, I applied foundation, then a blusher. Both were creams, applied with a sponge. Moving up, I turned haunted eyes into stylishly smoky ones by skimming a gel pencil along both waterlines, smudging shadow into the corners, and separating my lashes with mascara.

Satisfied, I straightened and stood back, brushed my hair, fluffed my bangs. Then, as I did each day, I turned away from the mirror wearing my new face and tried to forget the old one. Was this honest? No. But it was the only way I could survive, and survival was key.

This day, the rising March sun was paper thin but promising. I felt no threat, no premonition, not the slightest sense of unease as I coasted down Pepin Hill over frozen ruts and cruised toward the center of town. After crossing the river, I passed the elegant Federal-style homes of the town founders and turned left where the road I was on ended and South Main began.

The usual string of cars lined the block fronting Rasher and Yolk. Some were pickups with mudstained skirts that labeled them locals. Others were clean SUVs with New York plates, but with the state line only thirty miles away, I thought nothing of it. Rasher and Yolk served the best breakfasts around. Every New Yorker who knew Devon knew that.

Warmed by omelet thoughts, I continued south for two more blocks before turning left toward the river again. The pottery studio was in a cavernous mill that had straddled it for a century. Like the Inn upstream, the mill had endured its share of Vermont blizzards and the ensuing spring floods. The fact that the old mill was built of wood, rather than the Inn's stone, made its survival all the more magical. Not even the hurricane that had washed out so much else on the river two Septembers before had harmed the mill's ancient oak.

I found this inspiring. To live through trauma and thrive? That was my goal.

The pottery studio did thrive. I was one of a dozen sculptors here today, and it was barely eight in the morning. Half were students, in town for a week of clay immersion that was offered by the studio's owner in partnership with the Inn. The rest were experienced artists, drawn to Devon for its appreciation of fine craft. Some were throwing pitchers and pots to be sold at the studio store in town. Since moving to Devon four years ago, I had sold things there myself. None were billed as Mackenzie Cooper art, and I deliberately tried not to replicate that style. Little bits slipped; I couldn't fully escape myself. But my current work was more subtle than spirited, and I never sculpted the family groups for which I had been known. Understatement was what my life in Devon was about. I was happy to fly under the radar.

Devon was a perfect place for that. A small town in south-central Vermont, it was known for upscale art galleries, VIP sightings, and the Spa's signature hot stone massage. Though the best-worn path to town was from Manhattan, more distant visitors came to rub shoulders with the rich and famous. All were welcome. Guests kept the town afloat.

How to tell a guest from a predator? Should a clean SUV outside Rasher and Yolk have caused suspicion? Or a lone tourist wandering on South Main taking pictures with his phone have raised a red flag?

Not in Devon. We were definitely used to strangers coming and going.

Buy a house in our midst, though, and we were cautious. It had been months before the wariness that met me when I first came faded—and that quickly, only because I had done repeated makeup applications for the library trustee chair, the Town Manager, and the head of the Garden Club. These people had bonded with me. The fact of my bare hands on their skin was conducive to that, but the emotional clinched it. A makeup artist was like a therapist, listening quietly to a client who arrived barefaced, with defenses down and a need to vent.

I knew about venting to a therapist, and I could certainly relate to wanting to feel better about oneself. What I loved most about my job was that I could make it happen for others, if only until bedtime, when the new face washed off.

So I listened. I didn't offer opinions beyond whether to use corrector or concealer, blusher or bronzer, matte shadow or glitter, and I never groaned, sighed, or frowned in response to what was shared with me. Hell, who was I to judge?

I also understood vanity. As far from the mainstream as Devon was, there were occasions when a woman wanted to look her best. Most of us had spent time in the city. We appreciated fine makeup, right along with craft beer, high-tech down jackets, and good cell phone reception.

The pottery studio was an exception to the last. Cell phones were useless within its wood walls. Potters knew they were leaving the world behind when they came here. For me, that was part of the appeal.

I had used the studio enough to be known by the local potting community, which knew me as Maggie Reid, not the full Margaret Mackenzie Reid, certainly not Mackenzie Cooper. Mackenzie was the artist, the wife of a venture capitalist, the mother. Maggie was just Maggie. Her hair was a deeper auburn than Mackenzie's had been and was colored at the roots to hide new wisps of gray. She used makeup to soften grief lines and bangs to hide her scar. Wearing base layers of wool under a sweater and jeans, a voluminous scarf, and fleece-lined boots, she was more concerned with warmth than style. She also weighed ten pounds more now than when she had been in the news.

She? Me. I could blame being thin on nerves, but even before the accident, I had been that way. It was the look of the elite, to which, for a time, my ex-husband and I had belonged. I had put all that behind, as well.

"Hey, Maggie," one of the regulars called in greeting as I headed for the supply bins.

I smiled and waved but didn't stop. Many of us were here before going to other jobs, which meant time was short. Besides, my need today was less for people than for clay.

Clay was in my blood, the smell of it alone a balm. Granted, March meant mud season, which lent an earthiness to the entire town. But potting clay was earthy in a different way. It didn't spatter my truck or cause ruts deep enough to make my tires spin climbing up to my cabin each night. Potting clay held promise. A world of wonder could come in a few hands-on minutes, and I had spent far more than that in my thirty-eight years. I'd been first drawn to clay when I was eight. By the time I was fifteen, it had become a passion, and by twenty-two, I was sculpting full time. By twenty-eight, I was married to a man who not only had faith in my work but a growing business network. An agent resulted, and my career took off.

If that sounds seamless, it's misleading. My personal history reads like a timeline in which each phase is separate and distinct. There were the growing-up years with my family, the eight years of college and beyond studying art, the seven years I was with Edward, the year in which I had been alone in hell, and now, the four in Devon. I had friends here, but none, save one, knew of those other lives. Clay did. For me, it was the single entity linking present to past—truly, the only one I could bear.

I deliberately chose a workbench apart from the others. The sandy burr of the potter's wheel soothed me when I worked, but not so human voices. I wanted nothing to come between my focus and the clay.

Not that focus was necessary to decide what to make. Need determined that, and today I needed a teapot. I had known it the instant I saw honey scones on my Facebook feed.

As bakeries went, The Buttered Scone was fabled in Connecticut. Its daily specials varied, but its honey scones were the best. They were simple and dense, but just flaky enough, moist enough, sweet enough to make you weep.

I had grown up on them. My mother *was* The Buttered Scone, and she knew I loved her honeys. I often wondered if she thought of me now when she featured them. I had posted a comment on her site this morning, then deleted it before she could.

I might not be having a honey scone today, but I could make a teapot. They're actually a challenge. There is an element of engineering in creating one that can pour without spilling. The spout has to be mounted at just the right height and angled just so, the rim wide enough to allow for washing but not so wide that water leaks out when it reaches the spout. I know these things, because I have only made, what, a gazillion teapots?

Today, my inspiration is a honey scone. Last week, it was a green cupcake with a sugar leprechaun crouched on the top.

My mother was an artist, though she would never call herself that. Art was an abstract concept, and Margaret McGowan Reid saw life in absolutes. She baked sweets, she would say. She rented a commercial kitchen and employed ten people. Like the rosary beads always on her person, these were physical things.

So was a teapot.

Dipping my fingers in water, I formed a cylinder. The clay was cool under my hands, but pliable. I widened my cylinder as the wheel spun it smooth, then reached in and bowed the inside. Dipping again, I sped the wheel a tad and narrowed the top on a whim, loving the eloquent irony of a whistle-hole crown on a round little belly. Of course, no infuser would fit through what I'd made. Wetting my fingers again, I widened back the collar, then, using my forefingers, shaped the rim. The lid would sit here, larger or smaller. I couldn't decide which. First, I made it too wide, and it looked positively stocky at the top of the pot. Then it was too narrow, too spindly. In the process of adjusting it, though, something happened that I liked. My thumbs had nicked notches that undulated around the top of the pot.

Letting the wheel slow to a stop, I smiled and sat back. I often carved designs into the bellies of my pots, sometimes combing through the wet slip with my fingers, sometimes with tools. I wasn't one for precise symmetry, far preferring an irregularity that made each piece one-of-a-kind, but what intrigued me most was texture. Using any number of techniques, I could add clay or shave it off, shape it, carve it, or glaze it to create a texture with which the user identified. Teapots could be whimsical, joyful, solemn, serious, businesslike, or practical.

It was rather like decorating a cake. At least, to me, it was. My mother had first built her business decorating cakes. I liked to think we were connected this way.

Covering the body with plastic to keep it moist, I fashioned a spout, positioned it, and, after boring a dozen holes in the proper spot, scored it and slurried it to the body. The lid came next. I had just enough time to put a little bee knob on the top—pure whimsy, with honey scones—before setting the pot to dry and cleaning up.

I took extra care with my hands. I would wash them again once I reached the Spa, but clay there would clog the pipes. Here we had two sinks, one to catch clay from the first wash, and a second for actual cleaning. I didn't skimp on either. Once dry, even a trace of clay would be gritty against the human face, and I had three makeup sessions booked for today.

Hands clean, parka zipped, I stopped only to give Kevin McKay a hug. Kevin owned the studio and, being soft-spoken, understanding, and gay, was as close to a boyfriend as I allowed. Turning away from the student he was helping, he held his clay-wet hands off for an arms-only squeeze. "Another teapot?" he whispered and let his raised brows ask the follow-up.

Kevin knew me well. "Honey scones," I whispered back and, drawing away to leave that thought here with my teapot, I made for the door.

The stairwell leading to the street was cold, the March sun still too weak to chase off winter's chill. I pulled on wool gloves and, once outside, climbed up into my truck without looking at the muck that spattered its side. Going through the car wash during mud season—like scrubbing the soles of my boots every night—was futile. I had learned not to make the effort. Besides, mud held a certain cachet. It gave me a sense of belonging. Every other local car looked like mine. Not that there were many right now. I saw several more New York plates and one each from Washington, DC, and Connecticut. Given the nature of Devon, this was normal.

I drove slowly past stores that were chicly appointed, their goods in artful window displays, their names etched in gold across handsome headers of Vermont granite. They were open now, entertaining early weekend visitors. Bookstore, coffee shop, boutiques—all were doing a comfortable business, to judge from the movement beyond those window displays. Same with two art galleries and a silversmith's shop. And the studio store? Some of the craftspeople who sold there relied on their earnings to live, and although I did not, the artist in me had enough of an ego left to like checking it out.

But I was heading north. The studio store was on Cedar, which came in from the east as I had earlier. Since I had a booking at noon, I had to go straight now to the Inn. That meant continuing for another mile on the Blue Highway, a two-lane road named after the river it followed.

First, though, came the small roundabout at the spot where South Main and Cedar met the Blue. At its heart was a war memorial initially built for the Green Mountain Boys who died in the Revolutionary War. It was an obelisk whose stone was updated too often for comfort, most recently to mark the death of a local Marine in Afghanistan. I hadn't known him; he left town before I arrived. That made it easier for me to focus on the river birch, which was finally—*exciting!*—looking more alive at the obelisk's shoulder. Maybe it was my imagination, born of a need for spring, but the curl of its bark was looser, the tiny buds on its branches fuller, and while it would be a while yet before leaves appeared, these signs said they would. There were times in the dead of winter when that was in doubt.

Ah, and there was Officer Gill, parked as always in his black-and-white SUV at the spot where the three roads met. When I first came to town, I was convinced my probation officer had sent him to monitor me. In time, I realized he was watching everyone. Well, not always watching. He was usually playing Solitaire on his phone, but he didn't need his eyes to know who was out and about. For Officer Gill, it was all about sound. Keeping a window cracked, he listened. He could recognize the locals by ear. Once he had come to know the sound of my truck, he raised a hand in greeting without bothering to look.

In hindsight, perhaps he should have. Perhaps he should have wondered about those people in parkas and jeans who were wandering a little too casually around town with neither partners nor kids. Officer Gill knew that someone was hacking into school computers. The whole department did. But they had no clue how far the problem had spread until an hour before the Feds went public with it—though, in fairness, those agents walking our streets made no sounds that Officer Gill would hear.

Should I have noticed them? For all my usual vigilance, either I was too focused that morning on transitioning from clay to makeup, or I had grown complacent, in which case I was as guilty as Officer Gill. Not that either of us could have done anything had we known. When it came to the media, we were powerless.

I rolled to a stop at the crosswalk, mirrored his wave, and drove on. Once the stores fell behind, houses were increasingly spread out. They were large homes, a mix of Colonials and Federals owned by people who had either lived here forever or more recently moved up from the city with money to spare. These houses didn't go cheap. They were set deeply back on large front lawns whose landscaping ranged from a few aged trees to the designs of a high-end landscaper. All was tasteful, even understated. And while those of us in town knew who owned what, tourists wouldn't recognize names even if they had been printed on mailboxes, which they were not. Celebrities didn't live on the main drag. Actors, financiers, retired politicians, bestselling authors—we had our share, but those with big names avoided the spotlight. Drawn to Devon for its promise of anonymity, they lived for the most part in smaller homes on the country roads that undulated through forest tracts.

There. Ahhhhh. I could smell the Spa. It was in my mind, of course; I was still a quarter mile from the entrance, but thoughts of lemon verbena were triggered simply by the road sign announcing the turnoff ahead. It was a calming scent. From my first visit, my first interview, I knew I had to work here. The smell wrapped me in the kind of comfort I desperately needed.

The road curved, and broad stone pillars appeared on the right. Beside them, elegant in its simplicity, was THE DEVON INN AND SPA, carved into Vermont granite and edged in the same gold as the signs in town had been. This sign was larger and had a quiet dignity to it. This one had come first.

Turning in, I had barely passed under the covered bridge that crossed the river when the Inn took shape through the trees. Clad in stone, it sprawled over the hillside, defying the river much as it had when built in the late 1800s by a New York financier. It had been a grand summer home then, and while later owners tweaked its size and shape, the original stone structure had been the cornerstone for its final conversion into an inn.

Final conversion? I had to smile at that. Was there ever a final anything when it came to The Devon Inn and Spa? It was forever being resized, rebuilt, redecorated, rewired, relit—all to keep it as stylishly decorated and technologically sound as the highest of high-end resorts. Edward and I had visited a few of those, so I knew what I was saying. I couldn't begin to imagine the ongoing cost here. Apparently, neither had three previous owners. A fourth was about to take over, a group actually, but we didn't expect anything drastic by way of change. Savvy investors knew not to upend a successful formula.

Approaching now, I passed the gracious entry, with its stone pillars and well-groomed doormen. In its first transition from home to hotel, the main floor had been enlarged to allow for restaurants, meeting rooms, a ballroom, and a gift shop, all of which had been enlarged and improved upon in subsequent years. Second and third floors rose wherever the escarpment allowed. These upper levels were shingled and designed with a riot of windows. Prudent pruning of encroaching trees maximized the effect. Whether reflecting sun from without or lights from within, the glass shimmered.

The Spa trailed off the southernmost end of the Inn, where it could be reached by even the weak winter sun. It had skylights and a year-round, open-air hot tub that needed no piped-in music, with the bubble of the river so close. Tasteful landscaping offered privacy to those in the tub, but, as I passed by on this chilly day, security was enhanced by a wall of steam that rose into the trees.

I parked head-in near remnants of a dirty ridge of snow, crossed the employees' lot, and went inside. There was no imagining now. Thanks to candles, sachets, and scented oils, the smell here was pure. Add the flow of hushed music—yesterday a piano, today a bamboo flute, tomorrow perhaps a bouquet of strings—and the face of the Spa manager, which lit when she saw me, and had there been even a drop of honey-scone nostalgia left in me, it was forgotten.

Joyce Mann had been one of the first people to befriend me when I arrived. Nearing sixty, she and her dove-gray bob were as calming as the rest of the Spa. The ultimate diplomat, she handled even the most difficult clients with ease, and though I was never difficult, I had arrived in Devon feeling lost. Sensing that, she had invited me to her home and introduced me not only to the most beautiful spinning wheel I'd ever seen, but to fresh produce at the Farm at Lime Creek, the no-kill shelter from which I subsequently adopted my pets, and the best Spanish tapas restaurant in the whole of central Vermont.

Okay. Casa Bruno was the *only* place for tapas in central Vermont. But the food was good enough to warrant the exaggeration.

Since Joyce was in the process of registering a pair of clients, I simply raised my brows in response to her smile as I passed. Minutes later, fresh navy scrubs on a nearby bench, I was in the shower with my hair wrapped in a towel and my face avoiding the spray. I had already done my makeup; I never left home barefaced. I would touch it up along with my hair, which I wound in a knot while I worked, but I knew from experience that my concealer would hold.

The shower would add a dewy element. Dewy was good. Dewy was fresh.

Dewy was also healthy, which was the goal of my noon client. Having been through months of physical mayhem, she needed to see a face in the mirror that spoke of hope.

Hope is the future lined in gold, my mother used to say. I'm not sure who she was quoting, or whether she meant it in ecclesiastical terms, but I didn't agree. Hope wasn't the future. It was only a vehicle to get there.

This client needed that vehicle. She was a cancer survivor. Having just finished a double-whammy of chemo and radiation, she was at the Inn with two friends for a celebratory escape. One look at her, and I saw vulnerability. She was feeling frightened, tired, and not terribly attractive. After a morning of manicure, pedicure, and massage, she wanted her makeup done while her friends did their hair. Her own hair wasn't an issue; she wore a wig. It was a good one. I raved about it. But she did need help with her skin.

After settling her into a chair, I pulled up a stool. Her check-in profile gave me the basics, but I was always curious for more. When had her chemo ended? I asked, and when she was fine talking about that, I asked how sick she had been, how she felt now, and how the morning's spa treatments had gone. She relaxed as we talked, telling me her plans for lunch here at the Inn, an afternoon of shopping, and dinner at the steak place in town—all of which meant she needed makeup that would last more than an hour. Since she generally only used blusher and lipstick, I sensed she would feel gauche in anything heavy.

Not that heavy is my style. I prefer a natural look. Like the deceptive simplicity of a teapot, it was actually more challenging. Anyone can pile on makeup for a dramatic effect, but applying it with finesse, particularly when there are blemishes to cover, takes skill.

I learned that the hard way.

I had never worn much makeup. Artists didn't, and Edward had always loved that about me. But a naked face didn't work at a black-tie event. So for those, I had gone to the woman who did makeup for my friends. I didn't use her after the accident, couldn't bear the thought of her telling the others I'd been in, which would have invited talk. Besides, Edward and I had stopped going out.

But I needed coverage. I couldn't bear looking at the naked me, and felt that the world was staring at me wherever I went. So I found a woman at Bloomingdale's. Her counter was in a far corner of the cosmetics department, an afterthought to the Lancômes, Elizabeth Ardens, and Chanels. She was younger than I, but she had flair. I watched closely, and not only to learn how to apply makeup. Her face, her eyes, her way of assessing and refining fascinated me. She was an artist. I connected with what she did.

The timing was right. I hadn't been able to touch clay since the accident—too many memories, too many dreams suddenly lacking meaning, too many speculative looks from proprietors of galleries where my work was displayed. But I needed to touch something. Being tactile was in my DNA. So I immersed myself in makeup artistry. I enrolled in cosmetology school, took an accelerated course schedule, and finished in a record nine months. Once I completed the required number of training hours, I became licensed, and after that, did dual internships with representatives of two of the most prestigious makeup houses.

Edward had called me obsessed, and I suppose I was. As a mother, I had been constantly busy; suddenly I was not. Add in all the other bad stuff, and I needed a distraction. Being a makeup artist was perfect. Not only was creativity involved in analyzing skin and applying makeup, but I could focus on other people, not myself.

And now this client. I asked which features of hers she liked best and least, and showed her pictures of looks I thought she would like. To the tune of soothing spa sounds, we found a comfortable back-and-forth, and all the while, with my LEDs low, I studied her skin.

Dryness was her major problem, possibly as much from winter as chemo, so everything I used had to be moist. I started with a gentle cleanser. Its purpose was as much to cool and soothe as to clean, and, though I would have normally used a scented one to blend with the smell of the Spa, I knew from other cancer patients that sensitive stomachs couldn't deal with anything strong. I applied a light emollient, and when her skin absorbed that well, followed with a richer one. Had it been my own skin, I'd have used my fingers. Not only did fingers warm lotions and emulsify balms, but they neatly reached creases at the edge of the nostril and corners of the eye. New clients often had hygiene concerns, though, and while I washed my hands often during applications, sponges were safer.

Using a small wedge, I dabbed color corrector into the shadows under her eyes and pressed the tiniest bit of powder there to set it. The moisturizer alone had done wonders for the redness on her cheeks, so I chose a stick foundation to even the color, then layered it with a liquid foundation and blended the whole with another sponge. Since her skin was naturally pale and her foundation color light, blusher had to be subtle. I applied a pale pink cream, set it with a dash of powdered blush, and stood back to assess. It was too much. I sponged off a bit, then a bit more, until the blush worked.

She was a pleasure to work with, holding steady while I created eyebrows, closing her eyes when I brushed ivory cream on her lids, looking up when I drew the faintest, softest line along her lower lashes, not blinking through a round of mascara.

That was it. I told her what I was doing and why, making sure she was comfortable with each step. If my challenge was to make her feel healthy, confidence was as important as anything I put on her skin. She had been following the progress in my mirrored wall, but given the way she sat straighter and smiled when I gave her a hand mirror at the end; the way she insisted on writing down the various steps; the way, at my suggestion, she spread moisturizer on her hands and patted it on the driest parts of her face for a final glow; I knew I'd succeeded. She liked her new face. It had taken her from recovering to recovered.

My one o'clock wasn't as pleasant. She was a bride-to-be who had come to the Inn with her fiancé for a tasting and now wanted a trial makeup session in advance of the wedding. In my experience, brides fell into one of two groups. Either they wanted to work with me for the best result, or they came knowing it all. This one knew it all. I felt it the minute I greeted her in the lounge. By the time we returned to the makeup studio, she had shown me a picture of her dress, which verged on being gaudy, and was telling me exactly what she wanted by way of makeup. Subtlety wasn't it. She was the star of the day and wanted to stand out. To her credit, she had thick hair and okay features. But cat eyes with glitter lids to match the blue hydrangea in her bouquet? Hollows in her cheeks where none belonged? Angelina-red lips? My gut said to tone things down. Weddings at the Inn might be lavish, but they were tasteful.

Right now, I said in a gentle attempt to sway her, *makeup is heading in a less-is-more direction. You can be in the forefront of that. Your skin is naturally beautiful. If we put the accent on your eyes, we don't want your cheeks and lips to compete. Soft is definitely the way to go with those.*

She didn't want to hear that.

What to do? When it came to weddings, my job was to make the bride feel beautiful, even if my concept of beauty didn't jibe with hers. And then there was the commercial aspect. If the bride liked this tryout, she would hire me to do the entire wedding party, which would please the resort.

That said, my professional reputation was at stake. I cared about that.

High-definition makeup was a no-brainer. She had already told me who her photographer and her videographer were. I knew both. Both used high-def cameras. The difference in makeup, I explained, was the ingredients. HD makeup contained things like mica and quartz, which sat on the surface of the skin to scatter the light and give the illusion of an even finish.

She liked that. Still, I began slowly, feeling my way along with the basics before proceeding to bronzer and brows. When she asked for more color on each, I complied, but with more brushing motion than actual deposit, and once I had done her eyes—yes, cat liner but modified, with pale-blue lids, a smattering of filler lashes, and navy mascara—she was so taken with them that she didn't complain about the rest.

She wasn't about to say that I was right, but I didn't need her to. It was enough that she booked me for the wedding.

We took pictures of the finished product, using both her iPhone and my Nikon, so that we would have a guide to follow for her big day, and she left the Spa excited, which truly defined my goal when it came to handling brides.

Nina Evans, my three thirty, was no bride, but rather a local who was here in her capacity as Devon's Town Manager. Like so many of us, she had a past. Originally from New York, she had risen meteorically into top management of a company whose president hired her, bedded her, and praised her to the hilt until the quarterly reports disappointed investors, at which point she became his scapegoat and was fired. Armed with a comfortable severance package, she had taken refuge in Devon, licking her wounds until boredom nearly did her in. When the position of Town Manager opened up, she leapt at it, and Devon was lucky to get her. Six years into her stewardship, the town prospered.

Nina was in her fifties. She had never told me exactly where, but neither age nor sophistication could erase the jitters she felt in advance of every major meeting. Her humiliation in New York had been public, and oh, I could identify with that. The key, here, was giving her confidence. She returned to me time and again because I did that—and I wasn't just blowing hot air. Everyone had one feature or another that was strong. Nina actually had two. *I just love your hair,* I said truthfully as I wove the long waves into a cluster of knots at her nape. *And here,* her eyes, which were an unusually dark green, *the tiniest line of amethyst at the corners will make them pop.*

Totally aside from the aesthetics of heavy makeup, we both knew the danger of overdoing it; what worked in New York didn't work in Devon. But Nina had lived in the city too long to go without. My job was to find the balance between a professional look and one that said, *here is Devon at its competent best.*

Her meeting an hour from now was about budgeting for renovations to the elementary school. With the annual March Town Meeting—cap T, cap M, open to the public and sure to fill the church nave—coming up fast, the Planning Board had to reach an agreement on what should be done, how and when, and at what cost, prior to presenting the plan to the public. This group consisted of a dozen local business leaders, all of whom had lived in town longer than Nina had, so she had to look like one of them, but not. A business suit wouldn't do, since not even men here wore suits. Instead, she came to me wearing tailored wool slacks, a silk sweater, and a nubby scarf clearly recognizable as the work of a local knitter. She was armed with a briefcase of printouts to bolster her proposal and now simply needed a confident face.

There was nothing complex about Nina's makeup. She might have done it herself if she had a girlfriend for the confidence piece. But she didn't know how to do girlfriends. Working in New York, she had never had time. Social activities had to be productive. Even here, in Devon, with me, she was marginally brusque. When I did her makeup, it was like a work lunch, woman to woman, without the food.

I knew the drill. She wanted concealer to cover mild rosacea, liquid foundation to even her skin tone, blusher blended lightly into her cheekbones, eyeliner so thin that it didn't look like liner at all, those gentle amethyst corners, and a breath of mascara. Through it all we talked—about raising electric fees to pay for work on the school, about the recent sale of the Inn to a mysterious group, about the messy divorce that threatened ownership of the town's leading realty company. Our tone was low and intimate, consistent with the reverent atmosphere in the Spa and its whisper-soft instrumentals. From time to time, a vibration came from Nina's briefcase, but she ignored it until I finished. She had pulled out her phone and was frowning at it when my door abruptly opened.

2

Grace Emory was a massage therapist, one of the Spa's most requested for her knowledge of muscles, the strength of her hands, and her quick smile. She was also a little zany, if only in ways a close friend would see. She painted her living room red on a whim, alternated beef gorging with juice cleanses, and, in the four years I'd known her, had surgically-tweaked her face twice.

We were visibly different. She stood five-four to my five-six, weighed one-ten to my one-twenty-five, and spoke in a higher voice. She had also lived in Devon for twelve years to my four. Since neither of us had been born here, though, we shared the bond that came from being *other*. Grace was chatty, getting me going when I might have been still. But we never discussed the past. It was an unspoken agreement between us. Our friendship was about the here and now.

She was caring; when I was feeling down, she seemed to sense it and would pop into the makeup suite with fresh-brewed apricot tea. She was impulsive; if neither of us had bookings on a slow day, she dragged me to a movie, a restaurant, or a mall. She was shameless; when I needed a new roof, she called a one-time lover, who just happened to be the best roofer in town, and talked him down several thousand in price.

I was the more practical, certainly the more cautious of us—the one who turned off lights when we left a room, who double-checked our afternoon schedules before we left for lunch, who drew her past the pickup from which a wolf whistle had come. I drove her home from the hospital when she had plastic surgery and stayed overnight bringing ice and drinks, and making sure Chris got off to school on time. I had also done her makeup so that she could return to work sooner.

Grace Emory was a woman in search of herself. I knew about women like that firsthand. Searching for self implied either not liking who you are or wanting to escape who you'd been. I didn't ask Grace which she was. I didn't want her asking *me*—didn't want to have to explain why, when given a choice, I made her drive, or why I wasn't interested in dating, or why I vanished every year on the third of October and returned emotionally depleted.

Grace accepted me for me, asking questions no more threatening than, *Think I should cut my hair?* The Spa had dedicated stylists. But she knew I liked to play and was forever asking for help, whether it involved a straight cut, layers, curls, or an up-do. Likewise, color. Currently a brunette with auburn highlights, she was making noise about ditching the highlights and going dark. This day, her head was a riot of the long ringlets I had shown her how to create with pin curls. She looked stunning, if I didn't say so myself.

At least, her hair did. The fact that she hadn't knocked might have warned me, if I hadn't instantly seen that her face was ashen. Saying nothing, she pressed a hand to her chest. Her eyes—brown today, although occasionally green, copper, or gold—held mine with an odd nonfocus as I approached.

Startled, I touched her arm.

"Chris just called," she whispered. Chris was her fifteen-year-old son.

When I tightened my grip, she said, "He's been arrested." Her voice shook. "They say he's the hacker."

I drew back my chin. "Excuse me?"

She didn't repeat herself. The fear in her eyes said that I hadn't heard wrong.

Too often in the last few months for it to be coincidence, local high school teachers had reported incorrect student grades showing up on their computers, hence the birth of hacker talk. But Chris Emory? I knew Chris. He didn't have a mean bone in his body.

"That has to be wrong," I said. "He's only fifteen. He couldn't—and even if he could, why would he? He's a good student. He doesn't need help with his grades."

"There's more," Grace raced on, mildly hysterical now. "They're saying he hacked into Twitter accounts of other people—people from outside Devon—like *our clients*."

I gaped at that. If the accusation was true, there was reason for hysteria. Our client list included some of the biggest names in New York. They came to Devon trusting that the world wouldn't learn that the lead in a Broadway hit had very little hair of her own on her head, or that a tight end for the New York Jets liked having his toenails buffed. Their privacy was sacrosanct.

"Spa clients?" I asked, to be sure. Any kid could fiddle with school accounts and call it a prank. Fiddling with Spa accounts was a whole other thing.

Nina joined us. She was wearing her business face and used a low, firm voice to match. "That was Jason Gill. They picked up Chris at school."

"Who's they?" I asked in alarm.

"The FBI."

"*Federal* agents?" The stakes rose. Federal agents added an element of horror. My own experience was limited to state agents, who were bad enough when you were in their crosshairs. Federal agents were even more dogged.

"They have warrants—"

"Why Federal?"

"Internet crime is a Federal offense," Nina said and told Grace, "They're on their way over here. They want your electronics."

She jolted back. "Mine? *Why?* What can they get from *mine?* Am *I* a suspect?"

"Of course not. They just want anything Chris may have used."

"But if they take my things, his name will come out."

"He's a minor. He'll be shielded."

"I won't be," she cried and, visibly trembling, hugged her middle. "Everyone in town knows he's my son. Once they hear my name, they'll have his name—and *don't* talk about innocent until proven guilty. That's *bull.* If they take my things, Chris won't be protected. *I* won't be protected. Everyone will be *looking* at us. Our names will be all *over* the place."

I rubbed her arm. She was getting ahead of herself, but I understood her panic. As unorthodox as Grace could be, she was no exhibitionist. I might be her closest friend, but I had no idea who was listed in her phone contacts, who starred in her nightmares, or what she kept in a box under her bed. Her private life was private. She trusted Devon for the same reason our clients did. Everyone had secrets. No one wanted them exposed.

Nina simply said, "They have warrants for your devices."

Grace's voice was high and tight. "Fine. They can have the computers. They're at home."

"Computers, phone, tablets."

"No. N. O. Not my phone."

"Grace," I said, knowing that cooperation was wise.

Her eyes flew to mine. "Clients text me. It's part of my work."

"I know, and you'll have the phone back."

"They'll need the computer here at the Spa, too," Nina said.

It was only one more computer, but its implication reverberated, sending a tremor from Grace's arm to my gut and back. If Spa clients had been victimized, some part of the investigation would, of course, have to be here. But involving the Spa meant involving the Inn, which did not include scandal on its list of amenities. Management would not be pleased.

Grace had to be thinking this, too. What she said was a high-pitched, "Why in the world do they need the *Spa* computer? Chris doesn't use it. He's never touched it. He has no access to it *at all*."

"That's the point of hacking," Nina said. "Hackers take access where none is given."

"My son *isn't a hacker*," Grace cried and swung to me, eyes wild, voice reedy. Her hand was back on her chest, as if holding her heart in place. "They have him at the police station. I was his phone call, Maggie. What do I do?"

Run, I thought. *Get as far from this place as you can*, or so the terrified voice in my nightmare always cried. I sucked in a breath, wanting to sound like I was considering her options, rather than trying to calm myself. In those few seconds, I refocused. This was about Grace, whose big, brown eyes were imploring me now. For her, I had to be a voice of reason.

"First, a lawyer," I said and glanced at Nina. "Jay Harrington?"

"No!" Grace cried.

"He's the best," Nina said.

"Not Jay! Jay does leases."

"He did criminal work before he moved here," I told her, as my lawyer in Boston had told me. True, Jay did real estate work in Devon. After burning out in the city, he had taken refuge in a place where criminals were few and far between. He had handled the closing on my cabin, but he knew nothing of my past. Lawyer-client privilege kept that information in Boston. In the event that I ever needed him on that score, I had a letter of introduction from my Boston attorney, along with copies of pertinent papers. They were in the green velvet box that had been my grandmother's, stashed now under my bed along with other mementos of my life before this one.

"He's been here long enough to know the town," Nina was saying to Grace, "and he knows you."

"We had a thing once. It didn't end well."

I did know that. Grace liked men but never stayed with one for long. Jay wasn't alone in having a "thing" with her that hadn't ended well. My roofer was another, and still she had called him when she needed him. At this moment, she needed Jay Harrington.

"And anyway," Grace argued with a feeble glance behind, "I can't leave now. I'm working."

She wasn't thinking straight, I knew. But I also knew something else. She loved her son more than life itself. "Chris is waiting," I said. "I'll stay here and reschedule—"

"No—come with me, Maggie—*please?* I can't go alone!"

My stomach twisted. Being involved with anything law-related was risky for me. I had spent my time in Devon avoiding the spotlight. I didn't want to be anywhere near it—which was surely a selfish thought. This wasn't about me, I told myself.

Taking a steadying breath, I corralled my scattered composure and one-handedly pulled up the Spa appointment screen. "Okay," I said. "Joyce can reschedule your appointments. Layla was doing a stone massage at three. She'll be done soon, so she can cover for you at four and five, and I'm done for the day." I turned to Nina, who was putting on her coat. "Okay?"

She nodded. "You have my AmEx on file." As she moved to the door, she told Grace, "The Planning Board may have already heard rumblings of this. If I want to give them something more than gossip, I need to go to the police station first. See you there?"

The police station was the last place I wanted to be. Jay Harrington's office came in a close second. But if I didn't take Grace there, who would? Like me, she had no family nearby.

Actually, I didn't know whether she had any family at all. Family was one of the things we didn't discuss.

But, orphaned or not, she was my friend. I couldn't let her go alone.

Nor could I let her drive. She was shaky and distracted, and distracted wasn't safe.

So I drove. The safety issue would keep me focused, even though I was probably as shaky as she was. I hated lawyers' offices. They dredged up memories I worked hard to forget. When Jay had helped me with my closing, we always met at the realtor's place.

Once at Jay's place, though, I couldn't just drop Grace off cold. She had spent the drive down from the Spa making the same bewildered arguments, and though I repeatedly agreed, repeatedly cautioned her against imagining the worst, she was stuck in that rut. Until Jay took over, someone had to direct her. So I pulled into a diagonal slot, parked, and, gripping her arm, led her inside.

The setup here was nothing like the office in Boston where I had spent so many dark hours. That one had been a sea of gleaming chrome, sleek furniture, and shelves of leather-bound books that were never opened, thanks to whatever technology stood nearby. Add law partners, associates, paralegals, and clients, and the firm was a hive of activity. Granted, Jay Harrington's office had no crowd, no chrome, no glitz, and he practiced alone. But a lawyer's office was a lawyer's office. No amount of expensive décor or technological innovation could entirely obliterate the Old-World smell that seemed to come with a law degree.

Jay's suite consisted of a small, sparsely furnished waiting room, no receptionist, and three doors. Two were open when we arrived. The third opened seconds later, and if I hadn't been determined not to freak out, I'd have lost it then. The man emerging with Jay was my ex-husband.

For several beats, I couldn't breathe. I told myself I was wrong. Edward Cooper had no reason to be in town. We were divorced. We held no joint property. He had nothing at all to do with my legal status.

Besides, this guy wore jeans and muddy boots, not imported sweaters and slacks. His hair was longer than Edward's, and he had a close-cropped beard. Tall? Lots of men were tall. Lots of men held their shoulders straight. Lots of men had cheekbones so strong that facial hair showcased rather than softened.

In my life, though, I had only known two people with eyes quite that pale, silvery blue. His widened on mine just long enough for me to realize that he hadn't expected to see me either. Then he passed by with a nod and left.

A nod. That was it. Not that I had spoken either. I could barely breathe, much less speak, and in front of two other people, neither of whom knew where I had come from and who I had been.

If Jay wondered at my look of shock, all he said was, "New owner of the Inn."

New owner? I swallowed and nodded, like that explained it perfectly. *New owner? Not. Possible.*

So not possible, in fact, that I blotted it out. Narrowing my thoughts to Grace's crisis, I let the icy hold she had on my hand channel my words.

"We need your help," I told Jay.

"So I heard."

Grace blurted, "How did you hear, if this just happened? No one bothered to call me until five minutes ago, and I didn't call anyone else." Her high voice went higher. "This is *my* son they're saying did awful things— things which, by the way, he couldn't have done—but anyway, he's under age, so how did his name get out and where are the laws to protect him? Whoever called you is violating my son's rights, violating *my* rights. I'm always hearing crap about privacy. Who's protecting *ours?*"

"Grace," Jay said.

"I mean it." Her eyes were blazing as I had never seen them blaze before. I might have reminded her that this was Devon, where people did respect privacy, and that whoever had talked with Jay might have done it to help her—had she not been the mama bear just then. I didn't cross mama bears in the best of times, and this, right now, for me, despite my very, very best efforts to stay calm, was not.

Edward? *Here?*

"My son did nothing," Grace told Jay. "He's a good boy who's done a *damn* good job growing up without a father. These charges are bogus. The cops are going after him because *they* look like morons with no leads, so they're grabbing the first smart kid around. Chris wouldn't hack into anything. He *couldn't* hack into anything."

"The FBI thinks he did," Jay said.

"Well, they're wrong."

"They wouldn't be charging him if they didn't have evidence."

"What evidence?" she charged back. "How could they have evidence? Who did they talk to? And when? There haven't been any Federal agents around here."

"Not that we can see."

That stopped her. Closing a hand on her scarf, she said in a voice that was only marginally conciliatory, "You mean, they've been snooping around in people's computers—hacking into our accounts—doing the same thing they're saying Chris did? Isn't that illegal without a warrant or something?"

"Cybersecurity still has lots of holes. Clearly, they were following a trail and saw something that led them to Chris."

Grace pulled herself up straight. "And clearly you agree, which means you're not the lawyer for me. Come on, Maggie, let's go." She had started to turn when Jay caught her arm.

"I do not agree," he said. He went on slowly, firmly. "I don't know what evidence they have, but I know how to discredit evidence. That's what I do, sweetie. You need me." They stood staring at each other, Grace smaller but no less ardent, with Jay, thin of hair and round of face, the blander of the two. Oh, he was pleasant enough to look at, but sexy enough for Grace to have slept with? I couldn't see it.

Not that I was any judge. I was immune to sexy. I hadn't been with anyone since Edward—hadn't been *attracted* to anyone since Edward— and the Edward who had just walked out of here was older, more tired, and clearly no more pleased to see me than I was to see him—which raised the question of why he was here. I didn't buy into the new owner of the Inn thing. Edward was a venture capitalist, not a resort owner. There had to be a better explanation.

Sounding defiant, Grace said, "There are other lawyers in the state."

Jay sighed, seeming to weary of the fight. "Yeah, well, since you and I have already played the ultimate game, now we can get down to business. Do you want someone to get your son out of jail today or not?"

She gasped. "He's in a *cell?*"

"Not yet, but if we don't get down there pretty soon, he will be. Are we going?"

"Yes, you're going," I said, seeing my out. "Indulge her, Jay. She's frightened for her son. Grace, I'm going home."

But the eyes that flew to mine held sheer terror. "No, no, Maggie, stay with me, just a little longer?"

Jay took his parka from a hook by the door. "Tell you what." He shrugged it on. "Maggie will drive you to the station. I'll follow in my car. Keep her calm, Maggie. Make sure she understands that when we get there, she has to keep her big mouth shut."

I didn't know whether Grace was heeding his warning or simply too upset to speak. But after climbing into my truck, she huddled against the door with her legs tucked tight and her arms pressed to her sides. Her mouth was a thin seam just above her scarf. Her eyes focused on the windshield and didn't budge.

Mine did the same, if for different reasons. Forget Edward. Right here, right now, Grace was my responsibility. I negotiated the roundabout with care, waited for an opening, then fell into single file among the cars on South Main. There were more cars than usual for a Thursday afternoon—for *any* afternoon—in Devon. I told myself that it was rush hour. But rush hour in Devon? That was a laugh.

With traffic holding the speed to a stop-and-go crawl, I darted a look at Grace. She didn't see me in her periphery, didn't blink, didn't speak, any of which was so out of character that I worried she had gone to some far and irretrievable place. Needing her back, I said, "I'm sure there's an explanation, Gracie. Jay will iron it out."

She said nothing.

"Does Chris have his own computer?"

"You've been to the house," was her solemn response. "You've seen it."

"I've seen yours, not his."

"The one on the kitchen table is his. Mine's in my bedroom."

I considered that as we crept along. "If his is in the kitchen, you must see what he does."

"Like I understand it?" she said so quickly she might have been asking herself the very same thing.

"Homework, you mean."

"Any of it."

"Even social media? Games?"

She lifted a hand only enough for a noncommittal wave.

Computers were part of my life. I used them at the Spa for record-keeping, and used my home laptop for research on new products, cyber-shopping, and keeping up with my mother. I used a tablet for reading, sometimes in the middle of the night, when I woke fighting to breathe and needed a diversion. My phone was linked with my other devices, and I had done the linking myself. I could troubleshoot any one of them. But hacking? I had no clue how that worked.

"Does he belong to a club at school?" I asked. "A programming club or something?"

"It's a class."

"A class, with lots of kids? Then maybe they've mixed him up with someone else? Maybe with another student? Who's to say one of *them* didn't hack into *his* computer."

She looked at me then. "And go after our clients? Why would one of his friends do that? They have no connection to the Spa."

"But they know you work there," I said. "Maybe one of them has a crush on you. Chris emails you, right?"

"Texts. Kids don't email."

"He's never done it?"

"Maybe once or twice."

"So your email address is on his computer, and your email connects to the Spa. It'd be easy enough for his friends to get it. He must be online with them every night." I made it into a question, but wasn't sure Grace knew the answer. Her work schedule was demanding. Between her loyal following and the fact that she was one of the few massage therapists willing to work evenings, she was heavily booked, which meant Chris was often alone. I had asked her about it once; she said she had taught him how to cook, how to text her, how to call 911.

She didn't reply now, simply stared at the windshield. At the next standstill, I studied her. Jay had warned her against speaking, but I was remembering what my own lawyer had taught me prior to my first court hearing. *Dress simply, Mackenzie. Modest clothes, low heels, light makeup. Court people are plain people, so you need to downplay style.* Having been at work, where scrubs were required, Grace conformed in every regard but her hair. As beautiful as those curls were, they caught the eye, which wasn't a good thing right now. Had I been in her shoes, I'd have put an elastic around them.

Grace did the opposite, finger-combing them fuller and forward to hide her face, and I totally understood. The closer we got to the police station, the more the congestion and the longer the standstills. Cars were pulling over and parking on both sides of the street. Likewise, media vans with satellite dishes. Some had the call letters of Vermont stations, but a few spoke of national brands—*national* brands. It made no sense. But I saw the logos. Their presence made the situation even more alarming.

Hide, my instinct for self-preservation cried, and it was all I could do not to pull my own hair free of pins and use it as a shield.

But Grace couldn't hide. Her son was on the other side of the press. *"How can they be here so soon?"* she cried.

I didn't know. But if I had been uneasy before, I was beside myself now. There were three things I religiously avoided in life—law offices, police stations, and the press—and here they all were.

I gripped the steering wheel tightly, thinking only about dropping Grace off and getting the hell away. She might be hidden under all those curls, but I felt way too visible. Edward had known me. I was the one he had nodded to, not Grace. If he had so easily seen through the makeup and bangs, the press would, too. Oh sure, I had nothing to run from. My case was over and done—well, done except for these last few months of probation. My fear was irrational. But that didn't mean it wasn't real.

The police station was a mile from where the three roads met in the center of Devon. It consisted of a low set of buildings strung along the southernmost blocks of South Main, and was built of square stones the color of unbleached linen, with wide stone steps leading to a black double door. The Town Hall was directly across the street, built of the same local stone but with ivory pillars, black shutters, and nine front steps to the police station's three.

Desperate to be done with it, I drove through the parking lot and right up to the station's entrance. As onrushers merged on the steps, their numbers seemed to swell. I heard Grace breathe, *Oh God*, though the thought might have been mine. Frantic, I checked in my rearview mirror and saw Jay rubbernecking for a place to park. Finally, he just pulled up beside me.

I rolled down my window and spoke before he could. Call me a coward, but there was nothing more I could do for Grace.

"I shouldn't be here," I told him straight off. "Grace is going to get in your car now. You'll take her inside." I turned to Grace. "Jay can help you. I'll only be in the way."

I don't know what I'd have said had she argued. Mercifully, she simply swallowed, pulled up her fur-edged hood, opened the door and rushed around the front of my truck to Jay's car. If the vultures saw her, they didn't yet know who she was.

They had certainly known me once. The Massachusetts Attorney General made sure of it. My crime, while unintentional and tragic, was personal for her. Her father had been crippled several years earlier when his car was hit by a person who was texting, and while the state legislature subsequently made texting-while-driving illegal, the penalty was a fine so small as to be no deterrent at all. The AG was incensed—and she was right. I'm the first to say that. A slap on the wrist accomplishes nothing.

So she continued to make noise, louder each time a new car came on the market that offered enhanced access to technology.

Then I showed up, lost in a densely wooded area and—stupid, stupid, *stupid*—taking my eyes from the road to look at my navigation screen and missing a STOP sign just as a van sped through. That driver and my daughter were killed. It didn't matter that he hit us or that forensics showed him going faster than the limit. I was the only survivor.

Seizing on the case, the AG strong-armed a bill through the state legislature banning interactive technology from functioning in a moving car. Granted, auto manufacturers sought injunctions and have since won years to implement changes, but the legal maneuvers took the case viral. The Massachusetts AG had called it the Mackenzie Cooper Law, and the name stuck. As if the horror of losing my only child wasn't enough, I became the poster child for distracted driving.

And the press? Ate. It. Up. For weeks, the media was parked outside our door, crowding in every time I left home, intruding on our misery with telephoto lenses, even at our daughter's funeral.

I deserved it. I deserved every bit of the punishment. Still, here, now, the memory threatened to close up my throat.

"Text me," I managed to call, but to Grace or Jay? I was too desperate to escape to care which. Shifting gears, I paused only to make sure that none of those converging on the police station were anywhere near the front of my truck, before leaving the horror behind.

3

Driving against traffic, I returned to the center of town. Officer Gill wasn't there; he would be at the station, wanting in on any excitement to be had. I stopped at the crosswalk anyway before turning right onto Cedar. Then I kept a moderate foot on the gas, block by block, quarter mile by quarter mile, pushing against the walls of the past until they began to recede.

My window was still down. The fresh air was a must. This late in the day it was cold but so, so different from the city air of those memories that the farther I drove, the better I felt. One turn had me driving past the pretty yellow farmhouse that, even with fallow fields gone soggy, made me smile. Another turn opened beside the facsimile of a mountain that Devon called its own. It had no black diamonds, just a double chair to lift skiers to six downhills, and the Magic Carpet where every child in town learned to ski. There were no takers today. The only remaining snow lay in fraying mounds under the evergreens that bordered the slopes.

With the reassurance of familiar sights, my mind began to clear. I had a good life here. It was carefully rooted and logical. Guided by that logic, I knew that Jay calling Edward the new owner was a euphemism. Edward was in venture capital. He would simply be representing a group, which was exactly what people in town were saying—that a group had bought the Inn. A venture capitalist might head that group or simply be here laying the groundwork for its takeover of the Inn. Whatever, his presence would be temporary.

That didn't explain why he had grown a beard or wore muddy boots. It didn't explain why he hadn't let me know ahead of time that he was coming. That was the most upsetting. Did he seriously think I wouldn't be hurt seeing him? We had been married for five years and together for another two before that. Even through the devastating days at the end, he had never been callous. What had first drawn me to him, twelve years ago, was his ability to communicate.

His back was to me as he stood across the room. It wasn't a large room; art galleries on Newbury Street were never large. But the good ones carried weight, meaning that museum curators attended their openings. I recognized one of them now, talking with the friend whose work I had come to see. Her medium was colored pencils, which she bought by the thousands, sharpened, cut and arranged point out, end out, flank out—any which way—to recreate parts of the human body. Since my own medium was clay, I was considered more conventional, although conventional wasn't a word my parents would use to describe me. Tonight I wore a calf-length drape of a dress that was definitely more artist than patron. It had been created by another friend, who had given it to me in exchange for a set of mugs for her mom. The silk was a breathy-pale coral, painted with flowers and lines in surprisingly gentle burgundies and browns. It was sleeveless, had a deep V in the front, and clung at the bodice before falling in slim drifts to uneven points that overlapped the top of my boots. The boots were cowboy-style, but of slouchy leather with a bronze sheen. I wore an armful of bangles, a narrow scarf tied as a headband, and goose bumps.

In fairness, the goose bumps were there before he turned. But they spiked when his eyes caught mine. They were a startling light blue, almost iridescent. On a purely artistic level, they intrigued me.

Not wanting to stare, I quickly retreated to the sculpture before me. Minutes later, I felt a warmth at my shoulder. "Are you the artist?"

As pick-up lines went in my circle, it was clichéd. But his natty suit said he wasn't in my circle at all. His voice was deep and serious. I dared only the briefest glance at him before saying, "Don't I wish. This hand is amazing." With a soft jangle of bracelets, I raised my hand to a similar pose, much as I had done when the artist was making the piece. My hand—her hand—was relaxed, raised and turned at the wrist, fingers extended and graceful in an almost pious way.

We stood side by side. He held a wine glass as he studied the piece. "How many pencils are in it?"

"Seven hundred and thirty-three."

He sputtered a low laugh. "That was a rhetorical question. How do you know the answer?"

"I know the artist. I watched her make this."

"Seriously?"

I looked up at him then. We were still arm to arm, but his eyes were on mine. I felt a fast link. "Very. We knew each other at Ox-Bow."

"Ox-Bow."

"Chicago. Actually, it's in Saugatuck—that's Michigan—but it's affiliated with the Art Institute of Chicago. It's an artists' colony. We were both fellowship students."

"So you are an artist, just not of this piece."

I knew the difference between polite indulgence and genuine interest. My father was a master of polite indulgence; I rarely knew what he actually thought. This man was different. There was something . . . bare . . . about his face.

"I work in clay," I said. "The challenge for me would be replicating the sheer feeling of this." I nodded toward the hand. "Look at it—wrist, knuckles, fingernails, all in perfect proportion and pose. It comes to life."

He said nothing.

Awkward, fearing I'd lost him, I asked, "Don't you think?"

He remained serious. "I do. But I'm pretty dumb when it comes to art. I'm here just tagging along with a friend."

That made sense. His hair was neatly cut, his suit dark and sedate, his loafers polished. The only thing even remotely artistic about him was his tie, which had tiny flowers—ironically—in the same coral as my dress. I wondered if someone had put the outfit together for him. I had a friend who earned money doing that. Her medium was gouache, but she worked at an exclusive men's shop to pay bills. If this man used someone like her, the tie might be as far as he dared go.

Too late, I realized I was staring at it, at the pale-blue shirt that stretched fractionally with each breath, at the nearby lapel that was drawn into an elegant curve by the hand in the pocket of his slacks. Too late, I realized that we were facing each other.

The silence went on a beat too long. Trying to make a joke of staring, I said, "You look very grown-up."

He snickered. "As in boring?"

"No. I meant serious. Disciplined." Even the hand that held his wine glass suggested it. Long fingers supported the stem while his thumb and forefinger cradled the bowl. But there, there, was a tiny betrayal. That forefinger tapped the bowl once, then again, like the discipline only went so far.

I must have been staring again because he said, "Uh, oh, sorry, would you—?" He raised his glass and glanced at the server who was circulating with a tray.

"No. But thanks. You're not drinking yours. Not into champagne?"

"Not into wine. Beer's more my thing. I'm just trying to look the part."

"Of what?"

"Knowledgeable art admirer." He cleared his throat. "My business card says I'm a venture capitalist, but I'm not totally there. I'm working my way up. That requires looking confident."

"Aren't you?"

His lips lifted in a lopsided way, still not yet a smile, but sincere. "Not like you. You look bohemian through and through."

I wondered if I'd gone too far with the outfit. Maybe the top was too bare for proper Bostonians, or the many-stacked bangles were silly, or the cowboy boots clashed with the rest. "That bad?"

"*That good, no, it's good. Do you live here in Boston?*"

"*For a week now and then.*"

"*And the rest of the time?*"

"*Trying to figure that out.*"

"*Where are you originally from?*"

"*Connecticut. You?*"

"*New Jersey. My dad's a dairy farmer.*"

I smiled at that. I wouldn't have guessed it, though he could probably say the same about me. "*My dad teaches math,*" I said to even us out. "*He's buttoned up, very into formulas.*"

"*Which you are not.*"

"*Which I am not.*" I grinned at a friend who approached. A fellow artist, he wore his standard black T-shirt and jeans. For the occasion, he had added a scarf that my mom would call dashing but that I called simply the price paid for the honor of eating high-end canapes.

"*Hey, Mack,*" he said and kissed both of my cheeks, then tossed a hand back at the room. "*Is this cool or what?*"

"*Very cool,*" I said. "*Uh, Ollie, this is . . .*"

"*Edward,*" said the tall man and extended his hand. They shook, which seemed to exhaust Ollie's patience for nonartists, because as abruptly as he'd come, he turned and left.

I was about to explain that artists weren't always socially skilled, when Edward said, "*Mack?*"

"*Mackenzie. Edward? Ed? Woody?*"

"*Just Edward. Tell me about your work.*"

I thought about how best to explain it to a layman. "*I sculpt people, but in an interpretive way. I find a trait in my subject that I want to capture, and I sculpt the face to reflect it.*"

"*Then, you make head shots? Torsos?*"

"*Fragments of both. I've started doing family groups.*"

"*Singly or together?*"

"*Together. It's the challenge of finding an overriding trait. Some families are cohesive, some are disjointed. Some are matriarchal, some are blended. I spend as much prep time getting to know the family as I do sculpting them. You must do the same thing with your work." I paused. What I knew about venture capitalism could fit into one of my mother's tiny pinch-of-spice cups. Cautious, I asked, "Don't you?"*

"Oh yeah, I do." He cleared his throat. "But hey," he said with what might have been a smile, though it was small and tentative, "I'm not big on whatever it is they're serving here, and I'm starved. I passed an Indian place down the block. It looked interesting, and it wasn't packed, which may mean the food stinks, but at least it'd be quiet enough to talk." He dipped his head, seeming a little unsure but genuinely hopeful, and asked, "Want some dinner?"

Meals were incidental in my life. I had assumed that dinner tonight would consist of whatever I munched on here, but there was no reason to stay. I had come for my friend, and for the gallery owner, whom I had met several times and who I dreamed would show my work one day. I had already talked with both. There were lots of other people here I knew; we could talk about art all night. But I always talked about art. Venture capital was different. So was dairy farming. So, frankly, was a man who could talk easily and, despite his appearance, came across as honest and unpretentious.

Oh yeah. Edward Cooper could communicate. Looking back, though, that wasn't the very *first* thing that had drawn me to him. Honestly? What had first drawn me to him when I saw him on the far side of the gallery that night were his looks. I liked tall, and he was that. I liked dark, and he was that, too. I only saw his back at first, but he stood straight with ease. And when he turned? He wasn't handsome in the classical sense; his cheekbones were too high, his nose too thin. But the attraction was instant and as electric as those weird, wonderful eyes.

That night was a pivotal one. Once we hit the street, he took off his jacket and, without asking, draped it over my shoulders. The warmth, the smell, the gesture—I loved it, even knowing he'd take the thing back as soon as dinner was done. But he didn't. I wore the jacket until we were in his downtown apartment, when it came off with the rest of our clothes.

The memory was vivid. Feeling it deep in my belly, I slowly and deliberately inhaled. On an equally deliberate exhalation, I forced myself to remember my last view of him as his wife. He wore a suit, but the tie was bland. His hair was combed, but limp. His eyes were shadowed, like mine, and the shoulders that had once seemed so broad now sagged under a burden too heavy to bear. He was going to work, but I had no idea whether he got anything done there, or even whether he actually went. I didn't ask. We were closed down to each other by then. When he went through the door, he didn't look back.

Nor did I. After the movers finished loading my things in their van that morning, I climbed into my new truck, headed for Vermont, and stopped thinking about the past.

His showing up now screwed that. It was the last thing I needed, on top of the rest of the chaos in town.

But I had a job, I had friends, I had a home of my own.

Focusing on those things, I consciously eased my hands, stretching the fingers of first one, then the other, until they sat less rigidly on the wheel. The scents of my new life were a drug. I drew them into my lungs, held them there, and released them—drew them in, held them, released them. With each cycle, my tension eased. It was callous of me, for sure. Edward was reduced to nothing, and Grace was going through hell, while I was starting to relax. But what choice did I have? I couldn't go back. Just *couldn't.*

A vibrating came from deep in my shoulder bag. I didn't imagine it was Grace or Jay—way too early, but as soon as I turned off the main road, I pulled over just in case. There were two texts, but they were from other friends. Word was spreading. I knew it would. Devon wasn't into petty gossip, but news was news. Add Federal agents and the national media disturbing our calm, and there was bound to be talk.

Having none to share, I drove on until I reached the white post that marked Pepin Hill. There were no other cars on the road, but out of habit alone, I signaled before turning off and starting up. I didn't smell the Spa here but rather woods, water, and mud. Lovely smells all, they reinforced the sense of distance that I had worked so hard to create. By the time I pulled up at the cabin, I could hear Jonah barking inside, which was another special sign of my new life.

The path to my door was free of slush, thanks to the job done during last week's late-season snow by a plow guy who liked me. And UPS had come by. Several boxes were stacked at the door.

Nudging them aside with a boot, I had the front door barely open when Jonah bounded out, heading for the brush to do his business. He was a beagle and a small one, for the breed. Nearly twelve, his puppy years were well past, which meant he was okay being inside for large stretches of time. After nearly four years with me, he had grown even more okay with it. Though I still tried to get home in the middle of the day to let him out, he never seemed to suffer when I could not.

That said, I felt guilty watching his exuberance now. He ran into the woods and back for several minutes before making a slower, panting return to the cabin.

The cabin? My realtor had always called it that, so I did. But given that it had well-planed wood siding, a paneled oak door, and a gable roof covered, Vermont-style, with the best metal money could buy, calling it a cabin felt like a misnomer. It was really just a very small house, painted the same slate gray as the squirrels in the woods. The first floor, front to back, held an open living room, eating bar, and kitchen, while the second floor was split between a single bedroom and bath, and a loft. Driving me here the first time, the realtor had described it as rustic, perhaps to prepare me for the worst. She knew I was from a suburb of Boston, knew that the house I was leaving had every modern appliance built in, along with a wine cooler, a hand-crafted Italian backsplash, and radiant heat. By comparison, the amenities here were modest.

Modest suited me just fine. Modest I could handle.

Besides, there was an element of pride involved in owning something myself. Granted, the divorce had given me enough money to buy it, but, had it not, my art would have. This was my own place. I had never owned my own home before, having gone from my parents to college to nomadism to Edward.

Should I try to call him? Did he even have the same number?

Stacking the boxes on a bench just inside the door, I hung my coat on a hook above and was toeing off my boots when my cell buzzed again. Seeing the name of another friend, I was tempted to answer. Alexandra Smith taught at the local school and might have inside news. But something in me couldn't go there yet, especially not with Hex and Jinx rubbing against my legs, one cat per leg, and vocal.

All three pets were from the shelter. I had adopted Jonah, because, as sweet as his face was, he was old, and old pets were hard to place. The problem with Hex and Jinx wasn't their age, which was two, or their health, which was fine, but because too many people were superstitious when it came to black cats.

Having lost a child, which, as far as I was concerned, was the worst thing that could happen to a mother, I was past the point of superstition. Moreover, the comfort my cats gave was beyond measure. Snugglers both, they curled beside me when I was on the sofa and slept on my bed every night. I wished they were better with Jonah. They picked on him like he was a cat toy, and, good old boy that he was, he took it. His revenge, of course, was going out with me for walks and drives, neither of which the others could do without risk of escape and subsequent death-by-fisher.

My phone vibrated again. After a quick glance to make sure it wasn't Grace, I set it aside. I stroked the cats head to tail, one hand per cat, until they slipped free and made for the kitchen. Jonah was already there, waiting patiently after expending his energy outside. I filled three bowls with the appropriate food and spaced them apart on the floor, then, while they ate, filled a glass from the tap. My well offered pure spring water—no labels, no plastic, no cost. As I drank, I picked up my phone and began thumbing the screen to see the latest posts.

I followed makeup artists. Some I knew personally, some only by reputation, but the pictures they posted kept me up-to-date on new products and styles. I followed local restaurants and stores. I followed craftspeople. There was an amazing silk-screen artist whose posts alone were works of art.

I followed my mother, CNN, and the Devon PD, but none of those could distract me in a positive way, which was why I followed CALM. *Some think that holding on makes us strong; but sometimes it's letting go*, I read now and couldn't have agreed more. Sometimes, though, it was easier said than done.

Like now.

What *was* that noise?

I lowered the phone and listened in dismay as my pets alternately munched kibble and shuffled pellets to get their little mouths around more. They made the same sound every day, but it sounded different right now. That munch and shuffle, over and over, conjured the image of multiple cameras snapping multiple frames.

It was memory, of course. I hadn't been near enough to the cameras today to actually hear them, but the knowledge that they were lying in wait was enough to bring it all back.

Distancing myself, I sank into the living room sofa, tucked up my feet, and looked at those new texts. Joyce wanted news; I texted back saying I had none. It occurred to me that Nina might. I was debating calling her when Alex phoned again.

"Grace Emory's son?" she asked in hushed disbelief. "I thought it'd be someone from outside, maybe a parent with a grudge. But a *student?*"

"How did you get his name?" I asked. Grace was right about the unfairness of that.

"They came for him at school."

"He's high school. You're middle school."

"The teaching community is tight," she said as if that forgave the talk, and hurried on before I could argue. "I taught Chris in sixth grade. He's brilliant. Lazy, but brilliant."

"Lazy? How is he lazy? I've never seen laziness. He does everything Grace asks—"

"But nothing more," Alex broke in, "and I'm talking intellectually. He was a great reader when I had him, read fast and with total comprehension, but he would only read what was assigned, just the assignment, nothing more. I'll bet he never reads a book at home."

I opened my mouth to argue but nothing came out. She was probably right, given his role model. Grace wasn't a reader. I had invited her into my book group, but she wasn't interested. Same when I occasionally suggested she read a book that I loved. Her addiction was for fashion magazines and the never-ending search for a different look. But that was neither here nor there when it came to her son being a hacker. Besides, sharing this with Alex felt disloyal to Grace.

"If he doesn't read outside class," I said, "how would he know about hacking? Are there instructions online?"

"Pretty much. I'm not saying he did it, but he could have. He's a smart kid."

"Right, so why would he want to change his grades?"

"Oh, *his* grades were never changed."

That stopped me. "Whose were?"

"Random others. Maybe he was testing himself before trying something bigger. Honing the skill, y'know?"

I didn't find anything humorous in her turn of phrase. "Maybe it wasn't him at all."

"It sure looks it. Poor Grace. She was always the first one to sign up for parent-teacher conferences or send cookies for a bake sale. She must be terrified." She paused, waiting for me to confirm it. When I didn't, she said, "The police station's a circus. They say it'll make the national news tonight."

I shouldn't have been surprised, given the national brands I'd seen emblazoned on satellite vans in town, but that didn't mean I wasn't alarmed. Federal charges were a big thing, but the crime itself—*alleged* crime—was localized. Nationwide interest didn't make sense unless someone had an ulterior motive. I certainly knew about those.

"The judge is on his way," Alex said. "They want him locked up. They think he's a flight risk."

"*Chris?* Chris is fifteen! Who are you talking to, Alex?"

She offered three names, one reliable, two not, but my stomach was knotting up against the past again—a past that, like Grace and every other female friend here, Alex knew nothing about. So when she switched topics and said, "But hey, we're still on for this weekend, aren't we?" I was furious at how unconcerned she seemed. It was a minute before I could calm myself and pull back.

Alex, Jessa Hutton, and I were binge buddies, meeting Saturday nights whenever Jessa's hunter-husband did his upcountry thing. In the last two years, we had worked our way through *Homeland* and *Girls*. We were now into *Game of Thrones*.

"Wouldn't miss it," I managed and, with a casual, "Let me know if you hear anything more?" ended the call. Two seconds passed before another came.

"Grace could have a problem," Nina said without preamble. "Those Twitter accounts belong to some important people."

"Do you know who?"

"Griswold wouldn't give me names," Gary Griswold was our Police Chief, "but he's sitting in his office with his chest puffed out like he had something to do with the investigation, which he did not. This has been a Federal operation all the way."

"There must have been talk. The press would be panting for it." *Like rabid wolves,* I thought, but didn't say. "Did you catch any names at all?" I might recognize a few. I did VIP makeup often, had certainly done my share of visiting celebs. As flattering as it was to be asked, now I wondered at my own hubris. If a client of mine was the victim here, my probation officer wouldn't like it. His parting shot at the end of each monthly visit was to warn me to give trouble a wide berth, and though, after all this time, he made it a joke, I took it to heart.

"I didn't pick up a thing," Nina said, "and, trust me, I asked. But Griswold said *he*. *He's* in town. *He'll* be at the courthouse later. Want to meet me there?"

"God, no," I cried, trying to make light of the suggestion. My own clients were female, but Grace worked on a lot of men. Frightened for her, but not willing to go anywhere near the zoo of a press conference, I asked, "How was your meeting?"

"A quick vote yes. All they wanted to talk about was hacking. I saw Grace at the station. She's a basket case. Did you see the media trucks?"

I said that I had, and took a single, long breath to quiet myself while Nina gushed over the various news outlets that had come. I suspected she was having flashbacks to New York and loving it. Me, I was having flashbacks to Boston and not loving it at all.

"There's going to be a press conference later," she said. "No doubt Griswold wants to get the biggest bang for the buck. And hell, Maggie, it's not hurting the town. Guess where the press is staying tonight? The Inn."

I knew what the Inn charged. Rates were up there in the stratosphere along with rates at the Spa. I would be surprised if the average reporter's expense account allowed for the Inn—unless there was a press special going on—which would be a stroke of genius, come to think of it. Talk about generating goodwill.

By every other measure, this would be a PR nightmare for the Spa. Nothing good could come of illegal access to personal information that we had promised our clients would never, ever get out. The new owners couldn't possibly be pleased. I wondered if Edward was the messenger who had to bring them the news. Best case scenario? They called him back to wherever they were and canceled the sale.

By the time Kevin called, my insides were a snake pit. Needing him, I answered with a quick, "Hey."

"Devon is crawling with enemies."

I barked out a high laugh. "Tell me."

"What'd your friend do?"

"Absolutely nothing. Her son is the one in custody."

Kevin snorted. "That little shit? If anyone's the hacker, it's Grace." He and Grace had never hit it off. She was too drawn to straight men to allow for a friendship with one who wasn't. Or maybe it was simpler than that. My therapist suggested she was jealous of my friendship with Kevin. I suppose she had cause.

"What else have you heard?" I asked. As focused as the pottery studio was, Kevin kept an ear to the ground. It helped that his significant other worked at the police department.

"Not much yet, but I was thinking you'd need company. Meet me for pizza?" We often did that, and if there was anyone who could help restore my balance, Kevin was it. But the pizza shop was on the police station side of town, which meant it would be loaded with media snoops, which Kevin must have realized as soon as he said it, because he followed up with, "Too exposed? How about One-on-Tap?"

One-on-Tap was a small, dark, locals-only place that served good beer and amazing burgers. Best, though, it was located in Pelham, on the far side of Lyme Creek, a safe two towns away. "Better," I breathed.

"Seven-thirty?"

"I'll be there."

4

True to its name, One-on-Tap offered a single beer each night. The choice was always local and served by the keg. One might be subtle, another bold, citrusy, malty, or dark. I liked a few and only tasted others, but I always finished the burgers, which were made of Angus beef from The Farm at Lyme Creek.

Tonight, though, eating was the last thing on my mind when I entered the restaurant's foyer and saw Kevin's familiar chill-red cheeks, dark gold eyes, and pulled-back hair. Had I been able to cry, I would have burst into tears, which was what I had done several years before when the gentleness of those eyes said he would understand and I desperately needed someone who would. But I never cried now; I had run out of tears. I simply held him tightly for several heartbeats, before he took my hand and drew me to a booth. Leaving me there, he crossed to the bar—a freestanding oval in the middle of the pub, with tall stools on either side—and ordered beer and burgers for two.

Returning, he slid in across from me and unwound a puffy scarf that I knew, for fact, he had knit himself. He had barely pulled away the last of the mohair billows when he stuffed the fuzzy mass into his lap and looked me in the eye. "How are you, girlfriend?"

It wasn't so much a question as a command, and my first thought was to tell him I'd seen Edward. But that would be giving my ex-husband's appearance more weight than Grace's crisis. So I reined in my thoughts and said, "I'd be better if Grace called. What have you heard?"

"Not much. Jimmy couldn't talk. He said the station's a scene."

"Has Chris been formally charged?" At his blank shrug, I tried, "Do we know the victim?"

"I don't. Was it on the news?"

"I couldn't watch," I said. "I checked the PD's Twitter feed, but there was nothing."

Kevin snorted. "If Griswold's busy, forget Twitter. He can only do one thing at a time."

"I thought Jimmy posted for him." Kevin's Jimmy was the techie of the pair. Gary Griswold might have hired a more conventional assistant— still called "secretary" in his department—if he hadn't been fascinated with social media. Jimmy was an expert at that. It helped that his dark-rimmed glasses, Oxford shirts, and short-cropped hair gave him a conservative look. He was known in town as Jim.

Since I had met him through Kevin, who always called him Jimmy, and since I loved him for the way he adored Kevin, he would always be the softer, kinder Jimmy to me.

"He did," Kevin answered, "until last week when he posted about the DUI that turned out to be Griswold's cousin. I mean, it was part of the police report, which was what Jimmy was supposed to post, and he didn't name the cousin, but people connected the dots, so Gary was pissed. He'll have Jimmy posting again this week, you watch."

"He can't post Chris's name. He's a minor."

Kevin shot me a dry look.

Fine. Everyone here knew exactly who was sitting at the station right now. Still, "Chris is fifteen. They aren't seriously thinking of locking him up." I tacked on a meek, "Are they?"

"Not if his mom and lawyer are there. But Jimmy'll know for sure." He glanced at the huge face of his watch, then again at the door. "He'll be here as soon as he can get away, but he's trying to show Gary he's diligent." Leaning forward, he said a gentle, "It was good of you to drive her into town."

I didn't bother to ask how he knew. This, too, was the kind of word that spread through Devon like oil. I had never been bothered before. Local talk here wasn't malicious. It was news. An argument could be made that Devonites, being Devonites, simply kept each other informed. Still, I cringed on Grace's behalf. She wouldn't mind people raving about an amazing deep-tissue massage she had given. But the news being passed around now wasn't that.

"It was the least I could do," I said.

"Not fun, though."

"No." My chest tightened. Kevin was the only one who knew about my past, the only one who knew that I had caused two deaths. During my early days at the pottery studio, when I needed clay badly but could barely lift my hands, he used to find me alone at closing time, close to tears. On one of those days, the dam broke, and my sordid past poured out. He knew about the media frenzy, the conviction, the divorce. He was the only one who knew that I wished, time and again, that I had died in the crash.

The relief of sharing had been instant. But why Kevin? My therapist said that to make Devon truly mine, I needed to confide in someone here. But why this man, whom I had barely known at the time? Well, clay linked us. He loved its smell and feel as much as I did, loved the act of creation. More, though, right from the start we connected on a visceral level. I knew more about Kevin now than I did about anyone else in town. He had his own Achilles' heel, so we balanced each other out. We loved each other for the total acceptance that allowed.

Kevin also understood my need for secrecy. Seeing my horror when everything first spilled out, he had taken a paper and pencil, written the names of his parents, their address and phone number, and said that if he ever betrayed me, I could betray him.

I couldn't believe that in this day and age his parents didn't know he was gay. Then I thought of my own parents and realized how it might be. Parents could be narrow-minded when it came to dreams for their kids.

Our beer arrived in heavy glass steins. It was a deep amber color with a thick head—an American Amber Lager, the whiteboard said—medium bodied, toasty malt character, only marginally bitter. I removed my gloves to cradle the stein, but my hands were like ice, and cold beer didn't help, at least, not on the outside. Needing help on the inside, I grasped the thick handle, took a solid gulp, and put my gloves back on.

"Sit on them," Kevin ordered.

I did. The warmth was instant. Thighs. Crafty Kevin.

"Talk," he ordered next. "What were you doing between when I called and when you drove here?"

"Worrying," I said. "I don't think Grace has money for bail."

"No one does—well, except you, because your then-husband was loaded—but that's why they have bail bondsmen. So what were you doing an hour ago?"

Stressing about said then-husband? Nope. Not going there. Mentioning Edward would make him real, and, with any luck, he was on his way out of town.

"Worrying about Chris," I said. "How can a fifteen-year-old deal with this?"

"Maybe better than you. He doesn't see the big picture."

"But he will. What then?"

"I don't know, love," Kevin said, seeming sad to let me down, which made me feel worse.

"Okay, after that, I went for distraction. UPS delivered stuff I needed for work—replenishments of the foundation I use at the Spa, disposable sponges, mascara wands. Some of it went in my closet. It stays fresher when I can control the storage. I combined the rest in one box to take to the Spa tomorrow." I had a horrible thought. "The media is staying at the Inn. What if they come to the Spa? I mean," I added with dread, "they will. It's part of the story, isn't it?"

"Don't jump ahead. This may all end tonight."

"We hope." I pulled out my phone and checked the screen. "Nothing from Grace, but they've probably taken her phone. What's happening, do you think?"

Kevin took a long drink, set down the stein, and ran a hand over the foam on his upper lip. "They'll be waiting for the judge or the stenographer or the bondsman, or else it's paperwork, and something always slows them down there, either the printer is out of ink or the scanner doesn't work. It drives Jimmy nuts."

"It drove me nuts, too. It's like you're in a spotlight that just hangs there, one minute becoming ten becoming thirty, and you're totally naked and exposed to the world for what you truly are."

"Not what you truly are. What someone *alleges* you are."

"Same difference. If you've gotten yourself in this situation, you've done something wrong. It may not be all they say it is, but Grace was right, innocent until proven guilty doesn't seem to apply anymore." I took another drink and studied the foam streaks on the inside of the glass. I was vaguely aware of bar sounds, utensil sounds, and guitar sounds, all soft and relaxing, but focusing on them wasn't easy with so many other disturbing thoughts.

Kevin knew. "What?" he invited gently.

"No. This shouldn't be about me."

"Come on, babe. How can it not be? You've lived this before."

"Right, and I don't want to do it again," I blurted, giving in to my fear. "Devon is my safe place. I don't want this happening here. Make it go away?"

He laughed. "I would if I could, but they've come to town in droves."

"Why so many? I can understand local media, but why national?" But Kevin didn't know any more than me. Resigned to that, I sighed. "Anyway, thanks for meeting me here. I couldn't bear to see them."

With an eloquent sigh, he glanced at the handful of stools that were filled at the bar. "Well, you're safe in this place. Only locals come. The rest of the world barely knows it exists. If the owners get drift of a reviewer showing up—or worse a guide-book author—they dilute the beer and overcook the beef."

"They do not," I scolded. "That'd be professional suicide."

"Why? No one local cares. We all know what we get here. Besides, how else do you explain it?" He tossed his chin toward a couple eating nachos at the bar. "The Gauthiers from Lyme Creek," then a guy cradling a beer two seats down, "Jack Randolph and his daughter, who is going through a divorce bad enough that she had to take out a restraining order, Jimmy said." He winked at someone on the far side of the bar and murmured to me, "There's our local homophobe. It drives him crazy when I do that." Leaning toward the aisle, he rose up several inches. "I see three moms in one of the back booths. They come to the studio sometimes, but it's mostly just to play, I mean, no serious talent there. I'm telling you, you're safe here. They're all locals." Eyes shifting slightly, he drew in a small breath. "Oooooo, not that one," he cooed, seeming intrigued. "Who is *he?*"

Leaning around the edge of the booth, I followed his gaze, then whipped forward again. I sheltered myself in the center of the booth's high wood back and reached for my beer. Not only had Edward not left town yet, but here he was in my favorite haven of a pub, which he had no business even *knowing* about. The fact that he did shot safety to hell.

I took one generous swallow, then another. With a finality born of resignation, I set the stein back on the table and said, "That is the new owner of the Inn."

"The new owner," Kevin breathed in wonder. Eyes glued to that back booth, he must have thought my upset had to do with having a new boss.

"Well, he's not the *owner* owner," I said, needing to qualify it for me

as much as for Kevin. "He's part of a group. Likely the one negot:
the deal."

"He's dishy."

I was in no position to say. My judgment was colored by total dis
"It's dark back there. You can't see much."

"I see enough. He's a far cry from old Ollie."

"Most anyone would be," I argued. The fabled Oliver Hamilton
been an imposing gentleman with white hair and mustache. Having
vated the Devon Hotel to resort status in the mid-1900s, he was co:
ered the father of the present-day Inn and Spa. The life-size paintin
him that hung in the lobby of the Inn remained the centerpiece aro
which any redecoration was done.

"This one's still too old for you," I said, which was absurd. Kevin
thirty, Edward forty-four. The age difference was nothing, but it was
first thing I could think of to say.

He continued to stare toward the back. "Not too old for you,"
hummed distractedly. "You're what? Forty-three?"

I managed a weak smile. We often joked about my being older th
Kevin, but his soul was my age, or so I'd always felt. He was sensitive
yond his years. Usually.

"Thirty-eight," I said, "which you well know, having put that ma
candles on the birthday cake you baked me last month." The cake h
been an artistic confection, those many candles one more gesture aim
at taking my mind off my mother on the day that marked my birth.

Kevin slid toward the edge of the booth for what he likely consider
a subtler view—just sitting there on the aisle, one hand around his be:
nonchalant as could be.

"Kevin," I warned, but his gaze didn't budge. Struggling to be cool
said, "Please, don't catch his eye. I know him."

"Know him."

"Don't want him seeing me."

"Good luck with that, honey bun. If he's the new owner—"

"He's one of many—"

"But he's in Devon." The wonder was back, along with sincere curiosity. "He could have eaten at the Inn. Why do you think he's here?"

I might have shared the curiosity, if I hadn't been so rattled. I conjured up a quick CALM—*Surround yourself with positive energy*—and took a deep, hopeful breath.

"Maybe he just likes beer." I knew he did. Edward wasn't a big drinker, but he loved an interesting brew. One-on-Tap might have, in fact, been why he offered to visit Devon for his group. Sure, the pub was our best-kept secret. But Edward had always kept an eye on beer blogs, of which there were many more now than when we had been married.

Kevin kept staring.

"Maybe," I added, scolding, "he just wants privacy," and reached across for his arm. "I'm serious. Don't stare at him. The last thing I want is for him to come say hello."

"He thinks I'm hot. There's a connection."

I sighed. There was no avoiding the truth. Closing my hand on his slender wrist, I gave it a shake. "If there's a connection on his part, it's curiosity about who I'm with. Kevin, that man is my ex-husband."

His eyes shot to mine—*bam!*—his ruddy cheeks seeming suddenly more ruddy in the dim pub light. It was a minute before he put it together. "Edward? *Edward* is the new owner?"

"Not him. A group he represents. That's what he does." He usually worked with start-ups, and The Devon Inn and Spa was far from that, but if rumor had it and another expansion was in the works, investors were needed. Edward specialized in gathering groups of those.

"Did he tell you that?"

"No. Jay did. Edward was leaving his office when Grace and I arrived."

"What did he say to you?"

"Nothing. We didn't talk."

"You haven't seen him in how long, and you didn't talk? No words spoken?"

"Kevin. We weren't alone."

"Still."

I sighed. "I don't know how long he'll be here, but the sooner he leaves, the better." Kevin remained quiet, waiting for more, but what more could I say? "So he's definitely straight, and he's definitely temporary, and anyway, you prefer blonds. Ah." Saved by the blond who was sliding off his glasses as he picked up a beer at the bar and strode toward their booth. "Jimmy. Thank goodness. Sit." He slid in beside Kevin, took a great gulp of beer, and set the stein down with a *thunk*.

"Mmmmm. I needed that."

He grinned. Kevin used his own napkin to wipe the foam from Jimmy's lip.

It was a sweet gesture, but I was moving on. "What's happening, Jimmy?" I was eager to shift the focus. Edward's being here sucked the control out of my life. How better to get it back than by immersing myself in Grace's problems?

"The closest Federal Court is in Rutland," Jimmy said, court being a slurred *co-ut* in the way that marked Jim Pratt a Dorchester boy, "so the kid had his initial appearance there, but he's gone home with his mom."

Home was a relief. "What does 'initial appearance' mean?"

"Indictment is read, charges are filed."

"Bail?" I asked.

"None. Not in this kind of juvenile hearing. The prosecutors duked it out earlier this week to determine jurisdiction. Feds won. Ergo Rutland."

Kevin made a face. "Ergo?"

"The chief's word, not mine. Do you want to know what happened or not?"

"I do," I said. A naive little part of me had been hoping that the whole thing would be declared a misunderstanding, charges would be dropped, and the circus would end there and then. Apparently not.

"The hacking was traced to Chris's laptop," Jimmy said. "The evidence is strong."

I was appalled. "How can that *be*?"

"Hacking isn't hard if you know passwords. School computers are networked, and the kids here all have school accounts. They do homework online. They email the teacher, the teacher emails back. I'm sure they trade passwords. Hell, bunches of them probably use the same one, so slipping from account to account would be easy, especially for a kid who's into it."

"Which means it could have also been one of Chris's classmates."

"Could have, but prob'ly wasn't. One of the others wouldn't have been able to get into the Spa network. You'd have to have an entry point, like having access to a computer that has access to the Spa. Chris did."

"Allegedly," Kevin prompted.

"There's evidence."

"Allegedly," Kevin insisted and scowled at Jimmy. "You're becoming as absolutist as the rest of the force. You're supposed to keep their minds open. Isn't that the point of your being there?"

"The point of my being there is to be paid," Jimmy shot back. He and Kevin often bickered. I typically ignored it, even though it was sweet. Silence had pounded a nail in the coffin of my marriage—well, along with other nails—but communication was key. I appreciated that Kevin and Jimmy could do it freely, not to mention that this time I had a stake in the discussion.

"I don't have your fancy art degree," Jimmy was saying, making art *aht* and drawing it out. "All I did was go two years to tech school, so I know how to use machines, and I know social media because there are plenty of times when I have nothing to do, so I play. I'm just saying what they're saying." After a short huff for Kevin, he faced me again. "Sorry. This may not be what you want to hear, but it doesn't look good for the kid."

"But he is just a kid," I argued.

"He'll be tried as a juvenile."

"And put in prison?"

"A juvenile facility."

"But what harm did he do?" I asked, bewildered on behalf of my friend's son. My crime involved death, which was the ultimate in harm. But here? "The high school records have been straightened out. And the

Spa, what harm there? Okay, a crime is a crime, but how serious could this be? Devon isn't the Pentagon."

"He got into Twitter."

"And did what *harm?*" I had a Twitter account. I used it to promote my work at the Spa. I couldn't imagine harm that a hacker could do that would justify imprisoning a fifteen-year-old boy.

"It's Internet fraud," Jimmy said. "That's a Federal charge. The arraignment is Monday. We'll have to wait 'til then to know about other charges. They could charge him with wire fraud, too."

"Isn't that the same as Internet fraud?"

"They're different statutes. Add one to the other, and the penalty gets worse. They could also charge him separately for each post he made, so that could be a dozen counts, maybe two dozen counts."

"*Chrissake,* Jimmy," Kevin said.

"Okay, okay, let's assume they leave it at Internet fraud. The government has to prove deliberate deception, which there was if he hacked into school accounts to change grades. They also have to prove he used someone else's computer without permission."

"The school will never press charges," I said. I knew many local teachers through Alex, and each one had struck me as kind. I was sure they would prefer counseling or an internal school punishment rather than incarceration.

"Twitter's the problem. The victim is Ben Zwick."

Kevin and I exchanged blank looks. "Who is Ben Zwick?" we asked together.

"Benjamin Zwick," Jimmy said with relish. He drew a sharp line between what was confidential police business and what was not, and while he might slip with small details once in a while, this wasn't small. Given how brashly he said the name, I assumed that the identity of Benjamin Zwick was public knowledge to anyone who had watched tonight's news, which neither Kevin nor I had done. "He's an investigative journalist with *The Washington Post.* He has credits a mile long. He's always showing up on shows like *Washington Week* and *Meet the Press.* And he wrote a book."

A silent bell rang. Maybe I recognized the name, after all. "On anti-semitism in Scandinavia?"

"That's it."

"Oh God. He won a Pulitzer Prize."

Kevin directed an unimpressed, "So?" at his partner.

"So our friend Chris," Jimmy quickly corrected himself, "*allegedly* Chris, hacked into Zwick's account and made posts Zwick claims hurt his career."

"Like how?" I asked.

"Like saying there's proof the last presidential election was rigged by the Republicans. Like saying the Secretary of Defense is supplying guns to whoever wants to organize a home militia. Like saying the Prime Minister of Norway is a second or third cousin to Hitler, and then calling his editor at the *Post* an asshole for refusing to let him print that in a story."

"Those posts are over the top," I said. "Anyone can see that."

"Not anyone. The retweets were even worse, haters from every side coming out. It took Zwick a couple days to realize what had happened and close down his Twitter account, which is also pissing him off. He says his name is smeared and people don't trust him like they used to and won't answer his calls. He's hitting back hard. He wants whoever did this to him to be publicly skewered."

"A fifteen-year-old boy?" I cried.

"He says he didn't know who it was at the time, but that if a kid did it, he should know there are consequences."

Once, after the accident, when the only relief my mind could find was in books, I read something that stuck. *A big part of growing up is learning to be cautious. It's realizing that there are consequences to everything you do.* Like the character in that book, Chris Emory was fifteen. Death might not be involved in the charges against him, but the potential consequences were still pretty heavy for someone that age to bear.

"Is Zwick the one who leaked Chris's name?" I asked Jimmy.

"Nah. He's too savvy for that. He made sure a colleague did it before the judge issued his gag order. He is one angry dude. He says he's the victim and that this is about his reputation."

"It's about publicity," Kevin put in. I was thinking the same thing, but given my reasons for disliking the press, it was more valid coming from him. "He'll make the rounds of the morning shows and sell a lot of books."

"Prob'ly. He says this is the only way he'll be vindicated. I'm telling you, the guy has a big grudge and an even bigger ego."

That explained the media invasion. This wasn't the first time Twitter had been hacked, but it took a well-known name to draw so much attention. If the man behind that name was media himself, he might not even have to pull in favors to do it. His colleagues would look at him, realize that it could have been them, and jump on the bandwagon in no time flat.

This was human nature.

So was my own sense of dread as the severity of the situation seeped in. This wasn't something we could shrug off as a local incident. It went beyond the town limits, beyond anything that had happened in Devon during my time here, and it wouldn't be going away tomorrow or the day after that.

Feeling slightly panicked, I was relieved when Kevin took over the questioning.

"So Chris is back home. What happens now?"

"He registers with a pretrial probation officer. They talk on the phone once a week to make sure the boy hasn't skipped town."

"He could call from anywhere on a cell phone."

"No cell. Has to be a landline."

"Grace doesn't have a landline," I said.

"Then he uses one at the school or the Spa or my office. Boy calls officer from a validated number, officer calls boy back at that number to make sure he's there. Oh, and he isn't allowed to use computers, tablets, or phones."

"Not even a cell phone to call his mother?" I asked. Grace liked knowing where Chris was, and a cell phone was crucial for that.

"Yeah, sure, of course. But he can't use the phone to surf."

"How would they know?" Kevin asked.

"He's in the system. They'll track what he does. They'll be combing through his electronics to see what he used, where he went, and when."

"Collecting evidence for trial."

"Right. They'll talk with Chris's teachers and people at the Spa. They'll look for motive, why he targeted the people he did."

"There were others?" I asked. Grace and Nina had both implied as much, but I didn't want to believe it. One voice might be called a blowhard. A chorus was more damning.

"Zwick says so. He has his own investigators, and if he got names of other victims, you can bet he's given them to the Feds."

So Chris had two factions working to lock him up, the government and a powerful member of the press. Feeling Grace's pain, I pulled out my phone and, on the off chance she still had hers, sent her a text, then set it on the table to wait for a reply.

Our burgers arrived, but I could only nibble. My stomach was in knots. Jimmy ate half of mine before his own appeared, telling us between bites who all had come for the show. I tried not to resent his excitement. Crime in Devon rarely went beyond noise complaints, so the police station had to be a sleepy place to work. Now, it would be alive with big-time law enforcement officers, not to mention the media arriving from hotspots from DC on up. If Ben Zwick had his way, I feared, the invasion would grow.

When the conversation turned to speculation about the kind of money the press attention would bring to the town, I tuned out. When it turned to their own plans for Sunday brunch in Hanover, I sent Grace another text.

"Where is she?" I muttered under my breath, setting the phone down again and staring at the screen.

"Isn't *that* the pertinent question," Kevin remarked.

Feeling a twinge, I looked up. "What do you mean?"

66

"Where was Grace while her son was doing all this?"

"Uh, working?" I was mildly offended. "Struggling, like single mothers do?"

"Where's the father?" Jimmy asked.

"I don't know. He's never been in the picture."

"She could always call him."

"Or not," I said with more force than I might have had I been with Kevin alone. I liked Jimmy, but I didn't trust him like I did Kevin. It wasn't that I thought he was fishing for information to pass on to the police. But my loyalty to Grace was key. I figured if Chris's father was part of a past she didn't want to discuss, there was a good reason. Men weren't always a solution. There were times when they made things worse.

Suddenly too antsy to sit, I reached back for my coat. "I have to go."

"No," Kevin said in alarm, grabbing my hand as it closed on the phone. "Forget I mentioned Grace. It was a stupid question."

"No," I said sadly now, "it wasn't. I'm sure other people will be asking the same thing. But she's a good mother." Phone in hand, I slipped free. "She isn't answering my texts. If she's home with Chris, I want to go over."

"Maybe she's saying she wants to be alone."

"Maybe she's saying she's scared and confused. Maybe she's *overwhelmed*. Likely," I said with mild accusation aimed at Jimmy, "they took her phone, which means she's cut off from the world. Maybe they've disabled her so she can't think straight. Maybe she needs a friend who can." Arms in sleeves, I slid from the booth.

Kevin had to shove at Jimmy twice until he slid off the bench and let him out. As soon as he was upright, he pulled me in for a hug. "Are you okay helping her?"

"I'll have to be. She has no one else."

"But are you okay?"

I drew back and met his eyes. I considered the question, then nodded. "I am," I said and smiled to prove it. "I'm a master at blocking out painful thoughts, you know?"

I left without a single glance at the dark booth in the rear of the pub, but I walked quickly, even ran across the parking lot. My stranglehold on the steering wheel didn't ease up until the pub was well behind me.

Edward hadn't followed me. As I drove, I wondered if this was good or bad. He owed me an explanation for why he was here, and I didn't mean his being the voice of a group. He knew I was in Devon. This was my turf. He could have let someone else be the voice. But he hadn't. That made me really uneasy.

Let it go, Maggie. Pack it away. Inhale, hold, exhale.

As I cruised through the center of town, I repeated the exercise. The streets were their usual peaceful, quiet selves. On one of those inhales, I conjured up lemon verbena. I told myself that Devon was my ally. And it worked for a bit. When it came to denial, I was a pro.

Turning north on the Blue, I drove past the entrance to the Inn. A tiny little voice said the parking lot there might be filled with vehicles whose tires I wanted to slash, but I pushed that from mind, too, and drove on.

Grace lived at the far reaches of Devon, just close enough to the town line to allow Chris to attend our schools without having to pay, as students from outlying towns often did. I had been to her house many times. It was the fourth and last bungalow on a road that snaked around enough to set each home apart. She said she loved the privacy this gave, that she was barely aware of having neighbors at all, and I couldn't fault that. Hadn't I chosen similar isolation on Pepin Hill? The problem for me here was that the twists in the road hid trouble until I was smack on top of it.

5

The road was narrow. Rounding that final turn, I had to brake and plow left to avoid hitting the taillight of the SUV at the end of the line of SUVs parked half on, half off the crusted berm. The vans were parked head-in opposite these, their satellite dishes staggered on the uneven terrain. Some people remained inside, heads ghosted by phones. Others, at the ready, braved the cold to lean against bumpers.

I had slowed to avoid that first car and stayed slow in the narrow funnel they'd left of the road. That was my first mistake.

Doors were suddenly flung open, led by a person of indeterminable sex loping toward me, which meant that I couldn't exactly speed up again without risking hurt. I had my foot on the brake and was completely stopped by the time she—I saw that, though it was little comfort—came abreast and gestured my window down.

I might have yelled *Go away!* through the glass, actually would have yelled something more obscene, if that hadn't seemed like a cowardly thing to do. Thinking that this was *my* town, *my* friend, *my* new life, I rolled my window down to tell her to let me pass.

That was my second mistake. She had barely asked if I was a friend of the family when a camera appeared and a flash went off. I brought a hand up, but too late.

Raising the window again, I faced forward and accelerated only enough to let her know I wasn't chatting. I might have stopped had it been Ben Zwick, if only to tell him to go to hell. But I doubted he was here. The cynical part of me figured that, with the temperature having dropped into the twenties, he would be in a cozy suite at the Inn eating a flat iron steak—rare, with horseradish-dill aioli and a bottle of the sommelier's vintage merlot. I was sure he had underlings doing his dirty work here in the cold, dark night.

Others came forward as I inched ahead, a few running alongside my truck, but I kept my eyes on Grace's home. It was a frame structure consisting of a modest bottom topped by dormers that looked uncannily like eyes whose brows were raised as they watched the road. But arched brows were the end of notable where the exterior was concerned. Grace's show of spirit was on the inside, which, of course, these people would love to know, but couldn't see. Every curtain was drawn. The only light escaped from those upstairs dormers and was thickly diffused. These were bedrooms, not that I expected either Grace or Chris was asleep.

She had no bell, just a brass knocker in the shape of a frog. I used it at the same time that I texted to let her know it was me, which was a waste if the Feds had her phone. But I couldn't be the first person using the knocker tonight, and she wouldn't blindly open the door to this mob. I stood an arm's length back, where she might see me from a window, and kept my head down against the ghosts, listening for footsteps inside, a shouted *Go away!*, anything. After what felt like forever, during which time I was swarmed by moving mouths and cameras, I heard the tumble of three different locks. Then the door opened enough for her to grab my sleeve and pull me in.

Only when I was leaning against the closed door did I realize I was shaking. Blaming it on the cold, I breathed, *"Nightmare."*

"You don't know the half," Grace said as she rebolted the door, "but you can't stay, Maggie." She sounded exhausted, and though I could barely see her in the dark, the little light that seeped down the stairs suggested a wilted version of the woman I knew. Her curls were caught back in a scrunchie that left as much loose as not, and her face was glow-in-the-dark ghostly. Barefooted, wearing baggy sweats, she seemed smaller than ever.

Feeling her helplessness, I said a gentle, "I heard about Rutland. How's Chris?"

"Terrified. They booked him. Do you have any idea what that's like?"

I did. Terrifying was a mild word for it. "Is he upstairs?" She lifted one shoulder. "Can I talk with him?"

"Why?" She drew out the word, but it lacked inflection. I heard despair beneath it.

"To make him feel better? To tell him it'll all be okay?" Both were for her, too. I wanted her to know she wasn't totally alone. When her shadowed face told me nothing, I added, "He's home, isn't he?"

"For now, but they have it in for him."

"Did he do it?" I whispered.

She whispered back, "He says no."

"Do you believe him?"

"I don't know. His father was a liar."

I was a minute processing that. "You've never mentioned his father before." She gestured, like she would have taken the words back if they hadn't already hit air. But they had, so I asked, "Does he know about this?"

She shook her head. "He's not in the picture."

"Should he be—I mean, helping with legal costs and all?"

"No. I'm good." She folded her arms around her middle.

"Maybe—"

"I'm good."

Words, body language—she was shutting me out. But I was her friend. Needing to get her talking, I asked, "Was Jay a help?"

"Yes."

"He did this kind of work before he came here. He's good at it. His name was the one I was given in case I ever needed help."

She snuffed. "Like you'd ever need help."

"We all do sometimes. It was a strong recommendation." When she remained silent, arms crossed, shoulders hunched, I tried, "The town will support you. So will the Spa."

The dimness didn't hide her worry.

"Do you remember Ben Zwick being here?" I asked. "Did you ever work with him?"

"Jay said I shouldn't talk."

"This is me. I won't say anything."

"Not even under oath?"

She had a point. If I was ever subpoenaed—but I couldn't go there, could *not* go there. Feeling helpless and angry at that, I said, "I want to help, Grace. What can I do?"

"Leave. You should leave."

"You need someone here. Did you eat? You need to eat. So does Chris. I can make eggs or soup. I can stay the night and guard the door. I'll sleep on the sofa. I've done it before."

"No. Don't make it worse, Maggie."

I didn't imagine how my being there could do that, but I had to respect her wishes. "Did they take your phone?" She gave a short nod. "Did Jay get you another?"

"A burner," she said with a derisive snort and looked away.

"They're used for privacy, Gracie," I said, because I knew what she was thinking. Crooks used burner phones. But so did people who wanted protection from crooks. "I've used them."

"When?" she shot back.

"When I was selling furniture on Craigslist and didn't want to give out my personal number. Women use them for online dating." My lawyer hadn't had to give me one; Edward had done it. That was in the hours immediately after the accident, before the loss of our daughter had set in, before the anger, the resentment, the recrimination.

Grace said nothing.

Hoping that maybe, just maybe, what I said had helped a little, I added, "Are you sure I can't stay?"

"I'm sure."

"Will you call if you change your mind?"

"Yes."

"Please. Even if it's the middle of the night. I'll keep my phone with me in bed. I'll throw clothes on and drive right back here."

She smiled sadly and, in a moment's softening, said, "I won't call, Maggie. I need to work this out myself. There's nothing you can do."

"Call. Or text. You have friends here."

I thought I saw tears in her eyes and might have given her a hug if she hadn't so quickly flipped the locks, opened the door, and shoved me out. I was wondering if she knew I would have put this off forever, when I was surrounded again, at which point wondering was pointless. Raising my hood against the cameras more than the cold, I kept my head down and rushed to my truck. When the occasional body stepped in the way, I either brushed it aside or went around it myself, and the whole time, the questions came. *Does she have any comment—did she know what her son was doing—how long has she lived here—what does she say about the charges—is the boy suspended from school?* They overlapped, repeated, and fought for my attention with increasing insistency, until I was in my truck with the door locked. Clutching the wheel for all it was worth, I backed around and, heart in my mouth, slowly, carefully, drove back down the narrow strip until the road opened and I could breathe.

Since Devon only delivered mail to houses in the center of town, I had to go to the post office for mine. Thanks to the media, I might have skipped it today. Driving under cover of darkness was different from driving around town in the light of day. I chanced it with the pottery studio, because the studio, clay, and Kevin were essential to my sanity. Besides, I went so early I practically opened the place.

The post office was something else. It was barely nine and full daylight when I left the studio, a chilly Friday under a glare of clouds that didn't seem to know whether to come or go. And wasn't that an appropriate metaphor for the twist my life had taken in the last day?

But I hadn't been to the post office since Tuesday, and I had three bills with short turnaround times that needed paying before the weekend. I didn't like being late with bills, and it wasn't about the fees. It was about my credit rating—a.k.a., my *record*. I wanted it to be perfect. Our postmistress, Cornelia Conrad, encouraged me to go green and pay bills online. She claimed she did it herself, and that if an eighty-one-year-old could, I could.

Oh, I could. I used to. I just chose not to now.

And you trust the United States Postal Service? Cornelia asked with the wry smile that chided her employer without quite committing treason.

No. I didn't. But my life now was about control. I liked seeing a bill in the flesh, writing a check, stamping an envelope, and dropping it in a slot. After living in the fast lane, slow held an appeal. Paying bills by hand took time; I had plenty. And then there was my mother, who said, *See, feel, know,* on a regular basis. She was usually referring to brownies, or some such baked good made from scratch rather than from a packaged mix, but the trinity also applied to makeup and clay. I liked using my hands, my eyes, even my nose. When makeup went bad, I could smell it. The primal quality of that gave me comfort.

Same with sliding payment of one bill, then another into the mail slot.

Oh, I did shop online. I loved Etsy and Gilt, but was also addicted to beauty forums like makeupalley and beautypedia. And products I used at the Spa? All cyber-bought and delivered to my door by UPS.

Besides, if I paid bills online, I wouldn't have had cause to go to the post office, and if that was the case, I wouldn't have found my book group or gotten to know Cornelia, whom I liked immensely. Exuding quiet confidence with her long spine, square chin, and wise words, she was a source of inspiration.

The post office was midway between the pottery studio and the Spa, so I usually stopped there on my way to work. Since I had an appointment at ten this Friday, I was earlier than usual. But the media had awoken. I passed vans in the center of town, even saw a reporter doing a stand-up in front of Rasher and Yolk. Pulling my scarf higher on my chin, I drove steadily on.

The sheer volume of vehicles in the post office lot nearly scared me off. But I recognized most of the plates, none of the vehicles had satellite dishes, and I suspected Cornelia would have sent the press packing if she smelled them around. Having spent her past life in Boston, she was savvy on that score. She was also protective of Devon.

Cornelia had no use for outsiders. Her great, guilty pleasure was reading the magazines she sorted. But I had seen her put down *Entertainment Weekly* or *Time* or even the *ABA Journal*, which she claimed helped her follow crime shows, to quiet an unruly summer person with a quick, firm voice.

There were no unruly people now, just small groups of locals holding mail to their chests as they talked with each other. I could guess the topic of discussion. Not wanting to take part, I kept my scarf where it was and went straight to the counter.

A tall man in a heavy barn jacket, jeans, and boots was signing for several boxes from Cornelia. As I stood behind him, trying to be invisible to those locals, I studied the floor, then his jacketed back, then his hips, which were lean and moved with male efficiency as he shifted his weight.

The movement was subtle, barely a movement at all—but was suddenly, totally, improbably familiar. No matter that barn jackets were the covering *de rigueur* of men in Devon, I should have known who it was from the get-go. That height, those shoulders, the butt so neatly gloved in jeans?

Thinking still, again, that Edward wasn't supposed to be here. I was seconds too slow in moving. When he turned, his eyes—those shimmery pale-blue things—showed surprise, unsureness, maybe even guilt.

Good, I thought with a shot of defiance back at him. He *should* feel guilty. It was his *turn* to feel guilty.

But there were at least ten other people around, all of whom I knew. This was not the time for a confrontation. That said, I couldn't quite get myself to joke and say, *We have to stop meeting this way*, in part because a smile was beyond me. Having a beer at my favorite pub was bad enough. Now my post office?

He stared for several more seconds this time than last. We both moved right, then left before working it out, at which point he nodded and passed.

"Have you not met him yet?" Cornelia asked, having seen our little dance.

"Oh, I have," I replied without saying where. "What was he picking up?"

"Bedding"

"Bedding."

"From Wayfair."

"Why does he need bedding?"

"He has to sleep on something."

"But he's with the Inn. Isn't he staying there?"

"Not now that he has sheets. He bought the Barnstead place. Lord knows why. It's been empty for three years and is falling apart."

Bought. *Bought?*

"It needs major rehab," Cornelia said, "and I do mean major. Bill Barnstead did nothing but mourn after his wife died, so the house is in a state of disrepair. Oh, the place has good bones, and it's set on a good piece of land, prime waterfront property overlooking the Blue, but it's overgrown. If he wants any sunlight, he'll have to take down trees, and you know what the town thinks of that."

I probably did, but the buzzing in my head muddled any thought of trees. He *bought* the Barnstead house? Okay, he might buy it for someone else. But setting it up? With *bedding?*

He was moving here. But without letting me know? Without calling? Texting?

It didn't make sense. A venture capitalist might visit Devon; he wouldn't move here unless he was retiring, and Edward was too young for that. Besides, I was here. No way would he want to live anywhere near the woman who had killed his only child.

"Maggie?" Cornelia tested softly. "Hello?"

I blinked and refocused. "Sorry. What?"

"Everything okay?"

"Yes. Uh, yes." I had to think quickly. Cornelia wasn't easily fooled. "I'm just worried." I tipped my head toward the group gathered at the bank of steel PO boxes. "What are they saying?"

"Pretty much what you'd expect. Did the boy do it? Did Grace know? Will the Spa keep her on?"

"Then the talk is positive?"

"So far. They like her. They say she's a good mother. They're not pointing fingers."

Yet, I thought.

Yet, her cocked brow confirmed.

I assumed Cornelia's excuse for cynicism was age. Not wanting to get into my own, I asked, "Do we know anything more about the case against Chris?" I had been out of contact for several hours, and the post office was a hub for news. If anything had happened, Cornelia would know it.

"Officially, no," she said for my ears alone. "Those who are involved with the prosecution are being careful not to jeopardize it."

"They have Ben Zwick to say what they won't. He's a force."

"He's only describing what he perceives as his personal injury. That's his right."

Had it come from anyone else, I might have taken offense on Grace's behalf. But Cornelia had been a professor before retiring here—*a Radcliffe degree from way back*, was the word, and *on the Harvard faculty for years.* I wouldn't have taken that as proof of anything, if she wasn't always right.

"Isn't it libel?" I asked.

"Maybe, if Grace can prove that her life or livelihood has been damaged. Naturally, there's only libel if Chris is found not guilty."

"Then you do think it'll go to trial?"

Cornelia never frowned. What wrinkles she had were light, which was proof either of a dearth of emotional display or good genes. To my knowledge, she had never worn makeup, never even used moisturizer. And she didn't frown now, but still managed to look concerned.

"You mean, will he plead out? That depends on what kind of case the government has and the penalty for it."

"What's the range?"

"Up to five years for someone without a record, likely less for a juvenile."

"Grace will die if he spends a single *day* locked up," I said with dread.

"Have you talked with her?"

"Yes." The call had come at seven, while I was making myself up.

"I'm sorry," she had said. "I wasn't polite last night."

"Screw politeness, Gracie. I don't care. This is a horrible time for you. Just tell me how you are."

"How do you think? I'm lousy. My life is in danger."

"Your life is not in danger. Kids get in trouble all the time, and parents bail them out. You'll get through this."

"Okay, but I can't talk. Chris'll be down in a second, and we're going into town to meet with Jay."

"Are they still outside your house?" No need to explain who "they" were.

"Yup. My car's in the carport, so we may be able to sneak to it without being caught, but they'll see me back out. I'll be sure to—"

"Give them the finger? Do not do that, Grace. They'll photograph it. Is that what you want going viral?" When she didn't answer, I said, *"Your behavior reflects on Chris. Aggression won't hack it."*

"They're scum."

"I know that, you know that, but don't let them drag you down to their level. Please, Grace?" When she didn't respond to that, either, I could only pray that my message registered. *"Are you coming to work later?"*

"Garrett called." The general manager of the resort. *"He told me to stay home."*

One phone call and I could fix that. I knew the new, alleged owner of the

Inn, did I not? It would give me a good reason to call him, and, "By the way, Edward, what in the hell are you doing in my town?"

"Maggie?" came a voice from behind. It was one of the women who had been near the mailboxes.

I gave her a weak smile and, seeing no choice, acknowledged the others with a quick wave. I liked these women. The last thing I wanted was to offend them. Nor, though, did I want to discuss what I knew they had in mind. At one point or another, every one of them had seen me with Grace and Chris. As well-meaning as their inquiries might be, I had nothing to add.

Sensing my dilemma, Cornelia waved an imperious hand to shoo off not only the one at my side but the others as well. It might have been overkill, but when it came to ordering people around, she had a free ride. Once the women had left, she retrieved my mail from the back room and handed it over. "Be prepared when you get to the Spa," she warned. "Word has it they've been doing live shots from the station and Town Hall. The Spa is next. They'll try to interview you."

"They tried last night. I didn't say anything."

"Good girl."

"How long do you think they'll stick around?"

She didn't have to know my history to know I loved the serenity of Devon. We were of like mind in this.

Her smile was small and resigned. "Until something else takes front page."

Her warning was spot on. I had barely parked, shouldered the strap of my makeup case, and lifted the box of supply refills, when a pair of reporters swooped in. Whether or not they recognized me as Grace's friend from last night, it didn't take a genius to guess that I worked here. Who else would park in the employees' lot? Who else would be carrying a cardboard box marked EYEBROW WAX?

They were joined by a third and a fourth, all shooting questions as they crowded me toward the door. They had barely moved from requests for my name to my knowledge of Grace, when a linebacker in a blazer and tie emerged, closed a firm hand on my arm and pulled me out of the fray.

6

I was never pleased to see Michael Shanahan. Nervous, maybe. Uneasy, for sure. Lately, resigned. The sight of him now, though, brought pure relief—at least until that door closed and, taking the box from me, he guided me deeper into the Spa.

Michael had been named my probation officer when I petitioned the Massachusetts courts to let me move to Vermont. We met monthly at his office in White River Junction, but in these waning days of my probation, he was showing up unannounced in Devon too often for comfort.

Spot-checks were within the terms of my probation. But I knew that Michael's showing up was more personal than legal. He liked me. He had told me as much—had told me that once my probation was finished he hoped we could be in touch. The words were innocent enough. Not so the cologne he had recently started wearing, or the warmth in his eyes.

I should have been flattered. He clearly appreciated the new me, complimenting me one day on my hair, another on my sweater or my boots.

And he wasn't shabby himself. The few times we'd gone to lunch together, I had seen other women watch him pass. After playing football for BC, he had been drafted into the pros, but had spent the better part of two years on the bench for Indianapolis before accepting that football was not in his future. Following the example of a fellow alum, he had gone into probation, and the job fit him well. He was earnest and toe-the-line honest. His blazer and slacks were far from high-end, but they showcased his physique. He was triangular, as in ripped above and narrow below. He was definitely tall, definitely dark.

I might be drawn to tall and dark, but I was not drawn to Michael. His tall was too tall, his dark hair too short. I wasn't into buzz cuts—or into preppy, which he was. There was no chemistry on my part. Zero.

Those few lunches I'd had with him? Mistake. I had initially gone along because he seemed genuinely interested in being a friend, and having lost so many after the accident, I welcomed that. But I was never comfortable, given what he was. And though he never overstepped, never came on to me physically, I got the sense he might if I gave him a sign.

My sign was to gently refuse invitations. Work was a perfect excuse. I never lied; being caught in one of those wouldn't help my case. I just scheduled bookings that allowed for the required thirty-minutes with Michael and the drive back to Devon, with no time to spare.

Failing at lunch, he invited me to dinner. When I refused, he asked, "Are you seeing someone in town?" The question was within his rights as my probation officer. Knowing with whom I spent time was part of his job.

"No," I replied.

"You aren't dating at all?"

"I'm not looking for a relationship. I don't think I can handle one."

He finally got it.

So did my coworkers. They knew I didn't date. The first time Michael showed up here, I introduced him as a friend of my brother. Yes, it was a lie. I apologized to Michael the instant we were alone, but he seemed fine with it. Hell, his status was higher as a family friend than a tool of the corrections department. Besides, we had talked through the issue of concealment during our first official meeting. The resort GM knew I was a convicted felon; I'd had to disclose it when I applied for the job. He knew that the conviction was a vehicular one with no connection to applying makeup. But the references from my practicum advisor, from the makeup artist with whom I had interned, and from the specialist at the Bobbi Brown counter at Saks, where I had briefly worked, were stellar. That was it. He knew nothing else. My first year at the Spa, I lived in fear that he would tell someone even that, but at least I was covered with my boss if Michael's real identity ever came out.

Walking down the corridor with him now, though, was awkward. He was always serious. Today, he seemed angry.

Guiding me into the makeup studio, he set my box on a chair, drew himself straight, and said in his stern, I-am-the-law voice, "You were on the news this morning."

That alarmed me totally aside from his tone. "I was? When? *How?*"

"You were videoed at Grace Emory's. It was you, wasn't it?"

My first thought was of all the people who would see my face. Exposure was my nemesis. My second thought was that, of course, my probation officer would be drawn to anything crime-related on the news, and would link the Grace Emory in the clip to the one who was my friend.

My third thought was to deny it. Michael didn't want me anywhere near a questionable situation. He might not have to know I was there. The press didn't have my name, and night images were grainy.

But risking it all with a lie, with only a handful of months to go?

"Yes," I said and lifted my makeup case to the counter. "I was there. Grace is my friend. I was worried about her."

"You're not supposed to mix with bad guys."

"She isn't a bad guy. Her son was the one charged."

"Same difference, with a minor." He leaned against the counter, crossed his ankles, folded his arms over his Vineyard Vines tie. "Do you know anything about what he did?"

"What he's charged with?" I corrected but absently, as though I was simply lost in thought. "I only know what the rest of the world knows. Grace doesn't know anything, either."

"Did you ask?"

"Yes," I said and faced him. Michael wanted to be taken seriously. I couldn't do that in a romantic way, but I did respect that he knew his job. "She's as mystified as the rest of us."

"Then you've talked with others?"

Feeling the warmth of the room, I unbuttoned my coat and unwound my scarf. "It's hard not to. The whole town's talking."

"I like that scarf," he remarked and his sternness eased. "What are they saying?"

If he was fishing for something to pass on to the Feds, I wasn't taking the bait. The conditions of my parole said nothing about being a snitch. Then again, the defiant part of me liked helping my friend. "They're saying Grace is a good mother and a hard worker and Chris is a good kid, but that someone needed a scapegoat, so they grabbed him." The women at the post office hadn't actually used the word "scapegoat," but it sounded good. I followed up with a curious, "Do *you* know anything about the case?" Let him betray the Feds to *me*.

But he simply asked, "Did anyone else go to her house last night?"

"I don't know. No one else was there when I was."

"Did she mention anyone else coming?"

"No. But I didn't ask."

"Then you're her only friend?"

"No. She has lots of friends." Everyone liked Grace.

"But you were the only one bothering to drive out to her place last night."

"Maybe there were others."

"There weren't. Just you. I'm wondering why."

I wasn't. Forget the issue of friendship. Think *past*. There was a truth here that was as important for me to admit as for Michael to hear. Tucking my hands in my coat pockets, I said, "I've been where she is. I know what it's like to feel alone. Like something's happening and you can't control it. Like you're on display."

If he was personally moved, he didn't show it. "Wouldn't that keep you away?"

"But I feel for her. She's my friend."

"How close are you?"

I wanted to say that my friendship with Grace was none of his business, but unfortunately it was. "We work together. So we have that in common. And we both like to shop. She's into clothes, and I need to know what's new for my work."

He wrinkled his nose, clearly doubtful. "What do clothes have to do with makeup?"

"Everything," I said with enthusiasm, because this was safe ground. "Makeup providers change shades to complement what's on the runway in a given year. If the stores are big on soft pink, orange blusher is bad, and if the styles are dainty and sweet, heavy eyeliner doesn't work. I need to see how runways translate into retail. Some of the makeup artists in department stores are good. I pick up tips watching their makeup applications. It's about staying current."

"Does Grace help with that?"

"Staying current? Absolutely. She reads fashion magazines." He was looking stern again. "As addictions go, it's harmless," I tried, but his brow furrowed. "Am I in trouble for being her friend?"

His eyes held mine under those lowered brows. He radiated disappointment, like I had seriously let him down. "It may come to that. You know the terms of your probation."

"Yes." I kept my voice low. Docile was the way to go. "I'm not supposed to associate with felons."

"Or suspected felons."

That wasn't my take on the document in question. Unfortunately, my take didn't matter. Michael Shanahan's did.

"Be careful, Maggie," he warned as he pushed off from the counter.

He rose to his full height. "You've made a good turnaround. The Spa likes you. The pottery store likes you. You haven't ever been late paying your property tax. You don't park in handicap spaces, and you haven't been stopped for speeding. So far, you've done everything right. I'd hate to see you blow it with this."

The message, I knew, was that he checked everything I was doing, would continue doing so, and didn't want me having anything to do with Grace. That put me in a bind.

I was trying to decide what to do about it, when he gave a cocky smile. "So I thought I'd walk around town, maybe do a little snooping, y'know, see who's hanging out where. I can protect you from the press. Meet me for lunch?"

Big weddings didn't book at the Inn for mud season. This time of year, there were no photo ops on the veranda or carriage rides through town, no rehearsal dinners in the pine grove on High Hill or chafing-dish brunches on the town green. There was no skiing, no hiking, neither sleigh rides nor hayrides. Other than a maple syrup tour, which depended on the flow of sap and was thus iffy, off-property activities were limited.

Therefore, March at the Inn was for corporate and philanthropic events, which was lucky. Weddings were more emotional. Had there been even a single one this weekend, we might have had a panicked bride, a bewildered groom, and parents who were alternately horrified, angry, or litigious on our hands. The main Inn computers, which were used for reservations and check-in, stayed in place, though government agents hovered, searching their contents at every lull. The Spa wasn't so lucky. They had carted our computers off to parts unknown, leaving us grappling with a pair of laptops from the front office.

But press or no press, scandal or no scandal, the show had to go on. Members of a national women's conference were checking in today. A benefactor was picking up the tab for massages, manicures, and makeup, so I was fully booked. That gave me a legitimate excuse not to meet

Michael Shanahan for a quick coffee, much less lunch, and my Saturday was just as busy. From ten to six, I would be making up attendees of a cancer research fundraiser that was being held in the ballroom that night. This year, as in past ones, I was donating my time. My friend Joe Hellinger was a key organizer of the event. Even if I didn't feel for the cause—which I did—I would have done it for Joe.

He was a doctor, though not a cancer specialist. Like so many others there that night, he had lost a loved one to cancer. In his case, it was his first wife. Others that day told me of parents or friends. For me, it was the grandmother whose green velvet box, tucked away in the dark under my bed, held the disparate threads of my heart.

In daily life, Joe was a plastic surgeon in partnership with the man who had done Grace's first facelift. Though the two did all major procedures at Dartmouth-Hitchcock, just over the New Hampshire line, their office, like Michael's, was in White River Junction. Since that was Vermont, I didn't need permission, but could go there at will.

That first day, I had been waiting to drive Grace home from a post-operative appointment, when Joe emerged from an inside office with a teenaged girl whose face was severely scarred. I never quite knew what had drawn him to me, whether it was the fact that I didn't avert my eyes, that the waiting room was otherwise empty, or simply that Joe was end-of-the-day tired, but he took a seat beside me, and we began to talk. It turned out his specialty was kids.

Mine was not. But I found that I could conceal a child's bruises just as well as my own and was even more gratified doing it.

Joe didn't call me often, but when he did, I shifted appointments and came. A time or two, I had even crossed the state line without permission for a last-minute consultation that I deemed worth the risk. Over the last thirty-six months, I had worked with burn victims, accident victims, and children with birth defects. Each one was worth it.

That said, I was grateful that since his event was this weekend, nothing would call me away. I didn't want to leave the Spa. Michael was watching. The media was watching. Even, for all I knew, Edward was watching. He couldn't barge in while I was doing makeup; my studio was off-limits for interruptions. But each time I finished one client, I had to walk through common areas for the next. I did not want to see him there—did not want to see him anywhere. He threatened the space that I had so painstakingly carved out for myself.

I resented that. He and I had to talk.

But when? I certainly couldn't now, what with the Spa under attack, and not only because the media was waiting just beyond our doors, ready to pounce. Our clients had begun asking questions, so we were in flat-out defensive mode. I had already received three separate memos from Garrett on how to answer those questions or, more accurately, how to avoid answering them. His main strategy appeared to be evasion.

Edward would be proactive. But either he wasn't yet in charge, or he was up to his ears doing damage control from some central-command post.

One thing was for certain. Given the threat to the Inn's reputation, our security had to be twice as tight, our facilities twice as sparkling, our services twice as rewarding. We had to carry on seamlessly. For this, we needed all hands on deck, which was one of the reasons why Joyce—ever-calm Joyce, whose shiny bob swung by her chin with each turn of her head—nearly lost it when I told her that Grace wouldn't be working. *She* hadn't told Grace to stay home, which her call to the GM, while I stood by, bore out. She didn't *care* if the resort was in crisis; this was not the way to handle it. She was fierce in Grace's defense, going on about loyalty, unproven accusations, and bad precedents. Her most potent argument was that there were no massage therapists quite as good as Grace, certainly no last-minute ones who would be willing to work a full Friday and Saturday.

Joyce phoned Grace herself, and this time Grace answered. I knew she needed the money.

She showed up just in time for her first appointment, but had to be rescued from the parking-lot press by the firefighter now guarding the door. Once inside, she kept a low profile, moving from client to client with barely a break. When I tried to talk with her, she held up a hand, *later*, but later never came. I tried to text her using the number she had called me from that morning, but she didn't respond. I tried her that night and again Saturday morning. Nothing. I knew she was distracted, preoccupied, maybe even embarrassed, but if she shut *me* out, who did she let in?

The press didn't let up. When they were banned from the front lot, they doubled up in the back, which was definitely better for Spa guests, not so for employees. Whether coming or going, we had to run the gauntlet of reporters and cameras. Honestly? There were times when I hated Grace for that. Even when I was safe inside, I knew the press was lying in wait. They were a constant worry, which was good only in the sense that I had less time to think about Edward.

By Sunday afternoon, I was exhausted. I had been out late the night before with Alex and Jessa, knowing I needed sleep but needing the diversion more. I announced that discussing anything to do with Grace and Chris was off-limits, and they stuck to it for the most part. And I did love *Game of Thrones*, although, in hindsight, the three episodes we watched weren't the best. I immersed myself in them anyway and returned home for five hours of solid sleep, no dreams, then awoke to the knowledge that by midafternoon, life at the Spa would wind down. The women's conference was done. All signs of Joe's event had been cleaned up. Weekend guests of the Inn had checked out and left town.

There were a handful of late-afternoon appointments, but none were for Grace and, thank God, given how wiped out I felt, none were for me. I needed a lift, which was why I was in the lobby with Joyce when Grace headed out. She saw us, raised a quick hand, and strode on. She was with a man. A repeat client, he was her last of the day.

Coincidence, I told Joyce regarding the timing, though they went out the front door together and certainly looked like a pair. Her hood was up, her curls hidden. The press might recognize her or not. Her being with a man might actually help hide her.

She wouldn't, Joyce said, smooth hair brushing her jaw when her head swung to mine, *not with everyone watching her.*

I feared that she would. Grace liked men. They were her escape. I had always suspected she equated passion with adoration, and, confirming it to me once, she was unapologetic. She adored adoration. All her life she had struggled to find it, finally settling for little doses here and there.

Joyce didn't know of the admission, but as she had done with me four years ago, now she sensed something wounded in Grace and seemed to want to talk about it. Since I was eager for a sympathetic voice, I agreed to take a ride with her to a yarn store she wanted to visit. Mud season was ideal for knitting, and although I didn't do it myself, I regularly wore one of several pairs of socks Joyce had knit me. It was three in the afternoon when we left the Spa. The store was a forty-minute drive, but it was open until five. Tucking myself into her Subaru, I relaxed and let her drive, and even though nothing new came out about Grace—Joyce was clearly as tired as I was—it felt good to be with a friend. It felt good to be out of Devon, felt good not to be looking around for media vans or, nearly as bad, for Edward.

The yarn store was the messiest place I'd ever seen. Yarn was everywhere, although it apparently did have some sort of order, judging from Joyce's conversation with the owner. All I saw was chaos. But the chaos was colorful and soft, the warren of small rooms toasty, and the background Simon and Garfunkel music that my mother would like, hence soothing to me.

By the time we left, I was feeling mellow, so when Joyce pulled onto the drive leading to The Farm at Lyme Creek, I had no problem. There were several cars in the lot. Parking beside a Jeep, she ran inside for a wedge of local cheddar. Since I needed none, I stayed in the Subaru, stretched out in my seat, and looked out over the farm. There was a bucolic ambiance here that appealed.

The fields were still fallow, but they had been tilled in advance of spring planting. The barns were newly painted, and the farmhouse, farther back, held a lopsided charm. The store itself was a rambling affair with a long porch for warm-weather chairs and bins of fruit. Attached to its hip was a bakery, where bread and rolls were baked fresh daily and, just beyond that, a greenhouse whose windows were opaque with steam. Herbs would be growing there now, along with the pea shoots whose leaves were a standard in March salads. Just this week I had seen ads for them, along with firewood, frozen steaks, and fresh maple syrup, in *The Devon Times*.

The Devon Times. Not a comforting thought, that one. I wondered what Thursday's issue would have to say about Chris Emory. Jack Quillmer, the paper's owner and editor-in-chief, would respect the gag order and avoid mentioning Chris by name, but he couldn't ignore the issue altogether and still keep his publication relevant. That left the possibility that he might mention Grace.

Five minutes into imagining the unpleasant scenarios that might result from that, I grew antsy and glanced at my watch. Joyce was a resource, which made her good at her job at the Spa but required being in the know. She might be talking with the farm's owner, who typically worked the store on Sundays, about whether his cows had started to calve, what he knew about a new restaurant opening in Devon, or where he was filling his insulin prescriptions. They might talk for fifteen minutes. They might talk for *thirty* minutes.

Climbing from the car, I wandered toward the barn. Other than a handful of chickens pecking at the mud, the yard was empty. I braced my arms on the pen rail and inhaled. Beyond the familiar scent of moist earth, I smelled the musk of cattle, the sweetness of hay, the tang of manure. As a group, they worked. Bundled together, they sang of life and growth. I leaned back against the rail, closed my eyes, and took another deep breath.

When I opened my eyes again, I gasped. Edward was walking from the store toward the Jeep in the lot. Despite the mud on its side, the Jeep looked new, and didn't that spring another memory? He had owned a Wrangler when we first met. He had loved that Wrangler. It remained his dream car before our lifestyle demanded something more.

This Wrangler might be a rental—and wouldn't that be great, if he returned it to the Hertz stand at the airport before flying back home?

But who was I kidding? People from Boston—or Hartford or New York—didn't fly here. They drove. They didn't work at the Inn. They didn't buy a house or receive boxes of bedding. Add that muddy Jeep, the barn jacket and jeans, and the red scarf that hung on either side of his collar? Edward Cooper looked to be settling in.

One arm held a large brown sack. When he reached the Jeep, he put it inside and, straightening, raised a hand to the vehicle's roof. He took a breath, like I had done seconds before. He was smelling the same things I had. All were innocent, but suddenly not so.

It was fall. We always came in fall. The first time, I was pregnant. The trip was a last-minute one, just an overnight, but our eyes had met in matching desperation, unspoken agreement that we needed a break. Our parents were driving us nuts. Mine were scandalized that I was pregnant before I was married. Terrified that a bump might show when I walked down the aisle, they had rushed to make arrangements at the church, and although I was in charge of the rest, they phoned multiple times a day asking whether I had called the photographer, the caterer, the florist, the priest. Since Edward was paying for the groom's part himself, his parents should have just been along for the ride. But they were newly divorced, and neither one particularly wanted to see the other. His mother was trying to one-up his father by badgering Edward on where the rehearsal dinner should be held, what should be served, and who should give toasts. His father wanted to know what his mother was pushing so that he could push for the reverse.

We chose a getaway in upstate New York that, having a late cancellation, gave us a bargain rate. We had our own luxury cabin, our own butler on call, our own masseuse. The farm was a mile from the resort. We had to pass it coming and going, and Edward hadn't been eager to stop. He had grown up on a farm and, at that moment, didn't want a reminder of his father. Then we saw fields of pumpkins and kale, a corn maze, and cars filled with kids. There were no cows in sight, not a one. So we stopped.

That first year, we walked through the fields and bought a jug of cider at the farm store. The next year, with six-month-old Lily asleep in a BABYBJÖRN on Edward's chest, we picked a peck of Macouns and bought another jug of cider. Lily was eighteen months the following year and wanted no part of a carrier. She sat still for a hayride, but otherwise ran wherever other children were running. At two-and-a-half, she was helping with the picking, and a year later, after declaring that she needed not one, not two, but three pumpkins so that we could carve a daddy, a mommy, and a little girl, she made her choices from high on Edward's shoulders, one hand pointing out her choices, the other clutching his hair like it was the mane of a horse. By the time she was four-and-a-half, from the first pumpkin sighting at our supermarket, she was the one begging to visit the farm. We did it all that year—hayride, corn maze, apples, cider donuts—and it was so good.

We never got there again.

I returned to the present with a pain in my chest. How a memory could simultaneously be beautiful and horrific, I didn't know, but this one tore me apart.

Thoughts are just thoughts, CALM said. *Let them come and go.*

It was easier said than done. The pain in my chest remained, so I put a hand there to soothe it. The movement tipped him off. His head turned, gaze shifted, realization hit.

He went still, which was only fair, since I couldn't move, either. I didn't know what he was thinking, whether he was back in the past of his own childhood or Lily's, whether he felt happiness or angst, heard laughter or screams.

As he looked at me, though, memory began to break apart. Here and now, dressed down but standing tall, looking older and tired, Edward remained striking.

I don't know what made one man my type and another not—why only Edward's brand of tall and dark turned me on—why he had always done it when no other man could. I don't know why my pulse raced at the sight of windblown brown hair or lean hips in jeans. I didn't want to feel any pull at all. But there it was. I couldn't look away.

Then he hitched his chin, inviting me closer, and the spell broke. With a single shake of my head, I turned my back on him and faced the pen. In the next frantic breath, though, I spun back around. He had taken me off guard three times now, which was three times too many. I wanted to see where he was and know if he approached. He might have some new, mysterious, even vengeful purpose in Devon. But. Devon. Was. Mine.

I was about to stalk forward and confront him, when Joyce entered my line of sight. Having emerged from the store, she was crossing the lot. Beside her was another sack-carrying man, clearly heading for his own vehicle. I heard bits of an exchange between the three—saw the swish of her hair as she turned from one to the other—and guessed from the levity of it that they had chatted inside.

She peered into her car, straightened, and looked around. When she saw me, she waved me over. Naturally, she would want to introduce me to Edward—which was a total joke, I knew and felt a moment's panic. Did I acknowledge him or not? Would he acknowledge me or not? It would be bad enough to say we'd known each other before Devon, but if we admitted we'd been married? In no time, someone would add my first name to his last name to Boston, and my secret would be out. It was everything I'd worked so hard—*so hard*—to escape.

I was spared it when Edward said something to Joyce and then disappeared into the Wrangler. Seconds later, he backed out and headed off.

My relief was shallow. I had dodged the bullet, but for how long? If he was going to be here for any length of time, in the role of Inn owner no less, the link between us would come out. Sometime, somewhere, somehow it would. Our having been married and both ending up here was the kind of coincidence people loved hearing. They would think words like sweet, touching, and charming, until they got to awkward and painful, and if they ever got to wanting revenge? There'd be all hell to pay, with me being the target.

Oh yeah, Edward and I had to talk, but not with an audience around.

"He was late for a meeting with Hank Monroe," Joyce called as I neared the Subaru. Hank Monroe was the first name under Home Renovation in the Devon directory. I might have said he was a thief, if she weren't still talking, her voice returning to normal the closer I got. "That's our Ned Cooper," she informed me with a bright smile, assuming I would tie the name with the Inn. "He bought the Barnstead place. Did you know?"

"I heard," I said, but she was already nodding into the next thought.

"Extensive renovations *that* one needs. Apparently the guy has the money for it. Money is good, Maggie. You need to meet him."

"Money is not good," I snapped and quickly winced an apology for the sharpness, "and anyway, we've already met." Neither statement was false, I thought as I slid into the car, but I was surprised that she didn't hear my heart. It was thudding its way into my throat and on up to my brain. Or maybe what I felt were arrhythmic little bursts of anger. Life had been calm, quiet, and easy here, but no more. Try as I might to keep the past tucked away in its own little box, events of the past few days were poking tiny holes in the bottom and letting it leak.

Joyce closed the door and buckled up. "I think he's a little awkward meeting people who work at the resort, like he isn't sure what kind of professional distance to keep."

If she thought that was why he hadn't wanted to meet me, I was fine with it. "What's his role?" I asked with just enough curiosity. "Isn't he representing a group?"

"I understood he *was* the group," Joyce said and, starting the car, backed around.

"Just him? Uh, no. That can't be." Edward didn't have that kind of money. He didn't have anywhere *near* that kind of money. "The last two owners were groups of investors."

"Uh-huh, and you see how well *that* worked," Joyce remarked, cruising forward at last.

"It did," I argued. "Our name is more prominent than it ever was. We're listed in the best of the best for nearly every category that applies."

"We're losing money."

"Not losing," I said, but the look Joyce shot me, hair swinging, when she slowed at the end of the drive said otherwise. "We are?"

She turned onto the main road and accelerated. "Yup. Garrett let it slip when we were talking last week. Of course, it might have been sour grapes. He's interviewing for other jobs."

With that, the issue took on a larger dimension. "I thought our jobs were safe. Weren't we told that?"

"We were. Garrett wasn't. Apparently, Ned Cooper will be doing most of what Garrett does now."

"Ned."

"Cooper."

"His name is Edward," I said without thinking, then barely breathed, but Joyce didn't seem to have caught the slip. She kept her eyes on the road, relaxed hands on the wheel, and her expression benign.

"Maybe on paper," she said, "but he goes by Ned."

He never did, at least, not during the time I had known him. He had been Ned growing up, like I was Maggie growing up. But the sophisticated venture capitalist was always Edward.

"Is this a game for him?" I asked in annoyance. Joyce shot me a surprised look. More gently, I explained, "You have to wonder why someone with that kind of money would want to take over as GM."

"Maybe for the same reason Jack Quillmer bought *The Devon Times* or Nina Evans became Town Manager. Maybe he struck out in another life and needed a change. Maybe he's tired of the money thing and wants a new challenge." She sighed. "Who knows if it'll work out? At least he's not changing what the Inn is best known for. But he is changing other things. He was just telling me; that's why I was in there so long. He's bringing in upgraded computers to replace the ones the government has, but mostly we're switching to tablets. They'll be here this week. He hired a team to set them up and teach us how to use them. The security system is state-of-the-art."

"On a tablet?"

"That's what he says." She took a quick breath. "By the way, Elizabeth

Rossi was in the farm store just now. She said Grace knows the journalist whose account was hacked."

I frowned at the road, trying to decide how best to handle Edward Cooper—and he was Edward, not Ned. It wouldn't be so bad if he was buying the bookstore or the general store. But The Devon Inn and Spa were the town's major draws.

He had to have come here for a reason. I had no idea what it was.

And Joyce seemed to be waiting for a response . . . to . . . Elizabeth Rossi . . . saying . . . that Grace knows the journalist whose account was hacked.

"You told me that this morning," I replied. The Feds may have seized the Spa computers, but its files were synced with iPads already belonging to the GM and Joyce. Once they heard the name Benjamin Zwick, they did a search. "Grace does his hot stones whenever he's in the area."

"Beyond that."

We exchanged a glance. She, too, was remembering how Grace had left work today.

"I told Elizabeth that I didn't think it was true," Joyce said, with her eyes on the road again. "I never saw them together. He always requests her when he calls for an appointment, but most of her repeats do." She paused. The silence stretched as she waited. Finally, she said an uneasy, "Maggie?"

She wanted me to deny that Grace had had an affair with Ben, but I couldn't. "I don't know." I searched for something I might have missed, but all I could do was repeat, "I don't know. But does that have to have anything to do with anything her son allegedly did?"

Of course, it did. If you were looking for motive, resentment of a mother who was having an affair might work.

Joyce dropped me back at the Spa, pulling up close enough to my truck so that I was able to lock myself inside before the lone remaining reporter reached it. When he knocked on the window, I gave an angry headshake and motioned him off. As soon as he backed away, I gunned the engine, and left. My heart was in my throat until I wheeled out of the lot and modulated my speed, but it jumped right back there as soon as I passed under the covered bridge, turned south on the Blue, and heard a rustling right behind me—*inside* my truck. I was about to scream when the inimitable mess of sandy curls that was Chris Emory appeared between the seats.

7

"J*esus*," I breathed and, trembling, veered to the side of the road.

"Don't stop, no, no, no, do not stop, they'll be on our tails for sure!" The words came in a rush, aimed back, then front, then back again, and his voice cracked every few syllables. Puberty had it wavering between man and boy, still not yet sure which way to go, and stress didn't help. Between the press now and the arraignment tomorrow, he had to be terrified.

"No one's following," I said. I had been checking since I left the Inn. There had only been that one reporter, likely a lowly leave-behind, since the Spa lot had largely cleared out. I assumed the big guns were in the center of town, but the road behind me remained dark.

My heart slowed its racing enough for me to ask, "What are you doing here, Chris? And how did you get *in*?"

His hand appeared. My spare key was in his palm.

Had the situation been different, I might have laughed. The key. Of *course*. But in the seconds before it appeared, I had imagined him jimmying the lock, which didn't bode well for his innocence on the computer-hacking score, given the high-tech security system in my truck.

The key was the one Grace had forgotten to return when her car was being serviced and she borrowed my truck, which raised the issue of his taking it from her purse.

But that wasn't my worry. I had enough others. If Chris had been photographed entering or, worse, inside the truck, Michael Shanahan would be back.

"You weren't seen?" I asked. If he had been, media reinforcements would likely already be on the way. Hell, if *I* had been recognized, they might be. I looked in the rearview again, but all was dark. "How did you do it?"

Moving under cover of darkness was one thing, but we had just turned the clocks forward, so it was still light. Okay, there would have been more cars in the lot an hour or two ago, meaning more cars to crouch between and hide behind. But there would have been more reporters, too.

That said, I knew how cunning Chris could be. I had played hide-and-seek in the woods with him and, granted, he was eleven at the time, technically too old. But he had asked, and was totally into it, like he'd been waiting forever to play with someone.

He was good in the woods. What he lacked in athleticism, he more than made up for in smarts. He moved stealthily and with purpose. I imagined him now, behind the Spa, watching for an opening from the cover of nearby trees, waiting for the moment when something else drew reporters like a shark to chum.

"Hoodie," Chris said.

Hoodie. Of course. Like half the men leaving after a day of work at the Inn, the hardware store, or the highway department. Like half the boys heading home after a day of classes at Devon High.

Hoodie. Right. The hood was down now, but he'd kept it up going in and out of the police station, the courthouse, and Jay's office. And how did I know that? Since Michael kept tabs on the news, I had to keep tabs on what he saw. I had done it when I got home from Jessa's last night. As tired as I was, I was too keyed up to sleep, so, resting my laptop on my midriff, I retrieved every article I could. I hadn't seen myself in any more clips, but Chris was all over the place. Fortunately, his features hadn't shown. And his hoodie was the same nondescript gray worn by all those other high school kids who wanted more to look cool than feel warm. Huddling into himself in those clips, he'd had the look of someone who was either frightened, guilty as hell, or freezing.

When my thoughts reached the freezing part, I turned up the heat. The inside of the truck was cold, and he had been in it for God-knew how long, which raised an urgent issue. "Does Grace know you're here?"

"No. She's out."

I didn't want to ask out where—wondered if he knew—feared that if he had been hanging around the Inn for long, he might have seen her leaving the Spa with that guy.

I grabbed my phone. The call went straight to voice mail, which meant that Chris was just starting to protest when I said a louder, "Hey, Grace, your son's with me. I'm taking him to my place. You can pick him up on your way home."

I didn't ask her to confirm it, didn't want to wait for an answer that might be a while coming. She surprised me by texting *I will* within seconds, like she had her cell right there just in case, which restored my faith a little.

My periphery caught the flicker of headlights in the rearview. Heart pounding, I sank a little lower, watched, waited. The headlights passed, taillights receded. Only then did I dare take a breath.

Setting the phone down, I gestured Chris into the passenger seat. As he wormed up from the back, he was a lanky tangle of arms, legs, and torso, but I figured that if he had gotten himself in there, he could get himself out.

He did. Then he just sat, waiting to go.

I cleared my throat. When he looked at me, I looked at his lap. We had been through this before. I didn't care what his mother did, but this was my vehicle, and I didn't take chances. When I had to drive, seat belts were non-negotiable.

As soon as I heard the click, I checked the side-view mirror and returned to the road.

We drove in silence, actually were of like minds in this, Chris and I. Whenever I drove him places—like the times Grace had been stuck at the Spa and he had a hockey game or a dentist appointment—we didn't need noise. I didn't like his music; he didn't like mine. He didn't like sharing personal thoughts; I didn't like prying. Had Lily survived to fifteen, I would have wanted to know her music and, yes, would have pried if I felt she had something on her mind. But Chris wasn't my child, which freed me of responsibility. I was maybe an aunt, maybe a friend, in either of which cases, we drove in peace.

Tonight, though, peace was scant. Grace's absence was nearly as disturbing as the specter of tomorrow's arraignment. Chris had been released *into her care* at the court hearing, but his being alone now didn't feel like care to me. It felt like abandonment in a time of need. The tension in him was palpable. He didn't have much of a beard yet, but even if he had, I doubt it would have hidden the stiffness of his jaw, clearly visible despite the waning light. And then there was the jiggling of his leg.

Signaling at the obelisk, I turned left on Cedar. Once on the straightaway again, I said, "Want to talk?"

He didn't reply, just stared at the houses we passed. After we crossed the Blue and the space between houses increased, he shifted his legs in the foot well. It was only seconds before the jiggling resumed.

We were approaching the pretty yellow farmhouse, when, sounding brash, he said, "It isn't hard, y'know. Anyone can do it."

Hacking, I thought. *Here we go.*

"It's about tricking a person into giving up personal information," he said. His voice didn't crack as much as before. Nor did he push it deeper. I wanted to think he trusted me enough to just be who he was, but I suspected defiance was at play. Whatever, he seemed more focused on content than style. "Once you have that, you're in."

"But how do you get it?" I asked, treating it like a hypothetical discussion. We weren't talking about a crime Christopher Emory was accused of committing, simply what hacking was about, and I was curious.

We passed the farmhouse. Several weak lamps appeared in the windows, along with the vivid color of a flat-screen. For a split second, I wondered whether Devon was in the news again tonight, but the colors were quickly gone. As we drove on, the landscape was increasingly shadowed.

"First, you make a mock-up of a Twitter log-in," he said and snorted. "Takes maybe an hour to do that."

"Seriously? And it looks like the real thing?"

"The URL is different, but just a little, so most people don't notice. They're annoyed, they're in a rush, they see the little blue bird." He retreated to the side window again.

"Then what?"

He chewed on the inside of his cheek for a minute, like he was suddenly not sure he should be telling me this. But I sensed he couldn't hold it in anymore. Knee going up and down, up and down with the jiggle of his leg, he faced me again. "You write something that looks like an official message from Twitter. It could read, 'Maggie Reid just asked to follow you. Log in to approve.' You send it to the target."

"So you need either an email address or a phone number," I said. Grace would have both for Ben Zwick. "But if a person has a public account"—which I was sure Ben did—"wouldn't he question why he's being asked to approve a follower?"

"He'd think it's just a security precaution. Or maybe he recognizes the name of the person who wants to follow him. You can get names like that in a few clicks."

I bet. High school classmates, work colleagues, relatives—Google had it all. Someone as ego-driven as Ben Zwick wouldn't be able to ignore the lure of a long-lost friend or, even more, a professional rival who wanted to follow him.

"So," I said, "the target types in his log-in information. Then what?"

His shoulder moved under the gray hoodie in a dismissive shrug. "The hacker has what he wants, and the target is redirected to the real site. That's it. That's how you hack."

"Just like that?"

"Yuh."

"Is this, like, common knowledge?"

He focused on the windshield.

"Do all your friends know how to do it?"

He frowned.

"You do know it's wrong."

That earned a defensive, "I didn't say I did it."

"But just so we're sure, Chris, you do know it's wrong."

The guilty look on his face said he did. I left it at that.

We approached the ski slope, which seemed ridiculously innocent compared to the thoughts in my truck. So late in the day, it was a shadowed mass of evergreen spikes and gloomy swaths, some wide and straight, others narrow and curving out around the sides. Cables ran up the center of the hill, chairs dangling in a mild breeze, but otherwise all was still. That should have been ominous, but I had skied here enough for memory to add a gaggle of brightly colored parkas.

Chris Emory had taught me to ski. Oh, Grace would say it was her. And yes, she was the one who had made me do it. But after she got me outfitted and gave me brief instructions, she was skiing off, leaving bunny-land for steeper slopes.

Chris stayed with me. He wasn't the best skier—wasn't terribly coordinated, which was why Grace insisted he play hockey, like it would make him an athlete, like the coaches could make him a man. He did need male role models. But he never excelled on the ice any more than he did on the slopes. I always suspected that he loved teaching me to ski simply because it gave him an excuse to stay easy and slow.

The ski slope came and went. We drove on until I reached my turnoff, then the white post that marked Pepin Hill. I signaled, made the turn, and started up, all the while growing surer that this had been a confession. I should have been shocked, but was not. An odd part of me was proud that he excelled in this, at least. And to mess with the press? What he'd done to Ben Zwick was awful. But maybe, just maybe Ben deserved it.

Who to tell? Absolutely no one. Unless Michael had bugged my car, Chris's confession went nowhere.

I was concerned about him, about Grace, about me. But I was also flattered that he had confided in me, regardless of what Michael Shanahan said. I had my reasons for hating the press. If Chris had done what he was being accused of, he had his. Sometime, somehow, they would come out.

Right now, my caring gene said that Chris needed a breather. In that regard, my pets were a godsend. He stayed outside while Jonah bounded in and out of the woods, then came in and gave Hex and Jinx two lanky legs to wind around. I could hear their purring from the kitchen. The therapy they offered was priceless.

"I want a pet," Chris announced, bending over to scratch ears.

I had taken pizza from the freezer and was tossing a salad. "Ask your Mom."

"Like I haven't?" he returned, sounding annoyed. "She always says no. She says they tie you down. I keep telling her I'll do the feeding and stuff, but it's like she can't handle anything more than me."

She could barely handle him, I thought and, when his eyes met mine, knew he agreed. He looked away without saying the words, and actually said nothing more of substance until he'd eaten three huge pieces of the pizza, a large helping of salad, and half a dozen Oreos. We were cleaning up, me at the sink, him handing over glasses and plates, when he said, "She doesn't have many friends."

I put the last dish in the dishwasher. "She does."

"Not like close friends, only you." He paused. "Maggie?"

As I closed the dishwasher, I met his gaze and raised my brows in inquiry.

"You always talk to me like I'm a grown-up. I need you to do that now, because I don't know who else to ask. Since all this happened, she's been gone—I mean, like, not physically, at least, no more than she always is—but she's, like, in another world, and she's biting her nails. She never did that before."

I hadn't noticed. But then, I had barely seen her since all hell had broken loose. That said, it didn't take a genius to figure out why. "She's worried about you."

"Yeah, well, if that was it, wouldn't *she* be the one telling me how bad hacking is? Wouldn't she be the one asking questions?"

"Maybe she's afraid of the answers."

"I get that, but something's off, like it's not me that's giving her the creeps. When she's home, she sits there staring at the table or the floor or her phone, and she looks like she's waiting for something." He left the last word up in the air, like he was asking me to tell him what, but I didn't have a clue.

Feeling useless, I wiped my hands on the dish towel. *Hot chocolate,* said a little voice in my head. *He needs hot chocolate. With whipped cream. We both do.*

Opening the cupboard, I removed cocoa powder, sugar, and vanilla. They were on the counter and I was reaching into the lower cabinet for a saucepan when he said, "What do you know about my dad?"

Bent in half, I went still. I hadn't seen *that* coming.

I straightened holding the saucepan. "Your dad? Uh, nothing. Why?"

"She doesn't talk to you about him?"

"Never." I went to the fridge for milk. "You want to tell me?"

He was leaning against the counter on the far side of the sink, shifting his long legs like he didn't know how best to arrange them, but his face was suddenly all boy, all angry. "Like I *know?*" he blurted out. "I don't know *anything.* She won't talk about him. I mean, I get *nothing.* I've asked her a *bazillion* times, but she makes a face, like the . . . the"—he glanced at what I held—"the *milk* smells bad." His knee went in and out, in and out.

"Do I look like my mother? I'm talking hair, eyes, height—like DNA—and the answer is *no*. I look like *him*, but that's all I know. I don't know where he lives or what he does. I don't even know his name."

At the stove now, I said, "Maybe she doesn't know it herself," because it seemed like the only way to defend Grace's refusal to talk. I'd had a friend in college who got pregnant during spring break, ten shots, one night, no clue until weeks later. The only problem was that I knew better. *His father was a liar,* Grace had told me that first night.

I couldn't share that with Chris. I couldn't let it be the only thing he knew about the man.

And anyway, he was shaking his head. "She knows. She just won't tell me. Like I'll go try to find him? Why the fuck would I do that if the guy doesn't want me?"

"Chris."

"Birth certificate." His voice cracked under the press of emotion. "His name would be there, right? Wrong. Mine says I was born in Chicago, but I'm not sure it's true. Bogus birth certificates are easy to get. Were they ever married? Are they divorced?"

I poured milk into the saucepan and added the other ingredients. The silence was charged. He was waiting for me to say something.

I lit the gas and stirred, watching white blend to cocoa as it warmed. Then, looking up, I found his eyes. They were the same soft brown as Grace's contacts. It struck me that she wore these more often than the blues or greens. I wondered if aligning with her son was why. "I don't know the answers to your questions, Chris. I wish I did. I just don't."

He stared at me for another minute, then dragged his hands up his face and through his curls. With a loud exhale, he deflated. "Sorry."

"Don't be. It's only natural you'd wonder these things. At some point, Grace will give you answers."

"You think?"

"I do. Your mother loves you."

"You think?" he repeated, still doubting.

"I *know*," I said, because it was the truth. From the start, I had always known this about Grace. She might not exhibit maternal love as I would have. But over and above her quirkiness, what had drawn me to her from the first was her concern for Chris. I had seen her leave the Spa mid-massage when word came that a puck had hit him in the face. "She's just a private person. She has her own issues. We all have them."

"Not you."

"Yes, me. No one slides through life without bruises." I searched for a positive way to say it. "My favorite app is CALM. Know why? Because I'm not. So when I see something there that resonates, I remember it. Like, *Obstacles do not block the path, they are the path.* It's a Zen proverb—and no, don't roll your eyes, I'm not into Zen anything, only this makes sense. There are always hurdles in life. Getting over them is how we move forward. It's how we grow."

"Sure."

"Trust me on this."

"Oh, I do," he said with a sarcasm that was all wrong in a fifteen-year-old whose curls made him look like he was five. "It's my mother I don't trust. I mean, she sits there and stares, so I guess she's controlling herself, but then sometimes she gets this wild look in her eyes. It's scary. I mean, is she angry at me? Angry at the world? I don't have any fucking idea," he said with a wild look of his own. "But I have to be in court tomorrow. What if the judge sees that look? What if he says she isn't fit or something, and he puts me in a juvenile facility—"

"He won't—"

"Or foster care." His eyes widened, like he had an idea. I don't think it was premeditated, just a sudden brainstorm on the heels of the discussion. "Come with us, Maggie."

"Uh, where?" I knew, of course, just needed time to formulate my answer.

"To court. You're her best friend. You're always sensible. If anyone can keep her steady, you can."

He had no idea what he was asking. Even if I wanted to do it for his sake, I couldn't handle the press, which might focus on my being the only near-kin they could find and make me their next story. I couldn't risk that. It was everything I'd built a new life to avoid. I would lose it, literally and figuratively. And that was even before Shanahan had his say.

Smiling sadly, I reached for mugs. "I can't, Chris."

"Because you have to work?"

"No." Work would have been a lame excuse. Appointments could be shifted. "It isn't about work. I just can't."

"Why not?"

"Because—because it's inappropriate. Jay is the only one who should be with you."

"Jay's a lawyer. You're our friend."

"I know."

"Isn't this what friends do?"

"Yes—"

"If we ever, *ever* needed you, it's now."

"Chris—"

"I thought you liked me," he said, sounding hurt.

"I *do*—"

"Then how can you *not come?*"

Later, I would think, *KO'd by a fifteen-year-old.* At the time, all I could think was that once he personalized it, I had lost. Chris Emory needed love. He needed attention. He needed to know that you didn't have to pay for loyalty—like they were paying Jay—when friends were involved. This was a pivotal time in his life. He needed to know that someone who absolutely didn't *need* to be there *would* be there for him.

That said, I didn't fully commit, just told him I would try. I topped his hot chocolate with a mountain of whipped cream, thinking that my mother would never have used canned whipped cream but for all her whipping from scratch, she had deserted me when I'd needed her most. I couldn't desert Chris. He wasn't my child; I had only known him four years, had no more idea where he'd come from than he did. But what I did now seemed as pivotal to my life as hacking was to his.

Then Grace came to pick him up, Chris immediately said I was coming, and the look of hope on her face clinched it. She needed that kind of friend.

Maybe I did, too.

After they left, I sat in the living room in the warm and furry crowd of Hex, Jinx, and Jonah, and made mental lists.

The DON'T Go list had three points. First was the past, as in memory of courtrooms, judges, and the media. Second was the present, as in adding me to the spotlight now focused on Grace and Chris and jeopardizing my anonymity in Devon. Third, and legally crucial for my future, was Michael Shanahan.

The MUST Go side wasn't as me-centric. It involved keeping Grace moored. And freeing Jay from the distraction of an unhinged client, so that he could focus on his job. And, yes, being there for Chris.

But there was something else. It had to do with character. I tried to push it aside with arguments like, *It's not my responsibility, I'm too bruised myself, I can't save the world.* But I kept returning to it. My being in court to support my friends was the right thing to do.

Character? Oh, yeah. Who did I want to be in this life? Was I willing to stand up for something I believed in? I did believe in Chris and, even, in Grace. Neither was malicious. And what they faced? We weren't talking hurdles; we were talking roadblocks that could obstruct their entire future.

Sitting there, even with seconds of hot chocolate, my problems with Edward seemed suddenly mild.

I barely slept. The first time I came awake, I breathed deeply—in for five, hold for three, out for five, repeat. The next time I woke up, I made sleep tea—one cup, then a second. I dozed again, woke up, used the bathroom.

Barely sleeping wasn't new for me, but this night wasn't about Lily. It was about Michael Shanahan. If I went with the Emorys tomorrow and he found out, he might decide I had violated my probation and take me back to court, in which case I would be exposed. That, way more than prison, was my fear. I wanted to look at my probation agreement, just to check on what he could or could not do, but that meant opening the green velvet box under my bed to get it, and I couldn't yet, couldn't yet.

In an ideal world, I would have called Edward. He was one of the most rational people I knew. He had been able to think clearly on even the most emotional matters, until those emotions had grown bigger than us. But I no longer knew where he stood on me, much less on Devon or hacking. If he was part of whatever entity was buying the Inn, which would suffer negative fallout from this, he sure as hell would be no fan of the Emorys.

So, no Edward.

And no Mom.

And no Cornelia, though I did consider telling her everything, just for her advice.

That left Kevin. I waited until five thirty—just couldn't wait longer than that—and, telling myself that he would be up soon anyway, texted, *You awake?*

He replied a minute later. *Sorry. Couldn't find the phone. I'm calling.* My cell rang. "What's wrong?" he asked.

His voice was low. Jimmy would still be sleeping, but he wouldn't want to leave the bed's warmth. I didn't care where he talked from. He had been asleep himself, I'd woken him, and his first concern was for me. Talk about defining a true friend.

"I love you, Kevin," I breathed, then quickly told him what Chris had asked and the dilemma I faced. "Am I right? Wrong? Noble? Out of my freaking *mind?*"

"Not that, honey. Never that. But you're asking the right questions. The problem here is Grace."

"Please forget that you don't like her."

"I don't really know her," he admitted. "But do you? You say she has no one else, but why doesn't she? Where are her parents?"

"Where are yours?"

There was a pause, then a quiet, "Touché. Family rift. But this kid has a father somewhere. What's with him?"

I hadn't told him about that part of my discussion with Chris. "Funny you ask."

"Funny?

"Chris wonders the same thing."

"Well, he's how old? Fifteen? He *should* wonder. Lemme tell you, when I reached his age, I was looking at my father and thinking I had to be like him but couldn't. He was looking at me and thinking I didn't have his beard or his build or his guts. He was disappointed. I knew that. I told myself it was okay. I told myself that I must look like one of my uncles. Or my grandfather. That's what boys do at that age. They look in the mirror every time someone tells them to brush their teeth or use deodorant. It's like, who am I? Who do I *want* to be?"

Passion had driven his voice higher. I heard a groggy murmur in the background and a reply aimed away from the phone. "I'm good, I'm good." Back to me. "Sorry, the old hurts hang around." He paused. Then, softly, he asked, "Who are you, Maggie?"

The question wasn't a literal one. He knew where I had come from and who I had been. How he could zero in so perfectly at not-even-six in the morning, I didn't know, but it was why I had called.

"I don't know who I am. I'm trying to figure that out."

"Who do you want to be?"

"A good person. I want to be a good person."

"There's your answer." There was another background murmur, more input from Jimmy. Seconds later, he added, "A heads-up, doll. Zwick'll be there."

"Rutland?" I swore softly. "Not good."

"Not good," he confirmed. "Still want to go?"

Did I want to go, with a guarantee now that the media would be out in force? Absolutely not. The thought of it had my stomach knotting. But Chris's disillusioned, *I thought you liked me,* and *How can you not come,* followed by that look of hope on Grace's face?

Who was I? I wasn't a mother or a wife, and I was a daughter in name only. But I was a friend. Being a friend sometimes meant you left your own comfort zone for the sake of someone else. I wanted to be the kind of person who did that.

Grace texted me twice before seven. The first text told me to wear my purple herringbone tweed blazer. She had been with me when I bought it, and said that it was what was expected in court. I felt a stab of annoyance. I knew what was expected—God, did I. Since she didn't know how cozy courtrooms and I had once been, her remark was innocent in that sense, but not so in another. She was making sure I knew I was coming. The second text sealed the deal. It said that the hearing was scheduled for ten, and that Jay was driving "us all" and would pick me up at eight.

8

The Federal Courthouse in Rutland was modest by big-city standards, but seeing it through the tinted windows of Jay's back seat, knowing that I actually had to enter it, I felt a mild panic. The building was imposing. Standing three stories, it had tall, narrow windows, arched cornices, and double columns typical of the Italianate style. Red brick spanned its forehead, pale granite its mouth and cheeks. *Built in 1869,* Jay narrated, likely as a diversion, but no diversion could erase the media on the steps. They were clustered in the center of three sections marked by handrails. Alone near the top, positioned so that the backdrop would be the middle one of three massive doors, was Ben Zwick.

Grace swore.

So did I, though I kept it silent.

When Chris broke off from jiggling his leg and straightened to look, I rubbed his arm to remind him he wasn't alone. Back in Boston, I had needed that. All too clearly, I remembered the sense of being targeted, shot at, even *smothered* by the enemy. Fortunately, I'd had Edward.

Actually, I had not. For the first court appearances, yes. But by the time my trial rolled around, the silence in our house had driven us apart, the grief was so impenetrable that we couldn't get past it to talk. So Edward had been there in body but not spirit, and the pain of that? Salt on an open wound.

Grace swore again, now on a higher-pitched note. I wanted to touch her shoulder, hold her arm, do something to comfort her. Wasn't that why I was here? Wasn't that the *only* reason I was here? She had been silent through the drive, barely glancing at Chris as she burrowed into her coat in the passenger seat. Suddenly, she was back in force and upset, but I was sitting behind Jay and couldn't reach her.

I continued to hold Chris's arm, so the tremor I felt might have been his, might have been mine. Kevin had warned me that Zwick would be there, but his brazenness was still a shock.

"Is he really holding a *press conference?*" I asked. A wave of loathing took the edge off my nerves.

"Yup," confirmed Jay.

"*I thought the hearing was closed.*" This from Grace in a panicky shriek.

Jay remained calm. "It is. Zwick won't be in the courtroom, and he can't pull stunts like this in the hallways, but the front steps are fair game."

"Is there a back entrance?" I asked as Edward had five years before.

"Heading there now," Jay said and did just that.

We parked and made it through the back door with only a handful of reporters closing in before they were stayed by a guard. Were film crews scattered along those back streets? I'd bet on it. And though cameras weren't allowed inside, enough of the people we passed on our way to the courtroom were shifting phones in and around ears to suggest that there were at least a few surreptitious shots being taken.

Jay guided Grace, who held Chris's arm. The boy had his hood up, and her face was shielded between hair and fur hood. I had only my bangs, which weren't much of a shield. Had I thought ahead, I might have raised my own hood or worn dark glasses, though any attempt to hide at this point would only draw attention. I wanted to touch my bangs to make sure they covered the scar, but even that would be a tip-off. The best I could do was to keep my eyes straight ahead and my expression cool, like I was here in an official capacity, maybe as Jay's assistant.

The courtroom, surprisingly, proved a refuge. When I was a defendant, it had been mobbed, but since this was a juvenile proceeding, the only people allowed in were the AG and his assistant, the judge, the clerk, a court reporter taking notes, and us.

Jay and Chris sat at a table in the front, Jay wearing a respectable suit, Chris a shirt and slacks. Grace and I sat immediately behind them. Once we had our coats off, I took her hand. She immediately tightened her fingers around mine. Bitten nails? Oh yeah. She always kept her nails short; her work demanded that. But this was something else. I covered them with my free hand so that neither of us could see.

"All rise," said the clerk.

The judge entered wearing her black robe, and though her words bore the weight of authority, her voice was agreeable. *"Arraignment in juvenile proceedings . . . United States of America versus Christopher P. Emory . . . charges of Internet fraud and wire fraud."*

As I listened, I pushed memory away. Grace's death grip on my hand helped with that, as did the judge. Mine had been male, sharp-voiced, and grim. This one was younger and seemed kinder. If she was a mother herself, we might have a leg up when it came to sympathy. I suspected Jay had fought to get her assigned to the case. That was how it worked.

Facing Chris, she asked if he understood the charges. He nodded. With a small smile and a tip of her head to the court reporter, she asked Chris to speak his reply for the record. Once he had, she read the charges. Jay's influence showed here, too. In the course of multiple weekend calls, he had convinced the prosecutors to forego charges for each offending post, leaving only the two biggies. And they were big. As she read them, the words reverberated across the high ceilings of the near-empty room.

Chris pleaded not guilty. The judge ruled that the conditions of his release were the same as previously established. She set a date one month later for a status conference to hear motions.

Five minutes. That was all it took. I held it together until we left the courtroom, but once the media closed in, threads of panic returned. I lowered my head, likely a mistake given the vulnerability it showed, and the press pounced on vulnerability like no tomorrow. Recorders were shoved in my face along with demands for my name, my take on the accused, the hearing, the crime itself.

I couldn't have spoken if my life had depended on it. Jay hustled us along with a hand raised to fend off the press.

We were almost at the door when someone called my name—at least, I thought that was what I heard, though, upset as I was, it could have been any two-syllable shout with similar sounds. Whatever, it resembled Maggie, not Mackenzie, so it would have been someone from Devon. Everyone there knew Grace and I were friends. The only danger lay in a journalist picking up on my name.

Then again, it might have been Michael Shanahan.

Needing to know, I looked back. I didn't see Michael, but I did see Ben Zwick. Tall and sandy-haired, he stood off to the side with a wounded air and his eyes locked on Grace.

I had another rough night. For starters, even though I knew it was asking for trouble, I'd felt compelled to surf every local news outlet, read what was there, and then click through to related stories. My face appeared often, and while I was always in the background and never identified by name, it was upending. The last thing I wanted was someone from my past connecting the dots, coming to Devon to check, and destroying what was left of my privacy.

That fear brought dreams, which played out during brief spurts of sleep. In one, I was having a seaweed wrap at the Spa, unable to move as clients entered the room and took selfies with me; in another, the players in my Boston nightmare were trekking up Pepin Hill cradling semi-automatic weapons in their arms. There was an erotic dream that involved Edward and was frighteningly coherent. And then there was the one about Lily, which had nothing to do with the fear of exposure and everything to do with a loss so profound that, even sprawled in bed, I was brought to my knees. I could see her. She was hurt and crying for me, reaching for me, begging for me to help. But I couldn't get to her. First there was an opaque wall that allowed nothing through but the sound of her increasingly shrill screams, then a dense web through which I could see a distorted view of her face, then, more cruelly, a piece of plastic wrap through which I could see and hear perfectly but not pass.

I'd had this one before. Many times. As always, I woke up alone in my bed, my house, my life. When I was first here, I would wake up in tears. Now when I woke, I simply struggled for air. *Breathe in, breathe out, repeat. Breathe in, breathe out, repeat.*

Leaving Jonah asleep on the bed, I went down to the living room. The cats followed. Actually, the cats led. Seeming to understand that I didn't want to be alone, their warm little bodies crowded in, rubbing close, on my legs and in my lap the instant I curled up on the sofa. Burying my face in their fur, I held them for as long as they allowed.

No amount of makeup could hide what was inside, so while I looked outwardly normal entering the pottery studio, Kevin saw more. Half a dozen other potters were working and another had followed me up the stairs, which meant we couldn't really talk, but that was fine. It was all about his hug. It was about taking my hand away from my hair when I went to touch my bangs for a third time in as many minutes. It was about indulging me when I did nothing but wedge. Oh, I thought about making a teapot, but my mother's special today was butterscotch brownies, which seemed to demand a plate more than a pot, and a plate here would be empty. I thought about making a vase—the flower shop in town had fresh tulips—but my hands didn't move. I even thought about making something Lily liked, like a harmless little bunny. My therapist had been after me to just ease up on purpose and design, and let the clay take me where it would. I hadn't dared do that before. But I was already upset, so why not?

Apparently there was a reason why not, somewhere in the great subconscious, because I couldn't get past wedging. And that was fine. If wedging was all I could do, I would wedge. I had always found the pulling, pushing, and slamming to be therapeutic, and it definitely was now. By the time I left the studio, I was feeling grounded.

The Spa reinforced that with its infusion of lemon verbena and, today, the whisper-soft melody of a harp.

As always, Joyce's face lit up when she saw me. This time, though, with a small swing of her bob, she directed me to the sitting area. Michael Shanahan was rising from the sofa, resplendent in navy blazer, checked shirt, and a pink tie with little blue whales. His preppy soul was so out of place in a Zen world of scented candles, artfully angled cushions, and the tiny waterfalls that were part of the décor, that it might have been laughable, had the sight of him not brought a chill.

"Michael." I was slightly breathless, the peace I had found at the pottery studio that quickly gone.

"Where can we talk?" he asked.

The makeup room was the obvious place, but his cologne—Burberry Brit, he had proudly announced when I commented on it once—had an unpleasant way of lingering there, and besides, I had a client in half an hour and still had to shower and dress. Hoping to keep the talk short, I gestured to the cushions he had just left. Joyce was the only one in sight, and her desk was out of earshot. Between the trickle of water and the strum of the harp, we would have privacy until new clients arrived. Their appearance would remind Michael that I had work to do.

Rather than sitting, he moved to the open area between the sofa and the soaring windows that made up the wall. I joined him there.

"What's up?" I asked in a Spa-low voice, though I knew the answer too well. I had dared the devil, and here he was.

"I saw you in Rutland, Maggie. Why were you there?" He sounded personally aggrieved, like I'd disappointed him in a major way.

So he had been the one to call my name. It wasn't a total surprise. Nor was it reassuring, given the power he held. But I wasn't backing down. "Grace is my friend. She needed support. She had no one else."

"She had her lawyer and her son. She didn't need you, especially after I asked you to steer clear of her. Why didn't you at least call me to get an okay?"

"I didn't think I had to. I wasn't leaving the state."

He wrinkled his nose in distaste. "But this looks bad, Maggie, don't you see? The kid did some awful stuff."

"Not proven."

"Not yet, but the charges wouldn't be brought without evidence. And there you are all over the news? You're putting me in a shitty position."

I couldn't muster sympathy for him. For Grace and Chris? Yes. Even, considering nightmares and fears, for me. But for Michael? No. He was being unreasonable, tone-deaf about the meaning of friendship. So maybe he didn't know what it was. Maybe he didn't have friends. That was cause for sympathy, I supposed.

We stood with our backs to the rest of the room. Just beyond the windows were trees and shrubs that seemed manicured even in March. I studied them until their tranquility eased me.

Then I said a quiet, "I'm sorry." I did regret putting him in an awkward position. He wasn't a bad guy, and he was only doing his job. But I did not regret going to court with Grace and Chris. "I honestly didn't think it was a big deal. The hearing took all of five minutes. It was just a formality."

"The terms of your probation are clear," he said, all stern, I-am-the-law. "You're supposed to pick good friends and stay clean. You're supposed to avoid anything that is even vaguely smelly. And there you were in a courtroom with a guy who's up for two felony counts? That smells *really* bad. So what am I supposed to do, Maggie? I mean, I like you, but this is my job. Do I report it?"

"Excuse me," came a voice from behind, and goose bumps rose on my skin. Edward's voice would always be that familiar to me.

Suddenly he was right there with us, and how could I not compare the two men? Both were tall, but even though Michael had a couple of inches on him, Edward was more classy, more confident, more imposing, like he was the real thing beside a wannabe. He wore a quarter-zip sweater and slacks; the sweater was cashmere and black, the slacks a lighter gray and cut of fine wool; loafers had replaced mud-crusted boots. His long hair was neatly brushed but, paired with the facial hair, seemed somehow wild.

And there it was, like two days ago at the farm. Edward's version of tall and dark got to me every time. The jolt I'd felt hearing his voice became a slow thrum in my veins. I tried to shut it down, but it wouldn't listen to me, and that, alone, was cause to resent him.

He extended a hand to Michael and said in a voice low enough not to carry past us, "Ned Cooper. I'm with the Inn. You must be Officer Shanahan."

Michael shook his hand. "With the Inn?"

I could read Michael. He definitely recognized the name. He just couldn't place it, which put me in a bind. What to say? How much to reveal? What the hell did I *know*?

"I'm heading the new management team," Edward said and hitched his head back at the reception desk, where Joyce was talking with a woman and a man. Both were dressed for business. "They're PR people working on damage control. I was showing them around and saw you with Ms. Reid. Is there a problem?"

That was his story then. He was "with the management team," which could have meant anything but was better than an out-and-out "new owner." He had met me before and knew who I was. And, based on the "Officer" he'd attached to Shanahan, whose name he had just learned from Joyce, he knew who Michael was and, therefore, knew my legal history.

"No problem," Michael said. "Maggie and I meet from time to time."

"Not usually here, though, and not usually when Maggie has to work."

Edward rarely did anything without purpose. Using my first name after Michael had was a power play—like they were jockeying for position with me the pawn. I was suddenly annoyed at them both.

"I caught the end there," Edward said. "What are you reporting?"

Michael shrugged it off. "Court business."

"She's on my payroll, so any business of hers is business of mine. Does it have to do with her being in Rutland yesterday?" When Michael straightened, he said, "I know she was there. Most of the town does. I just know more about Maggie's past than they do."

"How much?" Michael asked, the implication being that he knew more, like it was a competition.

But Edward raised a *hold-on* hand and returned to the reception desk.

"Who the hell does he think *he* is?" Michael hissed the instant he was gone.

"My ex-husband," I hissed back, and why not? He would figure it out. And I was angry, too. I didn't want this, didn't want *any* of it.

He eyed me in shock. "Seriously?"

"Would I joke about something like that?" My whisper was harsh. I felt a storm gathering inside and wasn't sure I could contain it. The past week had been hell on my nerves, which were now further shredded by Edward's pale-blue eyes—Lily's pale-blue eyes—strikingly silver-blue eyes, both pairs.

"I didn't invite him here, Michael, he just suddenly showed up. I had no idea he had anything to do with the Inn, and I still don't know the extent of whatever it is. He didn't bother to let me know before he was coming. God knows he didn't ask my permission. Trust me, I am not a happy camper."

"What's his game?"

"Like *I* know?" I asked, feeling so many warring emotions that when Edward returned, the best I could do was to bury my hands in the pockets of my coat.

Without missing a beat, he picked up where they'd left off. "I know about the accident, the trial, and the probation."

"If you're her ex," came Michael's smug reply, "you know a lot more than that."

Edward seemed about to say something, but reconsidered. He eyed me in question.

"I just told him," I said.

Michael seized the upper hand. "The problem is the terms of her probation. She's not supposed to associate with felons."

Edward frowned. "Who's a felon around here?"

"Right now, the Emory boy is pretty damned close."

"To being a felon? There's been no trial."

"You know what I mean."

"I don't," Edward reasoned. "Her crime didn't involve the underworld. It was a driving accident, for Christ's sake. If you take the spirit of the law, not the letter, the felon thing would never apply to her. She's not a violent person. She isn't a criminal. But okay, fine. The words are in the probation agreement. But a felon, by definition, is someone convicted of a crime. Chris Emory hasn't been convicted of anything. If it happens down the road, she'll stay away. Right now, there's no need. I don't recall anything in the agreement that contradicts that." He glanced at his watch. "Hey, I have to run. My lawyer's waiting. We're reviewing contracts. Should I have him look at the probation agreement while he's here?"

There was no probation agreement in my file here. The former GM hadn't had it, and neither did Edward. He had read it back when I first received it, but the only people outside the Massachusetts AG's office who had copies were Michael, my lawyer in Boston, and me.

Michael stood stone-faced.

"We'll talk later," Edward told me and set off with that long stride of his across the reception area to the door that led into the Inn.

"Arrogant son of a bitch," Michael breathed and attacked me as if it were my fault. "You were awful quiet. Didn't you have anything to say to him, or were you always the passive one in the relationship?"

The words were all wrong. I was suddenly furious, both at Edward for barging into my life and at Michael for being a prick. My voice remained in the privacy range, but barely. "What would you have had me say? I have not talked with the man in four years. I did not invite him here, and I sure as hell didn't text him just now to say I needed help. I was doing fine before either of you showed up." I took a fragmented breath. "I am my own person, Michael. I live alone, and I live clean. If you want to report me, go ahead, I'll hire a lawyer to defend me on the facts. Edward is right. Chris isn't a felon. The terms of my probation say *felon*, not *accused of a felony*. And,*"* I barreled on, "for the record, I wasn't passive in my marriage. Edward and I were equals. I had strengths he didn't have and vice versa. We complemented each other perfectly, and we were happy. Had it not been for my accident—for my taking my eyes off the road for one *fucking* minute—we'd be back in the life we loved with our daughter Lily—and two or three other children," I added in a broken voice. "I wanted four in all, he wanted three. That was the worst of any disagreement we had."

Slammed with grief, I ran out of breath, but not before silently noting another mistake we had made. Between enjoying Lily and building my career, we had put off having other children. And then, after Lily died, our bubble of invincibility was gone.

I didn't often think about what might have been. My chest didn't seize up; I had that much control, at least. But composure? Slim to none. The sudden silence was too dense even for sounds of the harp to breach.

Michael seemed startled, like he hadn't expected an outburst from me, like my vehemence told him how upset I was but he had no clue what to do.

I had no clue what he would do, either. In the void, though, it struck me that I might have sounded unstable, which wasn't something I wanted my probation officer to think.

Swallowing, I took a slow, palliative breath. "Sorry. I'm on overload. It's been a difficult week."

"Him showing up? I totally get it."

He totally didn't, if he thought that Edward's showing up was all, but I didn't have the strength to remind him of the rest. In that instant, only one matter was prime.

"About my having been married to him, he and I need to talk. He knows that you know, but he needs to know that no one else does. No one here even knows my married name, and I want it to stay that way. I won't be telling people Edward's my ex, and I don't want him to do it, either." The message was for Michael as well, which was why I ended on a pleading note.

He got that, at least. "I won't tell."

"Thank you. It's confidential information. It's no one's business but Edward's and mine. And now you."

"I promise," he said, his voice distinctly personal, "but you have to promise to avoid the Emorys. I mean it, Maggie. This whole business is so frigging public. Your face is a hundred times prettier than anyone else on probation, so people remember it. Suddenly there it is in the news, and I'm getting calls from the head of the department saying, 'What the hell? Get on top of this, Shanahan.' That's what *I'm* dealing with."

I nodded. "I understand."

His smile was too kind. "Good. Just so we're clear."

We were. I understood his problem. That didn't mean I agreed with his interpretation of my probation terms. In that, Edward had won hands down.

I might have followed Edward right then and demanded to know why he was here. But I was still reeling from the little flashback of his eyes and Lily's, and didn't think I could bear seeing either again just yet.

Besides, I had one client, then another, then a walk-in. The last was a local bestselling author who wanted to talk about the possibility of my doing her makeup for a photo shoot in April. She was the most exciting of the three. Her genre was political suspense, which meant that she wanted to look like a hip forty-year-old from Washington, DC, rather than a crunchy sixty-year-old from Devon. We talked about makeup and hair and even clothes. By the time she left, I felt I had made another friend.

Which, ironically, made me all the more irritated with Edward. I had a nice life here. His coming threatened to destroy it.

I didn't call him that night because, frankly, I needed to *not* think about Edward—to pretend that he didn't exist and remind myself of the plusses in my new life. So I went to happy hour at the studio store with a group of fellow potters, then went home and took a long walk with Jonah. After that, I returned to the cabin and, with the cats worming their way around every leg in sight, be it those of the stools at my kitchen island or mine, I cooked. I didn't bake; my mother was the expert there, so anything I produced would be, by comparison, too salty, too dense, or too dry. Cooking was okay. I didn't do it often and was lousy at it, mainly because the creative me balked at following directions as written. But it was fun. Having chosen a recipe online and picked up ingredients on the way home, I spent the evening with Spotify, à la Katy Perry, Coldplay, and Adele, and made a lovely mess of my small kitchen. There was therapy in cleaning it all up and the tiredness the whole adventure brought.

I slept. I dreamed. I awoke Wednesday morning fresh from another erotic one.

Resentful of that, I might have called Edward then—even marched myself to his office to demand that he stay out of my life—if Joe Hellinger hadn't called. His patient was a teenage girl whose cheek had been badly burned when a chemistry class experiment blew up, and while he had done what he could with skin grafts, no way could you miss it. Laser treatments would help once she was healed, but I was able to show her how to hide the mess until it did.

I was good at hiding things.

———

Cornelia was only partly right. Another story came along and took over the headlines. This one was about a gun incident in Florida in which five people were killed. Talk of terrorism superseded teenage hacking any day.

But the press didn't forget about Devon. Our weekly ran a piece about the case; it was a straightforward report of what had happened, giving Jay's name, Grace's name, the prosecutor's name, even the judge's name but no others. The rest of the media? Breaking-news reporters were replaced by magazine journalists, some of whom were friends of Ben Zwick and clearly on his revenge team. Their stories would be longer and broaden the picture to include Chris playing town hockey not very well, and Grace having come to town a dozen years earlier from no-one-knew-where. They talked with shop owners and road workers; they talked with locals eating breakfast at Rasher and Yolk, and with tourists eating dinner at the crêpe place two doors down from that. They tried to talk with me as I left work, but I waved them away each time.

"Much better," my probation officer said when he called Thursday afternoon. "You're staying off the Emory grid."

"You warned, I listened," I replied. I didn't tell him I had sent Grace home the night before with a pot of beef stew, or that I had agreed to do her hair. He didn't understand what friendship meant. I wasn't sure a man could—well, except Kevin.

Kevin knew how much Michael Shanahan annoyed me, and though he couldn't do anything about the man's visits or calls, he could do something about the press. He refused to allow them anywhere near the pottery studio—literally, all week, repeatedly, insisted journalists were "scaring off his patrons" and had Jimmy wangle surveillance patrols. That made the studio a double haven for me, which is probably why on Friday morning I tried, again, to just let myself go and give in to the past. Lily used to play with me for hours shaping bunnies, dolls, her favorite fruits, even her profile.

Today? Nada.

Oh, I retrieved the bin with my name on the front, and, taking an isolated workbench that faced the woods, unwrapped the paper-clay that I saved for special things. I even wedged it, like I had done Tuesday. But I kept at it so long and hard this day, that Kevin finally came up from behind, gripped my shoulders, leaned low, and said into my ear, "You're killing it, babe."

I froze. With a last meek nudge at the clay, I let my hands fall. "Sorry."

"Don't be for my sake."

"Not for you, then. For her," I said. Though my voice was shielded by the room's sandy hum, chagrin kept it low. "I still can't do it."

Kevin turned my stool and hunkered down. "It's hard. You're not ready. And anyway, she's not expecting you to be ready." He frowned. "Uh, are we talking about your daughter or your therapist?"

I met his eyes. "Both. Lily, because there are times I think she can't rest in peace until I do this. My therapist, because she told me I had to confront the past if I want to move on." I read the question in his eyes. "No, I haven't Skyped with her lately. What's the point? She doesn't approve of my locking things away. She says it won't work." I put a protective palm on the clay I had wedged. It was cool and damp, and smelled of everything I loved, but I couldn't work it. "Maybe she's right. I'm sure as hell not making progress here."

"It's not the right time."

"What if I can't choose a time?" I cried softly. "What if the choice is made for me? What if the past won't stay packed away in a box with my name on it, just sitting on a shelf until I feel like taking it off and breaking the seal? This week has been brutal, Kev. I see reporters even when they're really just tourists. Officer Gill is in his cruiser, only he's not playing Solitaire, he's watching me, I swear he is, and he doesn't wave. I look in my rearview mirror as I drive. I pull over at the bottom of Pepin Hill to make sure I'm not being followed. And I keep seeing Edward. I saw him at the market yesterday. He was buying eggs. Why is he buying eggs at our market when he can raid the kitchen at the Inn any time he wants? Why is he buying eggs, when he doesn't even know how to cook!"

"He doesn't?"

"*No.*"

"Breakfast? *Eggs?* Any idiot can cook eggs." When I shrugged, Kevin said, "Maybe he wants to get to know the town. Maybe he's lonely. He doesn't have a girlfriend. He moved here alone."

Moved here alone? Well, there was another possible burr. How unpleasant would it be seeing Edward with someone else? "How do you know that?"

"Those women who come here to play with clay? They talk."

"How do *they* know?"

"Beats me."

"Maybe he's licking the wounds of a bad relationship," I said with a snort.

Kevin looked skyward. "Sounds like someone I know." His eyes returned to mine. "Have you talked with him?"

"No."

"Why not?"

"I don't want to."

"Maybe you should."

"Maybe he's only here for another day or two."

"He bought a house."

"Maybe for someone else. I mean, why would he want to be in the same town where I am? By the end of our marriage, we couldn't *look* at each other. What does he think he'll accomplish being here?"

"Don't ask me that. Ask him. You need to talk with him—you know, get it all out in the open."

"Talk about pain?"

"Yeah, well, it ain't going away by itself. It's festering in you, sweetie. I can smell it."

"Smell it?"

"Not literally."

I squeezed my eyes shut for a second, then, not caring that I sounded all of three years old, glared at Kevin and whispered, "I don't want him here. I don't want Officer Gill watching me. I don't want to be frightened every time I see a camera. *And* I don't want people talking at the post office about how Grace could have let her son do what he did, because that's where we're headed. People speculate, and she's next in their sights. Do they not have anything better to do? My eyes were on my GPS when I ran that stop sign. I admitted it. Know what the rumors were—no, you don't, because you weren't there, but every one of them got back to me. Either I was drunk—you know, a bored soccer mom taking shots at lunch. Or I was high on something. Or I was rushing to drop off my daughter so I could meet a lover."

Kevin didn't blink. "And you listened, why?"

"I thought friends were friends," I said, feeling the betrayal like it was yesterday. "I thought loyalty mattered. I thought other mothers would understand how it had happened." The pottery studio wasn't the best place for this, and my voice was low enough, but the words continued to spill, which said tons about my emotional state. "Oh, they understood all right, only they needed to convince themselves that it could never happen to them, because they were better than me. They didn't do shots at lunch or smoke weed before getting in the carpool lane, and they sure didn't have lovers."

"So what did you tell them?"

"Nothing."

"You didn't fight the rumors?"

"What was the point?"

"Uh, killing them?" he asked, but I was shaking my head before his mouth closed.

"Rumors take on a life of their own. Besides, my lawyer told me to ignore them." I snorted softly. "Lot of good *that* did."

"I hate it when you're cynical."

"So do I. It's ugly and mean-spirited and lowering myself to their level—"

"I get it," he broke in, squeezing my hand.

But I wasn't sure he did. "I've lived through this, Kevin. Seeing reporters and hearing gossip and knowing, just *knowing* where it can lead."

"Jimmy says the station is quiet."

"Uh-huh. This is the lull when lawyers are plotting strategy. Jay Harrington amasses pro-Chris legal arguments, while prosecutors amass anti-Chris ones, but *we* won't see any of that. What we will see isn't about legal issues. It's about headlines. It's about entertainment. It's about sensationalism."

"And memory," Kevin said, returning the subject to me. "Confront them, honey."

Well, there was that underlying theme again. It was easy to ignore my therapist, who had her head in psych texts. It was harder to ignore Kevin, who had a keen feel for real life.

That sent my frustration through the roof. *"How?"*

"Start with *him*."

9

Kevin didn't know the half. He didn't know that passion had been like lightning between Edward and me. Or that since the divorce I hadn't missed it—had barely *thought* about it—until now. Or that by the time Friday ended with a fourth—or was it a fifth or a sixth sighting of Edward Cooper, now calling himself Ned, I was upset enough to confront the man.

I did it that night in my dream. I yelled at him, yelled and screamed, threw the kind of tantrum I had never thrown in my life. I wanted to scare him off, but don't know if I did. The dream woke me too soon.

And still, when I left work Saturday evening, I might have avoided him if the parking lot hadn't been surreally dark and rainy, or if the first person approaching me as I dodged puddles hadn't worn a plastic poncho visibly shielding camera equipment. When Edward came from nowhere with his ball cap dripping, warded off the man and shepherded me to my truck, I was so grateful that when he said, "My place or yours?" I was lost.

"Yours," I whispered.

"Lock your door."

I did. Wipers going double-time front and rear, I backed around with care lest the photographer be lurking behind, and waited only until the Jeep Wrangler had done the same before following it out of the lot.

Lost was putting it mildly. I was insane to be doing this. But I was exhausted after a day of back-to-back appointments, and worn down after a week of fighting the past. I didn't know what I was looking for, didn't know what I wanted, didn't even know whether the simmering inside me was from anger or desire, only that it was there.

My wipers beat at the rain, muting the thud of my heart as we headed north on the Blue before crossing back over the river onto a lesser-used road. His taillights were my guide. When he put on his blinker, I did the same. Our headlights showed a brief sprawl of farmer's porch, shingled siding and mullioned glass, but all went dark when I pulled in behind him at the side door and shut down the truck.

I had a moment then, literally sixty seconds in which I might have changed my mind. I had been so prudent, *so* prudent since the accident. My life was about self-control. It was about discipline. Yes, it was about self-deprivation, and my therapist had tried to change that, to no avail. Self-deprivation felt better to me than self-indulgence.

So this was out of character. I felt a flicker of hope that acting now would kill the need, but if that gave me a lofty motive, it was quickly gone. The past was knocking as insistently as Edward's knuckle on my window, and my body ruled.

He held my gloved hand as we ran through the rain and, once inside, he quickly had me backed against the door. Our mouths fused. His kiss was forceful; so was mine. I was furious to be here doing this, but I truly hadn't had a choice.

Clothes were in the way. He pushed my hood aside to dig his fingers into the knot of hair at my nape, and, with better traction, kissed me again. Between my wet down jacket and his sodden wool one, though, skin was too distant to feel. And I did want to feel. That was all I wanted to do—not think, just feel.

We pulled at clothing, hands tangling at buttons, zippers, and snaps. I'm not sure we were completely undressed when he entered me, but it didn't matter. I gave a sharp cry. Oh, my body was ready, but it had been nearly five years without this, and the stretching, followed by his incredible fullness was a shock.

He paused only for a rough, "You okay?"

I didn't answer, just grabbed the facial hair I hadn't known and pulled his mouth back to mine. I was hungry. I was angry. Too much lately was beyond my control, but here, now, I was taking what I wanted. He might be larger and anatomically able to lift me against the wood with each thrust, but I was the one managing hands and mouths.

I came too quickly, still wanting more as he pinned my body to the door to allow for his own throbbing release. He was barely done when he bodily lifted me and half-walked, half-ran down a hallway, past dark rooms I couldn't identify to one that had a bed. In the next instant, with sheets against my back, he came down on top and was inside again.

The joining was easier this time but no less startling. I had forgotten what it felt like to be totally possessed, and we both were that, in every sense of the word. I couldn't touch or taste enough. We fought each other, rolling and shifting, and all the while he pounded into me with a fury I shared.

My release this time was no less fierce. I cried out again, a sound that erupted from some primal place deep inside. His own cry was more guttural but totally familiar. We had always been vocal, Edward and I.

Awareness of what we had just done must have hit him at the same time it hit me, because we fell apart. I assumed his breathing was as heavy as mine, though both were muted by the drum of the rain. Staring at the ceiling, I saw nothing. I turned my head on the pillow. He was looking up, too, but, feeling my gaze, turned to meet it in the dark.

For a few seconds I was bewildered, wondering where I was and how

I had come to be here. This was no dream. But it was unreal. I was wide awake and, with each passing second, aware of the fact that the eyes that held mine belonged to my ex-husband, and that little had changed, on this score at least. Despite the hell that had torn us apart, the attraction remained.

That fact infuriated me, but still, yet again, I avoided confrontation. Thinking only that coming here had been a mistake, I rolled away and stumbled up.

"Don't leave," he said, half-rising.

"I shouldn't have come," I murmured and searched the dark floor for what few of my clothes might be there. Seeing none, I grabbed at the sheet that was bunched at the foot of the bed and held it to my breasts. *Leave,* my gut cried. *Don't talk.* But I was too curious not to ask what I most needed to know.

"Why did you come here?"

He reached for the lamp.

"*Don't.*"

He withdrew his hand.

"Why, Edward?" I asked again.

He was on an elbow, in a limbo between sitting and lying. "I needed a change."

I struggled to process that and remain calm. There were many ways he would know where I lived, not the least being through our divorce lawyer. "But why would you want to be anywhere near me?"

"Owning the Inn was too good an opportunity to pass up."

"Edward," I said, impatient. "You're a venture capitalist. You don't own things. You raise money for people who do own things."

"I quit my job. This is what I do now."

"*Inn* keeping?" It defied belief. "Everyone here said it was a group."

"It is. I'm the managing partner. So I'll be living here."

"In *my town?* Why, Edward? There are inns all over the country!"

"Not like this one."

"I. Live. Here."

136

"I know that."

"And still you came? To punish me? Torture me?"

"No."

I wanted to throw the kind of tantrum I had in my dreams, but it would have demanded an energy I just didn't have. Instead, levelly, I said, "This isn't fair, Edward. I was here first. You need to leave." I backed away when he reached for my hand and, dropping the sheet, left the room.

My GPS tragedy notwithstanding, I had a good sense of direction. Returning to the kitchen, I fished through the clothes strewn about in the dark. No bra? No problem. No panties? No *problem*. I pulled on my sweater and was stepping into jeans when Edward appeared. He wore boxer shorts, which I saw because he did turn on the light. It wasn't a big light, just a small one over the stove, but it removed the last vestige of illusion. I couldn't pretend that I wasn't here, much less that Edward and I hadn't just had sex.

Frantic that the past was crowding in here too, I turned on him. "I don't want you around. This is my home. I have a good job and good friends. I've invested four years of my life building something different from what was before."

"I know—"

"Want to know why?" I asked, and suddenly my voice was shaking, suddenly my whole *existence* was shaking. "Because I had to. I had no other choice if I wanted to survive, because you all pushed me away. My mother disowned me, my brother distanced himself, my friends rejected me, my father died on me, and you *divorced* me."

"I know—"

"Mom blamed me for my father's death, my brother blamed me for her grief, my friends blamed me for making them look bad, car makers blamed me for being a reckless driver, you blamed me for killing your daughter."

"It was an accident—"

"And that makes a difference?" Even barefoot, he was taller than me by a head, but I was past the point of being silenced. "She's gone," I shouted.

"I can't bring her back." My voice cracked. "I nearly killed myself, Edward. Do you know that? I had pills. The doctor prescribed them after the accident to help me sleep, but I didn't want to sleep. I couldn't let go of the image of Lily lying upside down in that car, still strapped in her seat but crushed on the wrong side and bleeding and covered with glass, because if I let it go, I'd be letting myself off the hook. So I saved up the pills."

"I didn't know."

"Of course you didn't." I pressed a hand to my chest, working harder to breathe but unable to stop. "We were living in the same house totally apart, and you were wrapped in your own grief, but a mother's is worse, Edward." I gulped for air. "I carried her, I nursed her, I fed her and read to her and let her make perfectly horrible things out of clay, every one of which was beautiful, because she'd made it with her own little hands. Then it ended." I pressed harder on my chest, desperate to say it all. "Her bedroom went untouched, her Cheerios went uneaten, her clothes went unworn, the stuffed animals she loved went unloved, and it was all my fault. I held those pills in my hands more nights than I can count. I went so far as to pour myself a huge glass of water so that I'd have enough to wash them all down." That quickly, I was caught back in the horror of it.

He looked shaken. "Why didn't you?"

Coming from another man, it might have been an accusation, even a dare. But Edward had never been cruel. He simply wanted to know.

I spotted my coat on the floor, picked it up, and held it to my chest. It was my life jacket, a piece of the present that would keep me afloat. As I held it, I forced in one breath, then another. The tightness in my chest eased just enough. "I asked myself that a dozen times—*ten* dozen times. When you lose the most precious thing in your life, how do you go on?" Again, consciously, I inhaled. "But how do you not? I lost everything, Edward, not just my daughter but my marriage, my family, my home, my career. I was all alone and searching, *searching* for something good about myself, and the only thing I could come up with was courage. Killing myself would have been cowardly. It would have been taking the easy way out. I couldn't let myself do that." Defeated, I inched my arms into my coat. "But I couldn't stay where we lived. I couldn't wake up each day to the wreck of my life, so maybe I was a coward after all."

"No."

I raised my chin with remnants of pride. "When I first moved here, I used to cry myself to sleep, the loneliness was so devastating, and when tears didn't work, it was rocks in my chest. But I made it through, and now I can't go back. You can. You have a life in Massachusetts. You have colleagues and friends. You have a big, beautiful house."

Eyes glassy, he half-shouted, "Do you seriously think I wanted to stay there, just me and all those memories?" His tone leveled. "I sold the house. I bought the Inn."

"If you bought it, you can sell it," I replied. "Buying and selling is what you do best."

He started to say something but stopped. And suddenly there it was—a look in his eyes identical to the one Lily wore when she didn't know what to do. I had seen it the morning Lily died, when she hadn't known which dress to wear for her playdate, and the day before that, when she couldn't find her magic ring and couldn't *possibly* go to school without it. I had seen that look the spring before, when she joined a soccer class and found herself with twenty other kids and thirty soccer balls going every which way. I couldn't count the number of times I had seen it and *adored* that she looked like Edward. Her hair was blond to his sable, her legs lean to his muscled. But they both had silvery-blue eyes, and the looks that came from those eyes were the same. It had been that way from the moment of her birth, had surely been so even in utero—

I felt a sudden chill. My eyes fell to the wide-planked floor. One image and a quick calculation later, I breathed again. I wasn't on birth control, but if ever I had a safe time of the month, this was it. Had it not been, I'd have gone to the drug store first thing tomorrow. I would not—*could* not have a child—not again.

Edward knew what I was thinking. Used to be, all I had to do was conjure up fro-yo and he was on his way to the ice-cream shop. Our minds had always run in the same direction, and they did now. He stared at me for a painful moment before breaking away and reaching for his jeans. "It's pouring. I'll drive you home."

I felt a sharp stab of fear. "No! My house is mine!" I blurted. "You can't go near it!" I grasped at the rational. "If you drive me home, my truck will be here and I need it to get to work. My work is important, it's what I do now, I like it, and they like me." Just then, I couldn't have said what day of the week it was, much less whether I had bookings the next day. I only knew that I needed to get back to a life I could control.

But he continued to dress, reaching now for the pool of flannel that was his shirt.

"Edward!" I shouted. "*Listen* to me. I don't know why you've come, I don't *care* why you've come, but I can't live with you here. You have to *leave.*"

His arms were in the shirt, but it hung open. "I can't leave," he said.

"If you won't, I will."

I mean it, I fumed silently as I drove. I could leave. Between Edward's arrival and Chris Emory's mess, Devon wasn't the refuge it had been such a short time ago. I could *definitely* leave, could leave *in a heartbeat.*

When I saw the glow of headlights in my rearview mirror, I was angry enough to pull to the side of the road. I was out of the truck when the Jeep came alongside and was leaning toward the side window as it lowered.

"Go home," I told him.

"It's dark. You didn't know who it was. What if I'd been a rapist?"

"This is Vermont, Edward. We don't have rapists around here, and even if we did, no rapist would be out in this rain. I knew it would be either you or the police. Give me credit for that."

"Get in. We need to talk."

"Isn't it a little late for that?" I cried sharply, but added a saner, "I'm fine. I can take care of myself. Please go home."

I didn't wait for an answer, just climbed back in the truck, drove along the shoulder of the road until I was clear of the Jeep, and returned to the pavement. I was relieved when his headlights shrank with distance and, once I rounded the curve, were gone.

I mean it, I vowed more than once during the fifteen-minute drive, and thought it again when I turned onto Pepin Hill Road and started up. *If I had reinvented myself once, I could do it again.* My tires spun in the slick mud, then caught, spun again a few seconds later, then caught. *If I found work here, I could find work elsewhere. If I made friends here, I could make them somewhere new.* When my wheels spun and caught again, I thought, *If I can handle this road, I can handle any road.*

But I liked my road. I liked the way the string of a stone wall sang of early settlers, the way fallen trees lay in the woods and became homes for squirrels, fishers, and foxes. I liked the weave of the road as it climbed around rocks and gullies. I knew every one of these curves, which was a good thing tonight, since the rain had given way to fog, and visibility was nil.

But the cabin had lights. They were on timers so that my pets wouldn't be alone when I couldn't get back until dark. Muted now by the fog, the swath of those lights was dispersed at first but grew focused as I neared. They were welcoming. They were mine.

And there was another thing—*my* cabin. It had character and charm. Sure, I could find another home with character and charm. But why did I have to do that? I had come here first. I had a right to stay.

Edward was the one who should leave. He had known I was here but had come anyway. He had never been cruel, but how else to explain it? Did he have a sick need to punish me more by making me see Lily's face wherever I turned? If so, then the pain would be compounded knowing that in killing our daughter, I had turned a loving man into a shell.

He had to leave. *Had* to leave.

Would he? Logic argued against. The Devon Inn and Spa was far bigger than anything I owned here. He could try to sell it. But that would take time. My cabin, on the other hand, would sell quickly. From a purely practical standpoint, if one of us left, it would be me.

The unfairness of that rankled. This was *my* road, *my* cabin, *my* town.

Pulling up beside said cabin, I killed the engine and sat for a minute. My body felt strange—used in new places, bone tired in others—but my mind was the problem. It had been through a wringer, and the wash was far from done.

Then I heard Jonah's bark and felt a pang of guilt at having been gone so long. But he didn't bolt for the woods when I opened the front door, simply joined Hex and Jinx crowding my legs.

They were my home. Warmed by that, I leaned against the door to shut it. Smiling at their antics, I set my bag aside and, pausing only to shrug off my wet coat, knelt to hug, rub, and scratch. If I had to move, these creatures would come. But why should any of us be forced from a place we loved?

A male voice answered. "Hey."

My head flew up, and my heart stopped.

10

It took me several seconds. The man rising from the sofa looked so like my father that, at first, I feared he had come back from the grave to haunt me.

But no. Not my dad.

"Liam," I breathed, pressing a hand to the thud of my reviving heart. "What—w-when—how did *you* get here?" I hadn't seen a car, though I did now see the muddy boots that lay strewn beyond the cats.

"I was doing just fine"—he picked up where he might have left off had there not been four years of complete and utter silence between us—"until I started up your hill." He approached with a scowl. "What kind of road is that anyway?"

The cats ran away. Keeping an arm around Jonah, I sank from my haunches to the floor. "Dirt."

"Not dirt. Mud. I skidded off into the trees and couldn't get back, so I hiked the last stretch. I'm assuming someone can tow me out in the morning. Hell, towing cars must be a way of life up here. I carried my backpack, but the rest of my stuff's out there . . . wherever." The last word trailed. He was studying my face. "Geez, Maggie. You look awful. Bad date?"

I might have laughed, if I wasn't still so close to heart freeze. My eyes surely showed the wreck of my life, and what Edward's hands had done to my hair, the rain made worse. But I wasn't sharing any of that with Liam. It was none of his business. Nothing in my life was his business. He had made his choice.

My younger brother by five years, Liam had the red hair and freckled skin that our paternal great-grandfather had brought from Ireland in the early 1900s. Though I was the first-born, Liam had been raised the royal, loyal son. That made his appearance here troubling.

Guarded, I asked, "Is Mom okay?" I had often wondered whether I would be contacted if she was ill.

"She's fine," he said. "Bossy as ever."

"Is something else wrong?" I held off Jonah when he tried to lick my face.

"Why does something have to be wrong?"

"Because you're here," I said, wary still. "Out of the blue, Liam. You haven't called. You haven't written. I send you birthday cards every year, but you never acknowledged a one."

"Well, they accomplished their goal," he said with a grin. "They gave me your address. I sure couldn't ask Mom for it, but she'll be guessing where I am." He grimaced, *yikes*. "*That* won't go over well."

Seriously, I thought, but my sympathy was short-lived. He owed me an explanation for why he was here in my house—and yes, I was angry. With each year that had passed without any sign from him that I mattered, my hurt had deepened. Anger was what came of hurt that had simmered just a little too long.

Bracing my back against the door, I pushed myself up. Jonah sat apart from me now, regarding my brother as if he didn't know what to make of him any more than I did.

"I like your dog," Liam said. "He must have smelled family DNA on me, because he didn't bark when I came in. By the way, thanks for tucking the key behind the wreath. I wasn't sure you'd follow the custom, bad feelings for Mom and all, and I wasn't sure you'd still have a wreath on the door so long after the holidays."

"My friend makes seasonal ones."

"Then thanks to her. All I could think when I was trudging up that road was that if you weren't home, I'd be locked out. By the way, I have the best app on my phone. Your road was right there on the map."

I don't use apps to guide me. Ever. They come with too many reminders, none of which, apparently, registered with my brother.

I folded my arms and waited.

"It's a relief, actually," he went on. "There may not be many streets around here, but I wouldn't want to get lost in the woods—like I guess I pretty much, basically, already did." Brightening, he glanced back at my tiny kitchen. "Got anything to eat? I stopped at a taco place right before Devon, but it was crazy—no organization, people talking between tables, servers zoned out. I have to say, they were doing a good business. I just didn't care to give them mine."

I said nothing, simply stood with my arms folded.

He stared. "Geez. Do you ever look like Mom. If you've turned into her, I'm outta here. Edward can find someone else to be his chef."

That broke my freeze. My arms dropped. "You're here for *Edward?*"

"I'm his new chef."

"At the Inn?"

"At the restaurant he's opening in town. It's part of the resort consortium. Didn't he tell you?"

"Why would he? We're divorced."

"But he moved here."

"Yeah. We're working on that," I said, but I was sick. So it wasn't only the Inn. It was a restaurant in town, maybe more, if a consortium was involved. If he had hired Liam and done God-knew-what-else to dig himself in, the chances he would leave were slimmer than ever. "Of all the chefs in the world, he picked you?"

"I'm good," Liam argued, sounding offended, but I didn't care.

"I thought you were working at a restaurant in West Hartford. What happened to that one?"

His phone dinged. He pulled it out, checked the screen, put it back. "I quit."

"Before or after Edward hired you?"

"After. I'm not dumb, Maggie. I wouldn't quit one if I didn't have another. For what it's worth, he asked me, not the other way around."

"But how did he know what you were doing?"

"We kept in touch."

Slap. "You kept in touch with him but not with me? Now, that makes me feel good."

"Nuh-uh-uh. You know what Mom says about sarcasm."

"Oh yes," I sighed and toed off a boot. *"Sarcasm is the language of the devil.* Thomas Carlyle was one of her favorites. Know what else Carlyle said?" In my longest, darkest days, I had Googled the Scottish philosopher to try to understand what Mom had seen in his thoughts and maybe, just maybe find one to offer me solace. *"A loving heart is the beginning of all knowledge,"* I told Liam as I kicked the second boot aside. "And yet her 'loving heart' wasn't interested in knowing the pain or torment or loneliness her only daughter was suffering."

That silenced him. His eyes held mine for a minute before sliding away, which meant he did have shreds of a conscience. I wondered about courage. "Why didn't you tell her you were coming?" I asked.

Liam wandered to the bookshelf and tilted his head to read titles. "We've been on the outs."

I was half bent, scrubbing Hex's head. *"You* and Mom?" That was a surprise. Liam was her golden boy.

"Yes, me and Mom." He glowered. "She's too controlling. She wants me married, wants me having kids, wants me putting less salt in my *osso bucco.* I took an apartment in town, but she made me feel so guilty deserting her that I was still spending hours at the house. Like I had nothing else to do but fix leaky faucets or take out the trash? Like I had time to date? Like my job wasn't demanding enough?" His voice had risen with each addition. "Speaking of which, do you know how different she is at work? I couldn't believe it when I saw it. She's way more creative than dogmatic, and she's sweet. She's gentle. Her assistant thinks she hung the moon. Know how she always said you get more with sugar than vinegar? Well, she uses up all the sugar at work—I mean, fuck it, literally and figuratively—so all we got at home was vinegar." Seeming suddenly unsure, perhaps treasonous, he tucked his hands in the back of his jeans like Dad used to do, and said, "How did he stand it?"

"He loved her."

"He loved that she made the decisions. He loved that she was the housekeeper and the menu planner and the disciplinarian. So who was he? Was he the king, or just a wuss? Did she crack the whip because he didn't have the guts?"

"I don't know." Truly, I had stopped trying to guess. I had loved my father, but he went along with Mom. Then, when things got worse and worse for me, he'd had a stroke. Because he was so disappointed in me? Because he thought Mom was wrong? Because he missed me? Because Lily's death broke his heart?

I had stopped trying to guess that one, too.

Liam walked toward the kitchen, fingering a ceramic bowl along the way. It was the first thing I'd crafted when I could craft again. It was painfully primitive, like me back then. I kept it here as a reminder of how far I'd come.

"Well, I'd had enough," he said. "I was interviewing for jobs on the West Coast when Edward called. I had to get away from Mom."

"If that was what you wanted, you'd have been safer on the West Coast."

"Yeah." He eyed me straight-on. "But my being where you are makes a statement."

Rising, I asked in dismay, "I'm your rebellion?"

He didn't answer, but continued to the vase on the counter that marked the start of my kitchen. "Nice flowers."

They were alstroemeria, which not only lasted forever but were one of the few flowers my cats wouldn't eat.

Needing a comeback but not sure where to begin, I said, "Your hair is thinning."

"Dad was bald at forty. I considered shaving off what I have, but that look is more techie than master chef. I like the wild, creative, flyaway look. Anyway, it's under a hat when I work."

I was still at the door, feeling tired all over but firm on my turf. I swallowed once, then said, "I don't want to be your rebellion, Liam. I've built a life without family, and it works."

"Too late. I signed a contract."

"Contract? He made you? So much for trust."

"It was to protect me as much as him. I'm relocating for the sake of his restaurant. I want certain assurances."

"Like salary if it folds."

"It won't fold, Maggie. Why did you have to say that? See, there's another Mom thing, pessimism when it comes to her kids. Someone else can make the same move, and it'd be great, a *brilliant* move, but if it's one of us, she finds fault. The restaurant won't fold. Edward studied every angle of the town before he agreed to the deal, including the feasibility of a restaurant."

"But the Inn already has two restaurants," I said, "and it's not pessimism. It's pragmatism."

"Okay. Fine. Pragmatic, then. Of the two restaurants at the Inn, one is a family tavern serving comfort food, and the other serves high-end American cuisine. What else is there? Rasher and Yolk, which is an upscale diner and closes at 2 P.M.? A steak place that serves great steak and soggy salad? A pizza place that, frankly, sucks? I'm telling you, there's a market here for something else. Edward and I talked about it for months before deciding on a French bistro with a Mediterranean feel. It'll be trendy and healthy and affordable. I wouldn't have come up here if I hadn't thought it would succeed."

I had never heard my brother sound as passionate or articulate or *knowledgeable* about anything before.

"The contract," he went on when I had no comeback, "is in case of flood, fire, or Armageddon, and if it's the last, I probably won't care, but what the hell." Opening the refrigerator door, he leaned in. "Seriously. I'm hungry. What do you have?"

"Leftover beef stew."

"That's it?"

"I'm not the chef."

"I'll shop tomorrow." His phone dinged again. "After someone tows my car." He checked the phone, put it away. "Actually, I can use your car."

"Actually," I said, "it's a truck, and I need it myself. I'll give you the name of a tow guy. So." I took a tentative breath. "Where are you staying?"

He spread his hands, *here,* and skimmed my home with his eyes.

I laughed. "Uh, I don't think so."

"What do you mean?"

"This is my home, and it's small."

"You'd turn me out in the rain? With no car?"

"You can sleep here tonight, but if you're staying in Devon, you'll need your own space. There are some great places on the other side of town. This one's mine."

"Don't you want me here?" he asked.

"No, Liam. I don't. I'm not Mom."

"But I'm family," he reasoned.

I held his gaze hard. "So am I."

It was a minute before he got it. "Ah. You're holding a grudge."

"I'm remembering when I told Mom that Edward and I were getting divorced, and she said I couldn't live with her. You said nothing, Liam."

"She couldn't deal. Dad had just died. She was in mourning."

My eyes went wide. "So. Was. I."

We stared at each other for a long, awkward time, but I wasn't letting him off the hook. He had been an adult back then, no child, and he had been wrong. I could appreciate his loyalty to Mom, but when it was misplaced? With Dad gone and him her prince, he should have stepped up and tried to reason with her. If anyone had a chance of succeeding, it was Liam. And if he failed, he should have risen above and kept in touch with me whether she liked it or not.

He hadn't risen above. And yet, here he was, bringing a visceral familiarity into my home.

Truth be told, it wasn't an entirely, completely, totally bad feeling.

Startled by that little insight, I had another on its heels. No, he hadn't risen above. But I could. He was my brother. If feeling better about myself was a goal, I could house him for now.

He must have sensed my softening, because he slid me a teasing smile. "This place is small, Maggie, but it's sweet. I like your bedroom."

Ah. Still king of the castle.

Only, this wasn't *his* castle.

"So do I," I said. "That's why I sleep there."

"But I'm the guest."

My smile was serene. "Guests take the loft."

I don't know how I managed that smile. It might have been that I was tired. Or that Liam was a distraction from my having had sex with Edward. Visceral familiarity or not, he certainly couldn't stay here long. The place was too small. It did occur to me, shortly before I fell asleep, that he could have it—could *buy* it from me—if I left town.

When I woke up the next morning to the warmth of two cats on my legs and the most unbelievable smells coming from the kitchen, though, I wouldn't have been anywhere else. Sliding my feet free of the duvet, I wrapped myself in a thick robe and followed my nose down the stairs.

My kitchen counter, not large to begin with, was covered with an assortment of open boxes, tins, and utensils. Liam was bent at the oven, with a cautious Jonah watching nearby.

"What did you make?" I asked, intrigued, pleased, even touched. It had been a long time since anyone had made anything for me, and never in my own home. Granted, he would be wanting breakfast for himself. Still.

"Quiche," he said and straightened. "I thought I lost your dog this morning. I opened the door to let him pee, and he ran so far I thought he'd never come back. What kind of animals are out there?"

"Nothing lethal unless you're a cat, in which case your life expectancy is a total of twenty minutes, so do not *ever* let either of my cats out of this house," I said, but distractedly. Liam's hands held my potholders, which held a pie plate with a circle of golden crust and a dappled top. A fruit compote simmered on the stove. Something green sat on plates. "Wow." I slid onto a stool. "Did you go out early, or did you actually find all this here?"

"Here. I like the challenge. *Kitchen Dregs for the Gourmand.* Could be a book."

"Could be. You should think about that. I'll bet you have other cookbooks in you, too. Chef cookbooks are all the rage. You could take up residency in a writers' colony in New Mexico or wherever, and write."

Having set down the pie plate, he reached for the compote. "Nice try, but no dice. I signed a contract, remember? I got my guarantee, but so did Edward." Skillfully, he ladled compote on the plates shaping each mound just so with the flick of his wrist. "Restaurants in places like this have a hard time keeping chefs. Spring, summer, and fall are great, but winter they want to be somewhere warm. Me, I just want dry. Does it rain like this a lot?"

"In March? All the time. And it stays cold," I added, looking him over, "so your clothes are all wrong." Thin socks. Thin shirt. Jeans were jeans, but even the rain jacket on the back of the chair wasn't lined. "You need clothes. Start at Stoner's. It's the general store in town."

"Do you have an account there?"

"They take credit cards." When he frowned, I said, "Liam, you're thirty-three. You can pay for your own clothes." When he still seemed annoyed, I reminded him, "I'm not Mom."

"Are the prices sky high?"

"Some, but a local family owns it, so you'd be doing good for them *and* helping yourself if you want them to know who you are. Introduce yourself as the new chef at . . . at . . . does the restaurant have a name?"

"*La Bisque.* I actually wanted to call it *Chocolat Noir*," he added with a perfect accent, "but two syllables work better than four, and I mean, this town may be upscale, but *ce n'est pas Paris.* And anyway, the name is still a work in progress. So what do I tell the people at Stoner's?"

"That you're opening a French bistro here in town."

"Will they give me a break then?"

"No. If you want lower prices, there's an L.L. Bean in West Lebanon."

"Good," he said and cut into the quiche. "We can go there today."

"Not me. I'm working." I had no idea if I was. It seemed like an eternity since I had last left the Spa. Actually, yes. Now that I thought of it, I did have two bookings, though I would be done in plenty of time for a shopping trip with Liam. But I was not getting into that. Give Liam an inch, and he would take a mile, as Mom always said, and if that made me like Mom, so be it.

"You're working today?" he asked. "But today's Sunday."

"And you never work on Sunday? Will your bistro be closed on Sunday? Absolutely not. Devon is a tourist town, and tourists are here seven days a week. Will your restaurant be closed *any* day?"

"Mondays," he said and, frowning, set a plate in front of me. "Maybe. That's still TBD."

"This looks amazing," I had to say.

"I told you. I'm good."

Overeager, I took a bite of the quiche, then bobbled it in my mouth until it cooled enough to properly eat. The wait was worth it. "You're right. You're good."

Lifting a plate for himself, he straddled his stool sideways to face me. "What work do you have today?"

His blankness gave me pause. Given his closeness to Mom, who had wiped me clean of her life, he might be clueless. "Do you know what I do?"

"You sell makeup."

"I don't sell it. I apply it. I'm a makeup artist."

"So you put it on."

I glanced at our breakfast spread. "Like you sling hash? There's more to it, Liam. An artist is an artist, whether she's working with food or makeup. I studied to do this. I apprenticed, and I'm certified. I work at the Spa at the Inn." I added a dry, "You know, *that* Inn from which *your* restaurant will get most of its patrons?"

"I know the Inn, Maggie," he snapped, then softened. "I knew about it even before Edward approached me, and part of his pitch was laying out the numbers, so I know high-end dinner fare will sell. Still, I expected something sleepy—I mean, hell, this is Vermont. But it's been buzzing here lately. I saw you on TV, by the way—at least, I think it was you going into that woman's house and then, this week, going into court?" He studied my face, and suddenly, in my own home, I felt exposed. "You look different from how you used to."

I pressed my lips together, then nodded. "Older."

"That, too." His phone dinged. He pulled it from his pocket, took a quick look, slid it back.

"Did Mom see?" I asked, trying to be casual about it, like I didn't care. But I did. I wanted to know whether she thought I was being a good friend to a good friend or was still associating with the wrong people.

"You on TV? I don't know. I left a month ago." He lowered his voice, inviting the inside scoop. "So, did the kid do it?"

When I realized no more would be coming about Mom, I said, "I don't really know."

"But you know his mother. She seemed shell-shocked. Definitely a looker, though."

I wondered why men had to go with that first. "She also happens to be a good massage therapist."

"You work with her."

"We're both at the Spa."

"Does she work Sundays, too?"

I paused. "In what way is that relevant?" I dipped into my fruit. "Actually"—I relented, because the compote was warm, sweet, delicious enough to melt my pique—"she does. The best clients I get are the ones who come straight from her. They're loose and relaxed. I should be so lucky as to have one of those today. My morning appointment is the guest of honor at a birthday lunch. I'm not sure what the afternoon one is." I pulled out my phone to check and saw three missed calls. Two, plus a text, were from Edward's cell.

Talk about the past rushing back? I hadn't seen that number since the divorce. Funny that he hadn't changed it, though with his work and all, he wouldn't. I had definitely changed mine. The old area code would have given me away in two seconds flat. Edward must have gotten my new number from my file at the Inn.

The third call was from Grace, who had been so hard to reach that I returned it there and then, albeit in a low voice. "Hey."

"Maggie." She sounded winded. "Can you do my hair this morning?"

"Uh, I think so. I have a ten o'clock—"

"It's at eleven. They changed it. I'm looking at the schedule right now. If you get here at nine-thirty we'll have time. I know it's mean of me to ask this on a Sunday, but I really, really need something done."

Leaving the table, I turned away from Liam and quietly said, "Your hair looks great. You don't need—"

"*Want*. I *want* something done."

I might have argued that her current something was less than a month old and that too-frequent processing would hurt her hair. But how could I argue with *want*? *Want* involved emotional issues, and Grace, of all people right now, had a right to those.

"Not raven," I warned by way of concession.

"We'll discuss. When can you come?"

I took the phone from my ear long enough to see that my phone screen read eight. And that Liam had nonchalantly strolled close. And that Edward was trying me again.

Confront him, Kevin had said, but I wasn't ready. Last night's confrontation hadn't ended well.

Pressing ignore, I turned away from Liam, headed back to my breakfast, and told Grace, "Nine-thirty. See you then."

"Thankyouthankyou. Bye."

"Who was that?" Liam asked when I pocketed the phone. His own dinged.

"Someone I work with." I took another bite of the quiche.

When he typed for a few seconds, I thought he would let it go. But no. As soon as he lowered the phone, he said, "Her?" I wasn't sure whether he was seriously guessing or simply wanting to revive the discussion. I considered lying. An easy *no* would have done it. But having to lie in my own home, to my own brother?

"Yes, it was her, but that has nothing to do with anything that concerns you." I crossed to the small whiteboard by the fridge and scrawled the number of a guy who would tow Liam's car. "Use my name." I had a sudden thought then—a sudden, *awful* thought. "Liam?"

His phone dinged again. He was looking at it when he said, "There's great cell reception here. How'd you manage that? And Wi-Fi? Whoa. Full signal."

I caught his arms and shook them. "*Liam.* This is important. People here don't know where I came from or what I did. They don't know that Edward is my ex-husband. They don't know about Lily or the accident or my conviction. They don't have a clue who Mackenzie Cooper is. I want it to stay that way. You need to keep your mouth shut."

He twisted a lock at his lips too quickly for my peace of mind.

"Swear it, Liam," I ordered. "I've worked hard keeping the past out of my life here, but if you let it in, I'll leave—just move away and start over somewhere else. I can do it," I warned. "Edward had gall buying the Inn and you have gall signing on with him, so if word of the past gets out, it'll be on your shoulders. I'm Maggie Reid. Mackenzie Cooper doesn't exist anymore." I didn't like the look on my brother's face. "What?"

He held up his phone for me to see the screen. "Good luck with that."

11

I*'m almost there,* read the text, and at the top of the screen, Edward Cooper.

The words positively shouted at me.

I shouted back, *"I don't want him here."*

"He's been trying to reach you," Liam said.

"How do you know?" I asked, though I knew the answer. Guilt was written all over my brother's freckled face.

"He knows I'm here, so he texted me. He said you're not answering your phone and asked if I knew where you were."

Control was a major issue in my life. I had lost it along with my phone signal on that country road shrouded with fall leaves, had certainly been without it when that van rammed us and sent us into a flying roll. I hadn't consciously called for help; my high-tech SUV had done that. Control? *Control?* In my frantic effort to free myself from the car so that I could get to my baby? In the harrowing sound of police sirens and fire truck hoots, the glare of ambulance lights, the milling of responders keeping me from her? In the legal doings afterward? Control? Ze-ro.

Slowly, slowly I had returned it to my life. This, now, just wasn't fair.

I tried to remain coherent against a rising anger, though I shook with the effort. "You had no right, Liam. I do what I want when I want, and if I don't want to return a text, that's my choice. This is *my* house, and I don't want Edward here. You can tell him that when he comes."

"What's meant to happen happens. It's God's plan."

"Don't quote Mom!" I yelled, shooting to my feet. Then I just stood there, too bewildered to know what to do next until I actually heard the thump of boots on the porch. That got me going.

I had spun toward the stairs when Liam asked a disappointed, "Is that all you're eating? Didn't you like it?"

"Sorry," I said without looking back. "Lost my appetite."

I took a very long shower. Each time I thought I was done, I decided my body needed just a little more heat. Only when the water cooled to the dark side of tepid did I turn it off. I took my time toweling dry, blew my hair a little, brushed my teeth. My mug shot was there on the inside of the medicine chest—my old nemesis, never far—but I kept my mind on taking care of myself and getting out of the house.

It was a blend of escapism, defiance, and self-pity. It was also desperation. I wanted Edward gone by the time I was dressed.

When I left the bathroom, I heard voices down below. Since I wasn't dressed yet, I told myself that there was still time for him to leave.

Closing the bedroom door, I thumbed up Adele loud enough to drown out my thoughts. With my eyes out the window on the woods and my back to the door, I sat on the bed, pulled on leggings, a sweater, and heavy socks. Then I stood, turned, and gasped. Edward's back was closing the door—the door to *my bedroom.*

Every bit of the anger I had tamped down in the shower returned. "Leave," I said with what I thought was commendable composure. When he didn't budge, I said it louder, and when he continued to stare, I reached for my phone to silence Adele, and said it a third time, even louder, in case his hearing had gone bad in the years we'd been apart.

His voice was low. "Why won't you return my calls?"

"This is my house, Edward. I don't want you here." He was too tall for this room, too *past* for this house.

"We need to talk."

"This is not a good time. I have to get to work."

"Your first appointment isn't until eleven."

I could ask how he knew what my schedule was, but it would have been a waste of breath. He owned the Inn. He owned the Spa. He owned the new computers and would own the new tablets. He could search them at will. I had *no* control over that.

But here? Now? Crossing to the door, I moved him aside, returned to the bathroom, closed myself in, and flipped the lock. For a minute, bracing stiff arms on the rim of the sink, I hung my head. One deep inhalation later, though, defiance brought me upright. He might own all that at the Spa, but this was my house, my life.

He knocked.

"Not now," I said and reached for my makeup. If I wanted to feel strong, makeup was a must. I needed to look like the new me.

I half expected him to say something through the paneled wood. As I stood there, though, I heard nothing for a minute, then the sound of retreating footsteps. I heard him go down the stairs, and listened for either talk or the closing of the front door. Hearing neither, and not about to face him until I was good and ready, I carefully applied concealer, foundation, and blusher. I did my eyes and knotted my hair back. I brushed my bangs.

Realizing that I couldn't put this off forever if I hoped to meet Grace, I did a final check to make sure I was put together. After packing my blow dryer, best brushes, hair scissors, and clips in a tote, I went downstairs.

Liam was washing the last of the cookware while Edward ate what was left of the food. Both looked up when I appeared. Liam went still with the dish towel on the pan; Edward set down his fork and stood. Both looked wary. But then, neither was stupid. They had to see that I was fuming.

Driving home that point, my heels hit the wood hard with each step to deny the gentle sound my wool socks normally made without boots. "Glad you boys are enjoying each other's company," I said when I was half-way to the door. "Good breakfast, Liam." My tote hit the bench with a thud.

"You didn't finish."

"I had plenty." I looked back and smiled, not a particularly nice smile, but the best I could do. "Mom had it right. My eyes were always bigger than my stomach." Those eyes sharpened, daring him to say something smart. He seemed to think better of it. I checked my watch and made for the door. "I'm leaving now. I have a nine-thirty appointment that was not on the books. She's a paying customer." The currency was friendship, of course, but that meant as much to me as dollars and cents.

"It's with Grace," said Liam the traitor. I wasn't sure if he thought he was helping, but I didn't stop to find out.

"She can wait," Edward insisted. "This is important."

"Says the man who bought the Spa and is therefore my boss?" I asked, moving aside my bags only enough to make room for my butt on the bench.

His voice followed me. "Says the one who was married to you and has a crisis here."

I straightened the laces on my right boot and put my foot in. "*You* have a crisis? Sorry if I don't feel sympathy, because there's a no-brainer fix for *your* crisis. Leave town."

"I can't," he said. His voice was even closer. "I would have explained that last night, only you ran out—and I understand why you did. I didn't expect what happened to happen, either. I didn't lead you back to my place for that."

"Um, okay," Liam announced loudly, "I think I'll go out."

Reaching for the left boot, I gave my brother a disparaging once-over.

"Wearing that?" He had on sweatpants, a skimpy tee, and bare feet that were already moving toward the stairs, and we both knew that the rest of his clothes were just as pathetic.

"I'll go to the loft, then," he said.

"You'll hear everything from there," I called. "You could try the bathroom—but there's really no need. Another few seconds, and I'm gone."

"No, it's your house—"

"Excuse me?" Boots on, I stood. I looked in his direction. "Would you please say that again?" He didn't, of course. Point made, I reached for my scarf.

Incredibly, though, he wasn't done. "I just need socks and shoes. Then I'll hit the road."

"In *what*?" I asked. He might have found my front door key, but only that. When he appeared at the loft overlook, I dangled the others for him to see, dropped them in my bag, and wound my scarf.

"Let me take your truck now. Later I can call your tow guy for mine."

"I should walk to work?"

"Edward can drive you."

"I'm not going anywhere with Edward."

I had one arm in my coat when Edward said in a low, deep voice, "You said you weren't a coward."

"The new me is practical." I stuck the other arm in the sleeve but didn't bother with buttons. "When there's a pothole in the road, I go around it." Shouldering my bag and grabbing the tote, I went out the door.

The path would have been slippery after yesterday's rain if it hadn't been for the muddy boot marks underneath. After a few seconds of crunching over those shallow, ice-coated ridges, I was in my truck. I had just enough time to toss my bags on the passenger seat, buckle my belt, and press POWER, when the side door opened.

In one move, Edward shoved the bags to the floor and slid into the passenger seat. "If you want to do it this way, we'll do it this way," he said and slammed the door shut.

I glared out the windshield. "I don't want to do it at all."

"Not even after last night?"

"What difference does last night make?"

"We had sex."

"Really."

"Look at me, Mackenzie."

"It's Maggie," I said, with a glance in my rearview. The sight of his black Jeep blocking my truck did nothing for my mood. I could maneuver around it—lovely thing about living in the woods and having a driveway that extended to the trees—but it galled me. "You had sex with me to get me to talk?"

"*No.*" He added a more controlled, "No. I told you. I didn't plan on the sex. But the fact that it happened makes a statement."

"Which is?"

"That we both have unresolved issues."

"Sex means that?" My hands shifted on the wheel, itching to put the truck in gear, but how to get Edward out of the cab? "For the record," I said, "I might as well have been with a complete stranger, for all I know of the man you've become. For the *record,* if it hadn't been the safest, *the* safest time of the month for me, I'd be heading for the pharmacy right now for a morning-after pill. I'm not having another child, not with you, not with any man."

"Look at me and say that."

I looked at him and repeated the words. But then curiosity got the best of me—curiosity and an odd fascination—and I couldn't look away. He was as compelling as ever, if completely different, and it went beyond stray shots of gray hair. His eyes were tired, the lines at their outer corners deeper. His mouth was more tense, his beard a cropped mask on an iron jaw. His hair, which had always been short when I'd known him, had grown out thick and striking. Combed by fingers rather than a tool, it broke over his back collar and split in a natural part in front, leaving two broad spikes arcing over his brow.

I knew professional layering when I saw it. He hadn't grown it longer out of neglect but design. He wanted to be someone else, just like I did.

"You have bangs," he said.

"So do you."

"To cover the scar?"

"Yes." That raised the same urgent point I'd tried to make with Liam. "I'm a different person here, Edward. No one knows where I came from, because if they did a quick Google, it might lead them to Mackenzie Cooper, and if the truth of that comes out, I'll die—I mean, literally, die. I can't live through that again. So you and I did not know each other before—"

"We lie?"

"No one will ask. They won't suspect anything unless you give it away, which you have no need to do, unless you did come to punish me. Last night, you said you hadn't. Do you stand by that?"

"Yes."

I wasn't sure I believed him. Forgiveness was easier to discuss than to do. But I had to trust that his intention was there. "Then I beg you, do *not* offer information where none is needed. *Brainwash* yourself, Edward. Say it over and over again, like a mantra. *We did not know each other before. We were never married.* The story can be that we meet here through my brother Liam," I held up a hand, "the hiring *of* whom, the bringing to town *of whom* is a whole *other* issue, but I can't go there now."

Tearing my gaze from his, I returned to the windshield. In my current mood, the forest was a discouraging band of skeletal trees, with the occasional withered leaf clinging, even after the snows. I tried to take strength from those stubborn last leaves, but failed. My voice was as weak as the sun that struggled to filter feebly through a cold haze of clouds. "Your being here is a problem for me on so many levels I can't begin to see my way clear."

"I'm sorry."

"But you won't sell."

"I can't. It isn't just the resort." His voice was quiet. "The package includes property all over town, even the ski slope, which needs serious snow-making equipment, but that's *nada* compared to the crisis right now at the Spa. New computer security is the least of it. We're talking major damage control, posting newsletters on travel sites, sending personal notes to clients to tell them we're on top of things, working with travel agents to restore confidence. My group has a dozen investors. I'm the managing partner, which means I have a major responsibility for what's happened and a major incentive to make things work. I can't sell now. I'm in too deep."

I gave a short snort. "Bad time for a hacking scandal?"

"Ya' think?" he asked in disgust.

I met his eyes again, couldn't *not*. Yes, they were Lily's eyes, but that fact was clouded by my own despair. "What were you thinking, Edward?"

"Ned."

"Did you think I'd be happy? Did you think I was sitting here waiting for you? Did you never consider my side of this? Did it not occur to you that your coming here might be painful for me? Did it never occur to you to call me first and tell me what you were planning to do before the deal went through?"

Those silvery eyes grew intense. "I knew you'd say no."

"And you didn't respect me enough to respect my feelings?"

His lips were as tight as the small nod he gave. "I respect you," he said. "I've watched you—" He broke off.

There was dead silence, but the guilt on his face said I hadn't heard wrong.

"What do you mean, watched me?"

"Not the first couple of years, I was too upset then, but the last couple, I needed to know."

"Needed to know what?"

"How you were doing."

I was getting an uncomfortable feeling, another little razor-sharp tear in the fabric of a life I thought I knew. "How did you watch me?"

"Jay."

"Jay." I turned away, looked blindly out my side window, put my elbow on the sill and my chin on a shaky fist.

"He won't say anything without breaching lawyer-client privilege. I had to know you were all right." He stopped, but I refused to turn, was too upset to speak. His voice came from behind me. "He didn't tell me much, just that you had friends and a job and seemed happy."

Against my fist, I asked, "Did you learn this before or after you decided to buy the Inn?"

"Before. I figured maybe you were onto something, starting new and all, so when one of my partners learned about the resort package, I took over. You were my inspiration. You picked yourself up off the floor. Maybe that's why I'm here. I need this—"

"*You* need this?" I cut in, whirling back. "This is about *you?*"

"It's about us," he said, those silver blues defiant. "About the past, Mackenzie. I can't move on."

"It's *Maggie.*"

"There's no closure."

"Isn't death closure enough?"

"No!" He boomed, then lowered his voice. "This isn't only about Lily. Well, maybe it is. But it's about us, too. We stopped talking. Why did we stop talking?"

"Because I killed our child."

"You didn't kill her. If the driver of the van hadn't been going twice the speed limit—"

"Not that fast."

"*Yes,* that fast. When everything was over—the trial, our marriage—I went back to the police. I wanted to know exactly how fast he was going."

"Why did it matter? I was convicted."

"Yeah, and that bothered me, so I asked about the guy's speed."

"He was going between forty-five and fifty in a thirty-five zone." So we were told. So my attorney argued.

"Try seventy," Edward said. "I stood there with the forensics team.

I watched them re-calculate. The figure in the initial report was vague, but forensics are more exact, really a science now—and, sorry, but I didn't think that a van going forty-five would have killed a child who was sitting in the equivalent of a personal tank. If the thing had burst into flames and burned her up, I could've bought it. But kids are loose enough to survive a roll, so it had to be his front end hitting my child at a huge speed."

I tucked my hands in my lap, watched them clasp each other on the slick of my parka.

"He had a history of speeding. Someone pulled strings to cover it up. The AG didn't want anything polluting her case."

My fingers were freezing, but I didn't have the wherewithal to pull gloves from my pocket. Defeated, I said, "It doesn't matter, Edward. I ran a STOP sign. I was responsible. I could see it in your eyes every time you looked at me."

"Really?" He paused, like he was trying to figure that out. "Was it really there?"

"Does it matter? If I felt it, isn't that the same thing?"

He considered for a minute, then let it go, but the defiance was back. "So you shut down, refused to talk, agreed to a divorce, and left town."

"Whoa," I said. I had enough to blame myself for without taking sole responsibility there, too. "*You* shut down, *you* refused to talk, *you* agreed to a divorce."

"Fine," he conceded, moving a finger—long, lean, no more ring—back and forth over his denimed thigh. "So you came up here and became someone else. It sounds good, but what the hell does Jay Harrington know about bone-deep grief? What does he know about a woman who used to be able to bare her soul—who *needed* to bare her soul—to a life partner? New town, new job, new friends? How's that working for you?"

The Edward I'd loved had never aimed sarcasm at me—at other people maybe, but not at me.

Defiant in the face of his, I upped my enthusiasm. "It's working well! I like my work and I like my friends. I have a place of my own—*my— own*—and I have pets."

"But no soulmate. Not even a lover. Those two guys at One-on-Tap—"

"They're friends. They're caring and kind. They watch out for me."

"But intimacy with them can only go so far. Is that the appeal?"

"The appeal is their kindness and loyalty. It's their sensitivity. Their being gay is a bonus."

Going quiet, Edward gazed out at the woods. Spikes of hair on his brow, dark jaw, straight nose, lean lips—all were the same as moments before, but his profile was suddenly less stony. "I do want a wife," he finally said.

"Awesome. Go get one. No one's stopping you. You're totally free."

"Wrong," he said and met my eyes with a bleakness I hadn't seen before. "Oh, I tried, believe me, I did, and they were really cool women, smart and sexy, but no dice. Nothing worked. My personal life is stalled. I'm stuck in the past. I need to go back to the place where it went wrong."

"Then last night was an exercise?" I asked. "Something therapeutic?"

Another man might have grinned a sly grin or quipped something smug. But Edward had never been a chauvinist. Of all the things I didn't know about this new man, that hadn't changed. But then, if he wanted to take me back to the time when things went wrong, what better way than to do what he did—to smile a sweet Edward smile, the kind I had always felt was our secret, his and mine? I hadn't seen anything like it since before the accident. It made my heart ache.

"I really did not plan that," he said and looked down, actually seeming self-conscious. "I was thinking we were just going to talk, but then it was dark driving there, so I couldn't see where I was and what I was supposed to be doing, and by the time we got inside . . . well, you know." He paused and looked at me with something akin to hope. "But I wouldn't mind a repeat. It felt good, Mackenzie. It always did."

"Maggie," I corrected again, but sadly, because he was right. "So maybe that's all there ever was? Maybe that's why everything fell apart at the first sign of trouble, because there was nothing more than sex to hold it to-gether? I was pregnant when we got married. If not for that, we might not have gotten married. We'd have kept on living together, and when some other crisis came up, we'd have just gone our separate ways."

I said it. But seriously? No. The crisis that had torn us apart was the most extreme a family could suffer, but a lesser crisis wouldn't have ended things. We had been good together—*great* together—*light-years better* together than either of us had ever been with anyone else, including our birth families. And Edward had wanted marriage. He'd have insisted on it in time. My resistance had to do with my being younger, my friends being still single, and my parents being uber-conventional. They were sticklers for my doing things as they had, which meant legal and religious, which meant a high mass in church. But Edward was Protestant, not Catholic. They were concerned about that from the get-go, and grew more concerned the more committed he and I became. When we moved in together, they were crushed, and though they were relieved when we finally did marry, they weren't pleased that it took place in a hotel, or that Edward's pastor co-officiated with ours.

I told them it was that or a Justice of the Peace.

I did not tell them I was pregnant. When Lily was born six months later, they simply told their friends she had come early. She accommodated them by being small, but she was beautiful. They adored her from the start. They did not adore our house, which they thought was too big and showy—or our cars, which they thought were too expensive, or our friends, whom they thought too chic, or Edward's work, which they thought was shady at best. When the accident happened, they blamed our lifestyle.

So did I, in a way.

"What we were," Edward said, sounding wounded, "was far more than sex."

I shrugged. Fair was fair. In that retaliatory instant, I wanted to hurt him for the way his letting me go had hurt me.

"Do you really think that's all we had?" he asked and made a face, like I was an alien being. "Who *are* you?"

"Who are *you?*" I shot back.

He didn't move for an instant—didn't speak, didn't breathe. Finally, he blinked and shoved a hand through his hair, leaving his forehead exposed in a way that reminded me of the old Edward again. "Fuck if I know," he muttered.

And wasn't there perverse satisfaction in that? Misery loved company. My life right now was as messy as the mud in the woods. No matter how often I told myself that I knew what to do, my future was as much an enigma right now as the forest. Little shoots of green were out there somewhere—I knew they were—but it would take a lot of digging to find them.

We sat side by side—Edward, me, the future, the past—facing his mud-spattered Jeep, those naked woods, and a watery yellow sky. Finally, feeling like I was hanging on by a thread and desperate for firm ground, I said, "I have to get to the Spa."

He nodded but didn't move. "Is she a good friend?"

"Grace? Yes. Do not fire her, Edward. She's a decent person, and she did not ask for this. She has a son. She needs the money."

"I'm not firing her."

I wasn't thanking him. He wasn't doing me a favor, simply taking the advice from someone who understood the situation more than he did.

After a few beats, he asked, "Do you miss sculpting?"

"Edward," I warned, but still he didn't budge. So I said, "I sculpt. Just more now with makeup than clay. I have to leave, Edward."

"Are you okay, y'know, with money and all?"

"I'm fine."

"If you need anything—"

"I don't want money," I said more sharply than I planned but, that quickly, the past was back. "Money was what got us in trouble. If we hadn't lived such a high life, if Lily had gone to public school, if I hadn't had to drive to a godforsaken out-of-the-way place for a playdate—"

As abruptly as Edward had entered my car, now he opened the door and climbed out. When his feet were on the frigid drive, he leaned back in. "You think you're the only one who can't stop with the *what-ifs*? Think you have a monopoly on grief? Or regret? Or *guilt?* I was the one earning the money to put us in that place. I was the one who was supposed to be home to take Lily to the playdate that day, only I was too fuckin' busy earning all that money to do it."

Somewhere during the outburst, his eyes had filled with tears. With a last scathing look now, he slammed the door and stomped to the Jeep.

12

The one thing most vivid in my mind as Edward's Jeep tore down the hill and disappeared past the trees was the tears in his eyes. He was no actor. He could barely play gin rummy without giving away his hand. Oh, he could negotiate a business deal, but when it came to anything personal, you knew where you stood.

That, as my mother would say, was a double-edged sword. Knowing where he stood meant I had believed what I saw after the accident. As far as I could see, the sight of me brought him so much pain that he couldn't feel love, and without love, we had no future together.

I wasn't sure what to make of his tears now, but they did soften me. He had never expressed these particular feelings before, which said something about the silence that had choked us back then. It said something about the soul-searching he must have done since. Yes, I was touched— of *course* I was touched that he had dug into the facts of the case. I hadn't questioned them, and not out of naïveté. They simply didn't matter. I had been distracted; my eyes weren't on the road; I had run a stop sign. End of story. I wasn't ready—would *never* be ready—to share the blame of that with anyone else.

Still, Edward's raising the issue of guilt was interesting. That he felt it, whether right or wrong, said something about sharing responsibility. It had been a long time since anyone had wanted to share responsibility for *anything* with me. It had been a long time since anyone had trusted me enough.

I still didn't want him here.

But he was.

I could tell him to leave until I was blue in the face. But he wasn't leaving.

I could threaten to leave myself. But, seriously? If you want to talk about little green buds in the forest, that was my life in Devon. I liked those buds, liked the person I was growing into here. I felt for the people I knew—like Alex, who loved teaching but would give anything for her own kids—like Joyce, whose husband had left her years ago and whose children didn't often return.

Now I felt for Edward. In our old life, he'd had friends, but I wasn't sure he had them here yet. Liam sure as hell wouldn't be giving him advice on what to do here.

Considering this as I followed sanely down the road, I braked, stopped, and took out my phone. *Do not use Hank Monroe,* I texted. *He overcharges and underdoes.*

I was halfway to the Spa when he texted back. *Who then?*

I let him wait for a reply until I was parked in the employees' lot, which was comfortably filled with the cars of Sunday staff, no press van or black Jeep in sight. *Andrew Russ,* I texted, and, as a little reminder that I had a life here, sent a second. *Use my name. He loves me.*

Entering the Spa, I felt absurdly better, strong enough in that moment to want to work with clay—I mean, really work in ways I hadn't been able to do. My fingers ached to sink in, to feel its chill, tensile strength, to pound it and shape it and lose myself in creation.

But this was Sunday. The studio was closed. Where creation was concerned, the choice was between God and Grace's hair. Given that I was still angry at the former for allowing my child to die, the latter would have to do.

Grace was game. "I am so done with this look," she declared in her high voice, pulling on a cape over her scrubs, which were lilac and fitted. We were alone in the color room, as she knew we would be when she suggested this time. Freeing her arms from the cape, she dropped into a chair. She tugged an elastic from her hair and shook her head, freeing auburn curls to shimmer in a sea of chestnut waves.

The color was gorgeous. I couldn't believe she wanted it changed. But it wasn't my hair, was it?

Lighting a scented candle, I breathed it in and thought sweet, agreeable thoughts. They came with surprising ease. This, here, now, was my Devon life.

Taking a second slow inhalation for the sheer pleasure of it, I faced the mirror from behind Grace's chair and focused on her tension. It was in the fingers that were laced tight in her lap, in the shadow of lines on her brow and the tiny vertical ones between her brows. Her eyes, though, were the hazel I knew to be her own. Their normalcy made her hair all the more striking by contrast.

"This color really is beautiful," I said in a last attempt to change her mind, but she was having none of it.

"Too beautiful. People notice it. They remember it."

"But you like that."

"Used to like it," she said, her voice almost childlike. "It's too noticeable now. It gives me away wherever I go." The eyes meeting mine in the mirror were haunted. "The *People* article hits this week, Jay says. It'll be bad."

"He told you that?"

"Only that it's coming out, but I know it'll be bad. All publicity is bad publicity."

The expression actually was, *All publicity is good publicity,* but I knew what she meant. "Imagine that issue three months from now. Where'll it be? Long gone in the trash."

"After the whole world's read it." In her lap, her thumb picked at a cuticle. "At least you were right about Jay. He knows his stuff. He got the prosecutor to agree to waive a pre-sentencing report—family background and all. That," she said, with a wry twist of her lips, "would not have been fun." The twist faded, leaving her frightened and bare. "This is my worst nightmare, Maggie. I can't stand it. I want to disappear."

Oh, I knew *that* feeling. "You won't disappear with raven. It's too extreme."

"Okay, but this brown is too rich. I want dirty brown. I mean, *dirty*—like, mousy."

"And mousy is you?"

"I don't *want* to be me. That's the point."

I came around front for the sake of directness. "You can only disappear up to a point. If the press wants to find you, they will. So you go with a different color now, but what happens when they catch on? You can't change it every few days, and, anyway, if you did that, you'd only give the media something else to write about."

That seemed to register. "Oh God. Not what I want. But mousy is understated. Isn't understated good?"

"I'm not sure you could be understated if you tried," I said with a smile.

Her chin came up. "Excuse me. We can't all be as dignified as you."

Leaning in, I closed my hand over hers. "That's not what I meant, Grace. I love your flair. You're one of the few people I know who can pull it off. It's what makes you *you.*" I gave her hand a jiggle, let go, straightened. "And that's a good thing. Only a strong person can do it. Only a strong person can stand up to those cameras and say, *fuck you, I don't care what you think, I'm a good mother, my son is a good kid, these charges are bogus.*"

Her eyes held mine for a split second before shifting off. Guilt. Ah. So the charges weren't bogus. Chris had been able to tell me how hacking worked from firsthand experience.

Where to go after that silent admission? I wanted to ask why he had done it or what Grace had said when she learned it, but I couldn't criticize her when I knew the *People* story would. For now, "How is he?" seemed safe enough.

"Dense," she murmured. "He doesn't get that this goes beyond him to me. He keeps saying it's no big thing, but *he's* not the one whose life is at stake."

I might have argued. It seemed to me that Chris had more to lose with regard to future choices than Grace, who already had an education, a skill, a job, a home. Chris's life was up in the air in every regard. I wondered what he felt about that. I wondered if Grace had even asked him, or whether she was too conflicted to talk.

Actually, I wondered if they ever talked about things—deep things— things beyond what time to leave for school or whether to bring in pizza or Thai. My mother and I had often talked about those deeper things when I was growing up. College changed that, like I'd become some- one she couldn't relate to. She hadn't gone to college. She had married at twenty, at which point my father became her world.

"Maggie?" Grace prompted.

I wanted to yell at Chris, to ask what he had actually thought break- ing the law would accomplish. I wanted to tell *Grace* to yell at Chris. I wanted to lash out at both of them for dredging up issues in my own life, which would, of course, get us nowhere.

Instead, I said, "You're a survivor. You'll get through this."

But how, my past asked? In what shape or form? Life wasn't fair. Just when you thought you'd reached a good place, a crisis could boil up and over, spilling into even the corners you thought most secure. Grace's life would be forever changed, if only by the veil of suspicion that might linger in people's minds.

Her thoughts must have gone there, too, because she seemed suddenly withdrawn. For both our sakes, I brought the discussion back to color. We looked at charts. When she pointed to the blandest brown, I pointed to one several shades brighter. When she pointed at one up from the blandest brown, I pointed at one down from my original. Liver to milk chocolate, wood brown to russet, we bargained back and forth a minute longer before I hid the chart behind my back.

"I'll give you what you want," I promised, "but I can't ruin your hair. I'll do a quiet, woodsy brown. Do you trust me in this?"

Her eyes held doubt. "That depends. Do you understand my fear?"

"More than you'll ever know, but I'm also thinking about the cut. If you want a different look, you can do it with style. Leave the color as it is, but go short and straight."

She was shaking her head even before I finished. "The color goes. And I don't want short."

"Okay," I said, lifting swaths of her hair and letting them fall to imagine how her current layers would settle without curls. "A shag maybe? That would be easy. Unadorned. Very wash and wear."

"Maybe."

"Unadorned is big here. You'd totally blend in. You could still pull it up if you wanted, but it would frame your face and leave you enough to hide behind."

The word "hide" resonated, as I knew it would. "Okay," she said. "Go with that."

I told her exactly what I was doing as I mixed the color, which looked nothing in the bowl like it would once it oxidized on her hair, and even then, a leap of faith was required. Applying color over color took an understanding of the chemistry involved. I had it. I actually liked the puzzle part of this so much that I had initially considered being a full-time colorist. Then my classes turned to makeup, and the more personal, therapeutic part of it won hands down.

Wearing thin latex gloves, I used the pointy end of my brush handle to separate sections and the front end to apply color, taking care to cover the vibrant browns by starting at the very root and working out. We didn't talk. She closed her eyes, but I could feel the tension in her head and neck. Hoping to relax her, I turned up the wall speakers to allow for the soothing of soft guitar sounds.

After a bit, quietly, she said, "Three other men had their accounts hacked. Jay got their names."

My hand faltered for an instant. I waited. "And?"

"They're repeat clients."

"Yours?"

"Yes. All in the last year."

"Why did Chris choose them?"

She didn't answer at first. Then, reaching down, she lifted her satchel from the floor, opened it, and took out what looked to be computer print-outs clipped together. After removing the clip, she showed me one at a time. Each of the men was fortyish, light-haired, and fit. The last shot was a close-up of Benjamin Zwick, standing before a cluster of phones, record-ers, and mics. A similar one had appeared in the local paper.

"They're all good-looking."

"That's what Jay said. He said he was the exception."

It was a minute before I followed. "You were *with* each of these men?" The question came out more startled than condemning, though, given the circumstances, I felt a touch of the latter. I understood a woman's sex-ual desire. Oh boy, did I ever. I understood that the power of it could push her beyond reason. But the thought of being with one man after another after another made my skin crawl.

"Not all," Grace said. "With one of them, it was only dinner. My son didn't know that."

"What did he know? And how? And why would knowing push him to this?"

She pointed from my hand, which had stopped working, to her head. I went back to applying color, while she reclipped the pictures and re-turned them to her bag. Her hand reemerged with a snapshot. She kept it in her lap for a minute before holding it up for me to see. The man in the photo was as good-looking as the others. The details of his features were different enough, but still, yet, oddly the same.

"My ex-husband," Grace said.

I gasped. She had mentioned Chris's father the week before—and Chris had certainly asked about him—but in all the time I'd known Grace, she had never mentioned having had a husband. Never wanting to mention mine, I hadn't asked. But this, now, was significant. Had Chris come from a one-nighter or from an ongoing affair with a married man, Grace would understandably avoid the discussion. But a husband?

"He's obviously Chris's father," I said. The resemblance was marked. In the full color of a snapshot, rather than a black-and-white printout, the hair wasn't just light; it was sandy and had the waves that Chris might have if his hair was tamed.

"The other guys look a little like him, don't you think?" Grace asked tongue-in-cheek.

Not just a little. "Is that why Chris targeted them?"

"I don't know."

"Did you ask?"

"No. It's a tricky subject."

I took that to mean she was uncomfortable with it, which bothered the hell out of me, because if not now, when? Her son had committed a crime. Had she even told him how wrong that was?

"Are you in touch with his father at all?" I asked.

She shook her head, slipped the picture back in her bag, and dropped the bag to the floor. "We left when Chris was two, so he doesn't remember how bad the guy is. I didn't know he'd seen this picture until I found it in the back of my closet. I mean, like, who keeps real pictures anymore?" *Me*, I thought, but she went on. "I keep a few old things in a locked box. He jimmied it open."

If Chris's father was so bad, I wondered why she kept his picture. I also wondered why she was drawn to men who looked like him. But who was I to wonder that—me, who hadn't been drawn to a man in five years until tall and dark came to town in the form of Edward Cooper?

"So maybe," Grace said, "he was curious?"

Chris. About his father. "That'd be normal. Or jealous of men who take your time."

"Either that," she looked heartsick, "or he's as evil as his father."

I doubted that. I'd never sensed a mean bone in Chris's body, and while I was furious at him for doing what he had, he was only fifteen. "Not evil. Confused."

"*Dense,*" she repeated her earlier word. This time it sounded way more like *stupid.*

Part of me agreed. But he *was* only fifteen. "Puberty does things, Grace."

"Yep. Makes boys bad."

"Maybe shortsighted."

"Selfish."

"Self-absorbed. His features have totally changed in the four years I've known him. So he looks in the mirror and wonders who he is."

She seemed disheartened for a minute before conceding a quiet, "Maybe."

I went back to applying her color. The timing of it wasn't as critical as it would be if we were doing highlights, but oxidation in the bowl wasn't ideal.

"Or maybe not," she suddenly said, her voice shooting up. "How could he do this to me? He knew I liked Devon. People here let me do my own thing. They don't ask questions, or stare at me or talk behind my back. They trust me. Trust*ed* me. Now? Disaster. My son has an identity crisis and screws the whole thing up? Suddenly *he's* judging me?"

"Not judging—"

"*Yes,* judging. He thinks I sleep around too much, like I go from one man to the next, and they all look the same. He thinks I'm screwed up, so it's okay for him to be screwed up, like he can fool with computers and play at being someone else. And I'll never know, because I'm not smart enough or I'm too busy chasing men or working so I can send him to Montreal with the hockey team or buy him the high-tops he wants or fill a prescription for the zit cream that is *not* covered by my insurance, but he was the one who complained that he didn't have a girlfriend because of acne. He thinks I kept him from the one man he wants to know, and who in the hell was I to do that?"

"Has he actually told you these things?"

"No, but he's thinking them, I know he is."

I had stopped working again. Our eyes held in the mirror. Her out-pouring was pure guilt. Right or not, a mother always blamed herself when something went wrong.

"But why?" Grace asked, pleading. "Everything I've done in the last fifteen years has been for him. I've tried to keep him safe. I've tried to make a good home. So I'm not perfect. Are you perfect? Is Joyce or Nina? Where's the fairness of this? I've deliberately kept the men in my life out of his life. Isn't what I do on my own time my own?"

"Not when you have a child."

"How do you know?" she asked with just the slightest emphasis on the *you*.

I might have taken offense, if I hadn't known she was upset. "I saw it with my parents when I was growing up," I said. My mom had eased into baking, but once The Buttered Scone took off, she struggled with the balance. Though my dad liked the money she earned, he was always after her to do more for and with Liam and me. There had been some serious arguments, bits of which we had heard and, of course, discussed between ourselves. Our parents would have been good candidates for marital coun-seling. Actually, my father could have used counseling himself. He was decidedly passive-aggressive.

With that thought, I asked, "Maybe Chris should see a counselor?"

She cleared her throat. "He already is, and if you think I'm thrilled about that, think again. The court makes him see a forensic psychologist. They've had one meeting of three. I'm losing sleep over what was said in that room."

"He would never say anything bad about you."

"Like he would never search my closet for some sign of his dad? Hell, yeah, I'd love to talk with someone, too. I'd *love* to yell and scream about everything I did not plan. But I would never, never tell a counselor private things."

"Why not? They're bound by confidentiality."

"And you believe they keep it?"

I considered my own therapist. "Yes. You wouldn't have to see someone in Devon. Hanover has a ton of therapists—"

"No counseling. I'm telling you, Maggie, if it weren't for Chris, I'd run away in a heartbeat, just disappear and reinvent myself."

Hadn't I considered doing the same thing? Granted, it was the nuclear option, so I was holding off. Still. Returning the brush in my hand to her hair, I asked, "Where would you go?" Dreaming was as good a way as any to soothe emotions.

"Another spa. Maybe Canyon Ranch. You know, the one in Lenox? I could go there in a heartbeat."

I couldn't. Edward and I had often visited friends with second homes in the Berkshires. We had even been there with Lily. The memories would be too strong.

"Not the Berkshires," I said. "The weather is neither here nor there. Vermont winters are real winters, but if you want warmer, head south."

"What about Florida? We could do Fisher Island."

"We could," I said, "but there the work is seasonal. Here, we're booked year-round. How about San Francisco?" The weather there was moderate all year, and the spas were amazing.

"No."

"Austin?" Texans loved spas, and Austin was a fun place. I could do Austin.

"No. Nothing west of the Mississippi."

Her clipped tone implied it had something to do with her ex, and I didn't ask. Leaning around one way then the other, I made sure I hadn't missed even the smallest section, then applied the remaining color to what was soon a cap of goop swirled flat to her head.

"Virginia," I suggested setting a timer. "There's a Canyon Ranch at Hot Springs." I could go there in a heartbeat. Hot Springs had history. Anything with roots appealed to me.

Except, those were someone else's roots. Mine were here, now. I didn't want to pick up and move to Virginia. Or Texas. Or California. I liked Devon.

"New York would be safe," Grace said. "I could get lost in New York."

That was why I wouldn't move there. During the time I was at college in New York, I'd been surrounded by people, but lonely. "Philadelphia would be less anonymous," I tried. "Or Washington. Both have good spas."

But she seemed decided. "New York. I want to be nameless and faceless."

"You do not."

She gave me a strange look. "Why are you arguing with me?"

"Because I know you—"

"*Know* me?" she cut in, as though I had no sense at all. "You haven't been where I am. You don't know what it's like to run. You don't know what it's like to feel hunted. There are people in my past who would love to know where I am. You don't know what it's like to be hated so much that if the idiot who hates you had a gun he'd shoot you dead."

No. I didn't. Other than the accident, I hadn't known violence. I had never feared for my life.

Her eyes went wide, then she squeezed them tight. "Forget I said that. I'm just hyper-emotional."

But emotion alone couldn't explain away real fear. "Is the idiot your ex-husband?"

"Please, Maggie," she begged, eyes open now, "I shouldn't have said anything. You know how it is with relationships that go bad, he said she said, two sides to every story, yadda yadda. I shouldn't have mentioned him at all."

But she had. I couldn't imagine why anyone would hate her that much. "Would he come after you?"

She scrabbled the air with frantic hands. "It's over, finished, just stirred up by this shit with Chris, but *please* forget what I said. You don't want to know. Trust me. You're better off if you don't."

She was right about that. Hadn't Michael Shanahan already asked me about her? The less I knew, the more innocent I remained.

Of course, I knew now that she'd had relationships with the four men whose accounts were hacked, that they all looked like her ex-husband. I knew now that she *had* an ex-husband. And here I was, basically helping her hide behind a new head of hair.

That said, violence was something else. I couldn't shake the idea. Edward had never been violent—had never come *close* to being violent—not once, in all the dark days that had followed Lily's death.

Considering that, I felt more kindly toward him.

So when he wrote, *Can Andrew Russ handle major renovations?* I waited only until I finished cutting Grace's hair to write, *Yes. He's new, smart, state-of-the-art.*

I was midway through my eleven o'clock when he wrote, *Landscaping? Trees? Moldy basement? Bats in the attic?*

Why did you buy that house? I returned when my client asked for a minute to answer a text of her own. The woman in question had just turned sixty-five, hence the lunch in her honor, and she looked so like my mother that I spent extra time with her makeup.

Actually, she didn't look anything like my mother. The only thing the same was their age.

But I spared nothing—used only my newest products, layered luminous foundation over tinted moisturizer over multiple concealers. I did her eyes in the softest navies and grays, and her cheeks with a dash of peach. Mascara? Only enough to delineate the lashes.

She called me a genius.

I didn't feel it—should have known better than to encourage conversation with Edward—when I went out to get my next client and he waylaid me in the corridor. He had clearly been to that moldy house, since he had showered and put on clean jeans. He answered my question in a Spa whisper. "I needed a place to stay, and it was for sale."

Continuing toward the lounge, I whispered back, "You could have stayed at the Inn. It has a Presidential Suite—Bridal Suite—Honeymoon Suite—whatever you call it this week."

Edward kept pace. "I don't want the owner's suite at the Inn. I want a house. This one's a winner. It just needs a little work."

"A little? Is that what your text was about?"

"Okay, a lot, but I got the place dirt cheap, so the ROI will be good."

I stopped walking before we were visible to others. Edward would attract notice. He was that striking.

Quietly, I said, "Andrew Russ can coordinate everything. He's a great guy."

"You know him well?"

"He did my kitchen and bathroom. I've done his wife's makeup." I moved past him. "Sorry, but I have a client."

I spotted her the instant I was out in the open, and broke into a heartfelt smile. I knew this client. She was my absolute favorite. The appointment had been booked in her mother's all-too-common surname, Smith, rather than her family name, Kalmbach, so I hadn't made the connection. Seeing her in the lounge gave me an immediate lift. It helped that Edward disappeared, but I would have given her a huge hug regardless.

A referral from Joe Hellinger, fourteen-year-old Madelyn Kalmbach had been born with a port wine stain covering half of her face. She'd had laser treatments since toddlerhood, and the stain was greatly faded from what I had seen in early photos. What remained of it were stubborn areas that had either resisted treatment or that were too close to sensitive areas, like her eye, to allow it. Makeup made sense. That was where I came in.

The rapport between us had been instant. We joked that it was the Maddie-Maggie thing, but the truth had to do with my not being one of her parents. Understandably, they saw her as a child to be sheltered from a cruel world. Had they known some of the things her schoolmates said, they would have gone to school officials to complain and embarrassed her to death. She knew I wouldn't do that. So, while her mother either had a manicure or took a yoga class or walked into town to shop, she told me which girls excluded her and which did not, what they said, what they posted, and where. She told me which boys could look at her and which would not, and she shared her fear that the one she had a crush on would never see past the stain.

For me, it wasn't about hiding splotches of red. Once I got to know Maddie, I barely saw them, which I freely told her. But she knew they were there, which was all that mattered. I showed her how to shade them, how to draw attention away from them by highlighting her eyes. I had done her makeup prior to a party or two. Today, she was having pictures taken for her middle-school yearbook. While we waited for her mother to pick her up, I brushed her hair, braided one side at the temple and clipped it several inches back, used a curling iron on the rest.

We were both pleased with ourselves by the time she left.

And there was Liam at Reception, chatting it up with Joyce, whose wave for me to join them was far too enthusiastic.

"Your *brother*," she said, beaming. "I'm *so* glad he's here."

I was not. Right there, with Joyce as witness, Liam begged, positively *begged* me to help him pick clothes that *he* would pay for, he claimed, and how could I say no? I still didn't want him working for Edward. But what I wanted seemed not to matter. Liam was here. He had driven here in his own car, newly towed back onto my road. And if he didn't buy appropriately warm and weather-resistant clothes, he would catch his death of cold—which was totally a Mom thought. Anyone in his right mind knew that colds came from germs, not weather. But his clothes were wrong any way you looked at it. Advising him in this was the least I could do.

Not to mention that Joyce would have had my head if I refused.

So off we went, Liam and I, and naturally, with someone as needy as Liam, it didn't stop at clothes. He wanted a tour of the town, and though I pointed out apartments for rent over the stores on Lincoln, he was more interested in the shops themselves. When I pointed out available rentals in a condo community near the town line, he was more interested in the two eateries there. When I pulled off the road onto the drive of a small inn that I knew rented rooms by the month and, in fact, had a VACANCY sign prominently displayed, he was totally clueless.

"Okay, so, what is the appeal here?" he asked. "Do they serve anything other than breakfast?"

My phone dinged then. Not knowing how to deal with his denseness, since the message I was trying to send seemed crystal clear to me, I read Edward's text. *Who is Nina Evans?*

Town Manager, I replied and sent it off. I didn't ask why he wanted to know. Encouraging him only invited more, and I wasn't his wife—or his girlfriend, his facilitator, his interior designer—certainly wasn't the only one in town with the names of wildlife exterminators.

I didn't need a man in my life. Given the pain of the past, I sure didn't want this one.

Well, I did. Physically. Now, then, always—picturing how Edward Cooper had looked earlier at the Spa—he was something to behold. I wasn't sure what to do with that. But there it was.

"Jeez, who's at the other end of *that* text?" my brother asked.

My head flew up. "No one. Why?"

"The look on your face . . ."

"What?"

"Guilty. No. Hungry."

Says the chef who wants everyone hungry all the time, I might have said, misinterpreting the word just to get him off my back, but it wasn't worth the effort. He couldn't get into my phone. He couldn't see who I was texting. For all he knew, I was dating someone. Let him chew on that a while.

Dropping the phone in my purse, I murmured, "Yeah, right," and looked at the Inn. It was modest in amenities and, no, didn't serve anything other than breakfast, but it was high on charm. The owners were good people. I knew them. This was my turf.

"Nope," I said. "Not hungry. Not me."

13

Are you hungry?"

It was Edward's voice, of course. After seeing his number on my cell, I vowed not to answer, but it was a losing battle. By the third vibration, a progression of older, darker emotions had given way to the image of tears in his eyes, and I just couldn't . . . *not.*

Still, I was wary. I held the phone to my ear, waiting for him to say more.

"Mackenzie?"

Quietly, I said, "There's no one by that name here." Propping the phone between shoulder and ear in a private show of nonchalance, I capped a bottle of foundation and returned it to its shelf.

"Maggie," he said solemnly. "I'm just not used to that."

"Fair's fair. I'm not used to hearing your voice."

"Have you had lunch?"

I sealed a tube of mascara and returned that to its place. "I promised Joyce I'd cover for her at the desk. She has a doctor's appointment at two."

"It's only one now. Have you eaten?"

Collecting brushes, I slid them into disinfecting solution. "I've been with clients since eleven. The last one just left. But you know that." He was my boss. My schedule had to be right there on his screen.

"No. I don't. I decided not to spy."

I sputtered a dry laugh. "Isn't it a little late? You already have my address and phone number, and, okay, maybe you got that from our lawyer or from Liam, but I'm betting you've also been through my file. And if you pulled up the Spa schedule to compare today's bookings to a typical Monday before the scandal—which I'm sure you did, because that's the kind of info you'd want—my schedule is already on a screen in your mind. You have a photographic memory, Edward. Don't forget, I know you."

"You're the only one who does," he said without correcting the name. "That's why I'm calling. I have lunch here on my desk—Caesar salad for you, tuna sandwich for me."

Caesar salad for you, tuna sandwich for me. I tried to picture it, but all I could see was the risk. "You had your assistant bring lunch for two to your office, and you didn't think it would attract attention?"

"I got these myself at Rasher and Yolk. I didn't realize they were open 'til two," he said, sounding pleased, "but don't worry, they don't know who I am. My office is on the second floor of the Inn, so no one at the front desk will see. My assistant is gone for the afternoon, there's no one else around, and if someone knocks on the door, you can hide in the bathroom."

That distracted me. "You have your own bathroom?"

"It came with the office. You've never been up here? You have to see it. I actually could use your advice on the, um"—he cleared his throat—"décor."

Pulling the lidded trash bin from under my makeup counter, I swept in used mascara wands, Q-tips, and sponges. These things were more real to my life than this voice from the past. "Oh, Edward." I sighed. "What's the point?"

"Eating lunch. You haven't eaten, I know you haven't, and you're right, I did see you had a free hour, but I didn't go looking for it, I swear I didn't. It just kind of popped up."

I might have laughed again, now for old times' sake, because Edward could be sweet when he was earnest. But I honestly, truly, completely wasn't in the market for heartache. "What's the point of our being together?"

"You said you didn't know the man I've become. Here's your chance."

"Chance to relive a past?"

"Chance to live a future."

"I can't keep the past in the past, when it comes to you."

"Well, you sure as hell won't ever move on, if you don't get over that."

I should have been angry. But he was right. My therapist had said something similar. And it was common sense. The more I let the present unfold, the more the past would find its place. I just hadn't expected Edward to be in the picture. If he was staying in Devon, I couldn't ignore him. I couldn't fear seeing him everywhere I went. I had to face him.

And yeah, I was a little curious about that bathroom.

But then he sealed it with a bald, "Okay, it's me, I'm the one who needs to bridge past and present. You've never been in this office. You've never told me about your work or about the pottery studio or about Devon. Honestly?" he said with an element of pleading, "I feel lost. Okay, I know I just got here. I have to pay my dues. But people stare at me like I'm an alien." He paused, pleaded, "Lunch? Here? Please?"

It didn't take long to walk from the Spa into the body of the Inn and up the nearest stairwell to the second floor. I had to fudge my way from there, making one wrong turn that took me down a corridor of guest suites before heading in the other direction and spotting the glass double doors. They were frosted with a handsome pattern of horizontal bars, the name of the Inn, and a discreet BUSINESS OFFICE marking that was obvious enough to steer away even a tipsy guest. It would be locked at night, of course. And now?

There was still time to turn back. I didn't have to do this.

But he was right about layering new memories on the old. His needing it, too, helped. And then there were Mom-isms marching along to the beat of my feet, like *For old times' sake* and *Once and done.*

After knocking softly, I carefully lowered the brass lever and pushed. I slipped inside before anyone could enter the corridor behind me, and closed the door.

Edward was just coming from the inner room that had to be his office, but I was already looking around in dismay. The walls were maroon, though only small strips of it could be seen past a world of Currier and Ives. Large, small, etchings, oils—each one was beautiful but a throwback to an early era. Same with the carpets underfoot, which were Oriental and worn, and with the conference room, whose long table and dozen chairs were classic. "Chippendale."

"None other. It's a little much for me. Take it in, though. The best is yet to come."

I followed him to his office. The walls here weren't maroon but dark-paneled wood bearing oils with a fox-hunting theme. Names like Turner and Kilburne came to mind, but the claustrophobic feel of the room quickly squeezed them out.

"Well," I said, "they do say something about the founder of the Inn." None were Edward's style—or mine—but they were textured and rich. I approached a large one. "These have to be originals."

"Yup."

"Sell a few, and you'd have money enough to buy tablets for every employee and then some."

"Can't sell. It's part of the contract that's passed from owner to owner, but that doesn't mean I have to look at them. I may turn some of the larger guest rooms into theme suites and hang them there."

"Isn't there a theft risk?" Some of the pieces were small enough to fit into luggage.

"Funny you ask," he said, scratching the back of his head in a sheepish way. "The computers may have lacked security, but the art has always been sensor-protected. Everything that we display is for sale—except the ones in this office," he tacked on with resignation. "Obviously."

My gaze slid to the desk. It, too, was of an age and had the same heavy look as the rest of the room. The fact that its work surface held a large iMac, a smaller laptop, and overlapping piles of papers that had to be in some sort of order, though I couldn't see what, brought it firmly into the present.

An arm on my shoulder turned me away. "Don't look there. It's depressing."

"Confused," I blurted without quite knowing if I meant the desk, the whole office, or his touching me.

"Isn't *that* a statement," he muttered and steered me to the far end of the room. It was anchored by a large leather sofa, a pair of tartan club chairs, and a low coffee table, on one end of which were our lunches. *Caesar salad for you, tuna sandwich for me.* Some things never changed.

Escaping his warmth, I sank into one of the club chairs. My hand settled on its chubby arm, finger checking out the faded plaid.

"Yup," Edward said before I could. "It's seen better days." He slid the salad toward me, along with a plastic sleeve of utensils. "The last few owners were rarely here. Once they realized the foxes had to stay, they didn't care to redo the rest."

"Will you?" I asked and opened the lid of my salad. Taking a fork from the sleeve, I speared a piece of chicken. He wasn't eating yet, wasn't even seated. Manners dictated that I wait. But this wasn't a date. It was a work lunch. Eating first was my statement.

He didn't answer. Wondering if he planned to, I looked at him. It was the first time I had, and intentionally so. Sweater, slacks, loafers—he was amazing. I was getting used to the longer hair and the beard, which was just dense enough to lift it above scruff. Neither hurt.

"I'm not sure," he said, seeming surprisingly ambivalent. The Edward I had known preferred his office shiny and sleek. He was a clean, chrome, and organized guy, or used to be. But that was why I was here, wasn't it—to put a new face on the old one so that I'd be less threatened each time I saw him?

"Lots of papers," I said, indicating the desk with my chin. "Is there an order to those?"

He snorted a quiet, "I wish."

"What are they?"

"Reports on more departments than you'd think existed, contracts with more vendors than you'd think needed contracts—food, laundry, soap, gifts, pool personnel, pool *upkeep*, grounds upkeep, roof upkeep, linen replacement, insurance policies for fire, theft, weather damage, deranged-person damage—"

"Seriously?"

"It's an issue," he said. I heard defensiveness in the three words, but resignation—*reality*—quickly followed. "Someone breezes through the front door and opens fire in the lobby with a semiautomatic, and you got tragedy compounded by litigation, but hell, what're we supposed to do, arm the bellboys?" Standing there with his hands on his hips and his eyes on that cluttered desk, he looked suddenly weary. "There are times . . ." he began, but his voice trailed off. He chafed his beard with his knuckles.

"What?"

"Nah. Nothing." He sat on the sofa.

"You said I should get to know you. Tell me what you were thinking."

He unwrapped his sandwich, then sprawled back without touching it. His eyes met mine, shooting me into the past, but only briefly. The worry I saw there was all here and now. "I've done other on-site work since I left the firm, but nothing like this," he said. "There are times I wonder if I'm up to the job."

"Of course you are," I said.

"There are so many details."

"Plus a hacking scandal you inherited. It's trial by fire."

Coming forward, he picked up his sandwich. He stared at it for a minute before raising his eyes. "Why are you defending me? If I fail, I leave. Isn't that what you want?" He took a bite.

"Yeah, well, if you fail," I reasoned as he chewed, "the Spa suffers, and the Spa is my bread and butter."

"You like working here?"

"Yes."

"What's the best part?"

"The smell," I said. "It's soothing. And the people."

"Like Joyce Mann?"

"Yes."

"I can see it. She's warm and maternal."

She was a surrogate mother for me, which he was likely thinking but I did not want to discuss lest it lead to discussion of my own mother, which I *really* did not want. "I also like my clients. They need me."

His beard might be new, but his smile was the same. "You were always good with faces."

"This is different." I rushed to put space between that smile and my current life. "Back then, I did poses, groupings, relationships. I took pictures and spent time analyzing them before I decided on an approach. There's none of that now. My clients show up with their problems. The challenge is immediate, but so is the gratification." I returned to the art on the walls. "What'll you do with the foxes?"

When he didn't answer, I looked back at him. His brow had furrowed beneath those spikes of dark hair. He didn't want me returning the subject to him? Too bad. I was here for a glimpse of who he was.

I stared, waiting.

Finally, the frown faded. He hitched his head toward the paintings. "Each time I make up my mind to move them, I start thinking of what I'd put up in their place, and nothing feels right. These are growing on me. I've never had foxes on my walls. They speak of the history of this place. Maybe if there were fewer of them, it wouldn't be bad. Different is good."

Yes. Different was good. Wasn't that what my life in Devon was about?

Opening the plastic cup tucked in with my salad, I dribbled dressing on the lettuce, tossed it as best I could, and took a forkful. Rasher and Yolk made the best breakfasts, but their lunches were strictly utilitarian. The lettuce was crisp enough, the parmesan shavings fresh, the croutons crunchy. But the dressing? Not homemade. I had to tell Liam that.

"Do you miss clay?" Edward asked, but I wasn't letting him get off the hook.

"Are you still in touch with Adam Walker and Tim Brown?" They had been his closest friends back when we were married. Likewise, I had been close to their wives—at least, until the accident. I understood that people didn't know what to say when something as tragic as that occurred. But the truth went beyond headlines and shame. Those women had kids. I did not. The largest part of what we had shared was gone. We drifted apart.

"Nope," he said. "Not in touch. Says something about the quality of the friendship, y'know."

"That it was convenient." Certainly with those women, I realized now.

"Circumstantial. Shallow. But, hey, I withdrew as much as they did. After you left, I kind of, just, sheltered in place."

Shelter in place was a concept usually associated with mass casualty events. Lily's death hadn't been that. But it had been every bit as tragic, every bit as life changing. My chest tightened remembering that.

"But you," Edward said, "you're still in touch with clay. Do you ever think about going back to what you used to do?"

Pressing my fingertips to my breastbone, I took several breaths. When the tightness eased, I said, "Not now. I'm happy doing makeup. I like my friends. I like my home." I paused, thought, said, "And I *love* my pets."

He seemed puzzled. "Why didn't we ever get one?"

Then and there, I wondered it, too. "I don't know. We talked about it. But it was always a *some-day* thing. Maybe if—" *If Lily had lived.* I didn't have to say the words for Edward to hear. I could see it in those silver-blue eyes.

Telling myself to move on, I swallowed and forced a smile. "Lily wanted a rabbit."

"She had a dozen rabbits."

"Not real ones." I poked at my salad. "I thought having a real one would be too messy—pellets and cages and all. I mean, what's the point of having a pet if it's locked up nine-tenths of the time?" My eyes held the salad. "I should have gotten her one."

"We were busy."

I looked up. "Too busy to make a little girl's dreams come true?"

"Little girls can't have everything they dream about."

"Oh, come on, Edward. We're talking about a *rabbit*. How much work could one little *rabbit* have been?"

He let that one float, and took another bite of his sandwich. "Okay. We were too wrapped up in ourselves."

Feeling the start of stone inside, I tried to conjure a calming image—a gurgling stream first, then snow-capped mountains. When neither stuck, I studied one of the oils. But four frightened foxes fleeing dogs didn't do it for me either. Seeking an alternative, my eye inadvertently skimmed over cartons that were tucked in the corner, half-hidden until you looked. Though the flaps were open, only corners of things showed. I couldn't see if they were books or picture frames, but my gut said they were personal items, not the calming I needed.

So I thought of my own Hex, Jinx, and Jonah. "I'm sorry we didn't get a pet. They add a lot. It's about unconditional love." Which children gave, too. Which wasn't a safe thought, either, but that didn't prevent my middle from feeling the warmth of little arms. I sat straighter, but the arms only shifted to my neck, allowing the weight of a small body to curl in my lap.

"Do you think about her much?" Edward asked in a quiet voice.

My eyes flew to his. *Off-limits! Not why I'm here!* But my mind was already in the danger zone, and my silent screams didn't erase the feel of her arms.

He must have seen my panic, because he said a quick, "Okay. Tell me about Nina Evans."

Breathe, I told myself. *Breathe slowly.* A minute later, I was able to say a surprisingly calm, "Nina." The name brought me the rest of the way back.

"She calls every day," he said. "She keeps asking me how it's going—the job, the house, settling in—and can she do anything to help. The first time, I thought it was a Welcome Wagon thing. But she keeps calling, like she's waiting, like there's something I'm supposed to do back."

Well, there was a distraction. Amused, I stared at him, arched a brow, waited. When he said nothing, I tried, "And you can't figure it out?"

"No, I can't. I've never met the woman. I need you to tell me."

His belligerence added to the humor. Nina and Edward? I couldn't see it, but Nina apparently could. "She's in her early fifties and looks good. She's originally from New York, so she's as sophisticated as you are. She's our Town Manager, meaning that she's in a position of power, and it sounds like she's interested in you."

He had been sitting with his elbows on his knees, one hand holding his half-eaten sandwich. Now he drew back. "Interested."

"Well, I haven't talked with her about it, but, hell, Edward, you're the most attractive new thing to move to town in years."

Most men would have been flattered. This one was certainly aware of his looks—*of course* he was. I remember him combing his hair, shaving twice daily, frowning over whether this tie went with that shirt, checking the final product in the full-length mirror fronting our built-ins. There were times when he was so stealthy about the last that watching him was a hoot.

Not only was he attractive, but he was successful, personable, and unattached.

Right now, he was also impatient. "Is she a friend of yours?"

"Yes."

"Can you tell her I'm not interested?"

"How would I do that without giving away my relationship with you?"

"Then—then just tell her you heard I had a ton of baggage."

"That's no deterrent. Everyone has baggage."

"She's older than I am."

So? I was thinking. Then it occurred to me that he still wanted kids, which might put Nina out of the running. And that was okay. Once past the humor of it, the thought of them together bothered me.

Looking off, he scowled at one of the fox oils. When his eyes returned, they were narrowed. "Is she competitive?"

"She'd have to be, to get as far as she did in New York." Even here in Devon, when the opening for Town Manager had come, Nina had pulled out every stop. "So that's a yes. Why?"

"Does she compete with you?"

"Why ever would she?"

"Because you're beautiful."

"I'm not."

"You were too skinny before. You look better now."

I wasn't sure where he was headed, but it couldn't be anywhere good. Talk about baggage? There was so much of it between us, and it was *so dark,* that I just couldn't play games. He needed a reminder. I lifted my bangs to show him my scar.

He stared, frowned. "Where is it?"

"You don't see it? Right here?" I let him look for a beat before dropping my hand and rearranging my bangs. "You never liked makeup."

"Not on you. You never needed it."

"That was before."

"Well, I never needed a beard before, so we're even."

Pushing the salad away, I rose, went to the desk and etched my palm along its carved edge. "We'll never be even."

From behind, came an angry, "Jesus, Mackenzie," then, with more control, "Y'know, we can go back and forth about who's to blame, but you'll never convince me it's all you. So stop it already. We both feel guilt. We *both* feel regret. We both need to see someone different in the mirror when we get up in the morning."

I turned. I wasn't sure I could accept guilt on his part, but he clearly felt it. Nope, no actor, my Edward. There had been nothing staged about his wet eyes yesterday morning, and his fierce look now sealed the deal. He felt guilt.

Since arguing further would have been pointless, I studied his beard. "How long have you had it?"

"Three years," he said. His voice was quiet. "I started growing it when I realized I needed a change."

"Did it itch?"

"Growing? Yes."

"Take much work now?"

"Less than shaving."

"And it makes you feel different?" Hiding a scar was a subtraction. A beard was an addition. So were my bangs, I supposed, but I wondered whether seeing the beard in the mirror helped.

Actually, I wondered lots of things, only his eyes held mine, held mine, held mine with that irrevocably visceral pull. It had nothing to do with guilt or regret or grief, or any of the other emotions standing between us. I could raise any one of those, and it would instantly break the spell.

Actually, the thought alone did it. I looked away. At some point, we would need to have that discussion, but I couldn't squeeze it into an hour's lunch and then go to the most public job in the Spa without my face betraying angst. Besides, I wasn't sure I was ready to be so raw again, especially not with Edward.

When he remained silent, I glanced over to see him frowning at his sandwich. After jiggling it for a minute, he dropped it on the wrapper, wiped his hand on his slacks, raised his eyes, and shifted the fight. "Are you closer to Nina than you are to Grace?"

Back to the present. This was okay. Returning to the chair, I said, "No. I'm closer to Grace."

"Closer, how?"

I lifted my fork, waved it in dismissal. "Girl stuff."

"Does she know about us?"

"No."

"How do you have a friendship without sharing things like that?"

"Easily. You have ground rules. I don't ask about her past, she doesn't ask about mine."

"But you know she came here from Denver."

"Chicago. It was Chicago."

"Not according to her file. According to that, she learned massage therapy in Denver. Her references were from a spa there."

This was news. But my marriage to Edward would be news to Grace, too.

I forced a smile. "Glowing?"

"Glowing. What kind of mother is she?"

"What kind of question is that?" I asked, mildly offended.

"A normal one." Unapologetic, he reached for a take-out cup of fruit that had been hidden between the piles of papers and opened it. "Is she?"

Before I could answer, he was forking red grapes into my salad and cantaloupe chunks onto his sandwich wrapper. *Caesar salad for me, tuna sandwich for him, red grapes for us, cantaloupe chunks for him.* And that quickly, the past was back. The grapes were for Lily, who had loved them since the very first time I had fed her one. I used to cut each grape into small pieces for her to gum up. Gradually the pieces grew larger. A whole grape bulging in five-year-old Lily's cheek, taken with long, silky blonde hair and a mischievous look in those pale-blue eyes, was a memory to hold.

Had she lived, she would have been ten. She would be eating not just my grapes but my salad, or maybe something else entirely, because she would be reading the menu herself. She would be brushing her own hair, and curling up with me in bed on mornings when Edward left early, writing me little notes, texting kiss-blowing emojis. She would be growing into a friend.

"Maggie?"

His frightened voice hauled me back, but my whole being hurt. *Breathe,* I told myself, even as I felt a heavy lid lowering on my insides. Needing to flee it, I quickly stood, looked frantically around, and made for the bathroom that I had wanted to see.

It was spotless, if aged. The tiling was black-and-white checks that were cracked at spots. The sink was on a pedestal that spoke more of an earlier era than a current trend. The shower stall was dark inside, likely with a lone wall-mounted water head, no rain-head or hand-held. Fresh white towels hung from a vintage dowel, waiting.

I sat on the closed lid of the toilet, put my elbows on my thighs and my face in my hands. *Every shadow passes . . . every shadow passes . . . every shadow passes.* I breathed in, breathed out. It helped that this small room smelled different. In addition to a dispenser of hand soap, the ancient glass shelf above the sink held a fragrance diffuser. Half a dozen sticks, beautifully splayed, gave off a subtle aroma. It was pine, not the lemon verbena I loved, but it was enough to relieve the worst of the weight filling my chest. It couldn't touch the emptiness left behind, though.

The door sighed, and muted footsteps crossed the tile. I was aware of him hovering and might have appreciated his indecision, if I wasn't still seeing a ghost of that kiss-blowing emoji. When he drew me against his middle and held me there, I had no choice. I didn't hug him back. But I didn't pull away. Something was better than nothing when it came to deep loss.

We stayed that way for several minutes. Each time I told myself to end it, I allowed for just a minute more.

"I knew this wouldn't work," I finally said into his sweater. No pine smell here, just Edward's clean, male one. The familiarity of it was nice.

Same with his voice. "Maybe it is. Maybe this is what we need. I think about her a lot," he said in an odd, soothing tone. "She comes to me when I least expect it."

My own voice was muffled. "Like when?"

"When I'm having pizza. When I'm walking down the street and a little girl with long blond hair skips past. When I see rabbits."

Mention of Lily always brought back the compression around my heart, but being focused on Edward must have diluted the emotion, because what came now was a bearable spasm. "When do you see rabbits?"

"In the gift shop here. They're soft."

"You squeeze them?"

"Discreetly. Like I'm just picking one up to see how much it costs."

The image was funny. No, I decided, not funny. Sweet. And also familiar. I knew just where those rabbits were. They were tucked together in a bucket on a rotating stand that held buckets of donkeys, elephants, and giraffes.

"What about you?" he asked.

"I've squeezed those rabbits, too." But that wasn't what he wanted to know. He wanted confirmation that he wasn't alone in missing Lily. "I'm usually good during the day," I said. "She comes at night."

"Every night?"

"Pretty much. She loves my pets." Now, again, those pets were a lifeline, my link to the present. I drew back from Edward, but his hands were suddenly on my shoulders and when I looked up, our eyes met.

There it was again, a look heated by pure chemistry. In that instant, I wanted nothing more than to stand up against him, wrap my arms around his neck, and lose myself in his mouth. But that would *really* open a floodgate on the past. It would invite a repeat of what had happened at his place. And in his office bathroom?

"Nope," I said, denying us both, "not going there." When I stood, our bodies brushed, we were that close, but I quickly backed off and returned to his office.

It was a minute before he followed. One look at his face, and I swore softly.

He looked startled. "What?"

"You need to be less transparent, Edward. Actually, maybe you do need a Nina."

"Nope, not going there," he said, echoing me, and changed the subject with a curious, "You don't cry. Why not?"

He was the first one to ask. The first one. Because no one else knew. I was alone those nights in bed when it hit, and if I had been with someone, he would have thought me heartless and cold. That wasn't a risk with Edward. He knew I loved Lily. And he'd already noticed my dry eyes, so if he was going to think less of me, it was done.

"I ran out of tears a couple of years ago," I said.

"But you're in pain."

I nodded. "They tell me it's like having a heart attack."

"Like a panic attack?"

"No. I have chest pain."

He processed that while I forced memory aside and deliberately ate a grape. Cognitive Behavioral Therapy, my therapist called it. It hadn't worked in the past, but maybe with Edward here, it would.

"Tea?" he asked.

"Actually, yes. Thank you."

He crossed to the Nespresso machine. No, Edward couldn't cook, but he always made me tea. Back then, we had a Keurig. The Inn had a contract—yet another contract—with Nespresso.

Returning, he passed me a mug. I lifted it to my nose and inhaled. "Vanilla Oolong?" I asked in surprise.

"Yes."

"I didn't know Nespresso made Vanilla Oolong pods."

"I did some work for a start-up that made them. They give me whatever I want whenever I ask. These just arrived."

"Are you a tea-drinker now?" After he widened his eyes in an *are-you-kidding* way, I lowered mine and studied the clear amber liquid in its porcelain mug. Vanilla Oolong wasn't offered during high tea at the Inn. He had ordered it for me, which was thoughtful and sweet, totally touching. I just wish he hadn't. Kind gestures complicated things. Figuring out who I was—who he was—was hard enough without throwing a *we* in the mix.

He went back for coffee, but by the time he came back with his mug filled, I was no closer to knowing what to think. There was some solace in realizing he didn't either, because he didn't resurrect the tea-for-me theme, the chest-pain theme, or, thank goodness, the Lily theme, because the latter, especially, would have done me in. Once he was seated, he simply put his elbows on his knees, held the mug in both hands, and said, "Tell me about the Town Meeting."

14

Town Meeting was a Vermont institution. State law dictated that it be held on the first Tuesday in March, and while there was always business to discuss, it was as much a social event, giving people reason to slog through snow or mud to be with others of like mind. We Devonites were just defiant enough to have voted—overwhelmingly—to hold ours on the last Wednesday of the month, though it was also a practical move. We didn't like having to slog through snow, and by the end of March, the mud was drying. Besides, some of our most treasured members were snow-birds. This gave them more time to return, which they always did. Town Meeting was a reaffirmation of who we were. It was about self-identity.

Self-identity was a huge issue for me right now. In the life I'd built here, I was a makeup artist, a sculptor, and a friend. But that life had been hacked, broken into by two men I hadn't invited. Suddenly, I was a sister and a whatever-it-was to Edward. I didn't know how these roles fit into my life here, all the more so after Monday's lunch.

My emotions were the problem. I wanted to deny them; denial was my thing. When someone hacked into your life, you shut them out. So yes, I could tell Liam he had two days to find a place to live. But I couldn't shake the sense of family, that I thought I *had* shut out, but apparently missed, because I did like seeing him in my home. And Edward? I could demand he steer clear—could tell him that he stirred up memories too painful to bear. But seeing him brought good memories, too.

Besides, I could say whatever I wanted, but would my dreams listen? No!

Once upon a time, I had been a good sleeper. Then I became a mother and started listening for every peep from the baby monitor and, when the monitor was retired, from the room down the hall. After Lily died, I kept listening, hearing sounds that my therapist likened to the imagined pain of a severed limb. So I slept in short spurts, which meant that when I dreamed, those dreams were fresh enough to linger when I woke.

They were coming in droves again, and they were killers. Lily was in some, Edward in others. At times, I woke up struggling to breathe, when my only remedy was hugging whatever ball of fur lay closest to me. At one point Monday night, I even sat on the floor by my bed, pulling air into my lungs with my ear pressed to Jonah's sweet heart, and, fooling neither of us, studying the green velvet box under the bed. I didn't pull it out. I knew what was inside. Pandora's box? No. It held no evil, just all-too-real pieces of the past.

Yes, Town Meeting would remind me of who I was now.

But so would clay. I arrived at the pottery studio Tuesday morning in the mood to make another teapot. My teapots always flew off the shelves, which made them a win-win for me—loved making them, loved sharing them. Unfortunately, thanks to Liam's breakfasts, I wasn't thinking of raisin croissants, pecan buns, or anything else from The Buttered Scone. With my brother never far from my laptop and nosy as ever, I had no chance to check my mother's Facebook feed, which meant that Mom-as-muse was on hold.

That left a vacuum, which forced me to open my mind. *Let go, enjoy life and celebrate,* CALM told me, and, in theory, that captured the beauty of clay for me. Like clouds shifting in the sky, a mass being pushed around on my work bench could take on the shape of any little thing.

This day I did consciously let go, freeing my fingers to wander in, over, and around. I was once removed from it, watching with fascination as my hands formed a head and my fingers shaped its brow, eye sockets, and cheeks, before picking up tools to define a round eye, a slender nose, and long, wavy hair. The piece was small, barely four inches from crown to chin, but vivid.

"She's a looker," Kevin praised as he hunkered by my stool. "Lily?"

His voice, soft though it was, brought reality back. "Oh, no. No, no." I studied what I'd made, only then identifying the model. "Maddie. She's twelve. And she is beautiful." No matter that I had sculpted only one side of her face. The other side didn't matter. This was how I saw her.

"You haven't done a person before. You should do it more."

"Maybe," I said but let that go, too.

It was harder to let go as I drove to the Inn, harder not to think of Edward and wonder whether he would come by or call. What I needed was a day of nonstop work, but bookings were sparse. I was therefore relieved when Joe Hellinger called and, grateful for direction, I drove straightaway to his office to consult with the parents of a high school junior who had totaled the family car and seriously messed up her face. Also in White River Junction, I was able to connect with a freelance makeup artist who was hawking a line of organic skin cream.

So I didn't see Edward that day. Like a bug in my computer, though, his presence was felt in the form of updates to the Inn staff on the status of reservations and incentives designed to make up for the dip. He was both perceptive and proactive.

Liam was neither. Despite the tour I'd give him on Sunday, he showed no sign of leaving. I knew that he went out while I worked; his car was parked in a slightly different spot each time I got home. Based on his chatter, which filled my previously quiet cabin in ways that were alternately annoying and sweet, I knew he was meeting with designers and carpenters for the restaurant. But while he seemed to be mapping every market for miles around, he said nothing about finding his own place to live.

And how could I insist, given the cooking he did? Sunday night we had a hearty French onion soup with Gruyère rounds, Monday night beef bourguignon with a *bouquet garni* of heirloom carrots and herbs, and Tuesday night a Mediterranean fish stew. For Wednesday night, he was planning a skillet chicken cordon bleu with penne. But Town Meeting was that night.

"It's potluck," I said. "People bring casseroles and set them out in the social hall, so I'll have dinner there."

He made a face. "Mac 'n' cheese?"

I smiled. "In Devon? Not quite. Potluck here is high-end—like risotto, Mexican chicken salad, and black bean soup. Snowbirds bring recipes back from Boca and Palm Springs. It's pretty impressive."

"Can anyone bring food?" he asked, a little too-casually. I could see the wheels in his mind turning.

"Only locals. Guards will be at the door to keep out the press." Just when it seemed the attention might be waning, another media figure showed up, and the *People* piece wouldn't help. Even if it broadened to encompass computer abuse by teenagers in general, Devon remained ground zero.

Liam wasn't thinking about that particular circus. His sights were focused. "Do I qualify as a local?"

"Only," I warned with equal focus, "if you say nothing about my past. Do *not* breathe the name Mackenzie Cooper. Do you hear?"

"Yes, Mom."

I refused to give him the rise he wanted. Rather, with poise, I said, "Trust me, I am not Mom. Mom would be calling you out for putting heavy-duty tires on your car and adding them to *my* tab at the service station. Oh yes, brother, they did call me about that. I also got a call from the wife of one of *your* carpenters, who happens to be in my book group and learned from her husband that my brother is in town, and since she is not known for reticence, it's a safe bet that most of Devon knows by now."

Bless him, he was undaunted, and the irony of that? Five years ago, being related to me was poison. That I had become an asset said something about how far I'd come.

So I was feeling content when he asked, "Then my bringing food tonight will be okay?"

"Only if it's good."

"Slam dunk there. I'll double the amount I make."

"Quadruple it, Liam. Actually, make it for several dozen, and you're set."

It was a stroke of genius. Liam was in his glory preparing dinner for a large number of people, running to local stores for food and serving supplies, getting to know the town in a way that would pay off tenfold. He introduced himself alternately as my brother and as the chef of the new French bistro, which I learned when I was barely through the stone-arched door of the church where Town Meeting was held. The fact that he modified his initial recipe didn't hurt. His chicken cordon bleu roll-ups, held together with a delicate but sturdy puff pastry and sliced into easy-to-hold portions was the best-tasting, not to mention most beautiful dish there.

Typically, Kevin hovered over me at events like this, but when it came to the meeting itself, I liked sitting with Cornelia. Well ahead of the meeting, she would have pored over the agenda, which this year included not only making renovations to the elementary school, but funding a new fire truck, raising the police department budget, and allowing food trucks to park in the center of town during June, July, and August. Cornelia would give me a whispered commentary about each item that was alternately enlightening and hilarious.

This first hour, though, was social. I knew most everyone here, and while I saw some often, others had either been away for the winter, away just these last muddy weeks, or simply home with the flu, any of which reasons made me pleased to see them. If I'd wanted a reminder of what I loved about Devon, it was these people. They accepted me for who I was, right here, right now. Having never seen my scar, they had no idea it was there.

As promised, the press was barred from the church. I only wish the hacking scandal had been, too, because it was like one of us, slipping from group to group, at times waiting, at times butting right in. The latest news? Jay Harrington planned to file motions claiming that Ben Zwick and the media had fatally prejudiced the case against Chris. These motions would request disclosure of documents relating to media involvement, enforcement of the gag order, and dismissal of the charges entirely.

I figured the first and third were more feasible than the second, which, with the cat already out of the bag, was basically pointless. Others weren't so sure, but the debate was interesting. Intelligence was another thing I loved about Devon.

So was sensitivity. Quiet and concerned, the conversation typically began with Chris. Too soon, it turned to Grace. Had she appeared, it would have ended. When she didn't, there was speculation. Words like *self-consciousness, embarrassment,* and *fear* were bandied about.

But where is she? I was asked yet again. Like I knew? She loved Town Meeting, loved greeting friends with her big smile and her vibrant scarf, wild sweater, and spectacular hair. I knew that she'd had an afternoon meeting with Jay and had planned to come from there. But he arrived alone.

We figured, he and I, that she had lost her nerve.

I texted her, but got no response. *She may still be working,* I said to one friend and, to another, with resignation, *She knows there'll be talk.*

Catching the last as he came alongside, Kevin murmured, "You don't have to defend her."

"If I don't, who will?"

"It's her job. She's punting. Which is what you should be doing," he advised.

"You say that because you don't like her."

"I say it, doll, because I like *you*."

His deeper message wasn't lost on me. Michael Shanahan might have been a fly on the wall, for knowing what I said and to whom. But hadn't Kevin been the one, not so long ago, to tell me to do what I thought was right?

I was glancing back at the door, praying she was simply late, when Edward came through. He had left his jacket on the lobby rack and had come straight from work, to judge from his sweater and slacks. He was perfectly dressed. Other men wore versions of the same, though more often with jeans, and a few, like Kevin, were flamboyantly accessorized. There was nothing flamboyant about Edward, if you didn't count his eyes. His sweater was burgundy, his slacks gray, his hair brushed back with just those thick spikes on his brow. Other men had facial hair, ranging from scruffy to full. Others were just as tall. But Edward stood out.

Forewarned should have been forearmed; I had known he would be here. But how to arm myself against Edward Cooper? I tried not to feel anything that might give me away, tried to ignore the quickening inside, and the worry. Meeting him in private was one thing, but the risk of betraying our connection amped up with this many people around.

Kevin squeezed my arm. "I got this," he whispered and, divinely protective, strode toward the door. His back blocked the details, but body language was telling even from behind. I saw a greeting of some sort, then his hands were on his hips. Confrontation? I prayed not.

Nervous, I tried to disappear into my group, which was speculating on what the *People* piece would say and whether the media would be done with us then, when all eyes shifted.

"Hello," said Edward from my shoulder, extending a hand, in turn, to the owners of those eyes. "Ned Cooper."

Kevin had followed but refused to meet my gaze. After standing off for a minute, he turned on his heel and headed for food. Trusting that I would learn later what had been said, I tuned into Edward's audience.

"From the Inn?" said one, not really a question.

"Not the best time," mused her husband.

"I've seen you at the post office," remarked the stage actress who, without makeup, looked plain. I did her face when theater connections came to visit, but in all else Devon, she preferred to go without. Noting my lack of reaction to Edward's arrival, she shot me a curious glance.

"I already know him," I explained. "He's my boss."

"Huh. Of course."

"Am I interrupting?" Edward asked them.

"Absolutely not."

"We were just talking about, well, hacking and all."

"And it's not gossip," said the actress, almost in warning to the rest of us, lest we forget that Edward was not only Grace's boss but an outsider. "We love Grace. She's is one of us."

"Hel-lo," came a singsong voice and another proffered hand. "Ned Cooper? Finally. I'm Nina Evans. I'm glad you came."

She looked wonderful, *thank you, Maggie Reid.* Since the Town Manager was also the Town Meeting moderator, she had visited me at three to have her confidence applied. While I worked, she asked about Edward, and when I had little to say, she dove into Liam. She knew he was my brother. Now she wanted to know how old he was, where he had trained, whether there were other siblings, where we grew up, if my parents were still there. I would rather have talked about the night's agenda, but Nina had never asked personal questions before, and, given that nothing about Connecticut or the name Reid would betray Mackenzie Cooper, I couldn't think of a good reason not to answer, especially since I had stonewalled on the subject of Edward.

Tonight, her own sweater and slacks were professional, her wool Etro scarf powerfully New York, and her skin glowing.

Edward shook her hand, repeated her name as if he'd never heard it before, and smiled politely. He did nothing to suggest they had ever talked, and while he was gracious, I saw no particular interest in those silver-blue eyes.

Perversely, I was pleased.

That said, when Nina took his arm and insisted on introducing him around, I felt relief.

As soon as he was gone, our huddle shifted. The husband left, two other women arrived, and even from those who hadn't met Edward directly, there was a flurry of *He's awesome,* and *Would you believe those eyes,* and *Grace should be here just to see him.*

"She has seen him," I said. "Remember where she works?"

"Will he fire her?"

"No."

"Then he doesn't blame her for compromising the Spa network?"

"She didn't. Her son is the one who's charged." Not quite able to use the name *Ned,* I hitched my head after Edward. "He knows that," I added and quickly wished I hadn't. Anyone listening could tell that he and I had talked about Grace, which we would never have done unless we were friends, or so it seemed to me.

The good news? No one noticed. The bad? We seemed to have rounded a corner, and the tone shifted. I wanted to say it was an offshoot of curiosity, and, okay, I was supersensitive to criticism in situations like this. But the innocent *Where is she?* became the darker *Where was she?* And once aired, like the flu, it was contagious. This was on people's minds, just as I'd known it would be. It was human nature to want to explain things, even to blame. The people here might be one step above, but they were human.

I excused myself to talk with friends from the pottery store, then a coven of writers. But I couldn't escape it. Grace always returned. Where was she while her son was hacking into other people's computers? Where was she when he was alone in his room? Didn't she know what he did with his free time? Didn't she ask?

We were eating by then, at times seated at long tables, at other times standing with plates in our hands. At least I didn't have to worry about

Liam. Or maybe I did. He was surrounded not only by people wanting seconds of his roll-ups but by more than one available sweet thing, and he was loving it. No way would he be leaving town after this.

Nor, I feared, would my ex. The new head of the Inn was an important figure in town, and Edward—*think Ned, Maggie, think Ned*—was a beacon. People sought him out, curious about his vision for the Inn, the town, even the house he had bought. He could have easily stayed off on his own with plenty of company.

But he kept returning to me. Like we were a couple. Like in spite of people wanting to get to know him, he was apart. It was something I felt more than saw—felt, because I kept remembering those damn tears and knowing I had never fully considered the fallout of Lily's death on him. My own pain had been too great to allow for his. So now, here we were. Call it guilt. Call it atonement. However misguided his move here had been, he had abandoned old friends and didn't yet have new ones. Like advising him on who should renovate his home, I could help him with this.

Not that it was hard. Not that he couldn't comfortably converse with these people. Not that I didn't appreciate the admiring glances sent his way and feel just a little bit of pride that he chose to stand by me.

Nina noticed. When he left to replenish drinks, she said, "He likes you." Her voice held an edge. She was nervous about the upcoming meeting, but I couldn't tell if there was more. Edward had suggested jealousy. If so, it was misplaced.

"No," I assured, "he just knows me from the Inn. I'm a familiar face in a sea of unfamiliar ones."

But Jessa, too, noticed his attentiveness. She and her husband had joined us right before Edward set off, and she waited only until her husband was distracted talking with the head of Fish and Game, also in our current circle, before leaning close to me. "Is something going on between you and the Inn guy?"

I rolled my eyes, like the question was tiresome. "I work for him. He's paying me." In the broadest sense, it was true. Beyond that, I was only a vehicle, helping him break into Devon. Given our past, I could never be anything more.

And of *course* that saddened me. Hell, I was human, too. I had loved Edward through our marriage and could argue that I agreed to the divorce for that reason. I had become convinced that being apart was the only way we could survive. Divorce was the humane escape.

Still, my heart ached as I watched him pass out soft drinks and a plate of the Inn's signature chocolate chip cookies, like the host he had been when we entertained at our home. He might not have helped with the cooking, but he had always taken charge of wine, flowers, and—oh God, how could I have forgotten—the *grill*. All those cookouts, with or without friends, and manning the grill was his thing. He might not buy, season, or garnish the steak, but he did like his grill tools.

I hadn't thought about this in years. I hadn't allowed myself to. But a window had opened, lowering my defenses, so I was overly sensitive when, even with half-eaten cookies in hand, there was one more remark about Grace not seeing, knowing, stopping.

"Does any mother know everything her child is doing?" I replied with more bite than was necessary, because though I was holding a cookie in my own hand, though chocolate chip ones were my all-time favorite, and though this one was nearly as good as those my mother's bakery sold, my mind was still on cookouts at Edward's and my house. This time, I recalled being in the kitchen, slicing sweet peppers for him to grill, while upstairs and out of my sight, Lily used colored markers to decorate the walls of her bedroom, the hall, and the stairs leading down.

She was three. This was what three-year-olds did. But a dozen guests were arriving within the hour, so my first response was to panic. That was followed in succession by anger, frustration, and, finally, humor. Lily, even at three, could draw. As self-portraits went, hers was unbelievable. I had actually taken a picture. It was one of the items in my green velvet box. Not that I needed a refresher. The image was so vivid, even these seven years later, that my chest started to seize.

Edward touched my back just lightly enough, just briefly enough to help me breathe again. I was vaguely aware of responses, though truly more focused on regaining balance. And I might have done it, if someone hadn't used the word *distracted*.

"Okay," I said, letting my hand drop, cookie forsaken, "I'm really uncomfortable talking about this. Are any of us perfect? I mean, take any mother with her kids in the car. She looks away from the road to shoot a quick text to her husband to say she's running late, or to fiddle with Spotify, or to pass a snack back to the kids. One second, and, if another car suddenly comes from the side, there's an accident."

"Grace had more than a second," said one of several men with us then. "It took time for Chris to plan this."

"*If* he did it," I argued, "because we don't know for sure. Hacking isn't hard. There are other kids in town who could have done it and made it look like it was Chris. We haven't seen evidence, and I know that's for the trial"—I interrupted myself, needing to preclude that particular point—"but even if it was Chris, he's fifteen, for God's sake, which in some countries is old enough to be independent and leave home and even have kids, and as for Grace, she's done good for lots of us, so hasn't she earned the benefit of the doubt? And *besides*," I ranted on, "maybe we shouldn't be talking about her, because I'm not sure any of us is any better, and if you think she's feeling good about all this, think again. Mothers blame themselves"—I thumped my chest—"like the buck stops here when it comes to responsibility."

Feeling that large hand on my back again, I sucked in a breath. Only then seeing the startled looks around me and feeling appalled, I lengthened my second breath and managed a sheepish smile. "Sorry. Grace is my friend." I did believe she hadn't known what her son was doing, any more than I had known about the STOP sign hidden in a swarm of red oak leaves. But we both felt responsibility. I always would.

A tall beanpole of a man ambled up, and Edward quickly bent toward me. "Is that who I think it is?" He was a reader, so was clearly excited. Me, I welcomed the diversion. David Isenschmidt could be entertaining, in his gawky way.

214

The world knew him as Dylan Ivory. After years working with a hugely successful mystery writer, he was now writing on his own. He had just returned from a publicity tour that had included appearances on the biggest of the big talk shows, and, after I introduced Edward, who had read his two latest, they began talking books. Suddenly, though, the author looked at me.

"Who is she?" he asked.

I drew back. "Excuse me?"

"Grace Emory. You're her friend. What don't we know?"

That quickly, I was alarmed. "Um, like what?"

"Like where she came from or what she did before Devon."

"Does it matter?" Edward asked, but David's eyes held mine.

"If you want your story to be complete, there has to be a past."

"That's not how Devon works," I tried, but he talked right over my words.

"No one knows squat, like where she grew up and why she has no family—like who the kid's father is. For all we know, it's Zwick. Sure, the boy hacked other accounts, but they could have been red herrings. What he did to Zwick was pretty ugly."

"What he *allegedly* did, David," I said. "And nothing that happened to Zwick is any uglier than what he is doing now to a fifteen-year-old boy."

"QED. Zwick is known for ugliness. Maybe the kid inherited it."

"Are you planning to write about this?" Edward asked with a qualm I was glad to hear.

David shot him a glance, which wasn't the way *I* would reward a loyal reader, but the man was bizarre. "No. But it's an interesting premise, is it not?"

"It's a wacky premise," Kevin said, having walked over in time to hear enough. "Zwick wouldn't go public if he was Chris's dad. Why would a father put his son through this? Sorry, Davie. You won't get a bestseller out of this one."

"My point," said the writer Dylan Ivory, "is that things aren't always what they seem."

I wasn't laughing now. *Things aren't always what they seem.* Nor did I have a comeback. *No, they weren't.* He was building a story around Grace and Chris. Another time it might be around Edward and me.

In that instant, I felt like a fraud.

Kevin must have sensed it, because he slipped a comforting arm around my waist. At first I thought it was Edward. But no. Edward was watching, but the arm was Kevin's.

In the next instant, Nina's amplified voice rose over the rest of the conversation. Shortly thereafter, we were seated in the nave, and Cornelia was beside me, holding my hand, asking how I was with the kind of concern that might have made me wonder, if I hadn't been worried about Edward. I saw friends in pews front and back, but I didn't see him. I had to search, smiling when catching the eyes of others, and then search more, before I finally spotted him at the back of the hall with Liam. Only then could I face front and settle in.

The meeting itself was a settling experience. Cornelia whispered little facts, like how much had been spent on the last school renovation, who was supplying fire trucks to neighboring towns and at what cost, and the scene created by competing food trucks when last they had been allowed near the green. Kevin was in charge of munchies, alternately pulling candied walnuts, cookie halves, and Hershey's Kisses from his backpack.

We voted yes on renovations to the elementary school, no on funding a new fire truck, yes on both raising the police department budget and allowing food trucks to park in the center of town during summer months, but with restrictions on the latter relating to hours, size and color of truck, and type of food.

It felt trivial in comparison to a Federal charge of hacking, but the sheer normalcy of it revived me. Small matters were the currency of daily life here.

Actually, that told only half the story, I realized as the evening wound down. In the language of currency, trivial matters were loose change. The big money was being with people I liked.

For that reason, I lingered with friends after the meeting adjourned.

One by one, they left, but still I stayed. The church was the epitome of normalcy. I felt safe here.

"All set, babe?" Kevin asked when less than a handful of people remained.

I was in the outer lobby then, and, waving as those stragglers went out the door, I joined Kevin at the coat rack. Ours were the last parkas there. Hangers clinked as he freed mine and opened it for me.

"Your brother headed home. He said he'll see you there."

Liam. I grimaced as I inserted one arm, then the other. "I kind of forgot he was here." Such was the power of compartmentalization. With both Liam and Edward out of sight during the meeting, I had barred them from my mind and, in so doing, had recaptured a little of the me I was in Devon. But now came the other me, worming its way right back in.

"No sweat," Kevin said. "He did good, by the way. He's a fabulous cook, and people like him. I probably would, too, if he hadn't been such a shit to you."

I shot him a chiding look.

When he swung his parka around, his arms smoothly slid in the sleeves. "Yeah, I hold grudges."

"Isn't it my grudge to hold?"

"Not so long as you're my friend," he declared and, as soon as we were both gloved, looped an elbow through mine and walked me out.

The night was cold, thanks to gusts of wind that rattled naked branches against each other. Gaslights lit the parking lot, which resembled the coat rack in its sparsely filled way. In a far corner were vans of the set-up, take-down crew. My pickup was several spaces from Kevin's SUV. One row back and several more spaces over was a black Jeep.

15

Edward stood on the sidewalk at the bottom of the steps. Wearing only his barn jacket, he was huddled against the March wind with his collar up and his shoulders hunched.

I stopped, forcing Kevin to as well.

"And there's another one to begrudge," he said to me, then called to Edward over a whistle of the wind, "It's okay, I'm walking her to her truck. You can go home." Tugging my arm, he got me moving again.

When we were down the steps and close enough to see a nose that was red from the cold, Edward said, "I need to talk with her," but his eyes were on me.

"It's late," Kevin replied. "She's tired."

"Just for a minute, Maggie?"

Kevin's arm tightened in mine. "It's been a long night," he informed Edward. "Lots of drama."

"No drama here," Edward insisted. "Maggie?"

But Kevin wasn't done. Over another shush of wind, he told Edward, "It's freezing out here, and we can't go back inside because they want to close up. How about tomorrow?"

Edward's brows met in annoyance. "Can she speak for herself, please?"

"Why should she," I asked, "when the two of you are so entertaining?" I freed my elbow, pausing only to briefly squeeze Kevin's arm with a gloved hand. "I'm fine."

But his eyes were concerned. "I warned him, doll. I told him to leave you alone. I said you had plenty of support here and that he'd be in the way, and what did he do? Stuck to you like glue. He'll hurt you, hun."

"I will not," countered Edward, offended.

"You did."

"This is not your business."

"And it's yours? Last I heard, you two were divorced."

"Divorced means we were married once, and being married means I shared a hell of a lot more with her than you ever will."

"Excuuuuse, me," Kevin sang on an up note, "but that sounded suspiciously like a homophobic remark. Is that your problem?"

I might have laughed, if the two of them hadn't been so serious.

"Ah, Christ," swore Edward, who didn't swear often. "Are you seriously resorting to that? No, I'm not homophobic. I have gay best friends and gay business partners." Looking at me, he hitched his head toward Kevin. "Tell him, Maggie. Let's get this off the table right now, because I don't want to fucking hear it again."

"He's right, Kev," I said quietly. "Try something else."

"Okayyy. How about his showing up here like he owns the place—"

"I *do* own—"

"—like you're supposed to welcome him with open arms?"

"I didn't expect open arms," Edward shouted. He sounded exasperated—competing with Kevin?

"What the fuck *did* you expect?"

"Guys," I said to keep the hostilities in some kind of check.

Edward lowered his voice, though it remained directed at Kevin. "I expected to be able to talk with my wife without a go-between."

He was turning to me again when Kevin fired back. "She isn't your wife, she's your *ex*-wife, and why in the hell would I leave her alone with you? I've seen her knotted up so hard she's in pain. She came here all alone and got a good job and made friends, which was pretty obvious tonight, in case you didn't notice. She's finally getting her life straight, and now you show up, bringing her *brother,* no less, the two of you just messing her up again."

Edward stared at him, pale eyes lethal, voice grim. "You don't have a clue."

"I think I do. Maggie is my friend. I love her."

Edward opened his mouth, about to speak. At the last minute, though, he turned from Kevin to me and said, "So. Do. I."

Utter silence followed. The words were just words. But the eyes— those eyes—*Edward's* eyes held mine, adding more angst than the words alone could bear.

Kevin must have sensed it, because he said nothing at all, which made it worse. In that split second, I realized how alike these two men were. Both were perceptive. Both were guileless. Kevin's continuing silence was a recognition of the import of the moment, which made Edward's declaration all the more real.

Suddenly, I was neither entertained nor mesmerized. What I felt was that awful tightness in my chest, and in my mind, pure panic.

Flattening my gloves over my ears, I broke away. "Okay, I'm done here." I set off for my car as quickly as I dared, ears covered until I was clear of them, or thought I was. But there came the crunch of boots on the freezing pavement, growing nearer, and Edward's voice calling my name. I broke into a run.

The footsteps gained anyway, and suddenly I saw myself reaching the truck but making a mess of climbing in and locking the door. So, the instant I grasped the door handle, I turned. He was right there.

"No," I ordered. "*No,* Edward."

"That wasn't how I wanted to tell you."

"Do not say another word."

I pulled the door open and had a foot on the running board when he said, "I meant it."

"Which part?" I cried, because the past was right back with us. "The part where you asked how I could *possibly* miss a STOP sign—or the one where you said, forget the STOP sign, how could I not see the *intersection—* or the one where you said that everything changed, that nothing would be the same?" I climbed in. "Leave it, Edward. I had to. Let it *go.*"

"We need to talk. I'll come to your place."

"Can't. Liam's there."

"Then my place."

"Oh no. No, no, no. No sex."

"To talk."

I just shook my head, slammed the door, and started the truck. But then all I could do was grip the wheel with both hands and try to catch my breath. It had never been as bad as this before. From a far recess of my mind came the echo of a CALM order, but it was too distant to do much good. My chest was squeezing so hard it felt like my heart had nowhere to go but up and out my throat.

Wondering if that could actually happen, what it might look like, whether the truck would be spattered with blood the way my SUV had been that awful fall day, I barely heard the door open. My engine was humming but the heat hadn't begun to blow, so I didn't even feel the cold it let in. But I felt the hands. They were large, one on my back, one on my shoulder, tentative but purposeful. And I heard the voice.

"Breathe," it said with a kindness it shouldn't have had after what I had done, the pain and the loss. "*Breathe,*" it repeated, frightened now.

I tried. Really, I did.

But it wasn't until he said it a third time, with rising panic, *Breathe, Maggie,* that I managed to drag in enough air to begin to recover. I was breathing shallowly, ragged but consistent, when he pried my hands from the wheel and turned me into his jacket, where he held me, rubbing my back.

The jacket smelled of a Devon March night way more than of Edward. But the hands that returned to my back had an Edward feel, and the voice was his. It murmured words of encouragement that blurred together, because individual words didn't matter, only the tone, which was filled with caring and concern.

"I'm okay," I finally managed, but it was another minute before I managed to ease back, only then realizing that my gloved fingers were folded over the edge of his pockets. Muscle memory? It had to be. Taking them back, I refolded them on the wheel. "I'm fine," I said and drew in a long, only mildly stuttering breath to prove it to him. I looked at my purse on the seat, the heat panel, the rearview, anywhere but at him. "I'm leaving now."

He didn't argue. After a beat, he stepped back and closed the door. Once he had backed off enough so that he could watch me pull out, I put the truck in reverse and moved. I had no idea whether Kevin was still back under the gaslight, and I didn't look. I simply focused on breathing, driving, getting home.

Liam was in my living room. His new heavy boots lay just inside the door; his new flannel shirt and sturdy jeans covered his body on my sofa; his new Ragg socks warmed his feet, which were propped on the edge of my coffee table. Jonah was beside him, acknowledging my arrival by opening one eye before closing it and going back to sleep, but the cats came running.

"*That* was fun," Liam said. His mouth moved, but not much else. He was satisfied, but clearly tired. He had earned that right.

I wasn't sure I had earned a thing, but I must have been subconsciously holding it together for the sake of getting safely home, because one foot in the door and I was emotionally wiped. Toeing off my boots, I crouched down to greet the cats and just kept on going until my butt hit the floor.

The problem wasn't only my legs. My whole body felt drained. It often did, after one of my chest episodes—*panic* episodes, okay, it was *panic*, when the past came rushing back so fast that emotions clogged my veins, slowing the blood flow—but this one had been extreme.

The last thing I wanted to do now was talk.

Correction. The last thing I wanted to do was to think about what Edward had said. And here was Liam, so at home in my home and, just then, the perfect distraction.

"You did good," I said with a hand on each cat.

"So did you, Maggie." He shifted his head on the back of the sofa just enough to aim his apparently-*not*-so-tired voice my way. "I kept thinking you'd be in to check up on me, but every time I looked around, there you were with someone else. It's like you know absolutely everyone in town, which I guess makes sense, small town and all, but you didn't have so many friends growing up."

"I had friends."

"Not so many."

"Maybe you just never saw."

"True." He frowned, pensive. "Five years is a big difference. Why do you think Mom waited so long to have a second?"

"Two miscarriages," I said, but if my brother heard, he didn't seem touched. I'm not sure a guy could grasp the sense of failure that a woman felt when she had a miscarriage.

Sure enough, he babbled right on. "When I was in elementary, you were in middle. When I was in middle, you were in high. When I was in high, you were gone. You never brought friends home."

No, I hadn't brought friends home. My mother worked, and although I helped out, dinners were an effort, making an extra mouth an added imposition. Once I got to college, friends usually lived in another state, which would have meant spending the night with us, which would have been just as unwelcome. My father liked his evenings quiet.

Liam rolled on. "You had friends at the wedding, but we didn't know them, and anyway, they were different from the ones tonight."

"Artists," I said with a smile. "Artists are unique."

"Your friends were just bizarre."

"They were not. Their artistry was just different from yours, and you weren't an artist back then, so you had nothing to say to my friends. Devonites are diverse," I added, returning to the present as Liam's phone dinged. "They're good people."

He glanced at the phone but set it down again.

"Edward," I muttered.

"Oh-ho, no. Edward's past texting me. He'd text you directly."

"Then who?"

"The guy is totally hung up on you, Maggie. He was with you more than not. Didn't you notice?"

To answer him, I'd either have had to acknowledge it or lie, but I didn't want to discuss Edward at all. "Okay, so who's texting—uh, oops, calling you?" I asked as his phone jangled in a different way. I had heard both of his ringtones enough by now to tell them apart.

Liam glanced at the screen and, this time, gave a sharp grunt before setting it aside unanswered.

"Someone you met tonight?" I asked. "Someone you liked? Didn't like? Butted heads with?" I couldn't imagine who that might be—actually, I could. "Oh, cripes. Lizzie Steele?"

Liam made a face. "What *is* the problem with that woman?"

"Loneliness. She's thirty, give or take, moved from Pittsburgh—"

"—to Devon two years ago to market organic breakfast muffins in a smaller, more upscale community, blah, blah, blah." He had clearly heard the same story the rest of us had. "Is she self-absorbed or what?"

"She's self-absorbed."

"How are her muffins?" asked the chef.

"They're fine."

"As good as Mom's?"

"No." Hex sauntered over, so I scratched his scruff lightly enough to make him purr. I didn't want to think of Mom again. But then I thought of Liam's phone. "Does she call you?"

"Mom? She did when I first left. I was in New Orleans for Mardi Gras, so she could actually hear the noise of it. I told her I'd be traveling up the East Coast. I said it was a research trip. I said I had to broaden my perspective on food."

"Sounds lofty."

"It's true," he defended himself. "Culinary artists can't live in a vacuum."

"I believe you, Liam."

"Please do," he said, momentarily appeased. "Anyway, I told her I needed to see different restaurants before I found a place to live—not technically a lie, just the omission of a couple of details."

"Like Edward."

"You didn't want me leading her here, did you?"

"She'll worry until she knows you have a job."

"You'd think. But the calls have slowed down. We haven't talked since before I got to Devon."

"Does that worry you?"

"Not particularly," he said and yawned. "Margaret McGowan Reid can take care of herself just fine."

I might have argued that my mother valued family, having always professed to wanting *five* children before age and miscarriage got in the way. I might have argued that she had grown her career to take the place of the children she had lost, that she had lost my father and now Liam. And me before that.

But she knew where I lived, I reasoned, letting my open palm absorb the vibration of Hex's purr as a palliative to upset. My return address was clearly displayed on the cards I had sent. More than once, I had considered adding my new cell number, very small and unobtrusive, maybe on the back of the card along with the artist's information—the cards I sent were originals, usually done by someone I knew—so that if she was interested she could call. But I always decided against it. I hadn't wanted to wait for a call that might not come.

Not wanting to fall further into the quicksand of all that, I said, "Okay, then, if it isn't Mom calling, and I assume it wasn't Lizzie, because I saw that dumb smile on your face—"

"*Dumb* smile?"

"Bored to death but not knowing how to get rid of her. You wouldn't give her your number."

"Hell no."

"Who then?"

He was suddenly sheepish. "I did give it to Erica Kahn. Do you know her?"

I tried to place her, coming up only with a sweet thing who had been in Devon for no more than a year or two. "Personal trainer at the sports center?"

"Yes. *Amazing* body."

"And a nice person, I hear." My eyes touched his phone. "So why didn't you answer?"

"Because that wasn't her. It was someone I used to know."

His guilty look said more. "Used to date?"

"It totally ended when I left," he swore, defensive again, "and it was mutual. I don't know why she keeps calling."

"Maybe you should answer and find out?" I asked, remembering what Kevin had told me about Edward not so long ago. *Confront him,* he had said, so I did. It ended badly—well, not badly in the way that said good sex was never bad, but badly in the sense of emotional clarity.

And look at me now. Sitting on the floor. Using my cat to center myself and not quite making it. Emotional clarity gone.

Who was I to advise Liam?

I needed a cup of herb tea but was too weary to make it. Gently dislodging Hex from my lap, I managed to stand and head for the stairs.

"Where are you going?" Liam asked, only then sitting forward.

"To bed."

"But I need to know about Erica."

"Not tonight."

"She is adorable and available and toned. She may be the best thing I've met in months. In *years*."

"So call her," I said and felt my own cell jingle against my hip. At this hour, on this night, I didn't doubt who it was.

16

He tried calling first. When I didn't answer, he texted. I ignored the first few dings while I got ready for bed. But something about removing my makeup and seeing the scar told me sleep wouldn't come unless I had a silence that was totally Edward-free.

So when more dings came minutes later, I stared at the phone.

Call me, said one text, and a second, *Are you home?* When the third said, *Are you safe?* like I might have driven into a tree, I texted back, *Yes. Home. Going to sleep.*

His response was instant. *I do. Love you.*

Did, I corrected.

My phone rang. I picked up, just wanting to put it to rest.

"Do, Mackenzie," he said without preamble. "Do. I do love you. I tried not to, but how do you stop something like that?"

"With murder?"

"Where? When? What murder?"

"You know what I mean."

"I don't. There's no way, *no way* I'll ever believe you wanted that accident to happen, so can we agree not to bring it up again?"

I sighed. "Tonight."

"Forever," he countered. "Look. Tragedies happen. How we handle them is a test of character. So I failed. I needed someone to blame, and there you were, happy to be blamed, and where did it get us? Divorced. Living alone. Miserable."

"I'm not miserable."

"Is that why you live alone—why you don't date—why you freeze when the subject of being a good mother comes up?"

"I don't—"

"*Why didn't Grace see,* someone asked, and it triggered a memory you couldn't handle."

"It didn't—"

"Then you zoned out, maybe remembering the accident or—or the time Lily grabbed the scissors and cut her finger instead of paper because you'd left the room for half a minute because I was yelling for your help from the other side of the house—or the time I sat her on the kitchen counter and she pulled a *knife* from the butcher block in the few seconds I was pouring her milk."

"No—"

"And when you couldn't breathe in the truck just now—is that what happy people do?"

I hung up, then silenced the phone so I wouldn't hear it ring. Tossing it to the foot of the bed, I climbed under the covers.

The thing vibrated once, twice, three times, then stopped.

I turned off the light, rolled onto my side, and punched at the pillow.

When he tried again, the lit screen penetrated even my closed lids. Bolting up, I flipped it over to hide the light. Hiding. Yes, I was. And no, I wasn't happy when I had to deal with the past.

But the past wouldn't go away until I forced it to, I realized. So I snatched up the phone, clicked in, and said a tired, "Leave it, Edward. I can't deal."

He didn't speak, but I knew he was there. I could hear his breath, rapid but gradually slowing until I felt him beside me, like he used to always be. No, I hadn't had many friends growing up, and while that changed as soon as I got to college and found people who shared my interests, it wasn't until I met Edward that I'd felt complete.

It was a tapestry. *Life* was. A tapestry. Needlework had never been my medium, but the metaphor fit. Life was a bundle of loose threads, really just a flimsy canvas until a few, strong, basic cords were woven in. My parents had been two of those cords. Liam was one. Lily another. And Edward.

Quietly he said, "Neither can I. Deal, I mean. I've really botched up this whole thing. I'm sorry I said what I did after the accident. I'm sorry I thought that erasing this part of my life would work. I'm sorry I didn't call you before I moved here, and I'm sorry I said what I did tonight in front of Kevin, but I'm not sorry for the words. I am sorry we're talking on the phone right now, because I need to say those words again and keep saying them until they sink in. Christ, Mackenzie, you're stubborn."

"Damaged," I breathed.

"I heard that, babe, and you are *so* wrong. What you are is human."

I wanted to argue, but didn't have the strength.

Or maybe I didn't want to argue.

Maybe I wanted to believe what he said, because I kept the phone at my ear.

"And here's something else," he said. "I need to find a place for Lily in my life. I tried removing her. I mean, hell, she's dead, right? Only I can't just say goodbye and walk away. You can't just wipe out someone you made. She'll always be part of me."

A thread in the tapestry, I was thinking, but he continued to speak.

"When you left, I packed up my pictures, all those ones that you made frames for—hell, even your *frames* were artistic. But I thought it'd be easier to move on if I didn't have to see them every day—you know, to see her—us—to see what I'd lost. So what I have now is a big hole where the best of the past used to be. What I have is a carton—cartons, plural—filled with photos that I want to put out but can't."

"You can."

"Do you? I didn't see any photos at your place, not downstairs, not in the bedroom."

Pushing the covers aside, I slid from the bed to the floor, just far enough back to see the green velvet box underneath. I couldn't actually *see* that it was green or velvet or even a box. The night was too dark and the light from my phone too small. But I could have been blind, and I'd have known exactly where it lay. "It's too painful for me."

"And it isn't for me? But how does a cut heal if you don't give it air to scab over?"

The question hung for a minute before he said, "I want to put personal pictures in my office, only I can't, because people might ask about Lily, and I'm not sure I can hold it together enough to explain. And then there are ones of you and Lily, and you and me, and the shot of just you that your friend Juan-Louis took right after we met—remember that one?"

I did. Oh, God. Edward had *adored* that one. I had surprised him with it for our first anniversary. Lily was barely six months old, I was still carrying baby fat, still sleep-deprived, and I wanted him to remember me in better times. The vanity of that seemed ridiculous now, but it had been a lifetime ago.

Now, folding myself forward, I extended a hand, but couldn't quite reach the box.

The voice in my ear said, "You have bangs and different eyes now, but the face is the same Mackenzie for anyone with half a brain to see, so I can't take the risk, because you made me promise—"

"I get the point," I said and straightened.

But he wasn't done. "Do you? I want to be happy again, Maggie. I want to be whole. Is that too much to ask? Tragedies happen, but don't we make them worse by dragging them on and on?"

"I can't forget her."

"Neither can I, that's my point. I need to make a place for Lily in my life. I need to make a place for us. I want to be able to laugh without feeling guilty."

I didn't comment. Couldn't. He wasn't saying anything my therapist hadn't said back when I was seeing her, but coming from Edward, it held more weight.

The silence lengthened. Finally, worriedly, he said, "Are you there?"

"Yes."

I heard the creak of the door when one of the cats came into the room. I heard Liam's footsteps pass by on his way to the loft. I heard a coyote, distant but haunting.

I didn't hear Edward. He was waiting for me to speak.

"Okay," I finally managed.

"Okay, what?"

"Okay, speak."

"I have been. I need to know what you think."

"What I think is that you're the one with the ideas, so you need to suggest one."

"About . . . ?"

"What to do next."

"Is that interest?" he asked with what actually sounded like humor.

"Curiosity."

He was silent. Considering. "Okay," he decided. "Curiosity's a start. I want to go public."

"With our *relationship?*" I cried, scooting back against the wall and reaching for Hex or Jinx or whichever cat it was, black in the black. I clutched its little body to my chest. "You can't. That'd spoil *everything* for me. People here can't know what I did."

"Would that be so horrible?"

"Yes!"

"They would understand."

"But they'd know. And I'd know they did, so I'd be seeing it in their eyes whether it was there or not. I've thought this through, believe me I have, many times. You come to a new place, and you start making friends, and some of those friends become good friends. You want to share who you are, who you *were,* only you're afraid. I'm afraid, Edward."

"I'd be here to help."

"I'm *afraid.*" What more could I say?

"Okay. Then what if we kept the past a secret and dated? Just dated?"

"Which would surprise no one, given your performance tonight."

"Performance?" he echoed, more amused than offended.

"Edward. You were glued to my side. I mean, talk about making a statement."

"You were my guide."

"Like you ever need a guide," I said, but if there had been a smile in his voice, it was gone.

"I do here. We're in uncharted territory. I don't know what to do any more than you do. I know where I want to be, just not how to get there. And, by the way, in case you didn't get it before, where I want to be is happy. Five years of grieving hasn't brought Lily back. I loved her—we both did—during the time we had her, but she just isn't *here* anymore."

Maybe not. I couldn't see her eyes in Edward's right now, but she would be there in the light of day. Agreeing to what he said would mean opening a door and letting the agony in.

My heart was thudding. It wasn't quite the clenching I usually felt, but it was a hard *th-wham, th-wham, th-wham.*

His voice lowered. "Do you still have her ashes?"

We had put equal amounts in three ceramic boxes. One had gone into the ground under a stone that held her name. Of the remaining two, we each had one. Mine was in my green velvet box, being kept safe by my grandmother's spirit.

I took an uneven breath and willed my heart to ease up. "Yes," I said as softly. "You?"

"Mm. I haven't found a place where I wanted to set them free."

"Me, neither."

We were quiet then, even my heart. Given what we were discussing, the hush should have been filled with angst. Either I was too tired for angst, or discussing this with Edward had made it bearable. Not peaceful. But bearable.

After a full minute, he said, "So, can we do it?"

"What?"

"Date?"

"You mean, like go out to dinner?"

"Yeah. In public. There may be talk, but so what? No one has to know anything more than we want them to know."

"Michael Shanahan will have to know."

"How the hell would he?"

"He knows everything. I swear he has spies, and what he doesn't learn from them, he learns from me because when he asks, I have to answer. That's the rule. He says it's his job to know who I spend time with."

"So tell him. I'm sure he'd rather you spend time with me than with Grace."

Actually, I wasn't so sure. *Jealousy* was the word that came to mind.

"So, do we date?" Edward asked.

"It can't go anywhere," I warned. He might think he still loved me, but if he saw me often—if he saw me without makeup, with my bangs a mess and my scar showing, he might realize he couldn't wake up to that every morning.

And me? What would I feel? On one hand, I didn't ever again want to go through the pain of divorce. This time, though there was no marriage to be wrecked. I would always be coming home to my own place—well, my own, assuming Liam left—and my pets and my friends and my job. I would be keeping my heart to myself. But if spending time with Edward helped me work through the past, I might be able to move on, too.

"Is that a yes?" he asked.

I sighed. "I guess."

His voice held a smile. "Your lack of enthusiasm is a challenge, Mackenzie Cooper."

"Maggie Reid," I corrected. This mattered to me. That said, I would only ever think of him as Edward.

"Maggie Reid, can I come over now?"

"Right now?"

"Yes."

"No."

"I want to hold you."

"No!" I said, but I was smiling, too. "That would muddy the waters. This isn't about sex. It's about our helping each other through a rough patch in a way that keeps the past just between us. No one else is to know. I mean it, Edward Cooper."

The plan was sound. I remained comfortable enough with it to sleep better than I had in two weeks and wake up fully able to breathe. My contentment lasted through a companionable breakfast with Liam that included critiques of the Town Meeting, of Erica Kahn, and of his Morning Glory muffins versus Mom's. I did not go to the pottery studio. I did call Kevin. I did not tell him about my pact with Edward; I knew the pros and cons, and didn't need Kevin pointing them out.

I did tell him that I had to be at work at nine, also the truth. Hairstylists from all over New England were at the Inn for workshops on cutting, styling, and accessorizing. I would have liked to see the one on hair extensions, but with several hundred stylists and their models attending, we were in full Day Spa mode. Every treatment room was booked. Stylists called it research, but they loved being pampered. And makeup? Models needed it. Stylists wanted it. I had brought in an artist from Hanover to help. We had worked together before. Both chairs were filled from nine o'clock on.

The soundtrack today was little more than soft piano chords and the trickle of water, and the lemon verbena rising from candles was so light that only someone attuned to it might notice. I noticed. For me, it was the perfect, soothing backdrop.

Then Edward arrived.

The last of the morning applications was done, my coworker had taken off for lunch, and I was disinfecting the counters in advance of the afternoon when tall and dark appeared at the door. I felt a tiny quickening, but the expression on his handsome face discouraged it. A magazine was loosely folded in his hand.

People.

My eyes flew to his. Their silver-blue was solely in the here and now. "Bad?" I asked and, reaching forward, silenced the speakers.

He put a hand to the back of his head. "If that soothes, you may want to leave it on." He came toward me.

"Tell me, Edward. Is it?"

"That depends on how you define bad." Ducking in, he kissed me full on the lips before I could retreat.

"Edward," I whispered with an uneasy glance at the door, which remained ajar.

"Just so you know I'm with you." He stepped back but didn't hand over the magazine.

I swallowed. "Okay. So, I'm imagining the worst here, like there's some surprise reveal about Chris, or the government has decided to go after Grace. I don't need suspense, Edward. If you're with me, help me out. What does it say?"

"Not much, textwise. It's a recap of what's been in other articles, plus a larger perspective on teenage hacking. The problem is the photos." With a cautionary bob of one brow, he handed over the magazine. "Page seventy-eight."

I flipped through until I was there, and instantly saw what he meant. The entire right third of the right-hand page, top to bottom, displayed a trio of photos taken in the lobby just outside the courtroom in Rutland. The focus was on Chris and Grace, but Jay was in each one. So was I.

"Oh *hell*," I whispered.

"For what it's worth, you look great." When I shot him a quelling look, he added, "I know, not the issue."

"It actually is," I said. "I don't want attention drawn to me. All it takes is one person seeing something familiar and snooping around and my cover is blown. Am I named here?"

"No. You look like Jay's assistant."

"I was trying for that," I replied, all too clearly remembering that moment and how exposed I had felt.

"Your worst problem is probably Shanahan, but he already knows—"

"*Maggie,*" came a high-pitched voice as Grace barreled over the threshold and came to an abrupt stop. She wore red scrubs, which made her skin look all the more pale. Her eyes were very brown and very large.

Those eyes slid between Edward and me. "I'll come back." She turned.

Tossing *People* aside, I rushed over at the same time that Edward said, "Stay." While I wrapped my arms around her, he moved behind us to close the door.

"In print all over the country," she breathed in horror and drew back.

"We knew it was coming."

"But those photos are *so clear.* How'd they *do* that?" Her voice remained high, but had a confidential edge, like I was the only one who should hear. "What kind of phone takes pictures like that? Someone there had a real camera, Maggie, a real one, and if I'd have known there would be those inside the courthouse, even a chance of it, I'd have kept my hood up, but I thought they couldn't. I thought it was against the rules to take pictures inside. Can I sue them for that?"

"You could," Edward put in gently, "and maybe whoever took these would have to pay a fine, but this article would still be out there, and all you'd do is keep the story alive. Sue *People*, and you open the door to more pictures."

She looked like she wanted to argue. More, though, she looked confused. Again, her eyes moved between Edward's face and mine. She might not have seen him kiss me, but she was wondering why he was here. Which wasn't terrible. Which was actually part of Edward and my agreeing to date. It was only my guilt at hiding the truth from her that made me think she suspected the truth. More likely, she knew we were talking about her and wasn't sure if Edward was turning me against her.

Wanting to reassure her, I put both hands on her shoulders. They felt frail, not a good thing for a massage therapist. "He's right," I said, trying to sound convinced when a small part of me was chanting, *Fight, fight, fight*. I knew the anger. I knew the sense of violation. I also knew the futility of going against a Goliath. "Life isn't fair, Gracie. Things happen. People say things, and even when you want to hit back, it's sometimes best to just let it pass."

"But these go all over the country," she cried, hands together now, picking at her thumb. "Everyone sees them. *Everywhere*." She was thinking of her ex-husband.

I grasped her hand to stop the picking. "Your hair is different. You were smart about that. The hair in these shots is chestnut and curly. You're a smooth-haired brunette now."

"But the face is the same. I mean, sure, fine, great, you change your name and have plastic surgery—" She stopped short. She didn't look back at Edward, but I sensed only sheer force of will kept her from it. I hadn't known about the name change, but I did know that she was afraid of her ex, so it wasn't a total surprise.

Our eyes held. I gave a tiny headshake to indicate that Edward knew nothing.

But he had certainly heard what she just said. I wasn't sure whether he was making the connection between Grace's experience and mine, whether he understood Grace because he understood me. But he approached us and said with quiet confidence, "You're safe here, Grace. The Inn protects its own."

Again, she looked from me to him and back. "Okay," she said and pulled away. "Gotta go. I have a client."

"We can get someone to cover," Edward tried as she made for the door.

"No need." She didn't look back. "Thanks, though. I'm good." Opening the door, she slipped out and was gone.

In her wake came a brief silence, the exchange of nervous looks, then Edward's whispered, "Name change?"

"I didn't know," I said, only then seeing that *People* hadn't been the only thing under his arm. A newspaper was there, trifolded in a familiar Thursday way. "Is that *The Times*?"

"Devon. Yes." Something about the way he said it put me on the alert. "Luckily, *People* will overshadow it."

I held out my hand. "What's there?"

"A profile."

"Of Grace?"

"Of me."

I stared at him for a minute. Slowly, the meaning of his alert sank in. Unfolding the paper, I scanned the front page. There on the lower half, relatively small but still front-page visible, was a photo of Edward in his office. He was standing at his desk, seeming to be studying papers there. The fact that it was a profile shot taken from ten feet away, rather than a close-up face shot, took nothing from its compelling nature. Edward was eye-catching in any pose, but eye-catching here was dangerous.

"It can't mention me," I warned, knowing that if it was done, it was done, but I was shaken.

"No. I was careful with what I said. But Quillmer did his homework."

"His homework."

"He mentions where my wife and I lived, and that our daughter was killed in an accident."

"Edward, how *could* you—"

"I *didn't*," he cut me off, upset himself. "He already knew I was from Boston, because my work history is out there for everyone to see. I didn't tell him anything that hadn't already come out in press releases when we bought the Inn. We discussed the hacking scandal, and I detailed the steps the Inn is taking to restore the integrity of our computer systems—and I needed to do that, Maggie. I inherited a crisis, here. Anything I can do to rebuild public confidence is crucial. From that angle alone, I couldn't refuse the interview. But I swear, I focused on work. I told him what I wanted to do with the Inn, and I thought that was the gist of the piece. He didn't ask anything personal, and I didn't offer it. Maybe that made him curious." He slapped the paper with the back of his hand. "But here it is."

"Did he name me?"

"No."

"Nothing about the trial?"

"No."

"The Mackenzie Cooper Law?"

"No. He must have known that would have been overstepping. Hell, the Inn pays a shitload in annual advertising, so he needs me, too."

"But he knows."

Edward gave a short head shake. "How would he know? What would he see that would connect Maggie Reid to Mackenzie Cooper?"

"Uh, my face?" I asked in dismay.

"Hey," came another voice from the door. It was my coworker, back from lunch. Much as Grace had done, he looked from Edward to me. "Am I interrupting?"

I forced a smile. "Of course not. Ronan, this is—"

"Ned Cooper," Edward put in wisely. I couldn't think of him as Ned in the best of times, one of which this was not.

"Owner of the Inn," I managed. "Ronan Dineen, makeup artist," I told Edward. "He's helping me out today."

"Thank you for that," Edward said.

"Thanks for the opportunity."

"Where do you usually work?"

He gave the call letters of a Burlington TV station. "It's pretty quiet up there now."

"Well, we're grateful," Edward said and told me, "You need lunch."

"I'll get an apple in the lounge."

"That's it?"

"Yes." Collecting *People* and *The Devon Times*, I handed them back. As far as I was concerned, they smelled up the room as badly as a hot pastrami sandwich would have done. I didn't want them here.

Edward took the publications. He looked like he wanted to say something more but didn't know what he could, with Ronan there. So he simply nodded and left.

And what could he say? I was right. My face was the problem. Only it wasn't Jack Quillmer who connected the dots.

17

Nina Evans. I should have guessed it would be her. I knew she was interested in Edward. I also knew she was a product of corporate America, where being well informed was the key to success. In hindsight, I was surprised she hadn't researched him before.

But Nina was the last thing on my mind when I left the makeup studio late Thursday afternoon. My phone was loaded with texts. *Had I seen* People? *What did I think? How was Grace?* None mentioned the piece in *The Devon Times*, and while I feared the reprieve was temporary, I was relieved.

Only put off until tomorrow what you are willing to die having left undone. No Mom-ism this one, but a quote from Pablo Picasso that my art school friends and I used to laugh over. I wasn't laughing now. I would have happily died not reading *The Devon Times* piece. Dealing with *People* was enough.

I tried calling Grace. The call went straight to voice mail. I was in the reception lounge, about to ask Joyce how much longer Grace would be working, when Nina rose from a sofa and hurried over.

"She's been waiting," Joyce whispered, adding a mouthed, "Sorry."

Not your fault, I thought but didn't say, because that quickly Nina grabbed my hand and led me to a deserted corner of the Spa store, where the only eavesdroppers would be organic skin cream and silk eye pillows.

I had no idea what she was doing. The *People* article wasn't exactly a secret. I was unsettled when she began studying my features with intense curiosity, like she'd never seen them before, though it was true in a sense. I was the technician. When she was in my chair, the focus was her, not me.

The best defense is a good offense, my mother said each time she had to renegotiate her bakery lease. Her strategy usually involved threatening to move, and although fighting fire with fire didn't work in the art world, I was daunted enough by Nina's behavior to try it now.

I studied her right back, from the dark green eyes that had only smidgeons of eyeliner and mascara, and the faint splotches that weren't quite covered by the makeup she'd cursorily applied, to the large claw clip that held back her thick hair. Capping the casual look, she wore a short parka, yoga pants, and sneakers.

My tit-for-tat didn't seem to register as she continued to puzzle over my eyes and hair, and I had the sudden thought that she was comparing them to something else she had seen.

Like the picture of another woman.

No. Not *People,* I realized with a shock. Not *The Devon Times.* Hell, not even Google.

The Boston Globe.

I held steady. *Coincidence,* I told myself. *Guilty conscience,* I told myself. There was still a chance I was wrong. When she ducked her head to peer under my bangs, though, I knew I was not.

"Mackenzie Cooper," she breathed, a question but not.

I didn't answer. Didn't dare.

"I had no idea, none. I'm *so* sorry," she said with true feeling, and when I didn't react, added, "About your daughter."

At least her priorities were right. But this wasn't a conversation I wanted to have. It wasn't one I was prepared for, though I should have been. I should have known it would occur one day. But what kind of person assumed nightmares came true and had an actual, viable plan of attack?

Actually, most people would. I hadn't, because even though my mind had known it might happen, my heart denied it. Even with Edward's coming and my heightened fear of exposure, I hadn't thought far enough to know how to react.

So I focused on breathing. I didn't want to make it obvious; the tightness in my chest was only starting.

"I remember when you first got here," Nina went on in a voice that was kind enough. "It wasn't so long after me, maybe two years, but those first few times we worked together, you were quieter. I can't imagine what you went through, Maggie." She paused. "Maggie? Mackenzie?"

As the question hung, I wanted to curse Edward for coming to town and curse Jack Quillmer for interviewing him. I wanted to curse Nina for nosing around online, but it was done. And yet—and yet I couldn't quite get myself to acknowledge Mackenzie.

Nina seemed oblivious to my angst, clearly blinded by her own need to know. "If you and Ned are divorced, why is he here? Were you always in touch, even after you moved?"

Stay or run? I didn't know which to do, but my feet didn't move, so I was momentarily trapped. My chest wasn't getting worse. But it wasn't getting better. And now I felt a tremor deep in my gut. Wrapping my arms around my waist to hold things steady, I drew in a slow breath and, slowly, let it out.

"I go back to Cleveland to see my parents," she went on, "and my sister comes here every so often, but you've never left for long or had anyone here to visit—ah, but your *brother*." Her eyes widened in realization. "How did *that* come about?"

I felt no pressure to answer. She was doing just fine on her own.

"He showed up right around the time Ned did, and he's going to be running a restaurant owned by the Inn group. That can't be a coincidence."

No shit, Sherlock, I thought.

"Was it all part of a plan—you come here first to get set up and make sure it was the right place?"

I was incredulous.

But she seemed oblivious to that, too. "Do you have other family—like, parents? I didn't read about them being around."

I took the deepest breath yet, closing my eyes for a second longer than a blink. My exhale sounded like a sigh. Nina wasn't good with girlfriends. She had told me that, herself. But if she had an ounce of innate compassion, she would have shut up. Her questions were tedious. Actually, her questions were *infuriating*. She had to see that I didn't want to talk, had to see that her questions were causing me pain. If this was her idea of being assertive, I could understand why strong women got a bad name, which was patently unfair, since persistence was a good trait. But to be persistent at the expense of human decency?

"I think I should leave," I said as levelly as I could with my insides unsteady and my anger rising.

"Is Ned why you've never dated? Do you love him?"

"Nina . . ."

"Why four years? And why *Devon?*" she asked. "From what I read, you had a life filled with people, but you've been alone here. How do you do it?"

That was it, one question too many. "Is there a point to this?" I asked sharply and was startled when her voice became a hoarse whisper.

"There is. I had a life filled with people, too, but I don't here. Here I have respect and anonymity and nice people and perfect makeup"— desperation appeared in her eyes—"and a *shitload* of hours all alone with nothing to do but relive the past, which I can't do a thing to change. It's lonely and depressing, and I know you know what I mean. You've been on the unfair side of life, so you have to know the anger of it, and coming here is both the best thing and the worst. It's an escape but not. I want to know how you do it. I need help, Maggie—and I call you Maggie, because it's the name of someone I trust. I don't care what happened in Boston. How do you do it here, now?"

I might have laughed hysterically. Was she was actually looking for help from *me*? All the care I'd taken to protect my identity, to protect my *heart,* to what end? I'd royally botched it.

The thought lasted for only a split second, because just then Edward emerged from the innards of the Inn, passed Joyce's desk with a small pat—like a thank-you for calling him—and joined us.

The hand that touched my back was light, but not so light that I didn't feel it. I sought his eyes, actually hoping their pale-blue would take me to Lily and dampen my anger. But those eyes were all Edward, whom I liked but didn't, whom I wanted but didn't, and who by any account had helped cause this mess.

"Everything okay here?" he asked Nina.

She seemed nonplussed, like she hadn't anticipated his arrival and didn't know what to say.

But I did. "I'm leaving," I announced and, letting Edward's soothing hand fall away, strode off. I didn't look at Joyce as I passed her. Something about the way she'd contacted Edward said she knew everything, and, at that moment, I was too angry at the world for betraying me to be able to deal with the shame of my crime.

At least, Michael Shanahan hadn't shown up, although the day wasn't done.

I hurried down the corridor to the back exit, pushed the door open, rushed outside—and stopped short. Not Michael, but Chris Emory. With his gray hoodie, curved back, and gangly legs, he was propped barely six feet away on the split-rail fence that led to the parking lot. Though he had clearly tried to hide his hair in the fleece, wayward curls caught the late-day sun like a halo intent on escape, but that was the most benign thing about him. His hands were visible fists in the hoodie's muff pocket, his shoulders hunched, his brows tight.

I didn't look around for the press. Chris would have scoped the parking lot before exposing himself this way, not to mention that I was too irritated just then with all of it to care who saw me, him, us. As he stood, his expression went from forbidding to frightened. I should have been worried. But he was fifteen, no baby, and his face wasn't what I needed.

Willing sympathy away, I stood rock-still and stared. "Problem?"

"Yeah." He came toward me and said in a grudging voice, *"People.* Everyone's talking about it, and Mom won't answer texts."

The door opened behind me. That would be Edward.

"She's still working," I said, but Chris was eying Edward with unease. "Ignore him. He's with me. Does Grace know you're here?"

His wary gaze hung on Edward for a minute, before sliding back to me. He lowered his voice to keep the conversation private, though Edward was there at my shoulder. "I told her I was. She didn't say anything about that either—like, she doesn't tell me to stay or leave, just ignores me, but I have to see her. She's blaming me for everything."

I raised both brows. "Uh, who else should she be blaming?"

Forgetting caution, he reeled off the list with full resentment. *"People,* Ben Zwick, the media, and the crazies who listen to their stuff—*I* don't know. *I* didn't ask them to come snooping around."

"Christopher," I fairly shouted, *"listen* to yourself. You hacked into school computers, then you hacked into Inn computers, then you hacked into the Twitter account of a journalist with a national following. You are the reason this is happening. So, excuse me, but it *is* your fault." I was breathing fast, perhaps not thinking about the fact that this wasn't the best place to be talking, but I didn't see other people, just the three of us. So I asked outright, "Why did you do it? Were you trying to get someone's attention?"

"No."

"Trying to goad your mother into telling you about your dad?"

He shook his head, but his mouth was shut so tight that I figured at least part of the answer was yes. "What *did* you hope to accomplish?"

He stuck out his chin.

"Do you understand that what you did was wrong?"

He looked away.

"Are you *sorry*, Chris? Tell me that, at least, please, tell me that."

The gaze that met mine was liquid. "Yes, I'm sorry," he said, more boy than man now. "If I could go back and delete everything, I would, but it was like"—frantic eyes skittered away, then returned—"like this addictive thing, and being able to do it was awesome, because I'm a nobody—I mean, a nobody. I'm not a star at much, and I was feeling screwed over, so I wanted to show them—show *someone* I could—only it blew up in my face. So now I'm totally fucked, but I didn't know, I swear I never thought—never thought anything like this would happen." His voice stopped, but his throat continued to work, his Adam's apple bobbing at the hoodie's throat.

Anger notwithstanding, my heart did chip then. Stepping forward, I rose on tiptoe and hugged him. He smelled of ratty sweatshirt and boy, and his breathing was rough, but I didn't feel crying. He would refuse to do that with Edward watching.

I didn't speak, and it had nothing to do with the March chill, our audience, or the fists pressing into my back. Truth be told, I was too keyed up to say anything profound.

Truth be told, I was too *inexperienced* to say anything profound. I didn't have a child. Parenting anything older than a five-year-old was foreign to me.

When I pulled back, he was looking destroyed. The last two weeks had done that to him, and I hadn't helped. My sin here, now, was one of style, though, not substance.

"Blaming everyone else won't help," I said softly.

"But my mom—"

I turned, about to tell Edward to get Grace, when he nodded his understanding and went back inside.

"She hates me."

"A mother never hates her child."

"Then why is she being like this? Doesn't she know how I feel?"

"Have you told her?" I asked, but he couldn't hear past himself.

"I am suffering. I go to school, and it's like I have a disease. No one talks to me there, either."

"No one?"

"Well, except for people who think what I did was cool, but it wasn't, Maggie, I know that now, my mind just wasn't there when I did it. And okay, so the Feds are watching what I do, but that doesn't mean someone'll get in trouble for walking to fucking *class* with me."

"Language," I warned in the voice of Grace. When he pouted, I asked, "You have friends. What about them?"

"Friends." He rolled his eyes and, way too cynical for fifteen, said, "Oh yeah, friends. Well, we text sometimes, and they sound like they still like me, only they don't want to be seen with me, and that's okay, at least Mom's right about that. She says it says something about them, and that if they can't see past who I really am, the statement's more about them than about me."

"So she does talk to you." That restored my faith, at least a bit.

"Not today. Why won't she answer my texts?" He glanced at the door through which Edward had gone. "He's not coming out with her so fast. Maybe he can't find her. Maybe she's refusing to come out. Maybe she's not even in there. Maybe she's gone into hiding."

"She's working, Chris. I know this for fact. She's with a client."

"But she takes breaks. That's when she texts me back, only she's not doing it now. What was so bad about *People*? It didn't say anything new, but suddenly she's gone apocalyptic on me."

I had to smile. "Apocalyptic? I don't think so."

"Know what my problem is?" he asked and, before I could say the narcissism of being fifteen, answered. "Being fifteen. If I was eighteen, I'd run away, I mean, like, just disappear. I could do it now—there are a bazillion kids who run away from home every day. Only I don't have the guts. I'm pathetic."

Taking his shoulders, I gave a shake. "You are not pathetic, Chris. The fact that you say it—the fact that you've said all of what you just have, says something about the kind of adult you'll grow to be."

"But I'm serious, Maggie," he warned. His brown eyes were suddenly large. "I am not kidding about this. I need to be in a different place where no one knows me."

I was shaking my head before he'd finished. "Won't help."

"How do you know?"

"I know."

"How? Your life is sweet. You don't have psychologists trying to trip you up or government lawyers trying to lock you up or reporters trying to make you into a monster."

His description so fit! "But I did," I heard myself say.

He called my bluff. "When?"

I hadn't thought this through, clearly hadn't. Or maybe my subconscious had. Maybe my subconscious knew that the truth was out for Nina, possibly for Joyce, certainly for Jay, not to mention for other people who had seen the article on Edward, people who had seen us together at Town Meeting and wondered why I had come to Devon with no past.

Chris Emory, age fifteen and unlikely confessor, wouldn't be wondering any of that. He was too into himself. If I told him the truth, it would be all on me. If I told him, he would tell his friends, who would tell their friends, who would tell their parents.

I wasn't ready for that.

But if what I'd made of my life was a tapestry, the unraveling had already begun, and through no fault of my own. Maybe I needed to take control. Maybe I needed it now to *be* my fault.

Taking responsibility is a step toward redemption—and, okay, my mother had been talking about a serial killer then, but what the hell.

"*When?*" Chris demanded.

"Five years ago," I said flatly. "I caused a car crash in which two people died. It was a high-profile case—lots of press, lots of speculation. I didn't go to prison, but I've been on probation. My probation officer monitors everything I do. So I know what you're feeling, Chris. I had the psychologists and the government lawyers and the reporters crawling all over me, too."

His jaw had gone slack. It was a minute before he closed his mouth.

"I didn't know," he said, finally sounding contrite. "Mom never said."

"Mom doesn't know." I let that sink in for a beat. "No one does—or did until recently. It's not something I want spreading around."

"I won't tell anyone," he hurried to say, that quickly the innocent boy with whom I'd played hide-and-seek in the woods. "I swear, Maggie, I won't, I mean"—he scrunched up his face—"who would want to know that about you?"

I could think of a number of people, and, in fairness, it would be more curiosity than malicious intent. Nina was a good example. *I don't care what happened in Boston,* she said. The problem was that I did.

I cupped his shoulders again, rubbing gently this time. "The only reason I'm telling you is so you'll listen to what I say. As bad as life looks right now, it will get better. I know. I've been where you are."

"Not around here," Chris said, no longer ten years old and now way too smart. "You had to leave wherever you were before it could get better. So that's what I'm saying. I have to leave."

"Not now you don't," I warned, retrieving my hands and stuffing them in my pockets. "You do not run away, Chris. Once everything's done in court, you and your mother can decide what you want to do."

"What if I'm in jail?"

"Then you won't have to make a decision."

"You're supposed to say I'm not going to jail."

"You're not going to jail."

"Were you afraid of jail?"

"Terrified."

"Did you think of running away?"

252

"Then? No."

"Afterward?"

I paused, looking back and up at the beautiful stone structure that was The Devon Inn and Spa. "I did. I came here."

"*Gah,*" he sputtered, "that doesn't help me. What if I skip school until the trial?"

I gave a slow headshake.

"Mom could homeschool me."

Really? I asked with a look. We both knew the idea was absurd.

"Then I'm getting sick," he said. "I'll catch something . . . like Ebola."

"Seriously?"

"Yes." His eyes held mine. "No?"

"No."

"I'm telling you, running away is the best plan."

I grabbed his arms this time. "That would make things ten times worse. Promise me you won't, Chris? *Promise me.*"

"Fine. Okay." Jutting his chin out, he looked away. A second later, with bravado, his eyes returned. "Then I'll just shut myself in my room. I don't have to eat dinner if Mom isn't there. I don't have to *talk* if she isn't there. All I need's a bag of nachos. I'll get in bed and pull up the covers."

I was about to tell him how childish that was, when I realized two things. First, taking a bag of chips to bed was harmless. Second, it was exactly what I wanted to do, myself.

"There's a plan," I said and, hearing the door open behind me, looked back. Grace emerged, followed closely by Edward. He seemed to be shepherding her, meaning that he may have forced her to come, but I lacked the wherewithal to analyze her expression. Not that it mattered what she felt. As long as she was there, I could leave.

I gave Chris's arm a final squeeze, drilled him with a *remember-your-promise* look, and set off for my truck. I didn't look at Grace again, certainly didn't look at Edward. I blocked out everything but the sanctity of my home.

At least, I tried to block it all out. But the word *busted* kept popping up in my mind as I drove. Many, many Devonites read *The Devon Times* and were as computer-savvy as Nina. Thinking about it made my stomach twist.

I thought to call Kevin, but I couldn't bear to rehash the day.

I thought to call Grace, but she would be busy with Chris and, if she did answer—honestly?—I didn't want to deal with what I'd told Chris.

I thought to call Cornelia, just to tip her off in advance of comments she would surely hear. But she liked me. She respected me. My heart broke at the thought of losing that.

And then there was Joyce, who probably already knew everything, so what was the point?

And my girlfriends? My book group? My clay friends? Spa clients? Given how my phone continued to vibrate with texts, I knew there were questions. I didn't want to answer any of them.

Home was where I needed to be, safe and alone and in control of my life.

Unfortunately, I had forgotten about Liam.

18

Seeing his car brought it back, so finding him in the house wasn't a total shock. It was just disappointing. I really wanted to be alone with myself, my pets, and my furniture in my very own place. I really wanted to be alone with the silence, because too much had happened today, and too much static remained. I was used to silence. It was comfortable and safe.

But I opened the door to Liam's chop-chop-chopping and scents that were organic and raw. I identified onion, garlic, and celery. I thought I smelled rosemary—and melting butter—and lamb, not beef, but that was only a hunch.

"You're too early," Liam cried from the kitchen, his head bent over the cutting board, his thinning red hair actually combed. "I need another hour."

"No problem." I toed off my boots. "I'm going upstairs." Hanging my coat on a hook, I knelt. "Hello, babies," I whispered and hugged each pet as he crowded in. Then I went straight for the Ritz cracker sandwiches, which were my go-to comfort snack. The Spa offered apples, homemade granola squares, and organic coconut candies, but they didn't do it for me the way Ritz sandwiches did. I want to say I'd been raised on them, but with a mother like Margaret McGowan Reid? Nope. I had been raised on gourmet cookies and bars, from experimental to sublime. Prepackaged crackers were the antithesis of those, definitely against Reid family rules, which was likely part of their appeal.

Opening the eye-level cabinet where I kept them, I found one pack, angled it up to see the label, then pushed it aside. I stood on tiptoe for a deeper look. Reaching in, I felt around.

"Where are my Ritz sandwiches?" I asked Liam none too sweetly. "They were right here."

"There's one," he offered, a tad too innocent. His freckles were bright, which was a sure sign of guilt.

"That one's cheese. I want peanut butter."

"Cheese is healthier. Actually, celery is healthier." He held out a stalk.

I stared. "If you're trying to body-shame me, it won't work. I was too thin before. Know what happens if you're too thin? You get osteoporosis like Mom."

"You do not."

"You might. Thinness is one of the indicators. I know this, Liam. My doctor was after me for years to gain weight."

He drew in his chin and gave a huff. "You're in a snit."

I was. All I wanted was my own quiet little house back. No. That wasn't all I wanted. I wanted my nice quiet little *life* back.

Frustrated, I said, "I really want those crackers."

He went back to stirring whatever ground meat was frying in my pan. "I ate them after you went to bed last night—ate them right there on the sofa"—he indicated the place with his eyes—"but not to worry, I dust-busted this morning."

"You ate *all* of them?"

"There were only two packs, and I was hungry," he stated. "I can't eat when I'm serving other people, and in case you didn't notice, I served half your town last night."

No apology? *The best defense is a good offense.* My brother had learned that lesson well.

But I really, really wanted peanut butter crackers. Only two packs left, and I hadn't restocked? Didn't *that* say something about the distraction the last two weeks had been?

Settling for second best, I grabbed a box of graham crackers.

"Uh, Maggie, about dinner—"

"What *is* that?" I asked with a glare at the pan, disgruntled enough to suggest that it looked vile.

My brother was oblivious. His own agenda carried him blithely along. With a flourish, he said, *"Navarin Printanier."*

"Liam."

"Lamb stew with spring veggies, made with ground lamb instead of roasted because I couldn't find whole lamb at the last minute, but the turnips look great. I'll leave a little for you, but most of it is coming with me."

"Where to?"

"Erica Kahn's," he offered and waited, expectant, even anxious.

"Perfect," I said and headed for the stairs. My brother could have made *Navarin Printanier* for the *devil,* and that would have been fine. The idea of having the house to myself for even a few hours was heaven.

After closing the door to my room loudly enough to make a statement, I pulled up Spotify, set my phone in the dock, and climbed into bed fully clothed. Sitting against the headboard with the covers bunched under my breasts, I opened the box of graham crackers, removed a sheet and broke it in half. I munched happily, eager to redeem my personal space and relax.

But the first song was Adele's "All I Ask," whose lyrics made me lonely. I found Rihanna's "Stay" depressing, and Sarah McLachlan's "I Will Remember You" made me want to cry.

I identified with these songs, and wasn't that pathetic? My life was a playlist—sad, haunted, and filled with regret.

So music wouldn't help. Grabbing the phone from its dock, I was about to check Facebook to see what Mom's special had been, or Twitter to catch up on news beyond Devon. But the screen lit up with unread texts, and, even as I held the phone, another arrived.

I turned the thing off and tossed it aside.

Snapping another cracker in two, I listened to my woods, but the outdoor sounds were so low with the windows closed that I had to stop eating to hear. There wasn't much anyway; March was perennially stingy. I heard the coo of a mourning dove, or maybe an owl, hard to tell which. I heard the rattle of branches blown by the wind, softened only by the *susurrus* of pines and firs. I might have enjoyed the purr of the cats, but they were downstairs with Liam, whose cooking sounds had to be as deliberate as my door closing—the slam of a cabinet, the rap of a wooden spoon against my iron pan, the rush of water through the pipes as the sink faucet went on and off.

Call us both childish. But there was satisfaction in making noise when one was PO'd.

IMHO, I had more of a right to it than Liam did. The fact of his commandeering my kitchen for his personal cause only added to the anger of a day in which reality had seriously upset the basket of my life. The home-and-hearth smells that rose from the stove were little solace.

I waited, listened.

"Maggie?" Liam finally called.

I didn't answer.

"I'm leaving," he called.

Either he sensed my anger and didn't want a confrontation, or he was that eager to be at Erica Kahn's. He might have even thought I was asleep, though it was pathetically early for that. I mean, who went to bed at six-thirty? Only someone who had nothing better to do, and if *that* wasn't a depressing thought, I didn't know what was.

Whatever, he didn't try again. I heard the front door close and, more faintly, his engine rev. My bedroom was at the back of the house, so I couldn't hear the crunch of his tires on the drive, but I pictured him backing around and heading out.

Only when I guessed he would be halfway down the road did I open my door. And there were my pets, lined up and waiting in a way that both warmed my heart and hit me with guilt. "Oh guys," I said as I crouched down and reached out. "I am the worst mom." But not for long. I had a sudden stroke of genius. "Who wants lamb stew?" The smell out here in the hall was strong.

Me, me, me, I imagined them saying, because all three ran for the stairs.

I followed but paused at the top. Immediately to my right was the loft. It overlooked the open first floor of the house and in normal times held little more than a sleep sofa and lamp. Now it was a mess of strewn clothing, empty shopping bags, and dirty drinking glasses.

Resigned, I continued on down. Liam might be a pig in the bedroom, but the kitchen was spotless. A container sat on the counter, its cover steamed and warm. The pet dishes were dripping dry on the rack, so no one actually needed food. But I had promised.

When I cracked the lid, the smell hit me hard, and it was awesome, I had to give Liam that. I spooned out bits of lamb and knelt. Hex and Jinx each took a lick before walking away. Jonah cleaned the spoon.

Me, I wasn't hungry after eating . . . how many graham crackers?

I wasn't hungry an hour later, either, because something weird was happening. Nothing worked. I went through the mail, but threw most of it out. I flipped through the latest issue of *Makeup Artist*, but no article caught my interest. Spotting a small UPS delivery that Liam had brought in and set aside, I did feel a germ of enthusiasm. UPS brought me little gifts. I could use a little gift now.

Eager, I broke open the box, layered back the tissue, and wrestled with bubble wrap to uncover blush, shadow, liner, and brushes, all from a new brand that I'd wanted to try. The brushes were made of synthetic fiber, which didn't have quite the elegant touch of natural fiber, but natural fiber clumped when mixed with oil, and dry skin needed oil. I tested a blusher brush on the back of my hand, then my neck, then my face. Deciding it would be fine, I set it aside.

What to do then? My fingers itched, needing clay. But even if the studio had been open, I couldn't risk seeing people. I'd had a home studio when Edward and I were married. But this life was to be different from that one. As many times as I had been tempted to keep a stash of clay here, I'd resisted.

Right now, I wished I hadn't. I needed . . . *something*. The house was quiet all right, but it wasn't the quiet I knew. The quiet tonight, as darkness slowly settled over my woods, was lonely.

I walked around.

I reached for my next book-group book, settled into the sofa, and opened to the page where I'd left off. I read two paragraphs, but my mind didn't grasp meaning. I read them again, then put the book down.

I turned on the TV, surfed through the guide, turned it off again.

I lifted the lid of the lamb stew but covered it again without taking a bite.

Nina had asked how I handled the hours alone, the loneliness and depression. I used to do it fine. I had slogged through the worst and risen on the other side feeling good. No, not good. *Great.* My life had been *great* before all this happened.

I wanted that again. But I couldn't roll back time. What had worked two weeks ago wouldn't work now.

So here I sat, a prisoner in my own home.

And I deserved it, I mused, brooding as I lifted a ceramic bowl that I had thought so primitive at the time. I had enjoyed making it, though. It had been a sign of progress.

Today, I'd regressed. If my goal in Devon was being a good person,

I had failed. I had snipped at Liam, turned a deaf ear to Nina, walked right past Joyce, who had been so loyal to me. I had badgered Chris, then burdened him with a confession that might be too heavy for his already-burdened shoulders. I had let Grace down, putting my own obsession with *The Devon Times* before her obsession with *People*.

And Edward? I don't know what I'd done to Edward. I don't know what he'd done to *me*. The compartment of my life that contained him was a big, fucking mess.

Disgusted, I set down the bowl. I went to the door, put on my boots, parka, hat, and gloves, then went out into the night. I quickly returned for a scarf; the temperature had definitely fallen, but frigid air was what I needed to clear my head. No scent of lamb stew here. The forest was all moisture and earth and maybe, maybe new growth, though on a night like this, who knew if it would live? Native Americans did. They had a name for the moon, which this night shone full through the trees. They actually had two names, alternately calling it the worm moon, after worms that wriggled to the surface and invited robins, and the sap moon, for the flow from maples. Though I loved seeing robins and adored maple syrup, I was most grateful that this full moon was bright enough, so that even when it slipped behind a gauze of clouds, its sheen lit the road.

I walked down Pepin Hill to the bottom, turned around, and walked back up to my place. Those few nocturnal creatures that weren't still in hibernation were scared off by my footsteps. And the cooing I'd heard? An owl, to judge from the heavy whoosh of feathers when whatever it was flew off.

Black ice was a challenge. Snow melt on dirt made mud; snow melt on rocks made ice, and there were plenty of rocks on my road. I slipped a time or two but caught myself short of embarrassment. Not that there was anyone around to see.

And wasn't that the problem? As good as the exertion felt, the minute I was inside, the loneliness returned. At that point, I was just desperate enough for a distraction to go to my room, sit on the floor, and slide the green velvet box out from under the bed.

It was long and narrow, three feet by one and barely eight inches high. Its velvet was the color of spring leaves in all but the spots where the hand that loved it had been sweaty or soiled. Its corners were protected by gold filigree that matched the bracing around the latch. Lying flat beneath that latch was a worn leather handle. At its inception, the box had held my grandmother's art supplies, most notably the pastels she loved, and several remained inside, carefully wrapped in glassine, but they were only one of many mementos there now.

I ran featherlight fingers along its edge, one filigreed corner to the next. Then I opened my palm on its top. Nana's Treasure Box, I used to call it, because I had always found magic inside. I was ten when she died, but I remembered being as young as three, sitting cross-legged inside her crossed legs and holding my breath as she raised the lid. The past became real to me then, all those pictures and postcards and little tokens that wafted out and smelled of another time.

There was life in this box. Even after my grandmother died, there was. And now Lily was here. I pictured her flowing blond hair, pale-blue eyes, and impish grin. I saw her as a cat with face paint, and a princess with a tiara headband. I heard her high laugh when I tickled the side of her neck.

Heart beating wildly, I touched the latch, sliding my finger back and forth, back and forth.

Then I straightened. I told myself to breathe, and, touching velvet, that's what I did. After a minute, I folded forward. Putting my cheek to the spot where my palm had been, I felt warmth. It might have been from my hand. But no. My hands were still bone-cold from being outside. This warmth came from two spirits, one of a woman who had lived long, another a child who had died young.

When my eyes began to burn, I thought I might cry. Lord knew, I wanted to. Crying was the normal response. A good mother would *feel*. She wouldn't seize up like a heartless rock. A rock couldn't absorb bad— which, my therapist said, was why my body did this. When grief was too deep, the body shut it down. When I was strong enough, she said, tears would return.

And here I thought I was strong? Oh, I was. Just not in a way that might have kept Lily from harm. Nana could. Taking comfort that she was watching over my baby, I slid the box back under the bed and, alone once more, sat back against the wall in the dark.

Aloneness was what I deserved. Only it was worse now than it had been for a long, long time. Was the rock starting to crack?

Turning out the light, I climbed back into bed, pulled the covers to my chin, and just lay there. I thought to undress, but didn't have the strength. I thought to remove my makeup, but didn't have the strength.

Self-pity was a potent muffler, because it wasn't until after the fact that I realized the knocking sound drifting up wasn't heat in the pipes at all, but knuckles on my front door. Or not. When a key turned, I thought of Liam. If Liam was back this early, his date hadn't gone as well as he wanted, which meant that he would be making noise, if only to make his needy presence known. Whoever was down there now did not.

Only one other person would know that a spare key was always stashed behind the wreath by the door. I heard the door close behind him, and pictured him standing in my living room, looking around, maybe unbuttoning his barn jacket or rubbing the back of his head as he tried to decide what to do.

What did I want him to do? I wasn't sure.

No. I was sure. I wanted him to hold me. I wanted him to make me feel less alone, if only for a little while.

Barely breathing, I waited. I heard soft footfalls on the stairs, definitely Edward's. No intruder would leave his boots at the door to keep from tracking in mud, but these footfalls came from socks. They paused at the top, then started quietly down the hall.

He opened my door and stood for a beat before whispering my name. Hushed as the sound was, I heard its question.

"*Yes*," I answered, my own whisper a plea. Yes, I was awake. Yes, I wanted him here.

Approaching the bed, he was a dark silhouette, a ghosted shape in the ambience of that full moon. He hunkered down beside me. "Are you okay?"

I shook my head. Then I held out a hand. The instant he took it, I felt relief. I wanted to ask why he had come, but didn't dare. Coward that I was, I couldn't risk not liking the answer.

"You're freezing," he said and, sitting on the side of the bed, began chafing my hand between his two. The warmth was heavenly. So was the strength of those bigger-than-my hands.

I tugged on those hands. "Lie with me—just a little?" When he made to crawl over and stretch out on top of the duvet, I opened the covers instead.

Butt and legs came first. "Turn over," he whispered as the rest of him scooted in. He held me spooned then, knees behind mine, one arm around my middle, the other pillowing my neck, and his chin in my hair. It was comfortable. It was familiar. No matter that we were both fully dressed— perhaps because of it—*this* was heavenly.

I don't know how long we lay there. I matched my breathing to his— used to do that all the time, and the rhythm returned, like we had never been apart. I covered his hands with my own, one at my waist, one at my neck. Twice, he drew free, once to tuck a strand of hair behind my ears, once to wrap his forearm across my upper chest in a spontaneous hug.

I might have been fine lying like that forever, if he hadn't used his hand again, this time to move the hair away from my neck to allow for a nuzzling kiss. Suddenly I saw his words on the face of my phone. *I do. Love you. I tried not to, but how do you stop something like that?*

I needed to be loved. Didn't matter whether I deserved it. Just then, I needed it more than air.

Reaching back, I used my hold of his head to help me turn, and, grabbing his bearded jaw, I brought his mouth to mine. That was it—all I had to do—the sign he wanted. His kiss was thorough, and when it was done, he drew back for barely a breath before coming in for another. He touched my face and wove his fingers into my hair. He mouthed his way down my throat and chest, removing clothing as he went, so that when he reached my breasts, they were bare and aching.

What followed was light-years removed from what we had done last week. That had been angry and fast. I had resented the physical attraction and wanted to get it out of my system once and for all. Okay. Fine. Part of it might have been pent-up need. But lots of it was wanting to punish Edward for messing with my new life. That sex hadn't been pretty. In my right mind, I hadn't wanted it.

This I did. This was about being as close to another human being as was physically possible.

Frantic to hold and be held, I kept my arms around him, kept my hands running over whatever of his skin that allowed. The heat of his body was what I craved. Had I been able to disappear inside him, I would have.

Too quickly, his heat became mine, and I wanted more. I'm not quite sure I had ever appreciated the sweep of his cheekbone the way my lips did now, or admired his clavicle as my fingers did. I had certainly never before had facial hair to compare to the hair on his chest or his legs. I'm not sure I had ever been quite this dizzied by the nutty scent of his skin.

His pulse was the best. It meant life, and life was what I needed. I found its rapid beat at the side of his neck and buried my face there. I found it inside his elbow and even more strongly at his groin. I was licking the thrum at the back of his knee when he brought me to my first climax. It was barely done when he flipped us around and entered me, and the mind-numbing went on.

Edward Cooper was virility incarnate. I had always thought him so, whether wearing a suit and tie or a T-shirt and jeans. But here and now, with his dark, close-cropped beard carrying my scent, with his long body naked and hungry, with his hands knowing just how to hold and caress, and the rest of him dispelling what little remained of my loneliness with closeness and fire, he *was* my air.

I was in the last throes of a shattering climax when I felt him approach his. I could tell from his breathing, from the small catch in his throat.

Given a moment's lucidity, I gasped in warning, "Not inside!"

"Yes!"

"Not safe—"

"I want—"

"Please."

He pulled out. His body jacked, and he held his breath for the longest time before breaking into long, throaty gasps. Then he collapsed on me.

I couldn't move, could barely breathe. But I wrapped my arms around his sweaty back and held him, so that he wouldn't leave. His weight grounded me.

Finally, he slid to the side and drew me under his arm, holding my body flush to his with a hand at my hip. "I'm staying," he whispered.

I didn't argue. My cheek was on his chest, one leg wound through his. I wasn't about to move, and it had nothing to do with the part of him that my thigh touched, the part that was no longer erect yet still impressive. It had to do with his warmth, his scent, his pulse.

I didn't fall asleep. Nor did he, said his steady, sturdy pulse.

"You were sad," he whispered into my bedroom's night.

"I was lonely."

"Where's Liam?"

"On a date."

"Gone for the night?"

"Does it matter?"

"Not to me," he said, but, even in a low bed voice, his intonation reminded me that I was the one leery of taking our relationship public, and that Liam would talk.

At that moment, I didn't care.

Several moments later, though, I said, "It should. Matter to you. I'm bad luck."

He paused, sighed. "If you're talking about the accident—"

"No. Now. I mess things up."

"Uh-huh."

"I do. Like with Nina. I didn't handle that well. And Chris? He's frag-ile right now. I was too hard on him."

He gave me a sharp squeeze. "You're too hard on yourself."

But I wasn't. "I'm not sure I helped. I said way too much." That, even before my confession, which Edward didn't know about, unless Chris had blurted it out to his mother as soon as I left. "What happened with Grace?"

"She was okay."

"Did she stay with Chris?"

"I made her." There was a jolt on the bed, a dip, and Edward bolted up. "What the hell is *that?*" he asked.

"One of my cats." Needing to stay connected, I put a reassuring hand on his lower back, which was the part of him I could most easily reach. "They're not used to anyone else in my bed."

He exhaled resignedly. "Do they always sleep with you?"

"Apparently not when someone else does."

He lay back down, though it was a minute before his heartbeat re-turned to its pre-cat calm.

So low that it was almost to myself, I whispered, "I love my cats."

He was silent. Then, "Is that a warning?"

"Just saying." I reconsidered it. Yes, a warning. "I like them here."

"Where's your dog?"

"I love him, too."

"But where is he?"

"Probably asleep on Liam's bed. He likes lying in piles of clothes."

"Well, something else is here," he said, lying very still now. "Do you use a vibrator?"

"Excuse me?" It was a second before I understood. "Oh, God. My phone." Sitting up in the dark, I groped through the covers in search, but Edward found it in the rumple of sheets under his leg.

He handed it to me. Its screen was lit and a harsh intrusion. I put it facedown on the nightstand.

"Don't want to check it?"

Still up on an elbow, I looked down at him. "No."

"You sure?"

"Very. I don't want people telling me about *People* or *The Devon Times*."

"Maybe they're calling about something else."

I simply shook my head. My friends were wonderfully loyal to me and I to them, but for none of them was I the "person to contact in case of emergency," and if it wasn't an emergency now, I didn't want to talk, at least, not with them.

I started to lie down again but stopped, unsure. When Edward opened his arm, I went the rest of the way.

We lay quietly. For a time, I was content enough not to say anything. But the room was dark, and no, I didn't want to talk with friends, but maybe I did want to talk with my ex-husband.

"Edward?"

"Mmm?"

"Why did you come here tonight?"

He shifted his hips to get comfortable. "I knew you were upset."

Upset was putting it mildly. "I was bitchy to Nina and bitchy to Chris and bitchy to Joyce."

"Joyce?"

"She called you. So I walked right past her without a word."

"She understands, Maggie."

"How much does she know?"

"Most everything. I wanted her to let me know if Shanahan came again, and she asked just the right questions, no more, and she's like a mother."

I grunted. "Not like mine."

"Or mine. That's what makes her so appealing."

"She didn't say anything to me."

"Why would she?"

"I don't know." But I did. It was a whole other side of me, one that was neither pretty nor praiseworthy. Looking back, I didn't see anything she had done in my regard that was different. But I couldn't see into her deepest thoughts. They had to have changed. How could she not think less of me for killing my child?

He sighed. "Jesus, Maggie."

"What?"

"Get past it."

I wanted to tell him he was wrong. I wanted to say that wasn't what I'd been thinking at all. But this was Edward. So I just said, "I'm trying."

We were quiet for a bit. Then, he said, "You're okay with Nina knowing?"

"No." Funny, though, only now I remembered what Nina had said about her own loneliness. She wasn't upset with what I had done, just wanted to know how I had survived it. She wanted help. I had totally shut her out.

"But you're okay with me here?" Edward asked, so again I put Nina aside.

"In town? No."

"I'm not leaving."

"I know."

"You need me."

"You don't need me."

"Are you kidding? I need someone who knows who I am. Not who I am now. Who I was. Besides, you're a good lay."

"Good lays are a dime a dozen."

"How would you know?"

"You're right. I wouldn't." I was suddenly hesitant. "So . . . it was okay?"

"Better than okay. Better than *ever*."

I raised my head at that. "Was I not so good before?"

He pushed my head back to his chest. "You were great before. You're just greater now. That thing you did . . . the back of my thighs? No one loves me like you."

Seeming determined to test the theory, he took me again. And yes, he had a way of inspiring me. I had never been inhibited when it came to sex with Edward. Where he had size, I had finesse. Where he was athletic,

I was creative, which made total sense. Clay was my thing. I knew about kneading and shaping. I knew about fingering rough spots and smoothing others. I loved texture, and earthiness. I loved the beauty of the male form.

"Say it," he whispered when he was on the cusp of climax.

Right there with him, I could barely think the words, much less breathe them, so my plea was as internal as not. "Pull out."

That wasn't what he had in mind. "Say you *love* me."

I simply dug my fingers into his hips to keep them moving. I was close, so close.

"I love you," he gasped with one thrust, and with the next, "You love me. *Say* it."

I couldn't, not yet. And then it didn't matter, because he did pull out, and still we came together, and when he lay exhausted in the notch of my legs, he told me he loved me again.

It was an illusion, for sure. I was as flawed as a person could be. But it was what my damaged heart wanted, so for those few hours in the dark, I believed.

Morning arrived. After sleeping alone for more than four years, I should have felt a visceral alarm at the smell of a man in my bed. But my familiarity with Edward was so ingrained that from the first moment of awareness, I thought nothing of the soft snoring just above my forehead. We hadn't moved much during the night. My cheek was on his shoulder now, but the whole front of me hugged his side, and our legs remained entwined.

I didn't move at first. Having another beating heart with me was precious. With the forest sky starting to brighten, and the house quiet save the rush of heat through the vents, I listened to it until the reality of it brought back the reality of the night before. My reality was about being flawed, and it always returned.

Taking care not to wake Edward, I removed my cheek first, then my leg, and rolled slowly away. Easing open a dresser drawer, I lifted out clean clothes, then crept to the door, slipped into the hall, and reclosed the door.

In the bathroom, I removed my makeup. There was my scar, and, inside the medicine chest, taped right there behind the makeup remover, my mug shot. I had the lightest heat of whisker burn on my inner thigh, but if it was a contest for my attention, the scar and mug shot won hands down. Whisker burns went away. These did not.

Resigned, I took a short shower. Not knowing how much time I'd have until Edward woke up, I quickly put on my new face. For a split second, it occurred to me to let him see the scar—no, not *let* him, but *force* him to see it. Easy to say *I love you* when there were no reminders around.

But I couldn't. It was enough that I see the scar myself.

Once it was hidden, I redid my hair and quietly, very quietly went down the stairs.

My brother was slouched on the sofa. It was the first morning since he had come that he wasn't in the kitchen making breakfast. The presence of all three of my pets crowding in on the cushions with him would have been a tip-off, had his dejected face not said it first.

I approached. "Not good?"

"Nope."

"What happened?"

"Nothing much."

I waited for him to go on. It wasn't like Liam to be stingy with words. "And?"

"No chemistry."

It took me a minute. "Ah." Erica Kahn must not have wanted sex, which meant he'd been hit where it hurt.

"Yeah. Ah." He glanced toward the stairs. "You, obviously, do not have that problem."

"No, but I have so many others—" I stopped. This wasn't about me. Compassion wasn't a competition. I touched his shoulder. "I'm sorry, Liam. It's her loss."

He grunted. "That doesn't really help, y'know."

"How about breakfast? How about I make it for you this time?" I wanted only to make him smile.

He didn't smile. But he did show interest. "That depends. "What are you making?"

"Fried eggs."

He raised his brows. "And . . . ?"

I tried to think what I had. "Ham?"

"That's supposed to cheer me up? Fried eggs and ham is *so* Dr. Seuss."

"It's *Green Eggs and Ham*," I corrected on a wave of nostalgia. Lily had loved that book. She had "read" it to me before she even learned how to read.

If the ache I felt showed, Liam wouldn't have noticed. He was looking past me toward the stairs. Edward was coming down with the phone to his ear and a frown on his face. He wore boxer shorts and nothing else, clearly unconcerned with Liam's being there.

"She's not talking to media," he said into the phone then, "Yes, you said that, but how do I know for sure?" He listened as he approached me and inhaled to speak, only to hold his breath when whoever it was went on. As he listened, his eyes flicked to mine and half-mouthed, "Area code 860. Says it's personal."

860 was my mother's area code. But it sure wasn't my mother. If it were, Edward wouldn't be looking puzzled. He wouldn't be asking questions. He'd be handing the phone over ASAP.

I looked to Liam for a clue. His eyes were apprehensive, but they stayed firm on Edward, who began to repeat, like it was part of the conversation, what he was hearing so we would know.

"You've been trying to reach Liam and can't get through," he said, eying first my brother, then, after a pause, me. "You don't know how to reach Mackenzie." Another pause, eyes downcast now. "No, my number hasn't changed."

The person at the other end was upset. I could hear that much.

Finally, loud enough to get her attention, he said, "Okay. I believe you. Let me see what I can do. What did you say your name was?"

19

Edward held the phone to his ear for a last minute before lowering it out of voice range and asking me a skeptical, "Do you know an Annika Allen?"

I didn't.

But the low *Fuck!* behind me said Liam did. My eyes flew to his in time to see embarrassment. "She's Mom's assistant," he said, but the guilt slipping over his face told more. Annika Allen was Liam's relationship that had ended badly. Of *course,* she'd been trying to reach him. Of *course,* he hadn't answered.

The question—not reassuring at all—was why she was calling to speak with me, on Edward's phone, no less.

Taking it from his hand, I put it to my ear and said a cautious, "Hello?"

The relief on the other end was palpable. "Mackenzie? Thank God! I've been trying to call your brother for days, but he won't pick up. I'm sure he sees my number and thinks I'm calling because I miss him, but I don't. He can be a real shit, y'know?"

I did know, but he was my brother, so I wouldn't have said it even if she paused, which she didn't.

"When I couldn't get through to him, I decided to try to reach you, but the number listed in your mother's Rolodex wasn't in service, and I had no idea where you were living or what name you were using. I asked everyone around here, but no one knew, so I tried searching online, but all I got were articles about, well, from the accident. Then I was flipping through *People* last night, and there you were in Vermont. At least, I thought it was you, because your mom does have a picture of you in her wallet, and while it doesn't have bangs, the face is the same, y'know? Maggie Reid, makeup artist at the Devon Spa. Your mother never told me."

During her monologue, I had been looking at Edward. He seemed curious but calm. I clung to that. I didn't know what Annika Allen wanted, but the fact that she was my mother's assistant and had seen my picture *in Mom's wallet* raised a bunch of scary possibilities.

"I tried calling the Spa," Annika said, "but this was, like, really late last night, and it was closed. So I Googled the place and found an article about the new owner, and I guessed that maybe Ned Cooper was Edward, and remembered that his phone number was in Margaret's Rolodex, so I actually went back to the bakery really, *really* late last night, but I just couldn't get myself to call him so late, because maybe I was wrong that he was the right one. The names were all screwed up, and you're divorced, and his cell phone still had a Massachusetts area code, so if this one was actually in Vermont? As open as your mom is about things at the bakery, it's like there's a wall between that and her private life—"

"Has something happened to her?" I finally broke in. My thoughts were going every which way.

"She fell. That's why I was trying—"

"Fell how?" I asked and, turning my back on both men, wrapped my arm around my waist. I could have used the feel of one of the pets against my leg, but the cats were apparently smarting about my bed being taken by someone else, and Jonah was a lost cause. Or maybe Liam simply needed them more right then, though I couldn't focus on that.

"Down the stairs at home. It happened at night, so she was lying there a while, unconscious apparently, and then, when she came to, it took her a while to get to a phone. She broke her hip and a wrist."

I could see it clear as day. The house was a small Colonial, and those stairs were narrow. Liam and I had taken our share of spills on it, but a tumbling child was one thing, a sixty-five-year-old woman with a full-sized body, longer limbs, and osteoporosis another.

But sixty-five wasn't old. My mother wasn't old.

"How bad?" I asked. I shouldn't have been frightened, but I was. My chest shouldn't have clenched, but it did.

"The wrist was an easy set, but the hip needed surgery."

"Surgery? When?"

"Last week—"

"And you're only calling now?" A hand touched my back. The comfort of it calmed me enough to realize that I was being unfair, but my mother's assistant was on it.

"I've been trying Liam all week," she argued. "I left message after message, and told him to call back, *begged* him to call back. I didn't want to leave details on voice mail, but finally I did say that his mother broke her hip, and *still* he didn't call back. So either he didn't listen to my messages, or he just didn't want to call—because I don't lie, I have never lied, and that was actually a problem with us, my honesty was hard for him to take. But here's another thing," she went on, still in defense mode. "She didn't want me to call either of you. She said that Liam wouldn't be any help, and that you're too busy and not to bother you and that she'd do just fine, but I don't think she is. She's sleeping on the living room sofa because she can't climb—"

"How do they treat a broken hip?" I asked. "What did the surgery do?"

"They put in a single-compression hip screw. The procedure was straightforward, and Margaret had no complications. They had her up and walking the day after surgery, but they wanted her to go to rehab, and she refused. She says she has plenty of friends who can help. Only when her friends call, she tells them she's fine. I mean, I called one of them when I couldn't reach you or Liam. Alice Mahr?"

I knew Alice. She and her husband had been at my wedding. She would have known that Mom and I were estranged, but the fact that Mom hadn't told her where I was living now spoke volumes.

"She didn't know how to reach you, either," Annika said, "but at least she already knew about the fall when I called her. She talks with your mother a lot, but Margaret tells her not to come over. She says she's groggy from meds and needs to sleep. The church women bring food, but I don't think she's eating it. She's lost weight. Honestly? I think she's depressed."

That possibility upset me nearly as much as the image of my mother lying at the foot of the stairs in the dark. I knew about depression. I knew how paralyzing it could be. I also knew where it could lead.

Rationally, I asked, "Is anyone with her?"

"She has drop-ins. The VNA comes every morning to check her incision. A physical therapist comes every afternoon to get her up and moving around."

"Can she not do that on her own?"

"Oh, she can. She has a walker, but I don't think she's using it much. She really needs one of you there."

"Okay," I said and turned to stare at Liam. He would have to go. If Mom had told her assistant not to bother me because I was too busy, that was code for her not wanting me there. It hurt still, stung like a bad burn. But after four years of reaching out and being treated as dead, I accepted it as fact. "What about the bakery?" I asked.

"I'm on it."

"Is my mother on it, too?" This was my litmus test. The Buttered Scone was her baby.

There was a pause, then a hesitant, "Vaguely."

"Meaning?"

"I'm her second in command. I can do what she does. We talk a couple of times a day, so she knows what's going on, but honestly? I don't think she cares like she did."

Score one for depression.

"So will you come?" Annika asked.

"Liam will." But as soon as the words were out, Liam was shaking his head. So I said, "One of us will."

"Soon?"

"Yes."

"Thank you, thank you *so* much," Annika said with a gratitude as palpable as her relief had been at the start, which made me believe her when she said, "I've only been at The Buttered Scone for three years, but I really love your mother, and I know she's in pain. She needs family with her"— she caught in a loud breath—"but I won't tell her you're coming." In that instant, we became conspirators. "She'll be furious that I called you, and if I tell her I recognized your face in *People* from a shot in her wallet, she'll fire me for sure. I only went through her wallet because I thought there'd be some clue how to reach you, and I felt totally guilty the whole time. I'll tell her that I kind of put two and two together from the friends of hers I talked with—I even called her priest, I really did—but not one of them knew. Why didn't they know? Margaret is a proud woman."

"Stubborn," I murmured before I could help myself.

"That, too, but she wouldn't like me sticking my nose in her business. Only this really is an emergency."

The facts suggested it—assuming they were correct, and I had no cause to doubt Annika. She sounded coherent and genuinely concerned. I ended the call, promising to be in touch.

Edward and Liam had gotten the gist of what had happened from my half of the conversation. As I returned the phone to Edward, though, my eyes were on Liam.

He hadn't moved from the sofa—had a proprietary hand on my dog now and was sitting straight. "I'm not going," he said. "You're the girl. You'll know what to do with bandages and bathroom stuff. I can't help Mom in the shower."

I opened my mouth to argue. But the words didn't come. The issue wasn't Liam's being male. Many men helped their sick mothers. Many health care workers were male.

The issue wasn't even Liam's having been Mom's hero, until he was not.

The issue was me. I hadn't talked with my mother since she had blamed me for Dad's death and disowned me. I had tried to break through the wall many, many times and failed. The issue was whether I could try again.

I looked up at Edward. His hand had dropped from my back, but he remained close. I saw understanding in his eyes, perhaps even expectation. Beyond it, though, was just that little bit of distance between us saying that the decision was mine.

My gaze fell to his bare chest. The hair there had never been heavy, but seeing it for the first time now in the light of day, I saw a whisper of gray. It was the same gray that glinted in his finger-combed bed-head. It was also on his face, in the beard that was so short but so dense.

Five years later, he was the same, but not. He was five years older, five years more experienced, intuitive, sensitive—whatever. And me? I was five years older, too, and, if so, I had to be bolder. Sure, I could bully Liam into taking care of Mom. But she was my mother, too, and as independent, as self-sufficient, as stubborn, maybe even as angry as she was, she needed help.

We are our choices. It wasn't a Momism. Margret McGowan Reid was too devoted to the church to admire an existentialist like Sartre. But I had studied him in school, and my friends and I had glommed onto the words. *We are our choices.* Five years ago, I chose to take my eyes off the road. Then I chose to divorce Edward. I chose to reinvent myself as a makeup artist. I chose to move to Devon.

Those were all big choices. But this felt like one, too. I was at a crossroad. After behaving badly yesterday, I had ended up alone with my green velvet box and no one to love. Here, now, today was my chance to be someone new and different—someone better. The issue, I realized as I stood with my eyes on Edward's and my heart wavering, was responsibility.

"I'll go," I told him with quiet resolve and took a quick breath. "I'll have to miss work. Can we get Ronan Dineen to cover?"

"Joyce will handle it," he said, thumbing through his contacts as he started for the stairs. "Give me five to get dressed. I'm driving."

"Uh—"

He turned midflight, those pale-blue eyes spearing mine. They held past and present, maybe even future, but no matter what, they dared me to argue. And honestly? I needed him to make sure I got there.

"Call Shanahan," he said and, resuming the climb, reached the top of the stairs in two strides.

It was only seven-thirty, so I wasn't surprised when Shanahan didn't answer his office line. When he didn't pick up his cell, either, I texted. *My mother broke her hip. I just got the call. I have to go to CT. Yes?* He would allow it, and if he didn't, let him send the State Police after me. Edward was driving. I felt safe.

We were barely through the center of Devon, driving through a light, misting rain, when I texted Kevin an identical message. Within seconds, he replied. *Are you OK?*

My finger hovered over the phone. Kevin had issues with Edward. He had taken a step back after Town Meeting, seeming to accept that Edward's feelings for me were genuine. Still, I sensed a lingering element of something that was either protectiveness or jealousy.

Whichever, I couldn't lie, not to Kevin. So I typed, *Edward's driving. He's being good.*

I'd have driven, Kevin texted back, and in the midst of my turmoil, I felt a sweet warmth.

I know. Love you for that.

You okay seeing your mom?

No. But I have to. There's no one else.

That's not why you have to.

I smiled at the guy's insight before typing, *I know that, too. I love you, Kev.*

He sent two lines of kiss-blowing emojis. Buoyed by those, I dared check out who else had sent texts since *People* had arrived. There were the usual suspects—Alex, my book group, and—oh yes—Michael Shanahan from last night with a simple *Careful, Maggie* message. But there was nothing from Grace.

I tried calling. When she didn't pick up, I left a message with the basics, so that she wouldn't look for me at work. The message had to be shocking, first mention of my mother, then mention of her fall. Either should have been enough for Grace to immediately call back. When she didn't, I texted, *Are you there?* Then I set the phone in my lap and watched the road, but my mind was racing from Grace to Michael to Mom and back. *Breathe in, breathe out, repeat.*

"Music?" Edward asked.

"No—yes—uh, maybe." I breathed in. "What do you have?"

He passed me his phone. I scrolled through his stations. Aside from a few additions, the list was the same as when we were married. As was mine, I thought, and the absurdity of the situation struck me. My ex-husband driving me to my mother's house?

In some regards, it made perfect sense. Edward knew the situation and the players. He was rational and calm. I trusted him to get me there and back intact.

In other regards, though, it made no sense at all—no sense that the call had come to his phone while he was in my bed, where he had spent the night, with me. It made no sense that he had known to come to me when I was feeling so low, no sense that we still had such a strong emotional connection, no sense that the sex was so good. Our lovemaking had died soon after Lily did. But here it was, reborn hotter than ever.

I studied him without fully turning my head. He wore a black turtleneck, jeans, and his barn jacket, so only his head and hands were bare. His profile was strong, but his hands were what fascinated me now—

fingers that were solid and agile, that had touched every inch of my body last night and brought so much pleasure. That I should be so turned on by Edward in spite of all the grief we'd shared made no sense *at all*.

And yet, sitting here with him in a mix of new car, virile man, and misty rain smells, hearing the *shush* of the tires speeding over the road and a crescendo of *shushing* when we passed or were passed, it felt like the most natural thing of all.

I didn't need music. Between sounds and thoughts, there was plenty of noise. Handing back the phone, I focused on the road. Visibility wasn't great; we drove in and out of ground fog. The wipers kicked in every ten seconds or so, picked up when the mist became a drizzle, then slowed again.

My phone lit. Shanahan. *Seriously?* he wrote.

With my emotions in high gear, his doubt set me off. *Would I do this for kicks? My mother hasn't talked to me in four years. The call came from her assistant.* I punched Send before fully analyzing the wisdom of it, but was angry enough to add, *Trust me, I don't want to be going, but she's my mother.* I sent that one off with a huff and muttered, "Like having to ask permission helps . . ."

"Only a few months left," Edward said and gave my hand a squeeze. "Warm enough?" He stretched a long arm toward the middle console anyway, able fingers setting my heated seat to high. I hadn't thought to ask, but the heat was nice.

How long will you be there? Shanahan texted.

It was an interesting question. *I haven't thought that far. Just the day, I think.* Neither of us had overnight bags. *I have to see how she is.*

Let me know.

Returning the phone to my lap, I refocused on the road. We had joined I-89 heading toward White River Junction. It was a route I had driven many times, mostly to see Shanahan, which was part of my punishment and, therefore, welcome in its way. Only now, here, in Edward's car, with Edward and an illusion of normalcy, did I find having a probation officer humiliating.

I closed my eyes, pictured a mountain stream, inhaled and exhaled to the sound of trickling water.

"You good?" Edward's deep voice asked.

My eyes popped open just as his darted me a quick glance. I darted one back that held doubt.

"You're doing the right thing," he said.

"Tell that to my heart. What if she refuses to see me?"

"She won't."

"Why not?"

"She needs you."

My phone screen lit. *Barely,* I read.

"Grace," I told Edward and texted, *Is Chris okay?*

Contrite, she replied, but made no comment about my past, which she certainly would have, if Chris had told her. *Suddenly gets it. Realizes what a big deal this is. Did it take* People *to convince him?*

Possibly, I thought, though I wondered whether my confession had played even a small role. That would be redeeming.

How are YOU? I asked.

Nervous. Hiding. Angry at the kid.

I didn't respond. I got the nervous and hiding part, but the angry-at-the-kid part hit too close to home.

"They say a mother's love is unconditional," I said aloud, "but which is more abiding—a mother's love or a child's need for it?"

Edward was quiet at first. "You do need her love."

"But does she love me?"

"She's your mother."

"It's been four years. I've reached out. She doesn't respond."

"Emotions are complex."

"That's my point. Can she love me even if she can't forgive me?"

It was a minute before he said, "Can you love anyone, if you can't forgive yourself?"

The message was for me, but I wasn't there yet. "What if she tells me to leave?"

"I'll talk with her."

"She hates you."

His smile was crooked. "True. So maybe I need to be doing this, too."

But I wasn't there yet, either. "If she doesn't want me in her house, what can I *do* for her?"

"Make lunch."

That raised a whole other issue. "Annika said the church brought food, but how do I know it's still fresh? I should be bringing food myself. That's what a good daughter would do."

"A good daughter would wait and see what she has and what she wants. I can always make a supermarket run."

Now *there* was a distraction. Edward and I used to food shop together when we first met, not so much once we were married. My career had always been more forgiving than his, even after Lily was born.

"Well, yeah, that's another thing I did wrong," Edward said when his offer hung in their air. "I could've helped more. I've gotten pretty good at it since then. Necessity is the mother, and all."

"I would've thought you'd order online and have it delivered."

"Sometimes I did."

"When you were really busy."

"When I didn't want to be seen."

"Because people might recognize you?" I asked, thinking *collateral damage.*

But his expression held its own brand of shame. "When I felt like shit about me. When I hated work and missed you and couldn't see the future. I ordered paper towels online and had pizza delivered and watched *Homeland.*"

"*Homeland.* Not too real?" *Game of Thrones* was fantasy, which was the only reason I could bear the violence.

"Yes, too real. That's why it helped. It got me out of myself." He thought. "But the supermarket grew on me. Walking up and down aisles pushing a cart is mind-numbing."

So food shopping was his CALM. I used the reminder to take another slow breath, before returning to the subject of Mom. "Old people break hips. My mother isn't old."

"Falling down a flight of stairs can do it to anyone."

"What if my being there makes things worse?"

He reached for my hand. The Jeep was warm, so my gloves were off. When he linked our fingers and rested them on the console, I didn't resist. His touch made me feel less frightened.

We drove on in silence. He took his hand back when he needed both to signal and steer around a massive eighteen-wheeler. And then, way too soon for my nerves, we were on I-91, with Brattleboro in the rearview, Massachusetts ahead. Had I been driving myself, I'd probably have turned around, which was another reason I was grateful Edward was there.

We passed a family packed into a large SUV. *That could have been us,* I thought, and shot him a glance.

"Could've been us," he said. "Still can."

"You're crazy."

"It's what we always wanted."

"Once."

"Still."

"After everything I did? That takes a whole lot of forgiveness."

"You're the only one hung up on that," he muttered and added, "I need coffee," when a rest stop appeared out of the mist. When I declined his offer of the bathroom, he steered into the drive-thru lane. In no time we were back on the road with two coffees and two breakfast sandwiches.

We ate as we drove. Actually he ate. I was too tense to do more than nibble. When he was done with his, he finished mine.

"I used to send her things when I first moved to Devon," I said, "you know, postcards and cards silk-screened with scenes from Devon. She never acknowledged receiving them. I emailed. She never answered. I posted comments on Facebook. They disappeared."

After a minute, he said, "Your mother is a tough woman."

I sputtered a facetious agreement. The mist had cleared, leaving only the very palest of gray days. There was actually glare. Fishing sunglasses from my bag, I put them on, but the world felt too dark then. So I took them off again, tucked them in my lap with my phone, and said, "What she did—shutting me out—was like another death. First Lily, then my dad, then her. I couldn't be happy, so I blocked them out of my mind." I eyed him beseechingly. "Was that wrong, Edward? Is it wrong to want to be happy?"

"Christ, no."

"Then why is this happening? I survived by not thinking about her. Now I have to."

"Maybe it's time."

"To move on? Easier said than done. I'm so sorry—for what I did to her—for what I did to *you*. That whole scene," not the accident, but the fiasco it caused, "was a nightmare. I did that. I inflicted that on you. How can you forget?"

"You don't. Maybe you incorporate it into who you are and move on."

"But Lily—"

"Is dead. We have memories. They need a place in our lives."

I thought of the nights I spent with her, so many nights over the last five years. She felt so real.

I glanced at Edward. When his eyes flicked to mine, leaving the road for just that split second, they were sad. "You are the problem, honey."

"I know! That's what I'm saying."

"No. Not the accident. Not the media circus. Not even your mother's detachment. You're the one who can't move on."

"Can't forgive?"

"That, too."

The words hung in the air, along with the smell of man and car and drying pavement. We had crossed the state line and were in Connecticut. If the weather were an omen, it should have been raining like hell. If the weather were *kind*, it should have been raining like hell. Clearing skies? Clearing thoughts? Not a help, when we were moving closer to my mother, mile by mile.

"Maybe," he finally said, "you don't need to completely forgive. Maybe it's like memories of Lily. Maybe it just becomes part of who you are."

"Resenting someone forever?"

"Yes. A very small part."

"But can you be happy living like that?"

He leaned forward to check an overhead sign as we passed beneath. We were still several exits away. Then he sighed. "Okay. Here are the choices." One strong finger rose from the wheel. "You shut it all away, pretend none of it happened, lock the box, and never look back. That's total denial." Another finger rose. "Or you put the past on a pedestal—"

"Not a pedestal. That's too rosy."

"Dais, stage, front-and-center, whatever. You make it the first thing you think about in the morning and the last thing at night. You let it dominate everything you do. That's obsession."

I waited. "What's my next choice?" I knew there was one, because these two were extremes, and Edward was not.

He didn't bother with the finger this time, but said with resignation, "You accept what you can't change and move on."

"Is that what you do?"

"It's how I wound up in Devon."

"But you still resent me."

"No. I don't. I told you. I don't blame you for the accident. But I can't vouch for your mother. If she needs a scapegoat for her disappointments, you may be it." Grabbing my hand, he gave it a little shake. "Or not. We'll know soon."

I had grown up on a street of modest homes in Bloomfield, a suburb of Hartford, and there had been changes over the years, but they always seemed small. Signs of a new family, a new paint job, or an addition connecting house to garage were topics of discussion when I came home to visit. In my life, I hadn't ever gone a month without a visit home.

Now, four years had passed, and—like us—my parents' street was the same, but not. The ranch house where a high school classmate had lived was still there, but the one beside it had been torn down and replaced with a large arts-and-crafts-style home. The gorgeous hedge of forsythia that had positively glowed for three weeks each spring had been replaced with arborvitae. The plain shingle home across the street from the hedge had been dressed up with fieldstone, dormers, and skylights. And the maple trees I loved, the ones that had been planted before I was born, when farmland was first carved up into streets?

Gone!

Lindens stood in their place—spindly saplings with cords holding them straight, and while I knew that lindens were fast-growing and would interfere less with overhead wires than the maples had done, I felt a sense of loss.

The sense of loss, of course, included Lily and my dad, both of whom were newly gone when I was here last. And the feeling only intensified when we turned into the driveway I knew so well.

I put a hand to my chest, which had gone hard. "I can't do this," I whispered. If my mother rejected me now, I would be destroyed.

Edward turned off the motor. "Too late. We're here." In a gesture so casual it might have been a stretch, he reached out to massage the back of my neck.

"You're supposed to say I *can* do it," I said when I could breathe again.

"That's a given. You're a strong woman, Mackenzie."

"About to face a far stronger one."

"Maybe. Maybe not." He was leaning forward to study the house. "It doesn't look so good."

My own vision had been clouded by emotion. Now I took a clearer look. There were other Colonials on the street, many wearing the same gray-and-white, so ours totally fit in. But our gray body was peeling, our white trim stained, our front walk cracked, and our shrubs overgrown.

"Doesn't bode well," I said with a wince and sat back.

After a minute of silence came a quiet coaxing. "You can do it."

When I turned to look at him, his eyes held utter conviction—and how not to believe it? He certainly said everything right. Lord knew, his life in Devon hadn't been a cakewalk. And still he was here.

In that instant, I felt love, appreciation, even awe. For his sake alone, I had to face my mother.

Unbuckling my seat belt, I reached for the door.

20

And so I found myself—well, Edward and me—at my mother's front door. Was I supposed to ring the bell? Knock? Use a key to let myself in? I had always done this before—used a key. And that key was still on my key ring, which, since I hadn't needed car keys and had left in an emotional firestorm, was back in Vermont.

That said, times had changed. I was a stranger here. If my mother heard the door opening, she might be terrified. Might call 911. Might even have a *gun*.

I gave the wood three soft knuckle-raps, then waited, listening, but my heart was the only beat I heard. I knocked more firmly. Still nothing.

"Ring the bell," Edward said.

"What if she's sleeping?" And if she was? Would I turn away? Drive off? Chalk the whole thing up to a mistake and return to Devon?

"Ring the bell."

I rang the bell. I put my ear to the door, just to the right of a faded wreath. The silence I heard gave me permission to use the key. Sure, she might be out of the house, but if Annika was right about her refusing the help of friends, that chance was slim. And if she was home and not answering, not even yelling from wherever she lay, it could be that she'd fallen again or worse. I had to go in.

Slipping my fingers behind the wreath, I circled until I found the key. It turned easily in the lock. I opened the door.

"Mom?"

Typical of many small Colonials build in the 1980s, there was no front hall, just a small space framed by openings that led elsewhere—left to the living room, right to the dining room, forward to a narrow hallway leading back, with a flight of stairs straight ahead and up.

"Mom?" I called again. Behind me, quietly, Edward shut the door.

From the living room came a groggy, "Hello?"

Frightened by the sound, I hurried there.

Like the outside of the house, the only thing about the living room that had changed was its age. At its heart, two upholstered sofas faced off over an oblong table centered on the hearth; twin armchairs anchored the room front and back, two chairs each of the faux–Queen Anne sort. The chairs were empty, and Mom wasn't on the sofa that faced us, but a vague wave rose from its mate.

Swallowing hard, I rounded the sofa—and it was all I could do not to cry out. For all the times I'd imagined seeing my mother again, it was the vibrant, active, officious woman I pictured. This woman was none of those things. This one lay inert on the cushions, her lower half haphazardly covered by an afghan, her upper half by a wrinkled cotton shirt and skewed sweater that bulked over the cast on her left wrist, all of it crying *disheveled* as Margaret McGowan Reid never, ever allowed herself to be. But her face was what shocked me most. It was too drawn, too pale, seeming bled of life, like the florals around her.

My mother had always been a striking woman, with long legs, a straight back, vivid auburn hair, and eyes the color of spring grass. In my

290

mind, she would always be energetic and young. Today, though, she looked every one of her sixty-five years.

Her eyes were disoriented as they met mine. They flew to Edward when he appeared at my shoulder, and there was a flash of alarm before they returned to me, all without a blink.

Was she drugged? Half-asleep? Was she wanting to believe but afraid to—wanting to disbelieve but unable to? Was she confused? Frightened? *Angry?*

I couldn't begin to figure out which. I only knew that this was my mother, who, sternness and all, had raised me, clothed me, read to me, cooked with me, glowed for me on the day I'd become a mother myself. This was my mother, whom I had missed nearly as much as I missed my child. This was my mother, those whatever eyes in that hurting body.

My own eyes blurred, tears gathering as they hadn't done in many, many months. They didn't go far, too rusty to do more than gather on my lower lids, but it wasn't my chest that squeezed me breathless this time. It was definitely my heart.

In a beat, I was squatting beside her. "Mommy?" I cried, barely a sound. "It's me."

"I know that," she whispered, not unkindly. Her eyes cleared as reality registered. But clouds remained. "Why?"

"I heard you'd fallen. How do you feel?"

"Fine," she said but didn't move.

"Are you in pain?"

"I thought you were my physical therapist."

"What time does she come?"

"Two. What time is it now?"

I pushed at the sleeve of my parka to free my watch. "Ten."

Appearing surprised by that, she made to get up. When she fell back, I slipped an arm under her shoulders to help her sit. My mother had always been admirably slim, but now, through the sweater, I felt skin and bones.

One didn't turn to skin and bones in a single week, which was how long it had been since her fall. Nuh-uh. This had been a while coming. Like five years? For a split second, I blamed myself. If it hadn't been for the accident, those years would have been happy.

Or not, I could hear Edward saying. *Or not,* I could hear Kevin saying. *Or not,* even Cornelia would have said if I ever dared tell her the truth. *Life happened,* they would say, and maybe they were right. If it hadn't been one thing, it might have been another.

"My walker," Mom said, eye-pointing at the thing that stood between the sofa and the hearth.

"I'll help you walk." I slipped off my coat and tossed it aside. "Where do you want to go?"

"The walker is fine."

"I want to help. Are you hungry? Do you need to take a pill? Go to the bathroom?"

"They want me using the walker," she insisted.

It was a test of wills, I realized, and while hugs and kisses, even tears might have been nice, challenging me over a walker was better than, *Leave my house right now, you murderer.*

Gently, I said, "The walker is fine if you're alone, Mom. If the point is having backup when you put weight on your hip, I'm like a walker. Just tell me where you want to go."

She stared for an uncertain moment before conceding. "The bathroom."

I felt absurdly victorious when she let me help her up. Determining where to hold and how was awkward at first, but once we found it, we were good. She used to be two inches taller than me—literally five-eight to my five-six—and now we were closer, though, in fairness, she was neither standing straight nor wearing shoes. Her weight was negligible. She actually bore most of it herself, using me largely for balance.

This was a good sign. A person who was seriously depressed didn't do pride.

She let me guide her into the small lav, but once inside, she used her casted arm to nudge me out and close the door.

I waited for the thud of falling, but only heard normal bathroom sounds. Meanwhile, Edward was in the kitchen. The fridge door opened. I heard the crinkle of tinfoil as he checked packages there before closing the door. There were more tinfoil sounds from the counter. One cabinet opened and shut, then another.

He ran the water, filled the kettle, and lit the gas with a *tick* and a *whoosh*. All were familiar sounds, but of my mother's habitual doing, not Edward's. He and I had never used a kettle. A Keurig, Nespresso, or Instant Hot—yes. But not a kettle. I might have been fascinated by what he was doing and why, if I wasn't suddenly concerned with the silence in the bathroom.

"Mom?" I called against the wood.

She opened the door only enough to hold up her casted wrist. "Makes things harder," she said and set to washing her hands.

When she was done, I returned my arm to her waist. "I'd like tea. You?"

Her answer was a soft snort. Of course, she'd like tea.

"Are you in pain?" I asked as we approached the kitchen table. Something about the room was different, but not the table. It was the same one I'd grown up at, carried the same nicks and scratches on its aged oak face. That face now also held a laptop whose screen saver was emitting starbursts of color, suggesting fairly recent use.

"Some," she said, sounding vague. With a hand on either chair arm, she lowered herself, but it was a minute of gingerly shifts before she found the best spot.

"When do the stitches come out?" I asked, taking a seat beside her.

"Tuesday."

"Who takes you to the doctor?"

"Uber."

That broke my heart. "Not a friend? Someone from work?"

"The drivers are great," she challenged.

But not family, I might have said if she hadn't been daring me to argue. But I had won on the walker; I could let her win here. If this was a truce, I wasn't messing with it.

From the counter, Edward said, "Your friends brought enough food to feed an army, Margaret, but it's early for lunch. Did you have breakfast?"

She shot him a nervous glance but didn't answer.

Taking that as a *no,* he said, "You have eggs. I could scramble some."

Looking at me again, she screwed up her face. "Didn't you get divorced?"

"Yes," I said. "I moved away. He followed."

"When?"

"Two weeks ago."

"It was in the works for two years," Edward put in.

"Unknown to me."

"Unknown?" Mom asked me.

"She would have said *no,*" Edward said from behind. "Mackenzie, does your mother eat eggs?"

"Yes," I said.

"Yes," Margaret said and aimed her voice at Edward. "You don't really need to do that."

"I do."

She looked like she wanted to object but was at a loss for how. So again, she conceded. "Eggs. Yes. Thank you." Back to me, sotto voce, she said, "I didn't know he could cook."

"Neither did I."

"Is it safe?"

I smiled. "What he cooks? We'll soon find out."

I was trying to lighten things up, but my mother seemed too burdened for that. She looked as if she would have run in a split second if her hip had allowed it.

And me? For those times during the drive when I would have turned back, I didn't consider it now. I was exactly where I wanted to be. That said, it was a precarious spot. I didn't know what she was thinking; our landscape had changed. And then there was Edward, who, since showing up last night, was doing everything right, absolutely everything. I wasn't sure what to do with him either.

Mom's mind seemed to shift, eyes suddenly clinging to me in ways that had nothing to do with food. There was something in them that was so strong, so wanting—but gone as quickly as I identified it, so that I was left to wonder if I had simply imagined what I wanted to see.

I might have asked, but didn't dare. Feelings were crucial. We had to talk about them, but right now facts were safer. They were also major, given her health.

"How's your doctor?" I asked her as Edward cracked eggs into a bowl.

"He's fine."

"Do you have faith in him?"

"Yes."

"What do you take for pain?"

Her gaze pointed to the windowsill. "A half dose of whatever's in that bottle."

Edward stopped beating eggs and leaned forward to read the label. "Percocet."

"You never liked taking pills," I said.

"I still don't. They make me woozy. That may be why I'm having trouble . . ." She went quiet and frowned.

"Trouble seeing me?" I had known it wouldn't be easy, still I felt a sharp pang.

"Trouble believing you're here."

"How could I not come? You're my mother."

Her eyes moved over my face, taking in my bangs, the sheen on my cheeks, the balm on my lips.

"It's *me*," I whispered.

"You look different."

"I have to be," I said with enough apology to make it a perfect opening to discuss the past.

Margaret, too, was in the past, but not where I thought. Eyes haunted, voice unsteady, she asked, "If a mother sends her child away, is she still a mother?"

My breath caught. Uncanny how similar it was to the question I had asked myself so many times. My version differed by a few words, but the agony of puzzling out a new reality was the same.

"Yes," I said, because Margaret would always be my mother. "Same if a mother's child dies." I had to believe that. Otherwise, Lily wouldn't continue to exist.

"I wasn't a good mother."

"I'm the one who wasn't."

"It's an awful thing I did."

"No, Mom, *my* fault, all *mine*—" A shrill whistle sounded. Startled, I sat straight. But it was the kettle, just the kettle.

Edward turned off the gas, and the whistle died off, leaving the sizzle of eggs in the pan and my grandmother's soft voice in my mind. *Tea is my handyman,* she used to say. *He fixes everything.*

"Irish Breakfast?" I asked my mother.

"Please."

I found tea bags in their usual cabinet to the left of the sink, found mugs in their usual cabinet to the right, and poured water from the kettle that I had used hundreds of times growing up. As computer literate and social-media savvy as my mother was, in these things she remained a creature of habit.

When I brought the cups to the table, she was shifting carefully. "Is that chair uncomfortable?" I asked. "Can I get a cushion? Would you rather lie down?"

She didn't answer. Rather, seeming baffled, she was looking back at Edward. He had put toast in the toaster and was at the stove again. "I wasn't expecting you," she said. Her voice was timid, but at least she was addressing him directly. "You look different, too."

"More gray."

"More hair," she said, and seeming to have used up her courage where direct contact with him was concerned, returned to me. "How long is he staying in Vermont?"

From the stove, Edward said, "As long as my wife is there."

"Ex-wife," I told Mom.

"But you're together again?"

"No."

"Yes."

"Glad you're in agreement on that," she said and might have smiled. Instead, she refocused on her tea, dipped the bag repeatedly, as if answers would appear in the dark brew.

Behind us came the scrape of a buttered knife over toast.

I sighed. "Life is confusing."

"Very," she said quickly enough.

Before we could get into it, Edward gestured me to move the laptop, and was placing plates before us, then orange juice, napkins, and forks. As an afterthought, he added a jar of jam. It was everything I liked, which was everything my mother liked, which was likely why it was what I liked. Which of us was he trying to please? Did it matter?

"Impressive," I said and, feeling light-headed, sampled the eggs. When I realized that the other two were watching me, I pretended to gag.

To Margaret, Edward said, "There's one gone. More eggs for us."

I smiled. "Nope. It's good. Eat up, Mom. You need fattening." And that raised an issue that went beyond osteoporosis. Fattening wouldn't happen in one meal. She needed someone here to make it happen. Edward and I had left Devon on a few minutes' notice. We weren't even prepared to stay overnight. I had to go back. I would. No way could Shanahan deny this. If necessary, I would take it to court.

First, though, I needed to know what the typical recuperation from a broken hip was. But Mom had started to eat—hungrily, in fact—and I was suddenly famished myself. So we ate. She didn't ask about my life or about what Edward was doing in Devon, and she made no mention of Liam. It should have been awkward, but wasn't. We were in the same room. That was enough.

After a bit, I put down my fork. "How does a hip repair work? You get the stitches out on Tuesday, but what comes after that?"

She had either been lost in thought or simply too focused on eating to keep track of her surroundings. Swallowing, she set aside her fork and wiped her mouth with her napkin.

"Rest and PT," she finally said, and, to Edward, "Thank you. This is very good."

"How often is PT?" I asked.

"As often as I want. It's about flexibility. And strength." But she was looking at Edward again. "It isn't only the hair. You look rougher."

"Less slick?" Edward said and slid me a smug grin.

"He's become an innkeeper," I told my mother.

"A what?"

"Innkeeper," said Edward.

"Crunchy is the look," I said.

"Crunchy," Margaret repeated. She certainly knew the meaning of the word beyond the texture of cookies. When I was in college, crunchy was the only word Dad used to describe my friends. He had done it repeatedly, and not by way of flattery.

Lest my mother head in that direction, I steered her back. "How often do you see the doctor?"

She reached for the jam with her good hand. "After the stiches come out? I don't know."

Of course, she didn't. Uber wouldn't sit with her, making sure she asked the right questions and remembered the answers. Apparently not even Annika did, though I suspected my mother wouldn't allow that.

She needed me.

Feeling emboldened, I said, "How long is the recuperation?"

"Three months, give or take."

"With pain?"

"No. The pain is less each day. I'm about done with those pills. Tylenol will do."

"Can you get out? Go places?" I was thinking about church, and about all of those friends who might take her to lunch.

"I am *not* going anywhere with that walker," she declared. "As soon as I can, I'll use a cane."

"What's happening with work?" I asked. It seemed a normal follow-up to using a cane. If The Buttered Scone was my mother's baby, she would be in a rush to get back—unless what Annika said about her losing interest was true.

She shifted, then settled again. "Work is fine." Lifting her fork, she resumed eating without looking at me. I wondered if Annika was right.

I glanced at the laptop. "Who's been posting on Facebook?"

"Me. I only missed a day."

"Who runs the bakery?"

"Annika Allen," she said and reached for jam. "She's very good."

I waited for her to say something about Annika that might reveal either her knowledge of the Annika-Liam connection or of Annika having called me. When she did neither, I took the coward's route and let it go.

"Is there anything you're not allowed to do?" I asked.

"Run," she said. Edward snickered. She shot him an uneasy glance before adding, "Lift anything more than five pounds."

"Climb stairs?"

"I can if I want."

"Do the stairs make you nervous?" They were the scene of the crime, so to speak.

"Some." Her eyes rose, her voice vehement. "And don't suggest a stair lift. I am not *old*, for Christ's sake."

That took me by surprise, not the stair-lift part but the swearing part. It wasn't like Margaret to take the Lord's name in vain. But she was glaring at me, daring me to argue. And she was, in fact, looking more, with each passing minute, like the mother I knew. So I held up a hand, shook my head, backed off.

"What about swimming?" asked Edward.

"They suggested that, but I don't swim."

"You used to," I reminded her. "Way back. You used to do it every morning before work."

"That pool closed. I'd have to go farther for an indoor one."

I wasn't mentioning Uber. "When can you drive?" Luckily, the broken bones were all on her left side, not her right.

She picked up a piece of toast. "Not soon enough." She sighed. "The problem is reaction time. Surgery slows it down. If I drive too soon and cause an accident . . ." She pursed her lips and shook her head. Then, seeming to realize what she'd said, she dropped the toast and folded her arms.

I couldn't have asked for a better lead-in. Curling my fingers around her thin wrist, I whispered, "I'm sorry, Mom. Sorry for everything that happened. Do you know how many times I've relived those minutes and done things differently in my mind—like stopping and flagging down the first car to come along, or turning around and going back—but I didn't that day. I kept driving. Do you know how *sorry* I am?"

There were many things my mother could have said, but all she did was unfold her arms and wrap her hands around her tea.

"Mom?"

She sighed. "What can I say?"

"Something maybe about God forgiving our sins, or God having a plan?"

She let out a huff and looked into the distance. "I don't know about God." The eyes that returned to me were tear-filled. "I don't know. I just don't know what to say. I don't know why things happen or what to do when you lose what you always wanted and can't get it back. Is it God's punishment? Is God even *there*?"

"Of course, He is," I said because though my own beliefs were negligible, my mother's were not. Hers had never wavered. Until now. Which meant that her emotions were in *real* trouble. An intervention wouldn't help where religion was concerned since I was struggling with the Almighty myself. But there might be something else.

I looked at Edward, who seemed as alarmed with what Margaret had said as I was. Our eyes met and held. In that instant, that *second*, something passed between us. An idea. Something that made total sense without needing any thought at all, but that when even the tiniest bit of thought was applied, was the only thing that made sense.

"I think," he said, "your mother could use a change."

"Mom?" Leaning in, I grasped her arm, this time with both hands. "Come back to Vermont with us."

Margaret was visibly startled.

"Come back with us," I pushed. "I could definitely drive down here once or twice a week, even stay for a bit, but if you have to recuperate somewhere, why not there? Devon's an amazing place. It'd be a break for you."

"Oh, no," she said, eyes wide, "I couldn't do that."

"Why not?"

"My life is here. My doctor—my physical therapist—my bakery—"

"We have doctors. We have physical therapists. Your assistant is good, you just said that, so what difference would it make if you logged on from here or Devon? No one would know where you were."

"My friends—"

Aren't here now. Aren't driving you places. Aren't family. There was a cell phone on the coffee table in the living room, but it hadn't made a peep since I'd arrived.

"Your friends can stay in touch," I said, "but don't you want to see where I live?"

"I—oh no—you don't really want that."

"I do," I said and tried to sweeten the pot. "I work at a Spa, Mom. It's peaceful and smells wonderful. My friends there would wash and dry your hair. You could have a mani-pedi or a massage."

"I couldn't—"

"And we have a *pool*." I hurried on. "It's an indoor one at the sports center just down the road from the Spa. I could drive you there and back. I live on a beautiful hill and could schedule my work so that I can be home with you, and when I'm not there, Liam is." I stopped short.

She stared at me, then snorted. "Oh, Margaret Mackenzie, I know he's there. No way could that child survive without his mother or his sister. But *I* can't go there."

"Why *not?*"

"It's your place, and I've been horrible to you."

I'd been prepared for more of the creature-of-habit response. Or the I-like-my-own-home one. Or even the I-need-to-get-back-to-work one. Not my mother apologizing.

"But you were right—y'know, way back," Edward said, setting down his fork with a tiny clink. "Our lifestyle was sick. You got that before we did."

My mother looked baffled, but I wasn't being distracted.

"I want you to see my home. This is a perfect excuse—maybe even God's plan." She made a sharp slash with her casted hand. "Okay," I backed off, "maybe not His plan, but it's a good one. Think about it. It'd be like being on vacation. When was the last time you got away?" I didn't expect an answer to that. "You'd have everything you need, plus good people. My friends will love you."

"They're your friends."

"Some are way closer to your age than to mine." I was thinking of Joyce, but Cornelia would qualify, too. She would be onboard in a heart-beat. "They'd be thrilled to have you there."

She struggled, eyes moving here and there in search of an excuse. Finally, she just sank into herself. "It's too much. Really."

Not for me. This made more sense than anything had in a long time. It made perfect sense, actually, and the more I got into it, the more sense it made—the more I imagined it, the better I felt. The prospect of having my mother in Devon made me feel *happy*.

"It's a two-and-a-half-hour drive," I said. "We could leave right after your PT session. Front seat, back seat—you can sit wherever you're most comfortable. We can stop every half hour to get out and walk. Edward is a safe driver."

"That's not the issue," my mother tried.

"And here's another thing, Mom." She hadn't gotten up to walk away and end the discussion, which she would have done in the old days. I could blame her hip for that. Or not. Hopeful, pushing it, I said, "Devon is small, it's do-able. It's refreshing." I was thinking of the days when I had first come, way before the media had, but the media had pretty much exhausted itself, hadn't it? That was the art of the dream. "And it's different. You need a change. Devon is a change." I straightened and smiled. "It worked for me."

"And for me," Edward said.

She was torn. I could see it in her eyes, which went back and forth between him and me. I was startled to see shame. "You owe me nothing."

"Not owe," I insisted. "*Want.* I *want* you to come, Mom. It would be fabulous. For both of us."

"I don't know—"

"We could talk."

"Oh, Mackenzie—"

"Dad would want you to do this. He would want me to do it."

She seemed heartened by that, but only briefly. "Would he? I just don't know any more. Too much of what I want is different from what he wants."

"What do *you* want?"

My mom had always been a woman in control, but she had zero of it now. I'd never seen her bewildered. In a broken voice, she said, "I want to think. A little space, please?"

21

After tucking the afghan around her, I sat by my mother's hip. She wanted space, but I couldn't walk out. We didn't talk. I didn't even hold her hand, just wanted her to know I was there.

And honestly? The fact that she allowed it was a gift. Did I still want more? Absolutely. But I would have been naïve to think that our relationship would pick up where it had been before the accident. Too much had happened; we were different people now from the ones we had been then. Actually, if I were to dream, I would return to what our relationship had been when I was growing up. It wasn't all showy with hugs and kisses, more a meeting of minds. She was independent; I was independent. She was disciplined; I was disciplined. If I walked into the kitchen while she was making dinner, I set the table, not because she asked but because it needed doing. If I was cramming for an exam, she brought me tea, not because I asked but because it would help.

Things changed once I hit college and even more after I married

Edward. I remember, though, that when the accident happened, she had dropped everything and come.

Then she had gone back home to get my father, and by the time she returned, she was distant. So maybe the real problem was Dad. Maybe Liam was right. Maybe she was simply the enforcer. But my father had been dead for more than four years, during which time she hadn't reached out on her own.

I wanted to ask whether she still blamed me for his death. But what we had here, now, was too fragile. Besides, she had closed her eyes as soon as she lay down, giving her the space she needed. Her lids moved; I wondered what images flickered there. Gradually, the movements slowed, and she dozed off.

Cautious not to wake her, I eased off the sofa and crept from the room. She hadn't said yes to coming to Devon. But I was packing her bag anyway.

Then doubt set in. Halfway up the stairs, I turned and sat. There were two major problems here. I had barely begun to work through them when Edward appeared at the foot of the stairs, and, for a split second, that startled me, too. No matter that we'd been in each other's company since last night, for so long before this I had gone it alone. The idea that he was here for me, tall and dark, sensible and strong, still stunned me.

Sitting one step lower so that his head was that little bit closer to mine, he whispered, "It's the right thing to do."

"I know," I whispered back, but my hands were clenched between my knees.

"You're worried about exposure."

"For starters."

"That won't happen, Maggie," he whispered, looking sideways at me. "Nina was the only one who figured it out from *The Devon Times* piece."

"That we know of." And here I was today, AWOL with Edward. In theory, only Joyce and Kevin knew that, but theory only worked if no one else figured it out.

"Nina's the exception," he came back. "She's from a world where suspicion is a player. You know her secrets, so she wants to know yours. The rest of the people in Devon? They're not looking. You and your mother are Reids, but the accident involved a Cooper—and in Massachusetts, not Connecticut. There's no reason for people to make the connection."

"But I can't tell Mom not to talk. All it would take is an innocent comment, like, *Mackenzie had a bad time after the crash,* and I'm outed."

"She'll only be with good friends. Would it be so bad if they knew?"

Yes, the frightened voice in me said, but his pale-blue eyes were a beacon in the shadowed stairway, guiding me somewhere new.

"Explain the situation," he urged softly. "Ask her not to mention the accident."

"She'll say I'm hiding."

"Confess to it. Be honest. She's feeling things that you hadn't known, like the religion thing, so maybe she'll talk more if you do. Explain your fears. Get her invested in this. She'll be pleased to be drawn into the loop."

I wasn't sure. The meek Margaret down there on the sofa was an enigma. And that was only one of my doubts.

Edward got the others, too. Propping an elbow behind him, so that he was angled my way, he whispered, "You're also wondering where in the hell to put your mother in your house, because there's only one bedroom, which is upstairs, and the downstairs is small. If Liam is there, he may get in the way, but if he moves out, she'll feel isolated. Once you get past PT and doctor's appointments and Spa treatments, she'll be alone up there on your hill with not much to do or see and maybe or maybe not loving the forest like you do."

"Not. When my Girl Scout troop did an overnight in the woods—"

"I didn't know you were a Girl Scout," he said, pulling back with a captivated half-smile.

Unable to resist, it was still so new, I ran a fingertip over his mustache. "I was more artsy than the other girls, so I didn't really fit in. That's why Mom volunteered for field trips." I dropped my hand. "She didn't fit in either. She did the cooking. That's it. She's never been into nature."

He straightened and grinned. "Then she needs to stay at the Inn."

The words came so fast on my thoughts about Mom in the great out-doors, that it was a minute before they sank in. "The Inn," I finally said. "Oh, no. I was thinking I could rent a place in town."

"Why? The owner's suite is mine to use or not. I have my house, and if that weren't a major mess, I'd have both of you stay there. It's bigger than your place. But it's still raw, and it would be just as isolating. The Inn is ideal."

"That's yours, Edward. We couldn't—"

"Of course you could." His pale blues were intent. "The suite has two bedrooms, so you could stay there with her. It has a living room, plus a kitchenette, which she could use or not. Housekeeping would be in to help twice a day. She could call for room service whenever she wanted or come down to one of the restaurants, and it's a hell of a lot closer to the Spa than your house is for when you have to work. She could have PT in the suite. She could use the pool at the sports center. She could access everything without having to use stairs."

"It's too much," I scolded.

"What? Cost? There's no cost, no effort, no inconvenience."

"The *offer*. You don't need to do this."

"Need has fucking nothing to do with it," he whispered with force, then grew beseeching. "It's the perfect solution, Maggie. The suite is empty, it's on one level, and it's accessible to anything she might want to do. There's even a separate elevator." He added a singsong to his lure. "You could have your pets there with you."

"Me? *I* can't live at the Inn."

"Why not? It'd beat driving back and forth a dozen times a day, and she'd be more comfortable with you there. Even just for a week? Two, maybe, until you see how she does?"

But the offer was way too generous. Edward didn't owe us anything. We were the ones who had hurt him, not the other way around. "She doesn't deserve it. Neither do I."

His whisper held sound now, and the sound was angry. "So we're all feeling the blame, but it won't move us forward. Let it *go*, Maggie. I'm trying to on my end, but you have to try on yours. Guilt is pointless. What happened is over and done."

That quickly we were in the past—but not—with the pain of it hovering—but not. It was like a screen was superimposed on it, showing sneak peeks at a future I hadn't imagined when I took up with Devon, and the pain was the possibility that it wouldn't come.

"Is it?" I asked. "The past, over and done? Is it ever?"

"Ever changed? No. Ever accepted? Yes. It becomes who you are. That doesn't have to be a bad thing."

I wanted to believe him. He must have sensed how badly, because, with one lithe move, he was on my stair, pulling me to his side. I closed my eyes for a minute and breathed him in. His mouth touched my forehead with the barest grazing of beard before lowering until I tipped my head back and we were forehead to forehead, breath to breath. When he finally kissed me, it was featherlight, more soothing than heated, but just as precious. It spoke of a connection that went beyond chemistry. I could have basked in it forever.

"Just think," he teased against my lips, typically male in the end, "if you stay at the Inn with your Mom, you can meet me in my office after hours."

I swatted his middle. "You can think about that in the middle of a family crisis?"

"I can think about it any time. One look at you"—he breathed a rising whistle—"and there it is."

"You're bad."

"Not always."

"No," I conceded. "Not always." Because his offer of the owner's suite was really pretty good.

Slipping my arms around him, I fitted my head to its spot under his whiskered jaw. I was getting used to that scruff, was getting used to the longer hair and the idea that he, too, was different now. That said, I would never think of him as Ned. My need was to reconcile with Edward. And much as it terrified me to have and lose—again—I did want him there.

"Thank you," I whispered.

"It's a go, then," he asked against my hair, "you and your mom at the Inn?"

"Yes." I drew back to look up at him. "She's in a bad way. Pampering may help."

For some reason, a little subconscious tug, my eyes shifted to the wall by his head. Disturbed, I pulled back farther and followed one wall up and down, then the other. "Where are they?" I whispered.

"What?"

"Family pictures. She took them all away. Look at the holes." Though the grass cloth hid them, they were definitely there. But a niggling had started. Leaving Edward, I went down the stairs and circled the rooms. Oh, pictures still hung on these walls, but I had been too focused on my mother to notice specifics. I realized now that I had never seen any of them before. They were of the type sold at the mall, that looked like authentic oils but weren't.

Turning around in dismay, I realized that family pictures weren't all that was missing. My parents had been big on religious images, but those were gone now, too. Hoping that my mother's verbal dismissal of God was simply momentary bluster, and that she had simply shifted them to her bedroom, I left Edward and ran up the stairs. There were none in the room my parents had shared, none in the hall, none in either of the other two bedrooms.

At the door of the one that had been mine, I felt a little catch. Unable not to, I stepped in. It was much as it had been when I lived there, with its single bed dressed in pink, its matching curtains, my well-loved stuffed animals standing, some straighter than others, atop the bookshelf. And the shelves beneath? Clear as day despite the cracked spines were titles like *Number the Stars*, *Tiger Eyes*, and *Ramona Quimby*, and, on lower shelves, *If You Give a Mouse a Cookie*, *Hairy Maclary from Donaldson's Dairy*, and *The Very Busy Spider*. And there was *Lilly's Purple Plastic Purse*. It hadn't been one of mine, but one that my mother added to the collection when Lily was born. My baby had loved it. She had loved overnights with Nana and

Papa, returning home with tales of classic movies and cookie-making. My parents hadn't liked my life, but they adored their grandchild.

The familiar tightness was growing. This was ground zero where memories were concerned.

"Painful," Edward said from the door. He had a hand high on the jamb, supporting himself against memories of his own, and for a minute he seemed so . . . *wrecked,* that I couldn't breathe. Since our reunion, he had been the stronger of us. What I saw now was a glimpse of what his own past had been.

Crossing to him, I slipped my arms around his waist. Had we done this after the accident? I couldn't remember. Those days, weeks, months were a blur of shock and shame, grief and blame. But holding each other now felt right. And it wasn't only about my being held. It was about my holding him.

We didn't speak, just stood there feeling the memories, letting the pain have its way until, like the sting of medicine on a cut, it lessened, and my chest slowly relaxed.

"Thank you," Edward whispered against my temple.

"Ditto," I whispered back.

Then I heard the plop of mail hitting the floor from the slot by the front door and, pulling away, I hurried down to check on my mother. Mercifully, she hadn't woken.

But I did. There were things to be done while she slept. First, phone calls.

Knowing that Joe Hellinger would have to call me back, I left him a message, then called Annika Allen, who gave me the names of my mother's doctors, assured me that she could manage the bakery herself, and took my cell number.

I texted Shanahan, who had been sending annoying texts.

I texted Kevin, who had been sending endearing texts.

I was studying an unknown number on my screen, this one from area code 202, when Joe called back. He was thrilled to help after all I'd done for him—those were his words—and while I didn't see that I'd done anything I hadn't been glad to do, there was no time to argue. After I had explained the situation, he promised to get us an appointment with the best orthopedic person at Dartmouth-Hitchcock, plus the name of a good physical therapist to work with Mom at the Inn. He also insisted on coming over with his wife to meet my mother, which added two more friends to the list.

While Joe and I talked, Edward was phoning his assistant about readying the owner's suite. I caught phrases like fresh flowers, bowl of fruit, and Irish Breakfast Tea, before I tuned out to call Liam.

"You are *what?*" my brother said.

"Bringing Mom to Devon."

"Oh no. Nonono. If she knows I'm here, she'll be all over me!"

"She already knows, knew before I said a word. She isn't a stupid woman, Liam." I elaborated briefly on that and went back and forth with him for a time before cutting to the chase. "And here's the thing," I said, because he claimed to know nothing about the religious images, which meant that either he was oblivious of his surroundings or their removal had happened after he left, which meant that his departure had affected her as deeply as everything related to me, "she is our mother, and she's in need. You will welcome her to Devon, you will bring her food, you will tell her what you're doing. You will spend at least a little time with her each day and take her wherever she wants to go. If she feels up to it, you will walk with her. You'll drive her around on a tour of Devon. If she wants to eat out, and I can't be with her, you will be. You will take care of my pets until I'm sleeping there again—"

"Where will *you* be?" he cut in, sounding terrified.

"With Mom at the Inn." I explained that piece.

"Mom? At *our* Inn? She and Dad never went anywhere. She won't have a *clue* what to do with a luxury Inn."

I smiled into the phone. "Which is why we will show her. She is recovering from a broken hip, so she can't walk far or for long, but we will make things as pleasant as possible for her—and I'm serious about my pets, Liam." I ran through their needs to remind him. "*And* my house. I want it as neat as you keep your kitchen. Got that?"

"I'm not deaf," he grumbled.

"Just self-absorbed, but right now, this isn't about you or me, it's about her. She's given us a lot. We need to give back. She's our mother, and she's hurting. We owe her."

"Hey, you were the one who left. All those years, I stayed."

"Until five weeks ago, and that was the last straw."

"You're blaming me for her problems?"

I sighed. "No, Liam. We both let her down, so here's a chance for us to redeem ourselves. I'm hanging up now. I need to pack her things."

There was silence for a minute, then, because Liam wasn't dumb either, a cautious, "And she's onboard with all this?"

Wasn't *that* the question? But I wasn't giving him the chance to argue against the plan, so all I said was, "We'll be back in Devon tonight. Plan to be at the Inn first thing tomorrow. Actually, no," I made a few calculations, "be in the lobby by seven tonight. I want you there when we arrive."

My mother was not onboard with it, but when she started to argue, I listed the arrangements Edward and I had already made. Then I smiled. "It would be a major inconvenience if we had to cancel everything."

She stood by the front door, which was where she had been when she spotted her packed bag, and for an instant her expression held the kind of steel it used to. "That's unfair, Mackenzie."

I should have been daunted by that look. After my father died, it had pushed me away in the most hurtful of ways. Now, though, it felt more like spirit than censure, and spirit was good. So, smiling still, I said, "Maybe, but I'm betting Liam is already planning what to cook."

I waited for her to argue about that. After a minute, she simply said, "Liam puts too much salt in his food."

"Please tell him that before he opens his restaurant."

"I *have*," Margaret insisted, then blinked. "Restaurant? There?" So she might know where he was, but she didn't know what he was doing. Same with me. Apparently, her Googling had limits.

I gentled, even dared hold her arm. I imagined I felt a tremor, but she didn't pull away. "There's lots you don't know. I need to tell you."

"Why?"

"Because it's my life," I said and then, without thought to whether the time or place was ideal, I felt my eyes fill, and while the tears didn't spill, my words did. "Because you're my mother. Because I'm different from who I was, and I want you—*need* you to know who I am. Because Edward says he loves me, only I find that hard to believe after the accident, and because if I still blame myself for Lily's death, I have to blame myself for Dad's death."

She gave an angry huff. "It wasn't his first."

I pulled my hand back fast. "What?"

"Heart attack. He had one six weeks before Lily died."

"But he never said—*you* never said—"

"He wouldn't let me," she replied with surprising strength, and it struck me that her anger was at him.

"Why not? I was his daughter. I had a right to know."

Her green eyes held mine. "You tell him that. I tried. He wouldn't listen."

"But I could have helped. I *would* have. I'd have checked out doctors and treatment, and shifted things around to spend time here and maybe not even been on that road on that day at that time—" Catching myself, I closed my eyes. I inhaled loudly, exhaled loudly, inhaled again. The breather brought conviction. "And that," I said, opening my eyes to my mother's concerned face, "is why we need to talk. I can't keep on with the what-ifs—or maybe I just need to accept them into my life. That's what Edward says"—I palmed my chest—"only I can't if they're locked in here. So you coming to Devon would be good for you physically and good for me mentally and maybe good for you mentally, too." Feeling more sure of it than ever, I added, "Maybe we both need this, because we're neither of us going nowhere until we do." I hurried on before she could correct my grammar. "Opportunity doesn't knock twice. Who used to say that?" *She* did, mostly about small things to do with my schooling or her baking, but it sure as hell applied now. "This is our opportunity, Mom."

We were on the road shortly after three. The highway was dry, and, typical of late March, the air cooled as we drove north. My mother insisted on the backseat, where she could alternately stretch out on a pillow or sit. She began the trip sleeping, though whether from exhaustion after physical therapy or sheer escapism I didn't know. When she woke, she took to the phone to cancel her Tuesday doctor's appointment, alert a friend that she would be away, and follow up on a shipment of flour and sugar that was late reaching the bakery. Her voice was surprisingly strong during those calls. *I'm with my daughter,* she said at one point during each call, and while I wanted to hear relief or even pride, I could live with a simple statement of fact.

I held my own phone, but far preferred to listen to my mother's voice than hear mine or that of anyone else. An hour into the drive, when my screen showed another 202 call, I ignored it.

Mom was talking with Annika, sounding remarkably coherent and involved, seeming more invested now that she was headed away from the bakery, when Chris Emory called.

This one I did want. I had no sooner picked up when he began speaking. His voice was muffled, like he was hiding the call from Grace. "Something's happening," he said. "Mom's on a tear. She just got home from work and started pulling clothes out of drawers and making piles, like we're going somewhere, like we have to be gone in five minutes. Have you talked with her?"

"No. She isn't picking up. Is she there now?"

"Yeah, but—"

"Put her on."

"She'll be mad I called you."

"Put her on, Chris," I said, catching Edward's eye as I said the boy's name. He shot me a questioning look, but all I could do was shake my head.

When Grace came on, tension was thick in her voice. "I don't know why Chris called you. I'm just cleaning."

"Frantically?" I asked, because I could picture her going at it with her layered hair flying and her who-knew-what-color-today eyes as tense as her voice.

"So I have extra energy."

"Nervous energy?"

"Wouldn't you be nervous if your son had done something so bad he was facing jail?" She spoke the last word louder, clearly using it to punish Chris for calling me.

"That won't happen, Grace, but if it's making you nervous, you should have called. Talking helps."

"You're with your mother," she said with an odd accusation, like my having a mother when she didn't suddenly put me out of reach.

So much to say on that score, none of which I could say with the woman in question listening. I didn't even want to tell Grace that my mother was returning with us.

I simply said, "We're heading back to Devon. We'll be there in a couple of hours. Can I see you later?"

After a lengthy silence, came a quiet, "You don't want to be involved in this, Maggie."

"Involved in what?" I asked, because as far as I knew, I already was involved with Chris and his mess, but the way she said those words meant there was more.

I heard footsteps, then a coarse whisper. "Phone calls. From where I used to live."

"Who?"

"I don't know!" she cried before resuming her whisper. "Someone must have seen *People* and recognized me. I'm not picking up. I'm not stupid. Nothing good, absolutely *nothing* good can come of it, so I can't answer, but I can imagine, omigod, can I imagine. He's after me."

"Your ex?"

"Or someone he knows. It's not his number, but the area code is the same."

I remembered the code I'd seen twice now, and, feeling a twinge, wondered if there was a connection. "Washington, DC?"

"No." She paused, then whispered, "505. Santa Fe."

"New Mexico?" I asked in surprise. I don't know why, but I had always imagined her having come from somewhere north.

"Oh, yeah. I don't know what the hell to do, Maggie."

"Have you called Jay?"

"What can Jay do?"

"Tell the police you're being harassed."

"Like I can ever tell them why?"

"Even if it's a matter of life and death?" I didn't know all the details, but the little she had told me sounded dire.

She sighed. "Oh, God."

"Call Jay," I insisted. When she didn't reply, I said more gently, "I'll be staying at the Inn with my mother. I'll call when I'm back."

"Yup. Bye." She ended the call.

I looked at Edward, who didn't take his eyes from the road but asked, "What is life and death?"

"Like I know?" I asked, frustrated. Grace could be dramatic, but something in my gut feared that this drama had teeth.

"That"—came my mother's voice from the backseat—"being the woman whose boy is accused of hacking?"

I turned. She was sitting up, fully awake, definitely curious. The good news was that she looked better than she had when we'd arrived that morning. Whether it was from the food we had made her eat, the effort she had taken to clean up and dress, or just the fact that she had gotten out of that depressing old house, I didn't know.

"Grace is a friend." I was hesitant to say much. My mother was not prone to liking my friends. But Edward was right about being honest and drawing her into the loop. So I added, "A good friend actually."

"Who is her ex?" she asked.

"I don't know." But I was worried.

"He's in New Mexico?"

"Apparently. This is the first I've heard of it."

"How can that be, if she's a good friend?" Margaret asked and, yes, there was a touch of censure. Funny, though, it didn't shake me. She just didn't know how things worked.

"Devon collects wounded spirits," I said, smiling at my own melodrama. "I don't mean paranormal, just a kind place that lets people be who they want to be. It's forgiving in ways the rest of the world is not. I have no clue where half the people were before they came to town, and I wouldn't ever ask."

"So they don't know who you are."

"A few do. Most don't. I needed to be someone else when I first came."

"And now?" she asked—and oh, I had set myself up for that. A broken hip hadn't addled my mother's mind. Pain pills or not, she was astute.

I met Edward's eyes for a beat, before returning to her. "I still do. I'm different today from the person who drove that car."

"Do you like this new person?"

I considered my job, my cabin in the woods, my pets, my friends. "Actually, I do," I realized. I hadn't just fallen into an accidental life, but had actively chosen something better. "The challenge—" I paused, trying to decide how best to express it, "the challenge is reconciling the good from the past with what I have now."

Margaret seemed stricken. "I was not the good after Lily died."

"You were grieving."

"I was even worse when your father died. That wasn't your fault."

My throat tightened, then quickly eased. It wasn't an apology, exactly. But it certainly implied forgiveness for his death.

"No," I whispered. "Not my fault."

Wanting nothing to dilute the relief I felt, nothing to spoil the moment, I looked down at the phone in my lap. Seeming on cue, the screen lit. Area code 202. Washington, DC Again. Something in my gut was saying I should know who it was, but for the life of me, I couldn't come up with a name.

So this time I answered. "Hello?"

"Maggie Reid?" The voice was strong and resonant, definitely familiar, although I couldn't place it, either.

"Who is this?"

"Benjamin Zwick."

22

I caught my breath. Of *course*. His voice held the same assertiveness, the same *arrogance* it had in the interviews he had given when the scandal first broke.

"Why is Benjamin Zwick calling me?" I asked, repeating his name into the phone for the sake of Edward, who shot me a worried glance and mouthed *speakerphone*, which I quickly turned on.

"Because"—Zwick's voice filled the car—"I've been trying to reach Grace Emory, and I can't get through. You're her friend, right?"

My hackles rose. I wasn't about to say anything to a man who had gone after a fifteen-year-old boy in such a loud and vengeful way. "You're on opposite sides of a criminal case. Isn't it unethical for you to be calling her?"

"This is personal."

"Maybe she doesn't want to talk to you."

"Yeah, well, that's obvious, only something's come up. Trust me. She'll want to hear what I have to say."

"What something?" I asked and felt the same gut check I just had with Grace. These two calls were related. I waited to hear how.

After a moment's silence, he said, "Are you the same friend who was at her house the night all this broke and was then at the courthouse with her and her son?"

Edward nodded. And I agreed. Zwick wouldn't tell me anything unless I confirmed it. Besides, those pictures and tapes had already gone public. Anyone in town could confirm my identity. Michael Shanahan certainly had, which made my talking with this man risky. But how could I not, after talking with Chris and Grace? This wasn't about legalities. It was about two people's lives.

That said, I didn't trust Ben Zwick as far as I could throw him, which was a Momism of the first order, but was totally apt. In a voice making that clear, I said, "Yes. I'm her friend. What something has come up?"

"I'm getting calls from a woman who says she has a story."

There. The common thread. Coincidence? No way.

"She claims," Zwick went on, "that she worked in Grace's home way back and knew her when Chris was born. Do you know where Grace lived before she came to Devon?"

"Excuse me," I burst out, because, in that split second, my own distrust of the press trumped my worry for Grace, "what reason in *hell* would I have to tell you that?"

My vehemence didn't faze him. "Because this woman says that if I don't buy her story, she'll sell it to someone else, and I'm not sure you want her doing that. At least, I know Grace personally."

"Well, now, that was a big help two weeks ago, wasn't it," I remarked.

"Long story there, Ms. Reid, but this is different. I'm not the victim in this one. Grace is."

"Victim, how?"

"The caller wouldn't give details, just mentioned things like yelling and hitting, none of which would be anything new if she hadn't also mentioned kidnapping."

My mind went blank for an instant, before bursting into full color with threads of past conversations. *Evil,* Grace had called her ex. She had talked about fearing for her life and, just yesterday, about changing her name. And then, about Chris, *we left when he was two, so he doesn't remember how bad the guy is.* Given that Devon was a past-free zone, that Grace changed her look nearly as often as most people changed their sheets, and that she lived in a house that was hidden in an out-of-the-way place and had multiple locks on its door, kidnapping wasn't beyond the pale.

Victim? Perpetrator? *What?* If I was the betting type, I knew where I would put my money, though the thought of it was terrifying.

To his credit, Zwick didn't waste time gloating over my silence. "Look," he said, "I like Grace. Seriously. I did not know that her son was the one behind the hacking until it was too late to pull it back, but this one isn't about Chris. It's about her. I don't know where she came from or what she did, but if someone has a story that's worth the kind of money I was quoted, it may be something Grace wants to control."

"You mean, sell it to you first?" I asked, cynical to the core just then.

"I mean," he came back, sounding irritated, *"contain* it. Keep it from coming out at all."

"Why would you do that? Whatever you pay a source is peanuts compared to what you'd get for writing it."

"I won't write the story."

"Why not?"

For the first time, he seemed hesitant. "Because, whether you want to believe it or not, I do like Grace. Given a choice, she and I would have been more than just . . . well, more. She was the one who backed off. And sure, she hates me now—"

"Do you blame her? You went all out against her son."

"It's what I do," he ground out, like he'd already said it a hundred times, then eased up. "What he did really screwed me up, and I needed to hit back. So I made headlines, but like I said, had I known at the start that it was Grace's son, I wouldn't have done what I did. I'm trying to apologize now. I'm trying to make things better. If I buy that woman's story, it'll be to bury it, but that doesn't mean someone else from Grace's past won't go to another journalist. I don't know what that past is. She refused to talk about it. But if kidnapping was involved, that's serious stuff. Kidnapping is a felony."

The word shot to my gut. Michael Shanahan had used it too often for comfort. A quick glance, and I knew Edward was thinking it, too. Was Ben? Suddenly, I wondered what he knew about me. I sure as hell wasn't asking. With a crack journalist, and Zwick was that, one question was a tip-off.

I had barely four months of probation left. To be anywhere *near* the word *felony* was crazy. But this was Grace. Until I knew for sure that she had done something wrong, I couldn't abandon her.

"I think we should meet," I told Ben.

"With Grace. It has to be with Grace."

His vehemence made me edgy. "Why does that sound like a trap?"

"Maybe because you and most of the rest of the world think the media's scum. But in this case, I'm not, Maggie." He sounded earnest. Either he was a great actor, or he truly meant it. "Pick a place you want to meet. Your choice. Somewhere safe. I'll be alone. I won't have a recorder. I won't write anything down. I just want to talk. With Grace."

I wanted to buy into honesty here, because helping Grace was important. But it was only when Edward gave his approval by mouthing, *My office,* that I went ahead.

"The issue," I said, "may be getting Grace to agree, but the chances of that will be better if we meet at the Inn."

"When?"

I had to think quickly. The Inn was hosting a political conference that would keep Grace busy for much of the weekend. "Sunday afternoon at four."

"Sooner. I can't guarantee this woman will wait."

"Sure you can," I said, snarky maybe, but there it was. "She wants you. You're the best buyer she'll find. Promise her something. Lie."

He snorted. "Thanks."

"The office of the owner of the Inn is on the second floor. He and I will both be there."

"And Grace?"

"That's the plan."

Panic. That was what I felt. I didn't know what Grace faced; she didn't know what I faced. But strange callers from the past who mentioned felonious crimes were dangerous for us both.

Not that I could do anything about it now, other than to take a long, deep breath and realize that if ever I was good at compartmentalizing, I had to do it now. So I closed off my fear of what Grace was involved with and any related role I might have, and used my mother's impending arrival in Devon as a distraction from the sense that I had made a deal with the devil.

I pointed out to her a quaint shopping area on the outskirts of town, then a covered bridge that was painted red and glistened in the mist. I pointed out the police station and the Town Hall, both wearing bleached linen stone. A bit farther on, I pointed out the road to the pottery studio, and then, in the center of town, the shops where the three roads met. A quarter of a mile north, we turned at the broad stone pillars, passed the slab of Vermont granite, beautifully lit in twilight, that announced THE DEVON INN AND SPA in gold, and proceeded under the covered bridge that crossed the river. For an instant, when the Inn materialized through the trees, I was swept back to my first evening sighting. The place was every bit as imposing when lit by tungsten as by the sun.

Edward drove past the stone pillars to the front door, stopping under the porte cochére so that my mother would have less far to walk. The drive hadn't been as easy for her as she wanted us to believe. By the end, she was shifting often, clearly uncomfortable. Besides, the front entrance of the Inn, with its large doors framed in wood, was impressive in a classic Vermont way, and we did want to wow her.

Liam was waiting for us in the lobby. We had barely walked across the carpet logo when he came toward us, looking very Devon, in jeans, boots, and a tee under an open flannel shirt. His freckles were distinct, his hair combed. My mother stopped short when she saw him, and something about the startled look on her face suggested she was seeing my father in him, just as I had at first. The resemblance was uncanny tonight.

Once she passed the shock, though, he was a hit, and why not? He gave her a big hug, told her she looked great, asked about the drive. He was appropriately concerned about her hip without ever apologizing for his absence. In what I thought was a brilliant move, he had baked a batch of her fabled pecan sandies. This was not typically Liam. As a chef, he had always preferred entrees to desserts. I could never remember his baking, much less following one of Mom's own recipes. The fact that he had today was an homage to her, as was his warning that his weren't as good as hers.

My mother looked him in the eye. "You hate pecan sandies."

"Not always," Liam replied with just the right amount of deference. "You like them, which is all that matters."

She was flattered, which as far as *I* was concerned, was all that mattered.

The owner's suite was perfect. Rich in Devon charm with its custom wool carpets, blend of natural and painted wood, and rich leather accessories, it was done up in soothing shades of blue and tan, all of it warmly lit by lamps. Sofas and chairs were wool and chenille, a fine mix of plaids, solids, and stripes. The bathroom was marble, with a tub that was likely too deep for my mother to navigate, but there was also a stunningly oversized, glass-enclosed shower with a bench, hold bars, and a floor of embedded stones. And there were flowers—bud vases in the bathrooms, and in the living room and dining area, full arrangements of tulips to match the décor. Everywhere here, the smell was pine, much as Edward's office had been—pine lotion, pine potpourri, pine candles, pine fragrance sticks.

She walked around at first, both for her hip's sake and curiosity, and I let her tell me where to put her clothes, books, and medicine. After settling her on the sofa and ordering dinner from room service, I left her with Liam. Now that the ice was broken, he seemed delighted to talk about what he'd been doing since leaving Connecticut.

Since I had no car here, Edward drove me home. I needed to pack enough for a few overnights, but, even more, I needed my pets. Bringing them here would have been upsetting for them, and besides, they were only part of the picture. I needed my hilly road, my house, my old life, because this one seemed to be growing more complex by the minute. Once we left the Inn, everything I had denied earlier rushed back.

The car was dark, the night even darker. A light drizzle was falling again, and between the darkness, the rain, and the confines of the Jeep, my worries had nowhere to go but back into the gathering swirl in my head. When Edward reached out a hand, I pulled it into my lap and held on tightly.

"Having second thoughts?" he asked.

I glanced his way. Spikes of hair, straight nose, neat beard—his profile was vague in the murk, but what I couldn't physically see, my mind filled in. He was stability. I clung to that as I did to his hand and gave a mildly hysterical laugh. "About which part—bringing her here, meeting with Zwick, or consorting with you?"

"All of the above," he said.

"All of the above," I confirmed and let slip the noise in my head. "What if Mom hates it here? What if she finds she can't stand seeing me after all? What if Grace is into something serious—I mean, *really* serious—like something that overshadows anything Chris might have done, so her life is at risk?"

"Do you think that?" he cut in.

"I don't know, but what if something ticks off Shanahan, and he makes an issue of it, and my past comes out? What if Ben Zwick already *knows* my past? And this meeting? What if Grace refuses to see him or storms out when she hears what he says and then hates me for setting her up? What if you're pulled into it and the Inn suffers and your group votes you out? What if *my probation is revoked?*"

He was silent for so long that I wondered if he was having second thoughts himself. But he didn't pull his hand back. His fingers stayed around mine, tight as ever. We were turning onto Pepin Hill when he said, "I love you."

"That is not the issue."

"Do you love me?"

Though the forest cocooned us enough for the Jeep's headlights to reflect off wet fronds, I couldn't see his eyes, but I felt his presence keenly, just as I had this whole long day. If he hadn't been with me, what I thought to be challenging would have been ten times more so. This was what he and I had.

"I've *always* loved you," I admitted, "but *that is not the issue.*"

"It is."

I knew he was thinking that if we loved each other, we would get through whatever came our way. Only, we hadn't after Lily died. We had failed spectacularly.

"The difference," he finally said when he turned to me after parking at the house, "is that back then we got trampled by the outside world. We lost sight of what we wanted."

"We wanted Lily," I reminded him, feeling a visceral ache in my gut.

"We wanted each other first," Edward countered. "Lily came from us, but if there hadn't been a 'we,' she wouldn't have existed at all."

I killed her, I thought but knew not to say. Edward didn't like that wording, and maybe he was right. Technically, I had been responsible for her death. But I hadn't planned the accident. Had I seen it coming, I would have slammed on the brakes.

There was some consolation in finally accepting that. Still, a weight remained. "She was our child," I said. "She didn't ask to be born. We decided that. *We* took the responsibility."

He brought my hand to his mouth, kissed it, and held it there. The whiskers above his lip chafed, then soothed. His breath was warm, his voice sad. "Some kids are born with medical conditions and die within hours. Some grow big enough to be riding their bikes on the sidewalk when a car jumps the curb. There's no sense to any of these things—or maybe there is. Maybe Lily wasn't destined to live beyond five. Maybe she was a lesson we had to learn."

That sounded merciless. Affronted, I asked, "What kind of lesson?"

"Humility. Vulnerability. What doesn't kill you makes you stronger. My mother said that all through chemo."

"Actually, chemo killed her."

"Actually, cancer killed her, but maybe I didn't take my part of the lesson to heart. As hard as my mother's death was, Lily's was ten times worse, a *hundred* times worse. I never expected to have to live through something like that. But I did. And it didn't kill me. I'm here. And I have choices. I want to be better, Maggie. So yes. I'm trying to be stronger."

The strength of his belief resonated in his voice, which seemed suddenly deeper and, in that, soothing. I couldn't disagree with him, at least not entirely. Strength had been my major goal for the last five years—well, for four really, after that first year during which I'd been a hot mess. But weighing life lessons against cruelty was a toughie.

"When you talk about destiny, are you talking about God?" I asked.

He considered that with my knuckles to his mouth, then breathed against them. "I don't know. I struggle to find an explanation for what happened, and He's all I get." He looked sharply at me. "Don't you ever think that?"

I didn't. I was still angry at Him. But I tried to hear Edward. "You're saying we should be grateful for the five years we had."

"Yeah, I'm saying that. When we lose someone we love, we can either die with them or live on to celebrate their life. I'm tired of focusing on what we lost, Maggie. I want to focus on what we had."

I was about to argue that five years wasn't enough, that Lily had been a key part of our future, and what about *her* dreams—when I heard his words—and even then, it was another minute before they fully registered. When they did, though, they went straight to the soul of the person I was trying to become. He was talking about the photographs neither of us could put on a desk. Or nightstand or bookshelf. He was talking about the memories I had so fiercely locked away. He was talking about the same things my therapist had, until I got tired of failing at it, and stopped seeing her.

And where was I now? My ex-husband had stolen back into my life, my brother was occupying my loft, and my mother had become my responsibility. The past was crowding in. It was unexpected and, in many regards, daunting. And yet, there was something good about having family again.

If Lily wasn't part of it, she was forgotten. I couldn't let that happen.

In that instant, urgency hit—like I had wasted too much time and was suddenly on the verge of irrevocably losing her. Pulling my hand free, I dashed out of the car and ran through the drizzle to the house. Liam must have let Jonah out before he left, because the dog stayed inside, craning his neck on my thigh when I dropped to my knees and buried my face in cat fur. I felt like it had been a year since I'd been home, not twelve hours.

But I couldn't linger here, either. These three were my babies, but they weren't the only ones. Dropping my coat on the newel post as I passed, I was on the stairs when I heard Edward enter the house, but I didn't look back. I didn't stop until I was on my knees on the floor by the bed and had pulled out my grandmother's green velvet box.

I wavered then. There was pain in this box. I had kept it closed these four years not because I didn't want to see Lily; wasn't she with me in the dark most nights? But the physical somethings from her life, held in this box, were actual, touchable proof that she was gone. I hadn't been ready.

I wasn't sure I was now. But the past seemed destined to pop up, and focusing on loss was limiting. I agreed with Edward. I wanted to focus on the joy my daughter had brought. I did not want to lose her, *could* not lose her.

Touching the latch, I felt a spark and pulled my hand back fast. Not only grief, I told myself. Beauty, too. I reached out again, but hesitated. Fisting my hands on my thighs, I rocked back and forth, near the box and away, near and away. Then I raised my eyes. Edward stood at the door with his shoulders slumped, seeming as lost as I felt. And suddenly I couldn't do this alone.

"Help me?" I begged softly.

The question was barely out when he came forward, as though he had been waiting, as though he understood that a mother's grief—or joy— was different from a father's, as though he understood that I wasn't yet ready to make the commitment to him that he was to me but that, in matters of Lily, we were together.

On the floor, in the light of my bedside lamp, the green box seemed etched in amber. He hunkering down and eyed it. "In there?"

I nodded. Reassured by his nearness, I slipped the latch and raised the lid.

The smell hit first. It was my grandmother's trademark gardenia, con- juring summer and age. Though pale in comparison to the woman her- self, it had defied the years by clinging to her letters, to the sepia portraits of her parents and the sketches she had done of my mother as a child, of flowers and friends and the dogs she had loved and lost. I didn't see these things now, though. They were simply a nest for my daughter.

At my shoulder, Edward's breath tripped, because there she was look- ing up at us—Lily Reid Cooper, all blond-white hair, silver-blue eyes, and impish mouth, as real as ever. My chest tightened until he leaned closer. "We can do this," he said, and although his voice held a quiver, it was determined.

Only then did I realize that this was hard for him, too, and suddenly, being together had greater meaning. He needed me as much as I needed him.

Gratified by that thought, I picked up one photo. "How beautiful she is," I whispered and, emboldened by that first view, set it aside and went to the next.

"Look at her here," Edward said, holding another. It was taken by one of Lily's playgroup moms, who had thought it so special that she'd had it printed. The occasion was a birthday party, the setting a princess bounce house. The camera caught Lily mid-air, her hands and legs askew, her ex- pression the embodiment of glee. She was three at the time.

We had hundreds—no, *thousands* of digital shots. Most of these physical prints were copies of those we had either given to grandparents or put on our family room wall. I held up one of her grinning around a roasted marshmallow, Edward held up one of her scowling in time-out. I spotted one of her with Edward and pushed others aside to reach it, while he dug out one of her on her brand new, training wheel–less, five-year-old's bike.

I might have recalled that when she died, we donated that barely used bike to charity, if I hadn't just then spotted my old phone—not the one the police had confiscated, but the one I'd bought to replace it. We had always backed up to the Cloud, so restoring pictures had been a cinch. Not so easy? Reliving them. So I had packed away the phone, too.

Taking it in my palm now, I turned it on. Naturally, after all this time, it was dead. I nearly wept at that alone.

"We can charge it," Edward quickly offered when he saw the tears that hung, just hung on my lower lids. "I have them on my phone, too, but I haven't been able . . ." His voice cracked. Abandoning the thought, he returned to the box and lifted a photo of the three of us that had been taken by a professional photographer when Lily was one.

Blinking it into focus, I smiled. "She does not look happy here. Remember?"

"Oh yeah." I heard his grin. "Tantrum city. Did not want her picture taken."

"She didn't like her hair," I joked.

"What hair?"

"Exactly. Poor thing. It was late coming in, but the wait was worth it." I wondered whether that gorgeous white-blond silk would have darkened at ten, as mine had. And at eleven, twelve, or thirteen? Even beyond hair, I wondered how puberty would have treated her nose, her skin, her moods.

Rather than tightening up, my chest was suddenly empty, like a huge hole had opened where the future should have been. New tears welled but didn't spill. The purpose of this was to celebrate the life we'd had, not the one we'd lost.

My probation agreement didn't help. There it suddenly was with its business end peering out, that big, bold COMMONWEALTH OF MASSACHUSETTS in the upper left hard to miss. Like the mug shot in my medicine chest, I had meant it to be a truth in this box of truths, but it hurt in a different way from the others. It was a pollutant here, celebrating death far more than life. I saw that now. This was definitely not the place it should be.

"Move it," Edward ordered in a low voice.

Grateful for the direction, I snatched the envelope up and flipped it into the darkness where the light of the small lamp couldn't reach—and wasn't there satisfaction in that? For the first time, perhaps, I was separating what didn't belong from what did. That quickly, the green velvet box was pure.

One deep breath of gardenia had me fully back, and though the hole inside me remained, it, too, seemed more pure. Needing to be with my baby again, I moved aside the shot of Lily's wall graffiti to unearth pencil sketches I had made of her, and crayon drawings she had made of us. Under the layer of drawings were formal photos from preschool in which she looked stiff and photo-booth strips in which she looked irreverent. Edward chuckled at the last from my shoulder—but then there was Bunny! Tucked in at the side of the box, she was tiny, not much bigger than my hand, and oh-so-well-loved. There was a piece of the sleeper Lily had outgrown, but still cuddled. There was the ugly rubber rose barrette and a six-inch rendition of Sophia the First. She had loved both the barrette and Sophia, who debuted on TV less than a year before her death.

And there was a baggie. Victorious, I held it up. "First haircut," I crowed. "I took off two inches and thought I would die."

I stroked the hair through the plastic, then pressed it between my thumb and finger, as if holding it tightly would make it more mine. Her hair was real. It was part of her body in ways that the documents I found next—birth certificate, medical records, preschool papers—were not. But I had no sooner begun lifting them out when what I saw beneath stopped me cold.

"Her wish box," Edward said in a hushed voice.

I panicked. Oh, I had known it was there. I had packed it in myself, deliberately placed where Lily's things ended and my grandmother's began, and, knowing it was safe, I had pushed it from mind. That was where it had stayed, out of mind until now.

Lily and I had made it together. Since Nana's box was long and narrow, so was this one, but on a miniature scale, and rather than being green velvet, it was clay. I had done the basics, trueing up the sides and making sure the lid was snug, but Lily had added fingerprints and thumb spots, and splashes of color, a bird of sorts, and three rabbits, all of which I'd topped off with a rainbow and stars. The idea, she excitedly told Edward after it was glazed and fired, was that she could write anything she wanted and put it inside—wishes, secrets, notes to me or to him or to her friend Mia.

My tactic, of course, was to get her to write. But she hadn't lived long enough to learn how, much less to fill the box with wishes, secrets, or anything else.

So I had filled it with her ashes.

My strength vanished. I could take photos, dolls, and beloved shreds of a sleeper, but not my daughter's ashes. Granted, they were sealed in a bag. They might have been sealed in ten, but it wouldn't have mattered. They were Lily in the flesh, or what was left of the flesh after the flames had done their thing.

In that moment, I would have done anything not to have cremated her. But the idea of her body lying alone in the ground had been way too brutal. I wanted her in a gentle, loving place, and she was, but even this was brutal.

Hurriedly, I tried to replace what I'd taken out so that the clay box was buried again, but it wouldn't comply. Through a blur of tears, I mounded papers over it, and still it glared at me. I pushed it deeper, using both hands now to thicken the cover. When I could still see a corner, an edge, even a bright pink spatter, I thought to use my scarf to hide it. Desperate, I began tugging and yanking, nearly choking myself in my haste before an end finally came free.

From behind came Edward's arms, his hands closing firmly on mine. "Stop," he said in a broken voice.

Despite the warmth of him against my back, I couldn't begin to think CALM thoughts. "I can't—that box—I have to—"

"Shhh," he whispered as he pulled my hands away from my neck, "shhh, baby."

Twisting, I raised my eyes. His lips were a thin slash in his beard, his cheekbones severe over skin washed of color. And his eyes? Usually that startling pale-blue, they were flooded with grief.

Had he cried when Lily died? I couldn't remember. Couldn't *remember*. He must have, but with me? Possibly not, if he had wanted to keep a strong front. And then there was the public spectacle that our daughter's death had quickly become.

Edward was strong. There had been arrangements to make, and I was useless. I knew he grieved; I had seen it etched on his face, ever more deeply as the days without Lily dragged on. But tears? I don't recall seeing tears. Had he cried when he was alone, which increasingly he had been, since I was emotionally gone?

When the criminal case exploded and his stoicism remained, I interpreted it as anger, and we had gone downhill from there. I wondered now if I had been wrong. I wondered if stoicism had been Edward's own personal form of anguish.

If so, that had changed. Here in my little cabin, with the velvet box open and the remains of Lily's life laid out, it wasn't my suffering versus his grief. We shared the sorrow now. For the first time, we were absolutely, totally together in this. For the first time, it wasn't about how Lily had died, but the simple fact of her loss. Perhaps being apart had given us the space for this. Perhaps, over five years, our grief had taken its natural course, gradually evolving into something we could live with. Perhaps we were simply new people.

Whatever, his tears were my undoing. My own suddenly came in a torrent, gathering in my heart and erupting past my throat with such force that when they reached my eyes they had nowhere to go but out.

Edward barely had time to turn me into him when I broke into gut-deep, soulful sobs. I had no control at all. Clutching handfuls of his black turtleneck, I held on for dear life, helpless to stop what was happening—not trying to—not *wanting* to. And that was okay. Because he was crying, too. I felt it in the convulsive way he held me, in the tremors that came from deep within him and the strangled sounds that escaped his throat.

For so long, I had kept this to myself. For so long, *we* had. Now, finally, came relief.

I had no idea how long we stayed there. Somewhere in the back of my mind, I knew that my mother waited, that Liam would be growing impatient, and that I had to think up some way to get Grace to a meeting with Ben. But when the tears finally slowed, I had neither the strength nor the desire to leave Edward's arms. I was totally spent.

So we sat on the floor, me nested in the bend of his legs, saying nothing, just . . . *being*. I cleared my mind of negative thought, just settled into the here and now. Lily was before us, but it wasn't as painful as it had once been.

In time, my mind wandered. One of my first, cohesive, non-Lily thoughts, was of clay. I felt a strong compulsion to feel, touch, shape. I needed to escape into it. I needed to *create*.

But that had to wait. When we finally separated, it was to neaten up the Lily-things in Nana's box, close the lid, and slide the box back under the bed. We didn't speak, but there was no anger in the silence between us. Rather, I felt an unexpected calm where Lily was concerned. And where Edward was concerned? Shared tears had cemented a bond.

Over the last days, I had sensed that things would never go back to how they were before he had come. For the first time, now, I realized that I didn't want them to. I did love him. I did want him in my life.

I also did fear that when the next crisis arose, whether having to do with my mother, with Grace, or with something completely different, we might botch it again.

That raised the stakes.

23

As Edward and I talked it through, I realized that getting Grace to the meeting with Ben Zwick might be the easy part. Her last appointment on Sunday was a fifty-minute massage that ended shortly before four. In advance, Edward would leave a handwritten note at the Spa asking her to drop by his office when it was done. "Drop by" was casual, and something handwritten was less of a threat. Even then, our plan assumed that I would be talking with her beforehand, because Grace would likely assume he was planning to fire her. I could assure her he was not. I could even tell her that he had invited me to his office at four, too, which wasn't the whole truth, but would work.

So no, I wasn't worried about getting her there. Keeping her there once she saw Ben Zwick might be something else. She could be impulsive. And headstrong? *Totally.* I would have worried more—might have agonized that she would see my part in this as a betrayal—might have done something rash, like beg her to tell me about her past then and there, or make my case beforehand that she should hear Zwick out, or even enlist Jay to help—if I hadn't been preoccupied with Margaret.

Back at the Inn Friday night, I didn't sleep well, and not because of texting with Edward, though that went on for a while. After cementing a plan for Grace, we talked about ourselves—where each of us was physically and what we were doing, where each of us *wanted* to be and to do. Our tears had been cleansing. I felt closer to him than ever. I wanted him in my bed right now, and yes, I wanted sex.

But my mother was in the very next room—my *mother,* with whom my reconciliation was fragile and new. Lying awake in the dark, where things were always ten times worse, every possible glitch crossed my mind. For starters, I realized that Grace wasn't the only one who would be working this weekend; I had to work, too, and while Ronan Dineen might be willing to sub again, he wouldn't do it both days. And what about next week? I couldn't leave Margaret alone for hours on end. I could be with her between appointments, but how would she feel about my running in and out? Or about waking up in a strange place and realizing that she didn't know anything about it, or even about me? And how would she feel physically? There was the chance that when she woke up in the morning, her hip might be worse because of the drive, that we would have to rush to see the doctor Joe Hellinger had contacted, or that she would spike a fever and we would end up in the ER, all because I had insisted she leave her own home.

So I huddled between the soft white sheets that covered the pillow-top on the gorgeous big bed in my pine-scented room, and listened for sounds from hers. At one point, I crept across the hall and cracked open the door, needing to hear her breathe so that I would know she was actually there.

Naturally, in the dark where thoughts loomed, I thought of mothers and daughters—specifically, whether a mother was still a mother if her child died, which was my version of what Margaret had asked in Connecticut.

For the first time, I had an answer, because despite having been a hair's breadth from Lily's ashes, she felt more alive to me than ever. She was with me as I stood at Mom's door, pressed to my hip with her arms around my waist, just like she used to do. She was five, would always be five, and while that fact should have crushed me, it no longer did. The time I'd spent with Edward tonight had changed me. I accepted that she was gone—acceptance being different from simple admission. I found a peace in her presence now that I hadn't felt since her death. She was in my thoughts. No one could take her away ever again.

Secure in that knowledge, I finally fell into a dead sleep and awoke with a jolt as daylight ghosted through the drapes. But how to confuse my home bedroom with a room at the Inn? My watch said seven, which was later than I'd planned. Bolting up, I went for my mother.

She was already in the living room. Wearing an Inn robe and slippers, she had a hint of natural color on her cheeks. If the trip had set her back, it didn't show. She was typing on her laptop, but stopped, hands suspended, when she saw me.

She didn't smile. But neither did I. Being here together, after all this time and all that had come between us, was awkward. We were feeling our way along.

"How'd you sleep?" I asked.

She put her hands in her lap. "Very well, thank you. It's a beautiful bed." Her gaze circled. "A beautiful suite. Too generous of Edward." Before I could argue, her eyes were on me, speaking in advance of the words. "You look more like you now."

I'm sure I did to her. "You're the first person here to see me like this." Well, except for Liam now, but he didn't count.

"I like it."

I snorted. "No one else would. One look at my scar, and they'd run in the other direction."

"They would, or you would?" my mother asked. And hadn't she hit *that* nail on the head? I was going back and forth, totally unsure, when she said, "It's faded."

"I see it every morning. I need to. Sometimes life here is too comfortable, y'know?"

My mother didn't answer at first. Her eyes, such a fragile green, grew puzzled. "Is that wrong?" she finally asked. "To find happiness?"

Two soul-searching questions at seven in the morning was too much. Honesty was super when you knew what to say, which just then I did not. Thanks to Edward—and yes, to my mother—I had come a long way in the guilt department, but that didn't mean I was completely free.

"First, how does your hip feel?"

"Sore, but not enough to take a pill."

She had been typing with both hands. I eyed the left one, which lay still now.

She turned the cast over and back. "It's fine." As if to demonstrate, she reached for the nearby teacup and held it with the fingers of both hands.

"Oh, good. You got tea." I was relieved to see the top of the walker behind the sofa. I didn't care if she hid it, as long as she used it when she was alone.

"And I took a shower," she said with some defiance. "They told me to wait until the stitches came out, but it's been over a week, and I felt disgusting."

I had to smile. "You weren't."

"Well, I feel better now." Her face gentled some. It struck me that she, too, may have had her moments in the dark last night, imagining all sorts of negatives about coming here. "The flowers are beautiful," she remarked and, lingering on the nearest tulips, said, "I thought you'd be up before me. You always were."

"Usually am," I said, "but I didn't fall asleep until late." I crossed to the Nespresso, touched that Edward had thought to bring tea pods from his office. My own tea was brewing when I hitched my chin at her laptop. "What's today's special?"

"Cherry turnovers. Not your favorites, but Annika did the choosing."

"Would you have picked something else?" I asked, making it sound teasing, when really it wasn't.

She didn't blink. "I'd have picked salted caramel brownies. Or honey scones." She knew I loved the latter. I barely breathed when she added, "You didn't have to come for me yesterday. But you did."

"I'd have come sooner if I'd known," I said, and she did smile then. But what started shy turned sad, before fading into regret. She seemed about to say something, but stopped.

"What?" I coaxed.

Drying on its own, her hair was waving in a gentle way. Her furrowed brow was something else. She was struggling.

"Say it," I said. "Please?"

She took a breath, and in a voice laced with sorrow, said, "He was wrong." My father. "But it was wrong of me not to tell him he was wrong. The thing is, that isn't how it was between us."

"How was it?" I would never, ever, have asked that back in Connecticut—would never, ever, have asked it growing up. To ask would have been to challenge, which wasn't in the nature of our relationship. But that life was there, and we were here.

She must have felt the same distance, because she said, "Traditional. He was the head of the family. My job was to support him."

"You were the enforcer."

She made a small sound. "So to speak. Your father . . ." She studied her tea.

"Please."

"I shouldn't speak ill of the dead." She shot the sky a timid glance. "Not that He doesn't already think ill of me."

She was speaking of God this time, but I wasn't going there. "Why was Dad so angry at me?"

"Well, I often asked him that. He loved you, loved you very much." She sipped her tea.

Taking mine from the Keurig, I slipped into the armchair kitty-corner to her. It was too early in the day for this kind of discussion—but really, was it ever too early to discuss matters of the heart? What if the moment passed and never returned?

"Then why?" I asked.

"You did things he didn't understand. You made decisions without consulting him."

I waited for her to go on. When she didn't, I said, "That's it? He was offended?"

"Threatened. You broke the mold."

"But you did, too." If ever there had been an example of someone following her dream, it was my mother. "Look at the bakery."

She sniffed. "He barely knew about the bakery."

"Of course he did. You went there every day."

"He didn't see me there. I might as well have been cleaning toilets at the Town Hall. My bakers did the early morning work, so that I could be home and cook breakfast and make the beds. By the time I left, he was already at work. I got back before he did to cook dinner. He never saw anything different at home from how it was when you and Liam were first born."

"But you earned money. We couldn't have rented a place at the shore those summers without it. I couldn't have gone to college without loans. Liam couldn't have. The money you earned was crucial."

"We didn't discuss it."

I was floored. My face must have shown it, because she actually laughed. "Oh, Mackenzie. Your generation takes so much for granted."

"You're only sixty-five, Mom. Hadn't the women's revolution already begun by the time you were married?"

"For some." She considered. "Even for me. I was able to get a loan to start the bakery. Vendors would work with me, whereas twenty years earlier they wouldn't have." She returned to the crux of the discussion. "But your father was old school. He was uncomfortable with the idea of his wife helping support the family. Breadwinning was his job, and if he didn't do it, he would feel less of a man."

"It was ego, then?"

"It was the deal. He worked. I raised the kids."

"But how could he not see what you were doing?"

She shot me a did-you-not-hear-what-I-just-said look, and there was something so familiar, so *normal* about it that I nearly laughed. This was my mother. She didn't waste time repeating things. She was efficient, which was how she accomplished as much as she did.

Emboldened by the frank back-and-forth, I asked, "Did you love him?"

"Of course, I loved him. That was my job."

What I had meant was, had she loved him like I love Edward, meaning in ways that had less to do with expectation than a wildly beating heart. But that felt too personal, like I was asking about sex. So I went to what haunted me still.

"And when he died? Weren't you freed?"

She rested the mug on her cast. "I should have been. But he was my husband, and he was suddenly dead. I thought I was honoring what he would have wanted. I thought I owed him that. I wasn't thinking straight—" She stopped short. "Actually, that's not true. I was thinking exactly the way a woman with my marriage history would think. Now I'm not."

"What changed?"

"Your brother leaving," she said so quickly that I knew she had given it plenty of thought. "As long as he was around, I could tell myself the problem was you. When he up and left, too, I realized it was me. My failing. My fault. I couldn't even blame your father. He'd been dead too long by then. And suddenly I was alone, for the first time in my life, totally alone."

Now I was feeling sorry for her. "You have friends. And you have the bakery, you have Annika and the bakers and the high school girls who come in after school."

"Not the same," Margaret said with a dismissive wave of her casted wrist, and suddenly the way she looked at me was jarring. Mothers had answers. Right now, mine did not. There was uncertainty in her expression, in her semi-slouch, even in the generic Spa robe that was way too big for her frame. "The old model isn't any good, but I'm not sure what the new one should be."

"Nor I," I said with feeling, then qualified. "I mean, I can say the same thing about myself. I had it all figured out. Now I don't."

"If you're worried about the meeting with that reporter and your friend—"

"I am."

"Have a lawyer there," said the woman who might have lived a charade at home, but had single-handedly founded and managed a thriving business.

We ordered breakfast, which arrived in less time than it took me to shower, put on makeup, and dress. When I left my bedroom, the round eating table was covered by a crisp white cloth that held two formal place-settings and double servings of maple bacon, scrambled eggs, thick wheat toast, fresh berries, and clotted cream, not to mention garnishes of grilled tomato, three kinds of jam, and butter in its own small tub with the Inn logo embossed on the top. And almond milk for my mother. A full glass. I set it in front of her in a way that said I expected her to drink the whole thing.

It wasn't until we began to eat that I saw Margaret studying my made-up face, my knotted-back hair, my navy scrubs. "You're going to work," she deduced.

Had the statement held accusation, I might have called in sick, which would have been ridiculous, of course, since I would be immediately seen as a fraud when I went out, which I would definitely have done. I wanted to drive my mother around town. I wanted to show her my life.

But her voice held no accusation. She was a workaholic herself. I remembered once when I was home from college, I had found her in her sewing room late at night, typing on her computer while my father slept.

And didn't that take on new meaning now?

"Yes. Work." I bit into my toast, chewed and swallowed, then said a nonchalant, "You know what I do, don't you?"

"Makeup."

I nodded. "There's an event at the Inn this weekend. It's a statewide political thing, apparently boring, because the Spa is booked solid."

"You, too?"

"I get spillovers from treatments. So yes, me too."

"Will your friend be free by four tomorrow?" I was slow to follow, I was that good at denial. "Grace," Mom specified. "She does massage."

I was amused in a wary way. "How do you know that?"

"It was in one of the articles I read."

"Ah. Got it." But I really did not want to talk about Grace. The thought of meeting with Ben Zwick upset my stomach.

"Did you ever do massage?" my mother segued from Grace to ask.

"I actually started with it before gravitating to makeup. Makeup is more artistic."

"Why that and not clay?"

I studied my toast, before setting it back on the plate and raising my eyes. "I couldn't. I needed something different."

"Do you sculpt at all?"

If she hadn't been here, I might have been at the pottery studio right now. My sculpting Maddie Kalmbach felt like a corner turned. After last night, I might have sculpted another child, maybe even eventually Lily.

But not clay, not today.

"Only for fun," I said, adding quickly, "Makeup is kind of like working with clay. Every application involves a person, so in some ways it's more rewarding. But it's demanding. When you work at a resort, weekends are the busiest time. I have someone to help, but I'll still have to go back and forth today." I pulled out my cell. Joe Hellinger had done double duty. "Your physical therapist texted while I was showering." I scrolled to that text. "Her name is Janet Bolan. She'll be here at eleven. If you don't like her—"

"She'll be fine."

"Liam will be around. Edward will come by. And I'll come up between appointments."

"I'll be fine, Maggie," she insisted and, with barely a breath said, "I'm sorry you don't sculpt anymore."

I resumed eating. "Well, I do sculpt, just not on the same level." Between bites, I told her about the pottery studio. "I'm sure Kevin will come by, too. He's dying to meet you."

"Is he artsy?"

"Very, and gay, which his parents don't know, so he could use a mother." I watched for her reaction now, just as I had watched her meeting my friends at the wedding. Those friends had run the gamut when it came to sexual orientation.

She had been neutral then. Now, with quiet insistence, she said, "I was not the homophobic one."

"Good. Because Kevin is special to me. I don't want him hurt."

My mother could not have been nicer to Kevin, who came with my honey teapot, which, without my knowing, he had bought at the studio store, and a loopy scarf he had made of variegated green yarn, which she promptly put on. And to Joyce, who came with a basket of goodies from the Spa, tales of my pets, and enough praise of me to nauseate anyone other than my mother. Or to the physical therapist, who texted me immediately after their session to say how pleased she was to be working with Margaret.

I raced back to the suite between appointments, though it truly wasn't necessary. Between those guests, and Edward, who brought lunch and a bag of readables from the bookstore in town, and Liam, who brought purchases from my favorite clothing boutique along with the same argument I had made to him two weeks before, that what worked in Connecticut did not work in Vermont, Margaret was well-tended. She slept; she used her laptop for bakery business, and for personal business, a cane left by the physical therapist; she seemed content. By the time dinner rolled around, wearing her new jeans and sweater, Kevin's loopy scarf, and a relaxed smile, she was looking like a different woman.

Making up a new persona? Of course. That was what we did in Devon.

I had done it. Edward had. Now my mother. And Grace? As the weekend went on, that became more and more evident. After she blocked the first Santa Fe number, other calls came from the same area code. From the same person or a second? She didn't know. Though she blocked those, too, she figured it was only a matter of time before more came.

She told me these things in short whispers in the locker room, the hallway, the relaxation lounge, then outside the makeup studio just as I arrived Sunday morning. Her hair was pulled back for work, and she wore soothing celadon scrubs, but her eyes were strikingly copper and frantic. In a voice that was higher than her normal high, she told me about her summons from Edward, and yes, she was convinced he was firing her. I told her I had been asked there, too, but she wasn't mollified.

"He wants you there as a witness in case I go looney and accuse him of something," she said. "Someone from Santa Fe must have called him—I mean, I knew lots of people there. Maybe I shouldn't have blocked those calls. Maybe I should have talked and denied it all and been polite and confident, or . . . or threatened to sue for harassment or something. If Ned finds out, that's the end, absolutely the end."

"Hey, guys," sang another of the massage therapists as he breezed in from the parking lot.

"Hey," I said with as normal a smile as I could muster, even as Grace urged me into the makeup studio and shut the door.

"I really like it here," she pleaded. "I don't want to have to leave. Talk with him, Maggie? Tell him there are jealous women in Santa Fe who just want to make trouble for me. I've only always wanted to protect my son. Ned'll listen to you. He likes you."

I could have told her there and then what Edward was to me, but something held me back. Feeling like a heel, I simply said, "I've already talked with him. I told him he couldn't fire you, and he won't, but we'll have to wait for that meeting to know what he wants. Relax, Grace. Work. Actually, if you start worrying, go up and see my mother. I've talked about you a lot. She wants to meet you."

"Good God, no," Grace cried, as though the suggestion was preposterous. "I can't do that. I am not the kind of person you want your mother to meet."

"And you think she's innocent?" I shot back. "You think I'm innocent? You think neither one of us has done things wrong? Ask yourself why I've never talked about her or why she's never been here before. Grace," I said. "Everyone in the world is guilty of something."

"Not like me," she said, but gave me a quick hug before slipping out the door.

Cornelia came early Sunday to meet my mother and insisted, Margaret later told me somewhat wryly, on staying through Nina's visit. And how had Nina known my mother was there? Me. I had called her. I kept remembering what she had said about being totally alone, kept hearing the desperation in her words, and I figured that if anyone could handle her, it was my mother. Besides, it wasn't like Nina didn't already know the worst.

After the fact, I realized that Nina's questions might tip off Cornelia. But the questions hadn't gone anywhere near there. They had focused on The Buttered Scone, which fascinated Nina and which Margaret was only too happy to describe.

Then came Joe Hellinger and his wife, then Joyce again, then Edward with lunch, then my friend Alex. If I had wanted Margaret to see my life here, I couldn't have asked for better. These people gave her a glimpse of it without her ever having to leave the Inn. By the time I was done with work early Sunday afternoon, though, she wanted to see where I lived. I told her she ought to rest instead. The woman was recovering from a broken hip, for God's sake. She had been half-dead Friday morning.

But she didn't seem half-dead now. She was the Margaret McGowan Reid who kept going no matter what. She actually seemed exhilarated. And how could I fight that?

So we put on our jackets—Mom snug in the new little quilted number Liam had brought her. She had Kevin's scarf around her neck. The scarf was one-hundred percent merino wool, she informed me, though all I could do was wonder how Kevin knew that one of the dozens of shades of green in the hand-dyed wool would perfectly match my mother's eyes.

Walking slowly, elbows linked, we went down to the truck. I still had my doubts about what we were doing, but when she managed to climb up into the seat with some care but no mishap, despite the cast on her wrist and the cane that she hadn't quite mastered, I let it go. I desperately wanted her to see my home, and while it didn't have to be today, it actually did. I had to keep busy until four or I'd go nuts.

It was the second time in as many weeks that I had the responsibility of a passenger, the first being when Chris popped up in my backseat. I hadn't had a choice then; I was already on the road. I did have a choice now. I knew I needed to do this.

But if I was just the slightest bit uneasy, my mother was not. As blasé as could be, she said that Liam had offered to drive, but she didn't want to go with him. She wanted me.

And how could I fight *that?*

We talked more during that short drive than I believe we'd ever done in a car. She told me how much she admired Cornelia and how she sensed a lonely soul in Nina. She knew that Joe and his wife didn't let me spend a Thanksgiving or Christmas alone, and that friends like Alex and Joyce and Kevin were loyal and kind. Hearing it in her voice made me see how rich my life here truly was.

"They're very different from the friends you had before," she remarked with a flippancy that was so the old Margaret that I was momentarily taken back. I think she was, too, because she shot me an uneasy look, as if suddenly remembering where she was and why. "I didn't mean—"

"You're right," I said, because tiptoeing around didn't work as well as it had even a day ago. Too much in the past had been misleading. What I had taken for disapproval may well have been my mother torn between what she felt and what my father believed. He had been a good man in many regards; I wasn't speaking ill of the dead, either. But he was no longer here.

"I loved my art school friends," I said. "We were all different, but we accepted that. After I got married, the differences just seemed to grow."

"You were successful. They weren't."

"Maybe not commercially. Artistically, I couldn't begin to compare. But what I meant was lifestyle. Remember the Labor Day cookout we threw at our house that last year? You and Dad drove up for it."

"Oh, I do," my mother said dryly. "The flower arrangements were gorgeous. You had a caterer grilling everything imaginable, and the place was packed, one beautiful person after another."

"I thought you'd be impressed," I said, mocking myself, then braked sharply when a deer leapt from the woods onto the road. It had the antlers of a male and was quickly followed by a doe. I hadn't been speeding, still my heart raced, but the fear quickly ebbed. "Look," I whispered. It was a typical spring sight in Devon, but it never failed to enchant me. I watched until the elegant creatures disappeared into the woods on the other side of the road.

Accelerating again, I said, "My friends that Labor Day weren't real friends. They were part of a life, like the flowers and the caterer. And the house. And the cars."

"And the skinny," said Mom.

"Yup." I turned onto the hill road and started up, feeling an anticipation that had my heart clenching in its old familiar way. I wanted her approval, of course I did. It was only normal, right? And after all we'd been through, the years of my disappointing her?

"You drive this in winter?" she asked.

I shot her a nervous look, but she was more fearful than critical. And I knew that reaction, had felt it myself once or twice at the start, when the beauty of the forest had been offset by the rawness of the narrow road. Today, though, April was beginning, and I swear I could smell it in the drying mud, the new growth, the hope.

"Roads like this are a way of life here," I said. "So is plowing. My guy comes at least three times for each snowstorm. That's also why I have a truck." Only then remembering her broken hip, I asked in concern, "Too bumpy?"

"No, no. It's fine." But she sounded worried. "I shudder to think of you up here alone."

"You hate it," I said.

"I haven't *seen* it. Much farther?"

When we rounded the last turn, I didn't have to say a thing. There was only one road, one house, one forest in a dead end.

"Oh." She seemed surprised by the gray siding, the oak door, the gabled roof. "It's not very rustic."

I laughed nervously. "That's what I told my realtor when she first drove me here." Hurrying down from the truck, I ran around to her side, and helped her down and then up the walk.

There were no fanfares, but the moment felt momentous. I'm not sure I had dreamed of bringing my mother here; I'm not sure I had dared. The fact that she was here of her own free will—even at her insistence—was something. My eyes teared, which was better, I supposed, than having a chest freeze, but the tears disappeared the instant I opened the door and Jonah raced out, to which Mom said another surprised, "Oh."

His leaving was a good thing. By the time he returned from the woods, she seemed legitimately charmed by what she saw of the downstairs of my home, and while she remained oddly afraid of Jonah, she loved Hex and Jinx. Sensing that, they fought for space on her lap, which freed me to give equal time to my dog, while I answered questions about what it was like to live in the woods, how I got my mail, where my water came from, and whether I was ever lonely or frightened.

My mother had always asked questions. Some were innocent, some pointed, some accusatory as rhetorical questions could be. Looking back through a different shade now, I realized that many had been couched with *Your father wants to know* or *If I don't ask, your father will.*

Today, she might have asked for an hour and I wouldn't have minded. I could tell she was intrigued. There were times when I heard the same fear as when we started up the road—but hell, hadn't I told Edward she was no scout? Weaving through the questions, though, was a thread of acceptance. To my starved heart, a thread was a truckful.

When she absolutely, positively insisted, we climbed to the second floor. Given a choice, I'd have saved that part for another day. She had a broken hip, and while her PT encouraged stair-climbing, the jostling in the truck couldn't have helped. And then there was my bed. Mom was a stickler for hospital corners, and there was nothing here but a tangle of sheets. The last time I slept here—Edward and I, actually, though she didn't need to know that—was Friday morning, right before I learned about her hip, and I hadn't wasted time neatening up before we left.

She didn't say anything about the unmade bed, but when she saw Liam's belongings cluttering the loft, she wondered aloud, with distress, when he planned to get his own place. She spared me a response by asking if I had any Tylenol, which I did. I went to the bathroom and opened the medicine chest. After shaking out two pills, I closed it again.

And there, in the mirror, my mother's stricken eyes met mine. Her voice was a pained whisper. "Why is that there?"

My mug shot. I swallowed. "It's who I am."

"Who you were."

"I'll always be that person. I can't erase the past."

"Can't forgive yourself? Can't feel worthy of love?" she asked, capturing the gist of it in two quick questions.

How did you know? I might have asked if the huge knot in my throat hadn't blocked sound. My mother's arms came around me, then, and her weight settled against my back as if for support. When she buried her face in my shoulder so that I wouldn't see her shame, I knew she was talking about herself.

I forgave her. Absolutely, unconditionally, and irrevocably, I did. I now understood all she had given up of her inner self to keep her marriage intact, and I would have loved her for that, even if I hadn't loved her just because she was my mother. The apology she made in my bathroom—a silent, stoically poignant Margaret apology—was the icing on the cake, as she would have said.

And me? I wanted to forgive myself, truly I did. I wanted to feel worthy of love. But *worthy* went beyond Edward's declarations. It went beyond the love I did feel when his dark head rose, his pale eyes held mine, and he buried himself deep inside me. It went beyond my mother's tentative touch with the fingers that extended beyond her cast—my shoulder now, then my arm or my hand—as we drove back to the Inn. For someone who had never been a toucher, she was trying.

Worthy was about what I felt inside, and the closer we got to that meeting at the Inn, the more that feeling was dread. Right now, I had more than I deserved. Past and present were coming together in ways I couldn't have imagined just weeks ago. And it was good.

One missed STOP sign, though, and it would be gone. Five years ago, the STOP sign was hidden by leaves on the side of the road. This time, it was crystal clear in the shape of a meeting that I had myself set up to help a friend. Now, turning off the Blue, passing under the covered bridge that spanned the river, and approaching the gracious stone columns at the front door of the Inn, I had the awful thought that history was about to repeat itself.

24

I was complicit. Of the many negatives in my mind as I waited for Grace to finish her last massage, that topped the list. I was complicit walking her through the Spa, my cocoa-brown scrubs sedate beside her amber ones. I was complicit as we entered the Inn and climbed the stairs to the business wing, and again as I lowered the brass lever, opened the glass double doors, and strode past Currier and Ives. The conference room, with its long mahogany table and Chippendale chairs, was empty, but I had known the men wouldn't be there. Glass wouldn't do. We needed privacy. I was as complicit in this knowledge, as I was when I guided Grace into Edward's office, closed the door, and leaned against it so that she couldn't escape.

The scene inside was deceptively peaceful, as much the snapshot of a moment in time as the foxhunting oils that hung on the dark-paneled wood. There was Edward, leaning casually against the front of his cluttered desk, looking both in charge and gorgeous in a navy turtleneck and jeans. And Jay in one of the tartan club chairs, round face composed, legs crossed at the knee. Grace might have asked why the lawyer was there if Ben Zwick hadn't chosen that moment to turn.

He wasn't as tall or compelling as Edward, though his sandy hair and brown eyes were certainly attractive. Attitude was what gave him stature, and now, despite a glimmer of apprehension when he focused on Grace, his posture held as he left the window.

Grace's eyes flew to mine in alarm. I returned a tiny headshake, complicit in this, too. I might not know all of what Ben had to say, but I had certainly known he would be here.

Her gaze returned to the men, tripping from face to face in fear. "What is this?" she asked in her Grace-high voice.

"Thanks for coming," Edward began and gestured her toward the large leather sofa.

She was having none of that. Turning quickly, she reached for the door.

I caught her arm. "You need to listen to what Ben has to say."

"Hasn't he already said enough?" she cried. Twisting her head, she pinned the man in question with a killing stare. "You son of a bitch."

"Sometimes," he admitted.

"I don't want an apology, so if you're looking to feel less guilty, forget it. The damage is already done." Turning back to me in accusation, she tried to free her arm, but I held tight.

"He's getting calls from Santa Fe, too," I said.

That stilled her. After staring at me for several beats, she swallowed. Then, apparently not yet ready to deal with Santa Fe, she focused on my complicity. "You talked with him. You learned this and didn't tell me. You knew he'd be here."

"I love you, Grace, and I love Chris. I want both of you safe." When she said nothing, I stressed, "You are not alone here. It's us four against him. Edward will referee, Jay will protect your rights, and I will personally shut Ben down if he goes off the deep end."

She looked about to argue. Then her eyes slid to the side, where a coat tree held three very different coats, and although her back was to the men, I knew she was realizing that one controlled her job, one her son's legal case, and one her future. Her copper eyes met mine with resentment, but behind the contacts was worry as well. Putting her back to the door, she folded her arms to hold herself together and turned her glare on Ben.

A large manila envelope hung from one hand, but it stayed at his side. His voice was surprisingly quiet. Also surprising, I saw no arrogance. There was something sad about him, which might have made me think about his personal feelings for Grace, if I hadn't been caught up in his words.

"Thirteen years ago, a woman named Greta Brandt disappeared from Santa Fe with her two-year-old son. Someone called me to say you're that woman. I researched the facts of the case. Height, weight, smile—all the same. You look different in other ways"—he raised the envelope, suggesting there were photos inside—"but those ways could easily be cosmetic."

Edward and I exchanged a worried glance. Cosmetic? Easily.

Grace said nothing. Her hands curled into fists, knuckles white against the inside of her elbows as Ben went on.

"Greta Brandt had gone through an ugly divorce. Her husband was wealthy and well connected. He successfully made a case that she was an unfit mother, so he got full custody of the boy. When she took off with him, she was charged with kidnapping."

I felt a sinking sensation. But I had guessed it, hadn't I? The pieces fit. Totally aside from makeup, hair color, and contact lenses, it explained multiple rounds of plastic surgery.

Edward's eyes found mine again. They were uneasy, like he, too, knew where this was heading. I had driven Grace to the plastic surgeon. I had done her makeup and given her woodsy brown hair, which I had cut in layers to veil side views of her face. Before that I had given her auburn curls, and before that an ashy bob. I was totally complicit in helping her hide.

Grace raised her chin. "That woman couldn't be me. I am not an unfit mother. I love my son. I have done things for him that most mothers would never do. I've turned over my *life* for him."

"She was never found," Ben said. "Both of them gone without a trace." He dropped the envelope on Edward's desk, then rubbed his palms on his jeans. It was a nervous gesture, coming from a man who had surely been in far more threatening situations. "Here's the thing, Grace. The woman who called me was the Brandts' cook, so she saw what went on in that house. She says you're Greta Brandt; you say you're not. She has photos from papers back then and ones from papers now. She wants to sell me her story, and if I don't buy it, she'll show those pictures to someone else, so whether it's true or not, it'll come out."

"Libel," warned Jay.

"Not if corroborated," argued Ben. "For what it's worth, she said the boy's father was scum."

"*Batshit* scum," Grace cried in a burst of venom before realizing the admission. Her panicked gaze scanned the others before returning to Ben. Her eyes welled, and a tremor hit her voice. "Why are you doing this?"

"Because despite what you think," he said, sounding more sincere than I wanted him to, "despite what others think, I'm not the enemy. I don't make up stories. I do my research and report on it. Right now, I can only find one side of this story. There has to be another one."

In the silence that followed, I pictured the other side, which would be filled with a slew of details I didn't want to know. I looked at Edward again. His mouth moved just enough to share his silent, *Fuck.* Oh yeah, we were on the same page, right there in my probation agreement.

"Only one side of the story," Ben repeated, "and, trust me, I tried for the other. Can't see the court proceedings, because they're sealed. Can't ask the boy, because the boy was two when it happened. Won't get anything from neighbors and friends, because our man is that intimidating and that powerful." He screwed up his face at Grace. "Did you mount *any* kind of case in your defense?"

Jay neared Grace with surprising speed. "Don't answer," he told her. "Don't confirm or deny. He's media. He can't be trusted."

He was speaking as a lawyer, I knew. But I also knew he had slept with Grace, so his distrust of Ben might have been personal.

I stepped in. Hell, I was already in it up to my ears, so what was a little more? Besides, I was the one who had set up this meeting. "If anyone distrusts the press, it's me," I said, "but he claimed he wanted to help, and that all he wanted to do here was talk. He said he wouldn't even write anything down."

"Oh, he will," Grace argued, "if not here, then when he leaves. He smells a book, and what could be better than two opposing stories, lots of conflict, lots of drama, lots of injustice?"

"I *hate* the press," I told her, upping the ante. "I've seen them exaggerate and fabricate and lie. But I don't think he's lying now." To Ben, I said, "You promised you wouldn't have a recording device. Do you?"

He patted his pockets and shirtfront, held out his arms. "Nothing. I just wanted to warn you about what may be happening, and hey," he was addressing Jay now, "there's a risk for me, too. They find out I'm talking to you while Chris's court case is ongoing, and I'm in trouble."

"Damn right," said Jay, his second warning in as many minutes.

Ben came a step closer. He seemed oddly hurt. To Grace, he said, "You would never talk about your past. I told you I would never write about anything you said. I told you it was personal between us, but you never let me get close. I knew you were hiding—"

"You dreamed," Grace broke in, but meekly, like she had been badgered for hours, not minutes, and had simply run out of steam.

"Then tell me. Nothing you say leaves this room unless you say it does."

She was silent so long that I looked at her. Her face wore yearning, though I didn't know whether it was for Ben the man, or simply for unburdening herself of secrets that had chafed in her veins for too long— and, omigod, did I know how unburdening felt. Discussing the accident and Lily and loss with Edward these past few weeks, breaking down with him the other night, even broaching the forbidden with my mother—tears came to my eyes just thinking about it.

And here was Edward now, reassuring Grace. "We'll hold him to it. But he's right about containing this. We can't do that if we don't know what we're dealing with."

We. I loved him a little more each time he said that word, but my fear also grew. In hosting this meeting, he would be implicated if things went wrong. My shit would become his, again. I had never wanted that.

Seeing my tears, he shot me a silvery stare. Daring me to question his loyalty? Punishing me for the mess?

Unable to decide which, I refocused on Grace, who was going from face to face, bewildered, outnumbered, overpowered. My eyes cleared; I slid an arm through hers. I knew what it was like to be alone in a crowd of people with your life upended and no one at your back. In that instant, I didn't care about Shanahan. Being a friend in time of need was what I wanted the new me to be.

"I can't go back," she whispered, begging me to understand. "He'll kill me. As soon as he became a somebody, he wanted me gone, so my leaving with Chris meant nothing to him. He already had a new family. *That* started while we were still married. Smearing me was to justify his own infidelity. And the custody battle? It was just a power thing. That's what it's all about with him—power and ego."

"The problem," I whispered back, although the three men were close enough to hear, "is that you can't keep denying it, Grace. You've been found."

Her eyes darkened with momentary resolve. "I'll disappear again."

I remembered our discussion of places to go if not Devon, and understood now why she preferred to stay east of the Mississippi. She had most liked the idea of New York, where she might easily get lost. But starting over now wasn't so easy. Totally aside from his legal issues, her son was no longer two.

"Is that what you want for Chris?" I asked, and for an instant, she seemed to stop breathing.

"Low blow," she finally said. She looked crushed.

"I know. I'm sorry." But I wasn't. *I can't go back,* she had just said. But if she didn't go back, if she didn't finally tell someone the truth of the past, she could never be whole.

She?

Me.

I was barely grasping that—when her eyes flew back to mine. Her face was the color of chalk. She clamped a hand over her mouth, and her upper body convulsed.

"Bathroom," I murmured for the sake of the others, but when I put an arm around her shoulder and started to steer her there, firm hands eased me aside and took over.

I'm not sure what Ben said to Grace after she was done being sick. When they came out, her skin was newly washed, makeup nearly gone, and the soft brown hair around her face was damp. She remained pale but seemed marginally composed.

Composure was an act, of course. Grace was good at acting. You had to be, when you were in your thirties and restarting life with a new identity. By the time thirteen years, or four, had passed, you were a pro. You looked poised; you looked calm. You looked like you knew exactly where you were and what you were doing, like you had reached this point in a perfectly natural progression, even though inside you were terrified.

Grace had to be beyond terrified. I could see it in the way she went straight to the large leather sofa and sank into its corner as her legs gave out. Oh, I knew the corner gambit, too. A corner meant you were shielded on two sides—three, if you sat with your back to the seam, as Grace did, so that the only exposed side was your front.

Edward produced bottles of water from a low cabinet. He gave her one and put the rest on the long, low table.

Jay crouched beside the sofa, his fingers curled on its leather arm. "You don't have to do this," he told her quietly.

She nodded, but when she looked back at me, her eyes said she did. That look also held an apology, regret for what she had to say, fear that it would change everything, and it might. She might lose her son, her name, her job, her home. But not our friendship. Shanahan or not, that wasn't in play. Needing her to know it, I joined her on the sofa, sitting close with a leg folded under me so that I faced her.

"Tell us," I urged, and for a minute, seeing a last flash of panic in those copper eyes, I feared she might throw up again. But she stayed where she was, swallowed, and began.

She had met Carter Brandt eighteen years before. She was his massage therapist at a spa in Sedona, and the attraction was immediate. Later, when his dark side proved so dark that she wondered how she could have missed it, she blamed Sedona's heady vibe of red rocks, pine forests, and spirituality. Carter snowed her. She thought they had a special connection. He was good-looking and charismatic, turning heads wherever he went. What woman wouldn't be flattered that he chose her? she asked the men before returning helpless eyes to me.

"They wouldn't understand," I said softly and jiggled her wrist. "Go on."

She took a quick drink, tucked the bottle between her hip and the sofa, and folded her hands in her lap. He liked her spark, she said. He liked her independence. Within the year, she had moved from Arizona to New Mexico to marry him, and, soon after, was pregnant. She hadn't thought it would happen so soon, but his parents had been after him to have kids. Their business was a family one, and they needed promise of a next generation.

The Brandt family owned the largest car dealership consortium in the southwest. Despite being intimately involved with that, Carter built a separate source of power in politics. When he and Grace met, he was already a city councilor, although he kept a scrupulous finger in the automotive till. The dealerships he personally ran were the most productive; he used that fact to build connections beyond those of his family. This meant nights out, lots of nights out. Sometimes Grace was with him. Increasingly, she was not.

Soon after Chris was born, Carter was elected to the New Mexico House of Representatives. He had run as a successful businessman dedicated to honesty and transparency, buzzwords he knew resonated with voters, and he won by a healthy margin. Grace was at his side when he needed her, though she was starting to chafe at being "the little woman." She wanted to go back to work. The spa ambiance offered a warmth and serenity she didn't have at home. And Santa Fe was known for its spas.

Carter refused. He argued that she was the wife of a state representative, not to mention now belonging to one of the state's most prominent families. Touching men's bodies all day wouldn't look good.

Little by little, other things about Grace started not looking good to him. She wasn't good at political talk. She wasn't good at hosting dinner parties. She wasn't good at elegance. Her flair had become a liability, drawing attention away from him. And then there were her roots, about which his constituents often asked. She came from nothing. Her parents were working class, which hadn't bothered him when they first met, but suddenly did.

"He told you this?" Ben asked.

"Well, I sure didn't imagine it," she shot at the window to which he'd returned. "Do I look that insecure?"

She actually did, tucked in her protective corner, though I'm not sure the men sensed it the way I did. Confidence could be applied like makeup. I knew this for fact.

Jay had been pacing but now stopped before her. "Verbal abuse?" he asked.

"Not at first," she said and picked at a nail. "It started innocent, like, 'Can you do something with your hair,' or 'Maybe not that sweater.' Then it got worse, and it wasn't only Carter. His sister got in the act"—she made air quotes—"to help me out. She's a bitch in the best of times, which shopping with me was not. She kept choosing things that were totally not me then rolling her eyes at what I did want, like I was hopeless. Add that to all the nights he was out, and, well, yeah, I guess I did start feeling insecure."

"All those nights out?" Ben asked, leading her without quite saying the words.

"Of course. I mean, a guy with an ego way bigger than his dick? Of course, he cheated."

"And you let him?" Jay asked.

"What in the hell could I do, Jay?" she cried, but at least bits of color had returned to her face. "I asked him about it, but that only unleashed a long list of everything I was doing wrong. It was little nothing me against big powerful him." She considered that summation and let out a breath. Quietly, she said, "It went downhill from there."

"The abuse?" Again, from Jay.

"Yes. I kept thinking he wouldn't do anything major, because I was the mother of his son. But the words got more vicious, and he hit me where no one would see. I mean, women go through that all the time, right? I was *not* a great wife for him. I hated those political dinners, hated trying to look good and coming up short, hated the way he would find fault when we were out and blame it on my upbringing—I mean, right in front of other people." She looked up at her audience when she said the last. Every face held concern. "He said I broke my own arm tripping over one of the baby's toys, I was such a klutz." She looked at me. "Am I a klutz?"

I pictured her skiing those Black Diamond slopes. "Absolutely not."

"Thank you." She took another sip of water and tucked the bottle back in. Eyes downcast, she said, "I came to hate him—I mean, really hate him. I dreamed of leaving him, fantasized about it all the time, but I was worried he would take it out on the baby. Then he started losing patience with Chris, too—you know, complained that he wasn't walking early enough, wasn't talking early enough, made too much noise, didn't make enough noise. One spanking was all I could take. I said if he ever again lifted a hand to the baby, *ever* again, I would go public with it." She grunted. "Not one of my wisest moves."

"Why not?" I asked.

Her eyes met mine. "Because Carter Brandt loves a challenge. He needed dirt on me in case I went public with dirt on him, so he started having me followed."

"Followed," Jay said.

"He hired someone to go where I went and take pictures of anything that was remotely suggestive."

"Like what?" I asked, covering her hand to stop the picking.

"I had defied him and gone back to work, just a few afternoons a week while Chris napped, because I needed *someone* to say I wasn't a worthless piece of shit. So his guy planted a camera where it would capture my hands on men's bodies. Add those shots to ones of my talking with a guy at Starbucks or smiling at the pizza delivery guy or hugging my hairdresser— my *hairdresser,* for Christ's sake—well, you get the idea. But infidelity wasn't enough. He wanted to totally destroy me, which meant showing I was an unfit mother."

"How were you unfit?" I asked, indignant this time. Not seeing what your teenage son was doing on a computer wasn't being unfit. It was being distracted.

A tiny bell rang in my head. I hadn't been unfit, either. I'd simply been distracted.

But Grace hadn't heard the bell. "For starters," she said, "he claimed I drank. There were dozens of photos of me with a glass in my hand." She looked at me again. "Do I drink?"

"No."

"Thank you—but oh, I forgot to mention that most of the shots were taken at campaign events, which were a nightmare for me. I wouldn't have *dared* take more than a sip or two of whatever was put in my hand, because even with a clear head, I had trouble remembering who was married to who and which donor's son just got into U-N-M or U-A or U-S-C, because as far as I was concerned, that brownnosing is total C-R-A-P."

Throaty sounds came from Edward and Ben in varying degrees of appreciation, but Jay was brooding. "Carter Brandt? Isn't there a Carter Brandt in Congress?"

"That would be the *US* Congress," Grace confirmed in a voice laced with sarcasm. "But you're jumping ahead, Jay. Don't you want to hear about the videos?"

"Absolutely," Jay said and stepped back.

"There were videos?" Ben asked.

"Oh, you'd love to see those, Ben." She was running on anger now, reliving all she must have suppressed for so long. "His guy shot videos of me lounging at the pool while the soundtrack had Chris screaming inside. Forget the fact that the drink I held was an iced espresso because I needed the caffeine because we'd been at one of those godawful boring events the night before and Chris had woken up when we came in and hadn't wanted to go back to sleep, so he was overtired, too, and was screaming because I'd just put him in for a nap. There were videos of me laughing on the phone while, behind me, Chris was in a little floaty thing drifting toward the deep end of the pool."

"He was alone?" Jay asked in alarm.

Her head whipped his way. "No, he was not alone. The fucking *nanny* was in the water with him, only *she* was edited out."

"Experts can detect editing."

"I'm sure they can," she said slowly, as if Jay were the child here, "but when you have the judge and everyone else in your pocket, experts don't count. Did I mention," she added sweetly, "that every employee of his has to sign a confidentiality agreement? Did I mention that if any one of them breaks it, he or she becomes unemployable in the state? Did I mention that Carter makes that happen enough, so it's a lesson for the rest?"

"Well, someone's speaking up now," Edward said, reminding us why we were there in the first place.

"Our cook." Briefly, her voice softened. "She always thought Carter was a bully. She quit after I left."

"And you know this how?" Jay asked.

"Facebook."

"So thirteen years later she's suddenly not afraid of Brandt?"

"Oh, I'm sure she is. But she got her citizenship, and the family she's with are artists. They're politically active and *not* on Carter's side of the aisle, so if he goes after her, they'll go after him right back. But she has a special-needs child who must be a special-needs adult by now. I'm sure she needs the money, and I feel bad for her, really I do." Her eyes went to Ben, voice rising. "But if she talks with someone about this, I'm toast. If word gets back to Carter, it's all over. I was charged with *kidnapping*."

Jay was making rewind motions with his hand. "You're running away with this, Grace—"

"Well, wouldn't you?" she cried, starting to get up until I pulled her back. "Kidnapping means prison, with no hope of bail because I'd be a flight risk for sure, and what would happen to my son then, Jay? *If* my son isn't locked up himself—big if right now—he would be returned to his so-called rightful guardian, who lies and cheats and steals and is about as transparent as quicksand, all of which is what that asshole would teach my son"—her glazed eyes went to Ben—"my son, who made a gross mistake and needs to pay for it in a way that teaches him right from wrong. His father would teach him that his only mistake was getting caught. Is that what you want him to learn?" she asked Ben, then Jay, "Is it?"

Jay crouched at her side again. His voice was as gentle as I'd ever heard it. "We do not want that, none of us, which is why we need to know more. I'm trying to get a picture here, so I need you to go back to the divorce. When did you find out about the photos and videos?"

Like a balloon losing air, she sank back into the sofa. "When he told me we were getting divorced. He didn't ask. He told. He said I'd been cheating on him, said I was a lush, said I was a lousy mother, and he showed me enough of the pictures to let me know what I was up against. So I'm standing there in shock, and he hands me an agreement to sign. I would leave the marriage with nothing more than what I'd brought into it, meaning the clothes on my back."

"Did you sign it?" Jay asked.

"Hell, no. Chris was included in what I would leave behind, no visitation rights at all. Carter wanted me totally erased from their lives. I said no."

"What did Brandt say to that?" Jay asked.

"That he'd see me in court. He moved out of our house and into the new one he'd bought for his girlfriend, who, p.s., was pregnant. Impregnating women is his specialty. I think it's his way of controlling a woman, like once she's pregnant, she'll do whatever he asks. Only the new one would help his career. She was the daughter of a state Supreme Court justice."

"Did the divorce ever get to court?"

Grace snorted.

"You had a lawyer, didn't you?"

"Legal aid," she said and, when Jay frowned, added, "I had no money. Carter cut off credit cards, bank accounts, everything."

"So how did you get away with Chris?"

She folded her arms, and, for the first time, I saw an inkling of pride. "I might have been naive about how far he would go to annihilate me, but I'm not stupid. I told you I dreamed about leaving. Well, it wasn't all fantasy. While he was piecing together damning evidence, I was putting together documentation under an alias. Part of my backup was a stash of money. I kept adding to it, and it was never huge, but it was there when I needed it."

I was in awe. "How did you know how to get documentation?" It was such a ballsy Grace thing to do, one I would never in my life, not even in my darkest moments, have dared.

"Immigrants," she said. "They were all over Santa Fe, even undocumented ones on our property, and they had always liked me. I talked with them. Most employers didn't. So they shared. I was safe with them. For obvious reasons, they avoided the authorities."

I was thinking that as zany as she was, she could be remarkably resourceful, when Ben said, "So you and Chris left it all behind."

Grace smiled then. It was the first wide honest-to-goodness Grace smile that had come from her in days. "Not all of it. Carter wasn't the only one who gathered evidence, only mine was legit."

She stopped talking. Her smile faded as we watched, replaced by a look of pure . . . evil was the word that came to my mind, only I couldn't find fault. What I saw had to do with backbone and intent, with revenge, with justice.

"We're waiting, Grace," Jay prompted, as only the lawyer could.

"I couldn't prove that he hit me," she said. "There were no hospital records, and selfies wouldn't prove anything. He could talk his way around abuse. Not consumer fraud, though. He regularly turned back odometer readings and sold used cars as having significantly less mileage than in fact they did."

"Spinning?" Ben asked in surprise.

"Yup."

"That's a heavy charge," Jay cautioned. "Can you back it up?"

"I have papers."

"What kind of papers?" Ben asked, coming back from the window.

Staying him with a hand, Jay asked Grace, "Originals or copies?"

"Originals," she replied. "Records of used car sales, done in pairs, one legit, one doctored, same VIN."

Edward was looking as stunned as the rest of us. "Why would he do that? Why would he allow proof like that to exist?"

"Stupidity?" Grace asked. *"Ass-hood?* He showed them to me right after we were married, like he wanted me to know how smart my husband was. It was really just one guy, the head of the service department. He'd go in after hours to do his thing. Turned out, he had a gambling habit. Carter helped him in exchange."

"Carter told you this?" Jay asked.

"Oh yeah. Proudly. Like he was a good guy to be helping one of his men. Like that made what he was doing okay. Like *I* wouldn't even realize that any of it was illegal." She smiled her evil smile. "That was his first mistake."

"How did you get the papers?"

"He had a home office where he kept his private files. They were locked

369

up, but he took the key from its hiding place while I was standing right there. Like I wouldn't dare do anything about it." She huffed. "That was his second mistake."

"How many more mistakes?" Edward asked. He seemed less tense now. Physical proof was a bargaining tool, and while Grace was still in big trouble, apparently so was her ex.

"Well, let's see," Grace was answering Edward, "his third was leaving me home alone so much. His fourth was not having a surveillance camera in that office. His fifth was turning odometers back on so many cars for so many years that my taking a handful of records would never be noticed." She paused only to look expectantly, demandingly, from Jay to Ben. "Okay. That's my story. What happens next?"

"We see those papers," said Ben.

"*I* see them," Jay corrected. "At least with me, there's lawyer-client privilege."

"I said I wouldn't write her story, but I have to corroborate it first," Ben argued. "Once I've seen those papers, I can bargain behind the scenes."

"Bargain? You can also spill all if you're subpoenaed. I'm her lawyer. I'm protected."

"I know people in Washington, where the congressman works."

"Washington doesn't matter," Jay huffed. "The crime happened in New Mexico, and I know lawyers there."

"All of whom are in Brandt's pocket."

"Not the U.S. Attorney for the state. I went to law school with him. We were Moot Court partners. We get together whenever I'm west or he's east."

Ben frowned. "I called this meeting. Don't I have a say about what happens next?"

Jay said, "Sorry, pal, but no."

"Screw *this*," Grace said, rising so suddenly that I sat back in surprise. "What are you two doing? You led me on about needing to act quickly, so I spill my guts, and now you stand here duking it out to see who takes me to the prom? I am not the prize here. My freedom is, because if I'm not free, that bastard takes my son. I want both of us safe. Can't you two coordinate, or something?"

They coordinated. Jay would take custody of the incriminating evidence against Carter Brandt and meet with the U.S. Attorney in New Mexico. At the same time, Ben would use his contacts to sniff around Washington on the theory that if the congressman had used the threat of blackmail in business, he might do the same in politics, or, alternately, if he had cheated on his first wife, he might be cheating on his second.

The goal was to keep things quiet while working out a private agreement with Brandt's lawyers that would protect Grace and Chris.

It was a good plan. Jay plus Ben equaled contacts in enough high places to negotiate a deal—and it would have worked, had they only been one day ahead.

25

With barely a knock on the outer door, Kevin burst into our meeting. His face was ruddy, eyes frantic, voice shrill. "They're on their way here. You have to leave, all of you, *now.*"

Apparently, Jimmy had been called to the police station for a Sunday emergency and had slipped him word. The Feds were back in town along with the media led by Carter Brandt on his high horse, and they were gunning for Grace.

Jay barely had time to instruct her on what to say, or more accurately what not to say, when Federal marshals arrived with a warrant for her arrest. Looking at me in panic, she mouthed her son's name, before being cuffed and led out. Jay was on their heels.

Thinking only to get Chris and hide, I had started for the door when Edward blocked the way. "You can't go. I will."

"*I* will," Ben said, looking straight at me as he took his jacket from the coat tree. "If Carter Brandt is in town, he'll be at Grace's house right now filming his reunion with his son. He'll have his personal press buddies with him."

As warnings went, it might have been innocent, but whether Ben knew the truth about me was not the issue just then. Chris was. I couldn't begin to imagine what he might feel if a stranger claiming to be his father showed up at the house without Grace. And telling him that he wasn't Chris Emory at all? And that his mother was *locked up?*

Grace's panic became mine. "He'll take him away, we'll never *see* him again, everything she fought *so hard* for will be *lost*—and Chris doesn't even *know* Carter."

"He knows me—" Ben said.

"Hates you."

"Resents me," he corrected as he punched at his phone. "I was the one his mother would have been with if she'd been free, and since he didn't understand why she wasn't free, he blamed me."

"You were the one who kept coming back," I said, thinking of Grace's photos. "He thought you might be his father."

"Nah." He was typing again. "He just needed a target for all those blanks in his life."

"He does know me," Edward announced as he pulled on a leather jacket—and I felt a second's distraction. I knew that jacket. I had given it to him during our last year together. Not only was the leather like butter, but its pecan brown was a perfect foil for his dark hair. "I'm neutral," he said in a determined voice. "I'm going."

But that jacket had tapped into my other panic. "*No.* Grace is *my* friend, this is *my* mess." I had already complicated his life more than was fair, and my gut knew this was only the start. Slotted between the pages of Grace's story was the fact that exposure for her meant exposure for me. If she confessed to kidnapping her son, I was guilty of aiding a felon.

"Maggie, you know you can't—"

"Like it'll make a difference now?"

"Yeah, it will."

"The damage is already done, Edward. Don't you see?"

I'm not sure whether Ben got the subtext of our argument, what with his eye on his phone, but before Edward could answer, he made a frustrated sound. "Too late. Brandt is at the house."

The defeat in his voice was small consolation. Carter Brandt being anywhere near her son was the last thing Grace had wanted. Apparently, though, I couldn't have gotten to Chris in time even if I had rushed out when Jay had.

But where to go now? What to do? How to help? I drew a blank.

My sense of helplessness was even greater an hour later as live coverage of Congressman Carter Brandt's press conference filled the large-screen TV. The archetypal everyman in his rolled-sleeve shirt and jeans, he stood before folk art in the lobby of the Town Hall and spoke of his joy at being finally reunited with his son after these painfully long years apart. His eyes were moist, his voice cracked. Chris wasn't standing with him, but was "safe at last," the congressman said repeatedly, which meant he had been stashed where none of us could reach him.

"Sanctimonious fucker," muttered my brother, who sprawled in a nearby armchair.

My mother and I had the sofa. She was stretched out to ease her hip, but we didn't touch. I was curled too tightly into myself at the opposite end, trying to fill the hollowness inside.

The fact that she didn't comment on Liam's choice of words said something about her focus on Grace. She glanced up at Edward, who stood at the sofa's back. "How did the authorities know where you were meeting?"

"They showed up at the Spa looking for Grace," he said in disgust as he watched the screen. "They threatened Joyce with obstruction of justice if she didn't tell where she was. She had no choice."

Congressman Brandt was blathering on now about the tragedy of missing children.

"Merde," swore Liam. "This is a fucking campaign speech."

Again, my mother said nothing, but asked Edward, "What will they do to her?"

"Short term?" Tearing his eyes from the TV, he gentled. "Keep her locked up. Jay is working on what comes next." He pulled out his vibrating phone and studied the screen. To me, in an undertone, he said, "Good. Jay got her papers."

That was something, at least. Federal agents would be all over the house by now. Our fear was that in tearing the place apart for every last bit of evidence to incriminate Grace, they would confiscate what she had on Carter. We were praying she kept them elsewhere. Apparently so.

"*Quels papiers?*" Liam asked.

"Liam," Mom scolded. "Enough."

"Where?" I asked Edward.

"Her safe deposit box at the bank. The Feds took her key ring, but the bank gives you two keys. She told Jay where to find the second." When I raised a brow in question, he smiled. "Her spare set of house keys. Joyce had them."

"Ah. Redemption," I said but couldn't muster a smile. The congressman had ended his news conference. A reporter took over and began recapping the case. Clips appeared of Grace being led in handcuffs from the Inn, into a cruiser, into the police station. They were followed by clips from the day we had gone to Rutland for Chris's court appearance.

Not three weeks ago? How could that be? So much had happened, one domino falling, then another and another, each moving another step back in time. The past was the root of the rest of a life. I was coming to understand that.

"Is the coverage just because he's a congressman?" Margaret asked.

"And because of the hacking charge," Edward answered. "It makes for good drama."

"Look at *you* there, Maggie!" Liam cried in excitement. When Margaret snapped out his name, his head turned, freckled face fell. "What?" he asked, seeming oblivious.

"This isn't a game show. It's a travesty of justice. That doesn't call for glee on any level. Grace is Maggie's friend. She's a sweet woman."

"How do *you* know?" he shot back.

Margaret was unruffled, even serene. "She came to see me this morning. It was a quick visit. She was between clients. I wish we could have talked longer. She needs someone." Her eyes found mine. "When she left, she squeezed my hand and looked straight at me, and what I saw was raw and good."

I hadn't known. Grace hadn't said, nor had Mom told me when we'd been in the car. For a time, at least, it had been just between them, which somehow gave it greater meaning. Touched, I pressed a hand to my chest, not sure if I would cry or seize up. Had my mother been looking at me, I would likely have done the former, tears being my go-to since the flood over the green velvet box.

But she was looking at the TV again, then back at Edward. "Will there be fallout for the Inn?"

He shrugged. "The computer hacking was worse."

He was downplaying it, I knew. But the fact that he did it for my sake turned a little something inside me. Same with the sight of my mother and brother, staying with us, sounding for all the world like they were on our side rather than walking out in disgust. They were a blessing, so much so that I was suddenly overwhelmed.

Pulling my knees up, I closed my eyes against them. *Breathe in, breathe out, repeat. In, out, repeat.*

Edward's hand came to rest ever so lightly on my head. *It'll be fine,* that hand said, but I wasn't so sure. The other shoe hadn't yet fallen.

Keeping my eyes closed, I did my best to tune out the television. Those voices didn't matter to me. The only ones that did were here in this room.

Liam's voice came first. "Where do you think he's taken Chris? Did he book a room here at the Inn?"

"Not under his own name," replied Edward with a certainty that said he had checked.

Margaret spoke. "They're at the Town Hall now, but it's after seven. They have to eat somewhere. They have to *sleep* somewhere."

"He'll get the hell out of Dodge," said Liam.

"With his son in the middle of a court case?" Mom countered. "He can't just pick up and leave the state, can he, Edward?"

I had been listening with my eyes closed, trying to best absorb the confidence in Edward's hand. When that hand left me, I opened my eyes to see him clasp his hands at the top of his head. The motion made his shoulders look all the broader, though that certainly wasn't why he had done it. This was his frustrated pose. He was watching the screen again.

"The rules change when a US congressman is involved," he said.

"That's not fair," complained Liam.

"Life isn't," my mother told him just as my phone dinged.

My heart pounded when I glanced at the screen. I held it up for Edward to see. *Are you watching TV?* Shanahan wrote. *I warned you.*

There it was, the other shoe. Talk about life not being fair? I had finally reconnected with the three people who mattered most to me, and, four months shy of the end of my probation, I would be nailed for having befriended a woman with a past. I hadn't known who Grace was; I didn't intentionally help her hide. But the facts would say that I did aid and abet an accused felon, just as they would say that Grace did kidnap her son.

Heartsick, I rose from the sofa. My face must have shown the extent of my distress, because Edward was quickly beside me. His large hand was warm at the back of my neck. "Where are you going?"

With my throat tight from holding back tears, a hoarse whisper was the best I could do. "Home. My pets."

"They're fine," Liam called. "All fed and walked."

If I'd been able to speak, I might have thanked him. But I was crushed. I needed my own world, at least until the last of it fell away. Wasn't alone my default?

But my mother was sitting up in alarm. "Stay."

It was just one word, but I heard the rest. *Hiding won't help. Don't shut us out.* And there it was, a return to the time when she and I understood each other without having to speak aloud, which was exactly what I'd wished for not so long ago. And then came her "please," along with a look so vulnerable that my heart would never have let me leave.

But I did need a minute alone. So I gave the quickest little nod and simply went to my room. The door was barely shut before I began to cry. Swallowing the sobs as they came, I stumbled to the bed, climbed on, and curled up on the pillow with the scent of pine and my tears. Overwhelmed was one word for what I felt, but it didn't capture the extremes. I didn't think a person could feel so full and so empty at the same time.

The door opened, then closed. Had it not been for the click of her cane, my mother's faltering gait would have been lost in the carpet. She eased herself down on the edge of the bed. I tried to stop crying, but her nearness only made it worse.

"I'm not good at this," she said in a shaky voice. "You were always so strong."

That got me crying again, all the more when I felt her hand on my shoulder. She didn't tell me to stop, just sat with me until I finally quieted, sniffed, and brushed at my tears with the back of my hands. She left the bed then. I heard three pulls from the tissue box on the dresser—*whoosh, whoosh, whoosh*—then she returned and pressed them into my hand. I put them to my eyes, knowing they would come away mascara black, but what could I do?

I held my breath. No, she wasn't good at this. Would she leave?

The pillow-top shifted lightly as she sat again.

I exhaled a shuddering breath. "For months and months I couldn't cry. Now I can't stop. I'm not strong. I'm weak."

"You're wrong about that, Margaret Mackenzie. People don't cry because they're weak. They cry because they've been strong for too long." She touched my hair lightly, then caressed my whole head before pulling out a hairpin that must have been dislodged from the knot at the nape. "I'm sorry you had to be so strong."

I shifted the tissues to my running nose and said a nasal, "Not your fault."

"But it is. I wish I'd been a better mother. Softer," she said as her hand again moved in my hair. "I wish I were softer." She removed another pin and set it aside.

"You couldn't be." My father . . . *expected.* "I understand that now."

"But I want to be softer," she said with such paradoxical harshness that I almost laughed. Instead, absurdly, I cried. Again. She opened her whole hand on my head, then carefully, soothingly removed a few more pins before finger-combing my hair out of its knot.

"Is it too late to change?" she asked so quietly I wasn't sure if she was speaking to me or herself. When I didn't answer, she said, "There are two reasons people change. One is if they've opened their minds, the other if their hearts have been broken."

"Heart," I said.

"Mind," she said, then added, "So we have that covered. Tell me about your broken heart."

With a shaky sigh, I rolled to my back. "Oh God. Where to start? Lily. Always Lily."

"Yes," she said. Her silence urged me on.

"Lily, Dad, you, Liam, and Edward."

"Not five years ago. Now."

"You, Liam, and Edward. I like having you in my life."

"You do?"

"*Yes.*"

"But?"

"But Shanahan will file a report, I'll get a probation surrender notice, and everything I've found again will be gone."

"Why gone?"

"Because I can't put you all through that again."

"Is it your decision to make?" she asked. In the old days, the question would have scolded with more than a little indignation. Hearing only calm now, I really looked at her. Her skin was pale with just a hint of natural color. Her hair, a darker auburn than it used to be, waved gently behind her ears. She seemed confident, like she knew exactly what she was talking about.

Then she smiled. "Do me a favor, sweetheart? Take off that makeup? It's made a mess of your eyes."

It was also irritating my eyes. So I went into the bathroom, removed it, rinsed, and moisturized. When I returned to the bedroom, my mother was sitting on the bench at the foot of the bed. She patted the free space beside her. Hungry for her touch, even for just a little longer, I sat close.

"Better," she said as she studied my face. Her eyes first, then her uncasted hand went to my scar. "Better."

"Will it ever be over?" The nightmare of Lily's death.

"It'll fade more each year."

"But if a judge overturns my probation, and the press and the gawkers and the Mackenzie Cooper Law—"

"It's a good law," she broke in. "It's probably saved more than a life or two. And it has your name. Isn't that a good thing?" When I eyed her in disbelief, she moved right on. "No matter what happens, it won't be like it was. This time you'll have all of us behind you."

"No—"

"*Yes.*"

"But I don't *want* this. *You* can't want this. It isn't why you're here."

"Of course it is," Margaret said, as though only an idiot would think otherwise. "I might have stayed back home. I could have managed—oh, not as well, but I'd have eventually gotten going. Then you arrived and, in spite of my having been the worst possible mother to you at the worst time in your life, you invited me back here. That tells me something."

I paused, waited, asked, "What?"

"That there was a method to His madness." The light in her eye was a throwback.

I got it. Religion and Margaret had always been entwined, which was why what I had seen at her house—or not seen—had been so jarring. "God?" I asked.

She nodded. "I thought He'd forgotten about me. But there you were, walking into my living room and whisking me up here. I didn't want to come at first. I don't deserve your help. I don't deserve Edward's, either.

I was fixated on that until it struck me that there was a sign in your coming. He was giving me a second chance. This time it's just me, just me, and I'm not blowing it."

Her fluency, her belief—all I could do was stare at her in amazement.

"And if you dare," she scolded with indignation, indeed, "say you don't deserve this, I'll scream. If I can move past that, can't you?" She didn't give me time to answer. "Do you forgive me for what I did to you?"

"Of course," I said.

"Why?"

"Because I love you."

"Then why isn't it true the other way around? If I love you, why wouldn't I forgive you?" She hurried on again before I could respond. "You've worked hard for this new life." For a second, she considered. "Maybe I have, too, all those years of keeping the family going. I like it here, Maggie. I want to stay for a while—well, maybe not in this suite, because I still think it's far too generous of Edward, and I have a business to run in Connecticut. I love that, too. I can go back and forth. But I want to be with you," she said, and those spring-green eyes didn't blink.

Gradually, they blurred, because I was crying again. She put an arm around my shoulder and drew me close enough to smell the one visceral scent that had been with me from birth.

I didn't hear a knock at the door, but several beats later, she held me back. The end of her cast touched my cheek as her thumbs brushed at my tears. Then her full right hand cupped my cheek and, in a whisper she said, "It's Edward. He's a good man, Margaret Mackenzie. He loves you, too."

Her words did something to me, though it was only when we were in the car that I felt the change, and then it was so subtle that I couldn't put a name to it. I'm not sure I wanted to just then. Between the events of the last few hours and all that crying, I was wiped. The best I could do when Edward suggested taking a ride, was to put my arms in the parka he held and, without argument, walk with him out to the Jeep.

26

The night was quiet. Filling my lungs with moist, full-bodied April air, I felt soothed. If the press had been in the parking lot of the Inn earlier, they had either gone to bed or regrouped at the police station. We headed in the opposite direction. And yes, in sporadic moments, I thought of what lay behind. Grace had to be terrified. I had no idea what, if anything, they were telling her about Chris, and though I told myself that with the eyes of the world on the boy, he was physically safe, I couldn't begin to imagine his emotional state. Jay had already talked with the U.S. Attorney in New Mexico, but that was all we knew. I hadn't heard from Michael Shanahan again. He would file a probation-violation report the next morning, at which point my fate would be in the hands of the same judge who had sentenced me five years before.

I should have been panicked. The worst was happening. I should have been *terrified*. As we drove north, though, the reasons why drifted off in the night. It wasn't that I felt numb, certainly not mellow, though that word did come and go. Likewise, relief. With my greatest fear coming to pass, the wait was over.

But no, it wasn't relief, either. What I felt inside was deeper. It was as if a part of me could deal with this new fear, as if little threads of hope were caging it in.

I wasn't a total stranger to hope. I had felt it about many things in Devon. But this was different from finding a home for the holidays or realizing that I liked doing makeup. This was larger. Still, it remained just beyond my grasp as the tires spun over macadam and shadowed trees came and went.

I had no idea where Edward was taking me, hadn't asked when we left the Inn, hadn't *cared* when we left the Inn. Increasingly, though, the drive was a little too familiar. The farther we went on the Blue behind the headlights of this particular car, the stronger my sense of déjà vu.

"Sex isn't the answer," I warned over the engine's hum.

"No sex," came his deep voice. "I just want to show you something."

"At your house? There's nothing there."

"There is."

I studied him in the pale light of the dashboard. His jacket was open, collar down, turtleneck up. Above that, his profile was strong, those spikes of hair, his straight nose, and whiskered chin, but I saw nothing at his mouth, either smile or frown, to give a clue what "there is" meant. Then he reached for my hand, and something in the way he held it, squeezing and releasing, spoke simultaneously of excitement and concern.

Curiosity won over the purr of silence. "What's there?" I asked.

"You'll see," he said but said no more.

So I refocused on the night. Being in transit was a good thing. It allowed me to float, which wasn't to say there were no other random moments of thought.

"I have to call my lawyer in Boston," I said during one.

"Already did," Edward replied. "He says to let him know if the letter arrives."

I was adjusting the heat vent when the next moment hit. "If?"

"I'm not sure Shanahan will act. Nothing you did was intentional. He knows that. If he makes a BFD about it and the judge rules against him, he'll look ridiculous."

I might have argued, because the judge had been stern handing down his sentence, like he was doing me a huge favor and *You'd be wise to remember that, Mrs. Cooper*. But I was feeling calm without consciously working at it. This was new. I didn't want to jinx it.

After following the Blue for another mile, we crossed back over the river onto the lesser-used road that led to Edward's house. Thirty seconds more, and there it was again, the sprawl of a farmer's porch, shingled siding, and mullioned glass lit by the swing of his headlights as he turned the wheel. Pulling up at the side, he killed the engine and was jogging around to open my door even before I had my seatbelt released. As soon as I was out of the Jeep, he took my hand and drew me to the house.

Sensing in him the same anticipation I had in the car, I watched him unlock the door. When he stood back for me to enter, I hesitated. My last visit here had unleashed a firestorm of emotion. What with everything else going on back in town, I didn't want that now.

"Please?" he asked on a vulnerable note, telling me I had a choice here this time.

But really, what choice did I have? I trusted the man. I *adored* the man.

Stepping in, I stood aside while he closed the door and flipped on a light. I remembered the kitchen as being small and unsettled. With its checkerboard floor and Formica cabinets, it looked more old now than small and with the clutter gone, simply sad.

The bedroom wing was at the back of the house down a corridor on the right, but, true to his word, we didn't go there. Instead, he guided me left, through an open archway and into a room at the front of the house where moldings hugged ceiling and floor, and fluted columns separated endless shelves everywhere between. A smattering of books stood in random chunks, but far more remained in cartons below.

Edward's desk was the focal point of the room. Standing smack in the center, it was modern and spare, a simple mix of glass and steel set on an iron tube frame. We had bought it for our last house, and while Edward had done his share of late night work there, Lily and I also used its large surface for art projects.

This desk matched the sleekness of our lives back then. It didn't fit here, not with the decorative millwork. But here it was. An oversized computer stood at one end. At the other lay long rolls of architects' drawings in a pick-up stick mess. Seeming to know which of the rolls he wanted, Edward pulled one out, pushed the others aside, and unrolled it.

Then he rethought that. Letting go so that the edges curled up on themselves, he woke up the computer instead and pulled up the same plan, now in a full-color rendering. Positioning the desk chair, he urged me to sit—and oh, I knew that chair, too. I had sat in it many, many times with Lily on my lap. The memories warmed a little something in me. The familiarity of it was bittersweet, but not painful, as it once might have been.

Leaning over my shoulder with his free arm on the back of the chair, Edward moved the mouse. Starting with the front exterior, he talked me through the architect's rendering of the house, which showed a repaired and cleaned-up version with stone on the façade and dormers added to the smaller second floor.

"Local granite," he said, hovering the cursor over the stone, then sweeping it around a circular drive that was pictured with an artful gathering of plants and shrubs. "New drive, new landscaping. What do you think?"

"It's beautiful," I said. The drawing certainly was. I hadn't yet seen the house in daylight, but I could easily translate my night glimpses into what was on the screen. "I can't get my bearings. Where's the river?"

"Out back." He clicked to the next page to bring up a charming view that included a fieldstone patio, a large lawn dotted with trees, and a waterfront of sand and stones. The river itself was no more than thirty feet wide at that point. On the far side were woodlands. "Deer come out to drink. I've seen raccoons and once, at dusk, a really ugly cat—"

"Fisher."

"Really ugly?" He was looking at me with Lily-eyed distaste.

I laughed. Totally inappropriate with the hell back in town. But I couldn't help it. He was adorable. "Really ugly and *mean*, but not a cat, a weasel."

"What does it eat?"

"My cats if they ever got out."

"Not a pretty picture."

"Nope."

"What about foxes?"

"Same picture."

"But they aren't ugly. I saw one the other day from the kitchen window. It was handsome, a rich orange-red against all that green." His face had grown wistful. He might only be starting to know the good and bad of the woods, but he had liked seeing that fox and those deer.

Total agreement here. Our eyes met and held.

Then, with a quick intake of air and the shift of his arm to my shoulder, he returned the other to the mouse and used it to point. "As the crow flies, we're a half-mile from the highway. Those woods are a buffer. Car, truck, semi—don't hear a thing." With another click of the mouse, an interior floor plan appeared.

Though I hadn't seen much of the inside of the house last time either, my first impression was that the proposed work was extensive, transforming a traditional design of many small rooms into one with fewer, larger. In the drawing on the screen, the kitchen was joined with the room just beyond it—a den, apparently—to make a huge open space. Adding to that even more, the entire back of the house would be bumped out a dozen feet, significantly enlarging the master bedroom to allow for a sitting area, walk-in closets, and a huge bathroom.

As he narrated, Edward's jaw was at my temple so that he could view the plans from the same angle as me. His hand was deft on the cursor, his narration steady, but his voice held the same mix of excitement and nervousness I'd sensed in the car.

He had just clicked into closer views of these first floor rooms when he murmured, "Lift up a second." His hands elaborated, bringing me to my feet. In no time, he sat where I'd been and drew me back onto his lap. "Better," he sighed and stretched his spine.

It actually was better. Like my holding Lily on my lap, Edward's holding me in his lap was familiar, too. We had always fit together well like this, and being five years older hadn't changed that. My right arm fit his neck, his left fit my waist, and the narration resumed.

Other than refinishing the wood, he said, the library in which we sat wouldn't change. Nor would the living room or dining room. "She felt strongly about keeping the integrity of the original house, at least here at the front. Because I kept asking, she drew up one version that opened these rooms too, but it didn't work. She was right about that."

I drew back to see his face. Unable to resist his unique brand of soft and firm, I brushed a thumb over his lips. "She?"

"Andrew Russ's wife, Jillian. You know her."

I did. She did the design for the Spa renovation that had been done two years ago. "Does she know we were married?"

"No. But I did tell her you were the love of my life."

"Edward."

"It's true," he said, without remorse. "I could tell she likes you, so it was a motivator. And she likes the house. She's young, only a handful of years out of design school, so when she pushed for traditional over modern, I had to listen. What do you think?"

"I think she's right."

Eyes back on the screen, he clicked again. "Look what she's done upstairs. With the bump-out, the two bedrooms there are larger. Each will have bigger closets and its own bathroom. Right now, they share a small bathroom down the hall. She wants to turn that into a utility room with a chute to the first floor laundry." To point out the last, he clicked back a page and indicated the tiniest of the rooms along the hallway on the left. "What do you think?" he asked again.

"It's brilliant."

"Would your mother want to stay here?"

I drew back again. His eyes were expectant. "My mother."

"She'll come visit, won't she?"

I felt an inkling of unease—but what had I thought? Of *course*, he was renovating the house with the idea that I would be here. On some level, I knew that. He had been very clear about his feelings for me, and there was only one direction those feelings would lead.

The reality, though, had a few thorns. "Edward—"

"Wait," he cut me off and, squeezing my shoulder, returned to the screen. "It gets even better. Here's the new garage. The old one is detached, but from what I hear of winters here, I don't want anyone walking outside." Anyone. He had deliberately said that, but being vague didn't ease my qualms. "Jillian suggests adding an attached three-car garage that would be accessible through a mudroom off the kitchen." When I looked at him, his expression was all innocence. "For resale value. Everyone here wants a three-car garage. I mean, isn't that where they store the snowplow for the pickup, the riding lawn mower, and the canoe?"

I had to laugh—again laugh—at the image. He had nailed it.

And resale value certainly made sense. But I knew Edward. He was assuming I would be parking there.

Again I said his name. Again he rushed on, as eager as Lily would be showing me a sponge-art masterpiece from school.

"The pièce de resistance?" He pulled up a whole new page. Pointing the cursor to a small sketch in the upper left corner, he said, "The current carriage house." He moved the cursor to the center of the page. It showed a structure that was reminiscent of the first, but gentrified. "Raze the old and build this. It could have a guest apartment upstairs, like if Liam had to stay here, which would not be my first choice. Your brother may be a great chef, but he can also be a pain in the butt. Downstairs," he clicked to the next page, "a pottery studio." I heard the *ta-da* in his voice and would have stopped him then and there if he hadn't already been moving the cursor from one spot to the next. "Work tables, a potter's wheel, storage bins, sink. This end could be outfitted for finishing—tables, glazing supplies, and a kiln. Or two." He was cautious at the end, looking at me now with those striking silver eyes.

"Edward," I breathed.

"Kevin helped design it."

"Edward."

"This is a first pass. You can redesign it yourself. Redesign the entire *house* yourself."

"*Edward,*" I pleaded, cupping his bearded jaw. Our eyes held through a silence, until I finally asked, "What are you doing?"

"Planning our future," he said without a blink, a swallow, a breath.

"Now? Right now? With everything else that's going on?"

His arm went more fully around my shoulder, drawing me that little bit closer. "Yes."

"*How?* We don't know what's going to happen tomorrow, let alone next week."

"No one ever does." His voice toughened. "Isn't that what we learned last time? Through no fault of ours—and, no, don't look at me that way, Mackenzie, because thirty seconds one way or the other, and that accident would never have happened. But in that split second, everything changed, and I don't just mean Lily's death or the divorce. I mean the course of our lives." The toughness eased. "But our new ones are better. They're more honest. More meaningful. Even if we still had Lily, I would choose life here, but if things hadn't happened the way they did, I would never have known it." He stared at me. Gradually, his eyes moved to my bangs. Pushing them aside, he traced my scar with his thumb.

"I look awful," I said. No makeup. Pale skin. Naked eyes.

"You look beautiful." He leaned forward and kissed the scar. Then, returning to a place where he could see my whole face, he gestured toward the computer and asked a vulnerable, "Don't you want this?"

"More than anything in the world," I said, because it was seriously true. "But you're showing me something I may never be able to have. Don't you see? I could go to prison. If you're drawn into the mess, your group could vote you out. You were taking a chance buying a home here in the first place, but if you leave town," I gestured at the plans, "what's the point?"

"I'm not leaving town. I'm staying here, and, worst-case scenario, if Shanahan gets you locked up, all it means is that you'll miss the mess of construction and come back to something beautiful and new."

"An ex-con," I said, expressing the darkest of my fears. "A woman who has shared meals with felons and showers with murderers, one who has lost all dignity. And if you don't want me then?" I asked.

He gave a disbelieving huff. "Christ, Maggie, haven't we gotten past that?"

I paused. Actually, we had. Frowning, I looked away. The instant I'd asked the question, I had known it was wrong. But that was a change. When? Why?

In a flash of understanding, I heard my mother's voice. *He loves you, too,* she had said, and it wasn't that I needed her approval of Edward. But I trusted her judgement. That was why our estrangement had hurt me so much. Along with everything to do with mothering, it reinforced the idea, never spoken but implied, that my choice of life partner had been poor. She had never before shown any fondness for Edward, certainly had never praised him. That she did now registered.

But something else registered. *He loves you, too,* she had said, the *too* being key. *She* loved me. Despite the accident, the loss of Lily and my father and my name, she did love me. It had been right there in the comfort she gave back at the Inn. She said she wasn't good at that kind of thing, but she was. I had simply been too close to it to see it at the time.

That different feeling inside me? It had to do with healing. Something was intact where a ragged tear had been.

Weaving a hand into my hair, Edward angled my face so that he could look me in the eye. "You won't be going to prison, baby. There would be a riot in that courtroom if the judge buys into Shanahan's case. You have a ton of friends, not the least being Jillian Russ, who drew up these plans extra fast because she thinks you're the best. So do half the people in this town."

"Only half?" I asked, trying to make a joke, to lighten things up, to do anything that might explain why I was believing what he said.

"The other half don't know you. Once they do, they'll adore you, too."

"Well, there's another point," I said. "Once Grace's past hits the news and Shanahan does his thing, my secret's out. What'll the good people of Devon think of me then?"

"They'll respect you even more," he said without missing a beat. "Seriously, Maggie. How can you not see that? They'll be just as amazed as me that you were able to pick yourself up after a tragedy like that and rebuild a life. And you have. People here respect the hell out of what you've done since coming here. They told me this at Town Meeting when they saw us together. I was with your mother when Joe Hellinger told her what you do for his patients. Joyce thinks you're one of the Spa's greatest assets, which is accurate, according to online reviews. Cornelia loves you like a daughter, granddaughter, whatever, and your buddy Kevin? He thinks you hung the moon. I see the ways you've helped Grace and Chris— and don't tell me people here will think less of her for what happened in Santa Fe. They won't blame her for that any more than you do. So no, Devon people won't be fazed when they hear about the accident. They know how much you give of yourself. You put *you* into everything you do. They see that."

When his eyes grew too intense, I looked back at the plans. Something still didn't feel right.

Trying to figure out what it was, I said, "You want kids."

"And if they come . . ." Voice trailing off, he brought the cursor to the last unexplained space in the master bedroom wing. It was a small room, with a closet and a new small bathroom.

A baby's room. The breath caught in my throat. A baby's room was real. I wasn't ready for that.

"What if I can't?" I whispered.

"Then we won't."

"You'd be happy with that?"

"No. But better no child than no you."

And what could I say to that?

"Do you know," he said, "that when a couple loses a child, up to eighty percent of those marriages end in divorce? I don't want to be one of the eighty percent."

"We already are."

"Not here," he said, tapping his heart. He looked into my eyes, looked deeply. "Do we love each other?"

I nodded.

"*That's* what matters, Maggie. None of the other stuff is as important as us. Family matters. *We* matter."

And so he knocked down that argument, too. I was running out of options, but something was still off.

Feeling vaguely frantic, I asked, "What about my pets?" If we were talking about the future, my pets played a role. "You don't like cats."

He surfed through the plans again. When a detail of the kitchen appeared, he enlarged a small insert.

I leaned in, then glanced back at him. "What is that?"

"A pet-feeding station."

"Built in?"

"Better than tripping over food bowls. I told Jillian we had three pets. She has a setup like this in her own house." When I stared at him in disbelief, he said, "It isn't that I don't like cats. I just don't know them, but they're yours. They matter. And then there's your cabin."

"I love my cabin."

"Which is why we keep it. If you'd rather have your potting studio there, we can do that too."

"But I like going to Kevin's studio."

"Then go there."

"But I like doing makeup."

"So do makeup."

These were meaningful parts of the life I had built on my own. That life held its share of loneliness, but it also held independence and pride. And here was Edward, seeming to understand that, seeming willing to accept me on my terms, to take what I treasured and work it into a future.

I felt a stab of frustration. "How can you ask me to be happy with my best friend locked up?"

"I'm not—"

"You are. These things make me happy, Edward."

"Good," he said and gave a grin that stole my breath.

Suddenly, I needed space. From the start, back in that art gallery in Boston, Edward had been a force of nature in my life. It wasn't that I couldn't think straight when he was around, more that I simply wanted to go with his flow. Actually, no. It was more like his current was strong enough to carry my flow right along beside his.

That hadn't changed. It would be all too easy to jump in now and be swept along. But that wasn't what I had become. I needed a minute of separation to remember myself. Something still bothered me. I needed to figure out what it was. Edward's presence was too strong here to allow that.

Pressing a kiss to a corner of his mouth, I slipped from his lap. On my way to the built-ins, I traced the long edge of the desk and, then, because its texture was too tempting to resist, the fluted edges of the bookshelves. The millwork was striking. It just needed a little love. Edward would give it that. He had the resources and the desire. It was a good mix. But something nagged.

I went out into the front hall, which was wallpapered and bare. Money would fix this, too. Same with the living room, whose wide oak planks needed polish, stain, shine, something. Same with the winding staircase, whose newel post was worn and whose iron balusters should have been wood. Edward would fix all of these things.

I sat there for a heartbeat but rose in the next and went to the front door. The instant I opened it, I felt relief. Breathing in the cool air, listening to the night sounds, I reached out. Here were my woods, the distant gurgle of my river, my creatures, my Devon.

But my alone space wasn't out there, either. It struck me that being alone just didn't do it for me anymore. My happiness involved others.

Short term, that meant Grace, Chris, and Michael Shanahan. Long term, it meant Lily. I wanted to be happy, really I did and, yes, I could find happiness here, in this house, with Edward. Whether I had the right to it was something else—but even that wasn't the immediate problem.

Confused, I remained at the open door looking out at the street. There were no lights, no cars, no human sounds other than Edward's footsteps when he approached.

"Do you have neighbors?" I asked.

He came up beside me, a tall, warm presence with his arm brushing mine. "One," he said. "The house is farther down the street. It's a biggie, impressive since they're retirees. This is their summer home. They also have places in Palm Springs and Vail."

"Must be loaded," I said and stood straighter. This was the last piece, I realized, the only other qualm I had. Trying to put it into coherent thought, I looked back at the living room, the stairs, and the library. By the time he was done, Edward's house would be as impressive as anyone's in the town.

It was light-years removed from my tiny cabin, my modest life, even my pickup truck. I had chosen this lifestyle for a reason. The last one, fully loaded, had been a disaster.

I looked up at him. His face was shadowed. With the lights flanking the front door either non-functioning or simply not on, the glow of the moon on the edges of clouds had too big a job. But I could see he was looking at me. So I said, "We had a three-car garage once before. Is that a bad omen?"

He didn't frown or flinch, didn't seem to spend a single second weighing the matter, but said with utter calm, "Absolutely not. Our lives, our minds, our dreams are different now. They have nothing to do with the way we were. They aren't even about the way we are now. They're about the way we want to be."

There it was again, the issue of hope. That was what my mother's love gave me. It was what Liam's arrival had brought. It was what my friendships here in Devon added.

With that realization, the final piece very softly clicked into place.

I still had issues with me. But other people did not. They saw me as I was now, even as I might be in the future, not as I was back then. At some point, I had to hear what they were saying.

Only when I was silent did Edward show the slightest doubt, but it was more about wanting my agreement. No dictator, my Edward, no philosopher spouting lofty sayings. We might have failed to communicate after Lily died, but that wasn't the way we wanted to be.

"Aren't they?" he asked—our lives, minds, and dreams about the way we wanted to be.

Turning into him, I slipped my arms around his waist. I inhaled deeply, and, when his arms closed around me, exhaled into a smile. "They are."

EPILOGUE

Six months later, we were still in Devon, still together, still in love. But love was like wrinkles on the faces I made up. They could be frozen, peeled, and pulled tight. They could be moisturized and concealed. They could be minimized by drawing attention to other features, say, cheekbones or eyes. But they were the price of living, and they never fully disappeared. The older the face was, the more we had to work at keeping it smooth.

Same with love. Edward and I loved deeply. After losing track of that once, though, we were leery of kinks. And they did come. Take the third of October, the anniversary of Lily's death. Each year since moving to Vermont, I had driven down to Massachusetts to be with her on that day. This year Edward came with me, and much as we tried to be upbeat, the old litany of *what-ifs* was a shadow that followed us the whole way. We were silent in the car going, silent at her grave, silent in the car returning. It was only later that night, after lying in bed in separate crypts of grief, that I broke down, Edward reached for me, and we began to talk. It was about sharing memories of her and yes, sharing dreams of what might have been, because those dreams were valid and couldn't be ignored. It was also about sharing the pain of loss, understanding that it was different for each of us and, like crows' feet, could be temporarily hidden but would never be gone.

Our minds had owned that. Our hearts were simply slow catching up.

That was last week. But the very next day, something unexpected happened. I was stunned by the joy I felt, and it wasn't just an initial pop and fizzle. It lingered, giving each day since a little glow. I might have attributed the glow to autumn in Devon, which was a time of crisp apples, fields full of pumpkins, and leaves every shade of fire, if this glow hadn't come from deep inside.

I felt it even now, cradled in the hammock on our back lawn, where the river flowed more slowly now that summer was done, and the scent of drying leaves was strong. It was late Sunday afternoon. With barely two hours of daylight left, the sun slanted low over the dried leaves that littered the lawn. My head rested on Edward's arm. Behind me, his brow to my nape, he snored softly.

Slipping the cell from my pocket, I held it high for a selfie, then looked at the shot and smiled. Sweet, it showed two partial heads, Edward's lone visible eye shut, mine open, his cheek whiskered, mine clear, our jaws lined by a ruff of fall scarves, mine fuchsia, his heather blue. The air held a chill, though I was perfectly warm where I lay.

Pleased with the moment, feeling strong, I opened Photos and thumbed backward in time through a raft of construction shots. With the bulk of the inside work finished in the main house, the crew had moved on to the carriage house, garage, and mudroom, wanting to frame, roof, and rough those in before snow fell. For the sake of a before-and-after collage, I was documenting it all.

The shot I was looking for had nothing to do with home renovation. Swiping forward, then backward again in search, I found the one I wanted. It showed a clay piece, certainly construction but of a totally different kind. It wasn't a bust exactly, certainly wasn't a lifelike representation of Lily. It was more vague than not, more suggestive than exact, but it was definitely our child, whose life had never been static and whose memory mirrored that.

I hadn't been able to sculpt her before. So this was new. But I wasn't glazing this piece. I planned to bronze her and, after the last of the dust settled on the work in the house, find a special place for her to sit. It wouldn't be on a pedestal. Neither of us wanted a mausoleum. What we wanted was that Lily mix with our current life, because that life was rich.

Ten years ago, rich meant money. Neither of us had been rolling in it growing up, which may have been a way of rationalizing the lifestyle we had—and, hey, I'm not saying money can't buy happiness. When it means having a home, enough food, or medical care? Seriously. But wealth isn't wealth without family and friends. In that sense, we were rich now as never before.

Thumbing through pictures from the last few months, I stopped at one of Grace and Chris, and brought it full-screen. I had caught them from behind when they were leaving the courtroom after Chris's hearing. Chris seemed taller, perhaps simply standing straight, and his arm was around Grace's shoulder in what could only be interpreted as protectiveness. That was what I loved about this shot. Having learned who he was, he could finally appreciate what his mother had done for him all these years. More-over, after spending the week with Carter Brandt, who was also in the courtroom that day, Chris seemed neither impressed that the guy was in Congress nor, though he had little say as yet, particularly eager to be in his care. Call me perverse, but that pleased me.

The resolution of the case was equally satisfying. Given Chris's age, he had been charged with an act of juvenile delinquency. After studying the psychologist's reports, statements from Chris's teachers, and a plea of leniency from Ben, the judge suspended any finding pending a two-year probation, with the understanding that if Chris stayed clean during that time, all charges would be dropped.

Grace's case was more complex. She spent several nights in lock-up while Jay scrambled behind the scenes. He did manage to get her released on bail—huge victory there. Granted, the level of bail was high enough to terrify her. And Federal agents watched her day and night. Not that she would have run. Chris was the ultimate pawn. Short term, he was with his father. She knew that any attempt to flee meant she would never see him again.

If the analogy was to chess, though, she held the all-powerful queen. Her evidence against Carter Brandt was so strong—and Brandt's desire to keep it hidden so desperate—that he agreed to a deal. Kidnapping charges against her would be dropped and a reasonable custody arrangement agreed to in exchange for her surrendering the incriminating evidence.

Did she actually hand it all over without keeping any proof of its existence? Maybe, maybe not. No matter that she had Jay on her side, Ben on her side, so many others of us dying to testify on her behalf, she didn't trust Congressman Brandt. He had money and power, both of which held sway in a court of law, unless one had a weapon against them. I was guessing she kept a little something, just in case.

That said, old habits die hard, meaning that she did consider leaving town. Well after the legal issues were settled, the notoriety of the case made her paranoid when we left to shop the Manchester outlets or the Hanover boutiques. But Chris wanted to finish high school in Devon; he had become something of a hero among his friends. And besides, she feared that her past would be waiting for her wherever she went. At least here she was assured of a job, relative safety from gawkers, and a solid client base. She often disappeared when Chris was in Washington with his dad, though whether she was out looking for a new home or holed up with Ben, I didn't know. Our relationship still held secrets.

I did finally give her raven-black hair, though. I figured she had the right to look the way she wanted after the hell she'd been through. And it wasn't all bad, that raven hair, especially with a body wave to soften the starkness. Now, I studied the picture we'd taken when that session was done. She was a seriously striking woman. It was a miracle she had stayed hidden so long. Had it not been for the press . . .

But I couldn't go there. I had sworn to put that particular resentment behind me.

Yes, I received a probation-surrender notice soon after Grace's arrest, and, yes, I had to appear in court in Boston. But it was different this time. For one thing, my family was there rooting for me, as were not one, not two, but three carloads of friends from Vermont. For another, five years after my initial trial, the attorney general who had made headlines of me was out, and the new one didn't bother to come to court that day, which gave little incentive for press coverage—particularly after kidnapping charges against Grace were dropped, which made the case against me iffy at best.

Shanahan was humiliated. Was I sorry? Absolutely not. To this day, I'm convinced that his motivation in filing the probation-violation order was jealousy of Edward, whom I had chosen over him. His vindictiveness had caused me emotional and monetary pain. So no, I did not count Michael as a friend. He had proven himself neither reasonable nor loyal.

Cornelia Conrad, our savvy postmistress, was both. She sat front and center that day in Boston, exchanging smiles with the judge and greeting court officers like the long-lost friends that it turned out they actually were.

Everyone has a story, my mother remarked after the fact, because Cornelia certainly did. We knew she had been a professor in Boston. What we didn't know was that her professorship was in law and that she taught evenings. By day, she was a clerk-magistrate in Boston, presiding over probable cause hearings, issuing warrants, and setting bail, any of which promised less stress than the law firm from which she'd come. And for twenty years as a clerk-magistrate, she was fine. Then, one day, she set bail in a domestic violence case, only to have the defendant go home and kill his wife. Cornelia hadn't been any more responsible than the prosecutor or the defense attorney, neither of whom asked for greater bail. Still, she blamed herself. Soon after, she moved to Devon.

That total absence of wrinkles that I had speculated about? Definitely genes.

A movement caught my eye—a flash of beagle and the rustle of grass. Jonah was chasing a rabbit. The snap of my fingers brought him back, but it also woke Edward. He called Jonah's name in a groggy voice, which was probably what settled the dog under the hammock again. Did Jonah like it here? Honestly, I think he would have liked it anywhere Edward was. He had become man's best friend, which wasn't fair, since I was the one who rescued him in the first place, but there it was.

The cats, bless them, were all mine. Had we dared let them out, they would have been up here on the hammock, tucked against my body as I was tucked against Edward's. I had waited until two weeks ago to move them here, fearing either that they would escape through ever-opening doors, or that the construction noise would freak them out. Now, even with kitty condos placed in strategically sunny spots, I knew that if I craned my neck and looked back, two cat faces would be at the glass sliders, waiting for us to come in.

Edward's arm around my middle pulled me in deeper. "Feeling okay?" he murmured, still sleepy.

"Totally."

"Why am I so tired?"

It might have been that being an innkeeper was more time-consuming than he'd expected. The same addiction to the possibility that had made him a successful venture capitalist hadn't just gone away. It manifested itself in how he had dealt with the hacking crisis with an umbrella approach involving technology, personnel, and client incentive. As soon as the books showed stability, he started seeing other things in town that he could improve. There were three mansions on Cedar that, with renovation, could be turned into boutique B&Bs for large family groups. There was a mountain behind the current ski slope just begging to be developed. There were the elementary school, which needed a new playground, and the high school, whose tech lab was obsolete.

For all that, his group needed money. So Edward Cooper, as leader of that group, was now, again, heavy into client development. That meant entertaining investors at the Inn, basically putting on full day show-and-tells. Exhausting? For sure.

But Edward loved his work. I appreciated that. So I gave the exhaustion a different cause. "Uh, maybe because you were binge-watching *The West Wing* until two in the morning?"

"Mmm." His breathing lengthened again.

I matched mine to it for a bit, but, me, I had slept right through Netflix. Sleep was easier for me these days, now that my probation had ended and the future was free. I still had the occasional nightmare, but with Edward close, they had lessened.

Still, late this Sunday afternoon, I should have been tired. We'd had two weddings at the Inn this weekend, and although Ronan Dineen was now a regular, I liked doing weddings. I had worked both days. I had certainly earned the right to doze in Edward's arms before the night air sent us inside. But I was wide awake.

Raising the phone, I swiped again, landing this time on a slightly hilarious shot of my mother and brother. I had taken it at the cabin, where Liam continued to live, not that he spent much time there, now that his restaurant was open. A marketing team had named it *Basquaise*, after the simple elegance of the French Basque cooking with which he had grown obsessed. Thanks to cross-marketing by the Inn and word of mouth, its first two months were a huge success. I had pictures on my phone of opening night, of glasses of rustic reds from the southwest of France and trays of Basque-style tapas.

But the restaurant was closed Mondays. So, on the Monday of this shot, Edward and I had been invited to the cabin for dinner. Liam was cooking the entrée, Margaret baking the dessert. I should have known that one kitchen was too small for them both. Liam was Margaret's boy, as authoritative at *Basquaise* as she was at The Buttered Scone. A disagreement over the use of clarified butter had them arguing, which was the moment I snapped my shot—and hadn't Margaret turned on me then? *And what do you find so amusing?* she had asked archly. All I could do was to smile, as I did now.

I loved having her here. Six months after breaking it, her hip was almost good as new, and while she had returned to Connecticut to work, she regularly drove back to Devon. She liked the people, she said. Given how busy she was during visits, I believed her. But she also spent time with us. Since the new Margaret liked who she was now, she was more relaxed than I'd known her to be. Maybe it was growth. Maybe it was resolve. Whatever, she was easy to entertain. That said, she declared that she, not Liam, would use the guest room in the carriage house when it was done, if for no other reason than to make sure I was using the pottery studio below.

Ah. But that issue was still TBD. Clay had been my life once—too much, I wondered in hindsight. I had been a powerhouse wife, mother, and sculptress. But life in Devon was more laid-back. I had slowed down in ways that were good, and I feared that with a studio literally in my back yard, I would regress. And then where would makeup fit in? I loved the people part of that. I loved the Spa, whose scent alone still brought me peace. I loved knowing Edward was right upstairs.

I also loved Kevin and the pottery studio. Visits there several times a week worked for me. So the first floor of the reincarnated carriage might well end up being a game room.

For a brief minute, I pressed the phone to my chest and looked out over the lawn to the river. The sun had fallen behind the trees now, barely breaching their denseness, but, if anything, darkness was a better foil for the picture that was already clear in my mind. Lifting the phone, I thumbed forward and tapped into the cause of my glow, studying it full-screen for what had to be the hundredth time.

At eight weeks, a fetus was pretty amorphous. There was an oversized head and a bean body, together no more than raspberry size. Fingers and toes were visible, still vaguely webbed, but the tail I was told had been there at first was gone. We couldn't see the sex yet, which was probably good. We weren't sure we wanted to know. It was one of the things we hadn't decided. This had happened faster than we'd expected. My mother, who didn't yet know, would say it was meant to be. In this, I had to agree with her.

Hard to believe how determined I had been not to do this again. I was frightened. I was grieving. I hadn't wanted to put myself through the risk of loving and losing again—had feared I wouldn't survive.

But I had survived once. This was the message of that night when we cried over my grandmother's green velvet box. It was also the message of the tumult six months before. I had faced court hearings, the press, and a resurgence of self-doubt, and still I survived. This time around, I'd had better tools. Going forward from here, even more so.

And then there was the joy. I had forgotten what it was like to see the first image of my baby. Memory of that joy had been lost in sorrow. Studying this sonogram now, putting a finger to the beginnings of a nose and chin, to the indentation where an eye was forming and wondering what color it might be, to the tiny hand whose fingers would fully separate and one day not so far into the future close around mine, I felt the joy again.

That still stunned me.

But the past was like that. We might think we had it pegged, and that it was over and done. We might deny the pain, the fear, the sorrow. Deep down, though, it was there. Like DNA, the past was part of who we were. Only when we accepted that, were we whole.

There were still times when I felt guilty being happy, but those times were coming fewer and farther between. This picture on my phone, in my hand, was proof of the future, and it held promise.

ACKNOWLEDGMENTS

I owe thanks to the many, many people who helped me in the writing of *Before and Again*. Problem is, I don't know who most of them are! Our lives have crossed, however fleetingly, at one point or another, and something they said or did registered enough to appear in even convoluted form in this book.

I do know who my husband is. Before and again, Steve helped me with the legal aspects of what you read here. From the bottom of my ever-loving heart, I thank him.

I also thank Andy Espo and Derek Braunschweiger, for their very basic, very current, and down-to-earth explanation of how a person with evil intent can hack into my computer. This helped me not only in crafting *Before and Again*, but in protecting my own devices. I will never, ever, *ever* open an unexpected, unverified attachment again.

None of those, thank goodness, come from my editor, Leslie Gelbman. Everything she sends is legit and welcome. My very special thanks to her

ACKNOWLEDGMENTS

for her willing ear, her wise counsel, and her friendship. We think alike, she and I. Not only has she taken my writing to a new level with this book, but she has made it fun.

Before and again, I thank my agent, Amy Berkower, without whose care and expertise I would not be working with Leslie and, hence, would not be in this happy place.

And to all those at St. Martin's Press, from Sally Richardson on, my thanks for their faith in my work and their undying enthusiasm.

Finally, I thank my readers—before, again, always.